Defining

US

DEFINING US
THE
CALVIN & ERIC STORY

Zoey Derrick

Editing: Mandy Smith of Raw Editing - available at rawbooksbabe@gmail.com.

Cover Design: Parajunkee Design - available at www.parajunkee.net

Cover Art: stock photo purchased through Big Stock, Shutter Stock or similar site.

ISBN-13: 978-0996896610

Looking for More Zoey Derrick?
Check out these other Titles:

Love's Wings Series
Finding Love's Wings
Chasing Love's Wings

365 Days Series:
One Week

Reason Series:
Give Me Reason
Give Me Hope
Give Me Desire
Give Me Love

69 Bottles Series:
Claiming Addison
Craving Talon
Redeeming Kyle

Taming Dex
Devouring Raine

Ultimate Reading Order

While 69 Bottles can be read without reading previous books, for the ultimate fan experience, this is how I recommend you read these books. However, many readers have started with Claiming Addison or even Taming Dex and found themselves returning to the original stories afterward.

Finding Love's Wings
Chasing Love's Wings

One Week

69 Bottles Books:

Calming Addison
Craving Talon
Redeeming Kyle

Taming Dex
Devouring Raine

Defining US

Dearest Readers,

I cannot thank you enough for your purchase of Defining US: The Calvin and Eric Story.

I know that you have been waiting patiently for their story to come out and I am so happy to be sharing it with you finally.

A few notes about this story…

If this is the first book of mine or in the 69 Bottles Series that you're reading, ENJOY! There is no need to go back and read the first 5 books in this series before diving into this one. I've worked very hard to keep these stories all separate and while you will see some of the characters in previous books, I don't think that anything is ruined by starting here.

If you've been waiting on baited breath for this story, don't let me waste your time, turn the page and get sucked into the world of Calvin and Eric - Mouse & Peacock.

Thank you for all your love and support and most off all, you patience.

Love you ALWAYS,

XX
Zoey Derrick

Acknowledgements

Rachel - I'm truly running out of ways to tell you thank you, for everything. Without you, I couldn't keep doing this every day. You spark my imagination and fuel my fictional fantasies. Without you, these wouldn't be possible.

Parajunkee Rachel - You put up with my shit and design some seriously amazing covers and without you, my books wouldn't look this good.

Mandy - When I need someone to talk to, you're always there. When you need some one to vent to, I'll always be here. Thank you for not only being my editor, but a near and dear friend. Thank you for putting up with my bullshit and me leprechauns. **Did that on purpose, just to make her twitch**

Kelley - I know Calvin & Eric aren't your cup of tea, but I'm glad you're reading them anyway. Thank you for being my distraction, purposefully and indirectly. I miss our three hour chats… SOOOON we will be back at it. P.S. Thank you for being my Pimp!

Christine - My PimpQueen - My Ear - My Alpha, My Beta - my friend. You're AMAZING and I cannot thank you enough for all you've done to help bring these two to life, not only for me, but for you and the readers too!

XX
Zoey

For Emily -

For being there when I need you. For jumping in and taking over
even when I don't think I need you.
This one's for you!

prologue

calvin

14 years ago...

"You fucking tell anyone about this and I will kick your ass from here to China," Billy grunted out as he shoved me on a pile of hay on the far side of the barn. It's not the most secluded spot, but it will do.

"Your secret is safe with me," I whisper just as Billy's rough, chapped lips land on mine without preamble.

Though the connection I have with Billy is purely sexual, the passionate kiss doesn't stop me from getting worked up. My dick gets harder the longer his lips crush against mine.

Billy moans into my mouth and I run my fingers through his hair, holding him to me as he grinds his growing erection against my hip.

There won't be any sex, no, we never do that, but I know that eventually he will undo the fly of my jeans and start lavishing my cock with his mouth.

It's our way, it's our routine.

The first time we hooked up like this, I got him off first and he freaked out. Screaming and yelling at me in an attempt to make himself feel better about what we'd done. To try and convince himself that he isn't gay. I shrugged it off, even had a laugh about it, after he'd stormed out of the barn, this barn.

My father hired Billy a couple of summers ago to help around the farm and well, that was where it all started. Though prior to Billy working here, we were not friends. In fact, Billy is the quarterback of our football team. A member of the jock squad at school. You see, in my school, you're either a jock, a cheerleader or a not. I am a not. Or a 'not-not' because I don't associate with anyone. It's pretty hard to make friends when you're pretty sure you're the only boy in your town that's gay. At least that's what you think when you grow up in small town Iowa.

I'd never made a secret of watching Billy work, in fact, that's how this whole thing started. He'd set out to stop me, or scare me, and what ended up happening was the start of what's happening now. Sure, he has a girlfriend, but from the rumors I hear, he's "celibate" or at the very least, gun shy in bed.

Billy's fingers fiddling with my zipper, unzipping my jacket pulls me out of the memories of where this all began. I groan into his mouth as his tongue slides along mine.

When we're in here, in a position such as this, I do my best to stay as clothed as possible. It's rare that anyone comes in here unless they're working, but it's always a possibility.

In fact, the first time my father caught Billy and I right here, I ended up with a broken cheekbone. Luckily for me, that happened at the beginning of last summer, so I never actually had to go to school with the nasty ass shiner I had afterwards.

Billy's fingers reach the button of my jeans and he makes quick work undoing them and plunging his hand inside. He grabs a hold of my cock and strokes, hard. I groan as the pleasure engulfs me, my head falling back against the hay, my lungs gasping for air.

I open my eyes and watch him lick his lips as he slides down my chest toward his prize and he pulls my dick free of my pants.

My body is vibrating with the anticipation of his mouth wrapping around the tip and sucking me down like a hoover. That is one thing I have to give the boy credit for, he's damn good at sucking cock.

"Take it all, you filthy slut," I tell him and I watch as Billy shivers with excitement right before the head of my stiff cock slides past his lips.

My eyes close as he starts sucking, grunting and groaning when whatever he does feels good and my memories slip back to the fall of tenth grade, after spending the summer with a shiner from hell. I remember returning to school and falling right into Billy's asshole trap. He and his buddies had no problem calling me 'faggot', 'a hose lover', among other hurtful and derogatory names. I never gave them the satisfaction of knowing that what they were calling me was hurtful, but it killed me every day. Especially when Billy would spew the horse shit at me in school and come to work in the barn with me on the weekends. After a particularly awful week of his friends belittling me, I did my best to ignore him, but his constant staring drove me mad and made my dick hard.

Somehow he'd always manage to make it up to me and I'm naive enough to believe that he has a part to play. We all had our parts to play in school. Play it straight, don't let them know.

"Hssss...shit, don't fucking stop," I growl as his hands and mouth furiously work up and down my rod, enticing an orgasm from me.

Growing up in middle of nowhere, Northeastern Iowa means plenty of farm land, plenty of conservatives and way too many devout Christians who think their shit doesn't fucking stink. Being gay is the ultimate crime against family and family values.

"Shit. Someone's coming," I say as I try and back away from Billy, just enough so that I can...

"What the fuck are you doing?" I hear my father scream from the far end of the barn.

I freeze. Billy casually stands up, all calm and collected, turning toward my father before he strolls right on out of the barn.

"You dirty ass son of bitch, what the fuck are you doing?" my father growls as his face turns as red as a radish. "How dare you force someone to suck your pathetic excuse for a dick." My father reaches me then, leaning over and pulling me up by my shirts.

"He volunteered," I say back. Years ago my father intimidated me like no other man, but as I've gotten older, I've grown taller and far stronger than him.

"No wonder none of 'em girls come 'round here, you fucking faggot." My father continues his verbal tirade and I see Billy out of the corner of my eye. The son of a bitch has the balls to mouth "sorry" to me before he takes off for his truck.

My momentary distraction is what my father was waiting for as I feel the sharp sting of a slap right across my face. My head jerks to the side and before I can compose myself enough to fight back, he manages a kidney shot. I double over from the blow. My vision swims in red and I fight to breathe, calling on all my strength before I finally manage to fight back.

The next day, walking into school is a total disaster. My face is bruised, though nowhere near as bad as I expected it to be, my rib cage is a mess. He refused to take me to the doctor when we were done, but it didn't stop him from running off to the bar for the night, the same place he's gone every night since Mom died. Regardless, I cleaned myself up and crawled into bed. I'd heard him come home somewhere around four in the morning, but I paid him no mind.

As I strolled through the halls of our little K-12th grade school, I could hear the comments and commotion about my appearance. When I hit the jock squad, one of the running backs says, "Well, would you look at that, he really is a pussy if he looks like that."

Then someone else said, "The faggot probably hit on the wrong guy."

"Shut up," I hear Billy say. "For fuck's sakes, how old are you idiots? Grow the fuck up."

Despite the swollen, cut up lip, I manage a small smile as I pass by them. Being thankful that it was about time Billy finally stood up for me.

The weeks passed and I started to heal up once again. The bruises faded away into ugly ass green and yellow splotches. Everyone knew that it was my father who beat me, but in a town like this, in this day and age, it's not at all uncommon. After that fight, I'd managed to stop looking at Billy when we were working together. Though I could feel him staring at me regularly, neither one of us advanced it beyond that. I had a hard time forgiving him for running away, not once, but twice, and I wasn't going to go back down that road again.

So I got my hands on a fake ID and would drive about forty five minutes into another small college town called Decorah. It was far enough away from home where no one would know me and I could easily blend into the college scene.

It became a great stomping ground and I managed to find myself hooked up with a few really great looking guys. Most of them knew I was a minor, but they never seemed to care. I didn't turn into a slut by any means, but here seemed to be the one place I could be myself. So I was.

"It isn't something I can just turn off."

"Bullshit. You can and you will, or you will get the fuck out of my house."

Those were the last words I heard before my father knocked me the fuck out, breaking his hand and my jaw with one punch. It would be the last time my father would hit me. At that point in my life, everything changed. Years of confusion, years of frustration and misunderstanding finally came to fruition, only to be beaten out of me at regular intervals by my father.

After that, I tried to suppress my natural desires and turned them into false ones in order to please him, but it proved to be too difficult.

That was until he caught me kissing a boy I'd met at one of the many bars I frequented.

It was at that point that he realized his fist was no longer punishment enough and his own right wing views were aided by doctors of a similar mind. Doctors who believed that being gay was a choice and that, with intensive therapy, they could "cure" the gay from who I was.

chapter 1

calvin

For me, picking up girls has never been easy. Hell, I was lucky if I could manage to carry on a conversation with them, let alone get in their pants.

Until I joined 69 Bottles.

Whether we were performing in a bar in the middle of some Podunk town or some major arena somewhere, the chicks threw themselves at us. Picking up chicks became easy for an awkward, sexually repressed man like me. It was easy enough that I could manage to talk very little and get what I was after, though ninety percent of the time, I ended up in the bathroom spewing my guts out into the toilet when it was over.

"What about her?" Eric says to me as he points out some chick. I shrug it off like I'm not interested. In fact, I'm not interested, not tonight.

"What's crawled up your ass and died?" Dex shoulder checks me.

"Forget it," I grumble and put my hands in my hair. In an exasperated huff, I get up from the couch and head for the back door. I feel trapped inside this bar. Trapped inside myself.

Something about today has triggered this uncertainty. Something about today has me on edge, and I don't quite understand it. I feel like beating the shit out of something, or forgetting my name with pussy or drugs.

I rub vigorously at my arms, attempting to scrub away the creepy, ants under my skin feeling, but it's pointless.

I'm restless and I'm itching…twitching, desperate to wash the memories of the past away.

I'm gay.

I'm gay… Eric's words when we were in New York continue to ring through my head. The words that I somehow desperately needed to hear him say without knowing that I needed to hear them. Words that have brought back everything that I've ever desired, along with the reasons why I can't have it.

Eric and I had talked that night, after the concert. He pulled me into a quiet room at the bar we were in and…

"I have to tell you something," he tells me.

"Dude, you're gay, I get it."

"No Calvin, listen to me, please?" he pleads.

"How drunk are you?" I ask him and he smiles.

"I'm not. I just feel…" he shrugs and then starts pacing around the room, it looks like an office area, there are filing cabinets and yeah, whatever, it's not important. "…Free," he finally finishes.

"Free of what?" I take a pull on my beer.

"Everything, all the burden of wondering what people will think, free of the fact that I no longer feel I need to hide who I am from people."

I snort, "Dude, you've never hidden who you are with us. So you like the dick, no big deal. Honestly, Eric, we all knew." I shake my head dismissively at him. It's not entirely true that we all knew, I suspected, of course, but… I shiver involuntarily and fight the bile that rises in the back of my throat and my blood runs cold with hatred, hatred of myself, and of my father. Hatred that this conversation is going to turn ugly faster than I'm sure Eric intended it to.

"Did you?" he asks.

I give him a sideways glance as I take another sip of my beer, hoping that it will wash down the bile and give me something else to think about. Yes, in a way I did know, in another way I truly hoped I was wrong. I could deal with loving someone when I didn't think they could or would love me back. I could easily sit back and let him have his own happy life while I sat quietly in love with him. It was easier for me to admit my love for Eric when I thought nothing would actually happen between us.

He shrugs off my glare and goes back to pacing. Without saying anything.

I was safe without knowing for certain that I really was in love with a man who didn't stand a chance of loving me back. How is it possible that I could be attracted to someone who wasn't capable of feeling the same way toward me?

That was how I rationalized all this until now.

My inability to talk to Eric drove him mad and he stormed out of the room, leaving whatever he came in here to say unsaid.

Sex is something I take a lot of pleasure in, until I come.

Orgasms are the trigger of conditioned therapy. A belief that was ingrained in my brain for far too long. So much so that the idea of giving into being with a man, I have to swallow the bile rising in my throat, is enough to set off the little triggers my body and mind were conditioned to have as a response.

The never-ending knot I get in my stomach anytime I'm around Eric, alone with Eric or I'm really struggling with holding myself back, returns with a vengeance and I keep attempting to swallow back the bile that keeps creeping up the back of my throat as I pace behind the bar.

Why do I have to be in love with someone I can't fucking have?

How did I ever manage to fall in love with someone without once connecting with them on a deeply personal level?

The answer really isn't all that simple. I honestly can't tell you at what point in our friendship, pseudo relationship, that I actually fell in love with him. I just know that I did. A feeling that, until his coming out back in New York, I'd been able to ignore. I guess there was a part of me that wondered if he'd try and make a play for me after coming out. Sometimes I wonder if he's still trying to figure out exactly how to do just that.

"Goddammit," I growl as I kick at an imaginary rock on the ground.

"Care to talk about it?" I hear Eric's sympathetic voice and I slouch. All the fight I felt moments ago drains from my body in a rush. His voice carries a calming effect with it. A voice that has always managed to calm me down, addicting to the rolling waves of emotions running through my fucking body. Emotions that will send me running in the opposite direction, looking for a place to hurl, if I even attempt to act on them.

Denying who I am is much easier than admitting to myself or anyone else, the truth. It is impossible, physically and mentally, to give in. I have no choice but to let something so unbelievable wipe out any and all ability to love and be loved by the one person I want and the only person I know I need.

"No," I finally manage to work out past the rising lump in my throat.

"Okay then," I hear him say. Despite looking away from him, I have no doubt that he shrugs behind me. He doesn't leave, though I never expected him to. Eric has a way of quietly probing, a strange way of making sure he gets what he wants, or at least what he wants to hear. But, he also knows me well enough that if he probes me, in his silent, 'I'm here, I'm listening' kind of way that I will more than likely start talking.

Resisting the urge to tell Eric everything is becoming increasingly difficult. Desperate to tell him why we can never be together, I am not. You see, there is something about him, aside from his sexy as hell good looks, his quiet demeanor and his outspoken opinions on things he's passionate about that I fell in love with long ago.

How do you tell the one person you're deeply attracted to that you can do nothing about it without becoming violently ill?

"You know..." Eric says softly, the worn out bench I'd passed when I came outside creaks under his weight as he shifts. "You've been telling me since New York that we needed to talk, promising me that we would..." He doesn't finish his question, he doesn't have to.

After our impromptu meeting that followed his admission, he'd left me alone with my thoughts and it was then that I realized I needed to tell him. I'd found him a little while later and promised him we'd talk, but that night, in New York and while on tour was hardly an appropriate place to do so.

Even now it's not the right time. I know that when I manage to muster up the courage to tell him about my past, he needs to be able to escape me. He needs to be able to run away screaming. He cannot do that while we're on tour. Though I know that we can't have this discussion until we're back in California, off the bus and off the tour, I can't tell him he has to wait until then. I can't do that because the more time we spend together, quietly talking or not talking, the harder it is becoming for me to hold it all inside.

I also needed time to come to grips with the fact that he'd finally come out of the closet, finally confirmed what I thought I needed to hear. I often wondered if Eric admitted it to the rest of us, thereby admitting it to him and myself, if it would be the catalyst that would drive me over the edge to figuring out if I'm capable of wiping away more than two years of ingrained ideas about gay men.

"I'm not ready," I finally manage to tell him quietly. I can't bear to see the hurt in his eyes again, so I don't look at him. "And honestly Eric, I'm not entirely sure you're ready to hear what I have to say."

"Is that supposed to give me hope, Cal?" he says angrily.

I whip around, staring at him. "Hope for what, Eric?"

He just shrugs.

"You know, I don't understand you sometimes, man," I snap at him. I'm trying desperately to let the anger roll off of me without pushing it at him. He doesn't deserve my wrath, but fuck, he knows how to turn this into something to do with him.

God, I wish Dex was here instead of at some 'all-exclusive' club with Raine. He'd fucking help me with this shit. "One minute you want to know, you want me to talk, then the next minute you're pulling out the 'pity-me' card. I don't understand exactly what it is you want me to say, Eric."

I watch as my words sink into his heart, the longing, aching devastation washes over him.

"If you haven't figured it out by now, I don't suspect you ever will, Mouse." My nickname on his lips sends ice through my veins as I watch him stand up. My nickname coming from him is a rare occurrence anymore. Unless we're around everyone else.

He threw down the line in the sand; built the Great Wall of China between us. Neither of which I can cross unless I'm ready to talk.

I stare after him in astonishment wondering what in fucking hell crawled up his ass and died.

This isn't the first time he's turned the tables on me, bringing himself into the center of the conversation. It's also not the first time I feel guilty for not coming clean with him. For not telling him that I wish he could be to me what he wants me to be for him. Why it is that I can never have him.

chapter 2

eric

"What's the matter, Eric?" Jess asks through the phone. I'd walked straight through the bar and onto the sidewalk in front of it. The streets of Nashville are bustling, people walking from bar to bar, stumbling around, screaming, hollering, whatever they do when they're drunk. It's almost comical to watch. "He still won't talk to you, will he?"

"No," I grumble. "Tonight he got pissed at me, rightfully so, I was being an idiot," I tell her. I met Jess in San Diego, after our very first show on the tour. A tour that would prove to be more challenging to me, emotionally, than I ever thought it could be.

Jess is one of Addison's friends. She came to that first show and somehow we'd managed to hook up afterward. And no, we didn't have sex, though I'd wanted to, at first. Having sex with women is easy, not entirely unpleasant. But when you're trying to hide, miserably I might add, that you're gay from your friends, it becomes necessary.

We talked almost all night. For some strange reason, talking to her was like talking to myself in the shower. It was easy, effortless and freeing. I unloaded a shit ton of dirty laundry on her that night and she's been here for me ever since.

"You, an idiot?" She snorts into the phone and I can't help but laugh a little.

"I just don't know what to do anymore," I tell her, and it's the truth, I don't. "I just get more and more hurt every time I try and talk to him and he shoots me down.

She sighs into the phone, "Is it really worth it?"

"Jess," I reprimand her.

"No Eric, listen to me for a minute, please?"

I slouch and round the corner of the bar, it's a little quieter back here. "Fine." I roll my eyes even though she can't see me.

"You thought that coming out would be the kick in the ass he needed to finally bring him into your arms, right?"

I grunt.

"And that's not what's happening. At least not that you can tell. Maybe he really isn't into guys, Eric."

"Into guys or into me?" I retort.

"Does it matter?" she counters quickly and continues, "Have you honestly thought about that? Or come straight out and asked him?" I don't answer, I don't have to. She already knows I haven't. She's just trying to make me think. "Until you know, you can't judge him like this. Instead, pull him out, make him jealous, or grow a fucking pair and ask him, make him talk to you."

"Jess!" I scold her again.

She laughs, "Look, you cannot sit around and wait forever for him to figure his shit out. You need to be able to find your own happiness, you deserve it. But you need to find out for yourself, Peacock. You can't sit here wondering whether or not he is, whether or not there is ever a possibility of the two of you getting together unless you ask him. Talk to him about it. Unless you ask, how do you even know he's gay?"

My hand tightens around my phone and I hear it creak in protest. I sigh, "That's just it, I don't. But I think it would be pretty fucking unfair if I feel this way about him and he isn't attracted to me the same way."

"Oh, I wouldn't go that far," she tells me. "It happens to us girls all the time. We fall in love, or maybe it's just lust, with a guy who has no reciprocation whatsoever." I can tell she's grumbling and remembering her last little fling.

"Don't sound so bitter," I tease her with a little laugh.

"I can't help it. It comes with the territory of being a truly selfless person. Willing to give up everything for what? I've done it for years, Peacock, it's made me bitter."

On one of our many nighttime phone calls, Jess confessed to me that she was always ready and willing to give men what they wanted, usually just a blow job. The men never reciprocated. They simply had their orgasm and rolled over to go to sleep, leaving her high and dry, but yet she'd still go back the next time they called on the hope that something more would happen. It never did.

When she told me all of this, I felt awful for her, but I could easily understand what she meant, hell, I've had a few of those myself or been that way toward more than a few people. Needless to say, I apologized on behalf of dickhead men everywhere. We laughed it off, but I often wonder if she's gotten over being a doormat.

Remembering she had a date the other night, I ask her how it went.

I hear her sigh before answering. "My vibrator was more entertaining than he was."

I snort, "That bad?" I raise my eyebrow at nothing, knowing she isn't going to answer me. "Well, I would tell you that I'd find someone for you to hook up with, but they seem to be falling off the market faster than I can even mention your name," I tell her.

She giggles into the phone. "How is that going...you know, Dex and Raine?"

"I wish I could tell you, but I haven't seen them a whole lot, which may be your answer. Hell, they didn't even come out with us tonight."

"She's becoming more insistent," Jess says to me. I don't need further explanation. Jess has been keeping tabs on Sam for me, information that I've been feeding to Mills when he asks for it.

"Are you still ignoring her?"

"Yes, but she's calling all the time. It got worse after that article came out." She pauses briefly, "I don't know what else to do."

I sigh into the phone as I rub my fingers across my forehead. "Nothing more you can do. She knows you have an inside track to the band and she is dying for any information you might have and that you will give to her."

"But I won't."

"I know, love. I know. You don't need to explain it to me, but that is what she's after. Just do what you can to let it go."

"It's getting really bad." Her voice is interrupted by total silence on my end. I hear the phone shift. "Fuck me, that's her."

"Ignore it. Does she know where you live?"

"Mhmm and where I work."

"Is she a violent person? Would she do anything physical?" I ask her with the unexplainable urge to protect her, to protect my friend.

"No, Peacock, I don't think she would."

Jess and I finish talking, I let her go. I head back into the bar to find someone to take me back to the hotel. I'm tired and drinking no longer sounds appealing.

I've barely crawled out of the shower and into bed when Calvin finally returns to the room. He doesn't say much as he's emptying out his pockets. From the tightness in his shoulders, I can tell that he's stressing over something. It's not hard to read a man you've roomed with for some time, not to mention the man that you have what feels like an unhealthy, unwanted attraction to. My infatuation with Calvin started years ago, long before 69 Bottles became the name it is today. Why we never managed to ask for separate rooms was beyond me. It started way back when we could usually only afford one or two rooms if we were traveling. The one room nights were hell on earth with Kyle on the floor, Dex and Talon in one bed and Calvin and I in another. I shudder at the memory. Then when we could finally afford two rooms, it was usually Dex, Mouse and I in one and Talon and Kyle in another. Huh, it's a wonder they never hooked up before this.

Once we got down to being able to afford three rooms, Talon usually got his own and Dex and Kyle would room together. When we had the chance, and with previous tours, Calvin and I still shared. Why we never separated was beyond me, and while I'd asked for it, Calvin would tell Mills or me it wasn't necessary. I guess the little voice in my head took Cal wanting to share a room with me as a sign that maybe, one day, things might change between us.

With his back to me he says, "I'm sorry about earlier. I lost my head."

I shrug it off like I do all the time. Sometimes 'PMS' comes to mind with him. His moods will shift unexpectedly and sometimes I feel eggshells follow him like dirt.

Despite all that, the tone in his voice has my whole body humming with a need to reach out for him, to comfort him. Instead, I settle deeper into the bed I'm lying on. "I just want you to tell me what's going on, but despite what I want from you, I'm not going to push you, Calvin, but you also need to be aware of the fact that no matter what, I'm here to listen, always. If it's not me you want to talk to, let me find someone you can talk to, like Jess."

He snorts a humorless laugh. "She'll just turn around and tell you."

I sigh. "No, we don't work that way. We're not a couple of gossip mongers, Cal, we don't talk about stuff unless it affects one of us."

"Well, this might affect you, more than you know..." He leaves the thought hanging in the air before he walks out of my line of sight. What the hell is that supposed to mean? I don't ask the question out loud. It feels like prying and the opposite of what I just said I wouldn't do.

I hear the bathroom door click shut.

There is a newfound hope that wells inside me at his words... a hope I have no business feeling, a hope that I know will shatter me and keep me hanging and stop me from moving on. Jess is right, maybe I need to find it somewhere within myself to let it go, move on, attempt to move on at least. Once this tour is over and we're not cooped up together, it might be easier.

It's with that thought that I drift off to sleep to the soothing sounds of the shower. The thought of him naked on the other side of a rather flimsy door brings back the loneliness as sleep takes me.

chapter 3

calvin

After my shower, before crawling into bed, I couldn't stop myself from watching Eric sleep. The soft snores, the steady rhythm of his breathing, the warmth and comfort found in watching him sleep. Loving Eric from afar, that's the way this has to go. It won't be easy, but in the end it's going to be much better, for him.

I crawl into my bed facing him and click off the light. Plunging the room into darkness means I can no longer see him, but I can still hear him breathing softly. I shiver though I'm not cold. Loneliness creeps inside and I drift off to sleep.

"What now?" I ask Dr. V. as I call him.

"You've got to decide that for yourself, Calvin, no one else can do that for you. If he's opening the door to listen to what you have to say, let him."

"That's easier said than done, Doc," I say as I switch ears with my phone.

"Yes it is, it took you nearly three years to tell me everything and even then, I'm not entirely convinced I know it all." I can hear his determination.

At one point in all of this, he cracked a joke, saying that maybe my revulsion to women was because I was really meant to be with men. That sent all kinds of wild thoughts and impulses through me that sent me running to the bathroom. Needless to say, he dropped that subject and while I was pleased he'd tried to sway me the other way, he felt guilty for igniting a reaction from me. Thereby allowing me to open up to him about everything. Since then, Dr. V, Vincent, has been working with me on my issues, helping me to overcome the fear of intimacy and helping to reverse the impulse of revulsion when it comes to orgasms in general and sex with women.

He was finally able to put a name to what they'd done to me. Conversion Therapy, they successfully converted my homosexual tendencies in an attempt to make me straight. But I still have an aversion to women or maybe it's just orgasms in general, that was the crux of the joke at the time.

He thought that they'd turned me against sex period, but only to realize that homosexual thoughts and actions had more impact on me than women did, period.

I sigh, "You know more than enough and the stuff you haven't been told is irrelevant to any form of treatment plan you can concoct."

"Well, you need to decide what is more important to you. You can decide if being with him is most important or if you want to be with someone else. Women no longer seem to be an issue for you, but I also know that you struggle emotionally with them, so ultimately, is he what you really want?"

"I like to think so. But I can't say for certain. I can't allow myself to think about it too much without triggering a reaction. Something I've worked very hard to control."

"You just don't want people to know," he counters, and he's right, I don't. It's not so much that I don't want them to know that I'm pretty confident that I'm gay - well okay, there is that aspect of it too, but that's beside the point. I don't need to try and answer a million and one questions about why I seize up, why I throw up or why I freak out.

I continue, "Eric and I have known each other for so long, I'm pretty sure, at some point in this journey, we've crossed the friendship lines and I no longer know where those boundaries are with us. Not to mention the fact that I've been around him for ten years. I know a lot about him, but I don't know intimate things about him. Neither one of us has ever dated anyone while the other is around. I never became that friend he confided in when shit hit the fan with whoever he was dating, therefore leaving me a very small window of knowledge on how he'd be intimate with someone. Let alone the fact that intimacy, on any level, scares the hell out of me. It's nearly impossible to be sexually attracted to someone when you can't get it up at the mere thought of them." Dr. V and I have no secrets, he knows everything about the issues I have whenever I fight my converted nature, when I tamp it down long enough to attempt to feel anything. While mentally I can process a lot of it, the physical side of things is nearly impossible for me to achieve. In other words, my dick stays limp.

In an attempt to try and curb the problem I have, turning things strictly sexual, I watched porn once with two bisexual men who had no issues touching one another. I was great, it was hot, I was turned on until the two guys in the video kissed each other. I immediately went soft and ran for the bathroom. Which, even if it is straight sex, it comes up, but I rarely get off.

"What do you think stops you from 'getting it up'?" Dr. V asks, interrupting my disappointing trip down memory lane.

I can picture Dr. V's sheepish look on his face as he asks me that question. For being a psychologist, he's quite the prude. It makes me smile. His clinical talk gets old fast, and I imagine he spends most of his night at home either updating patient notes or playing some random computer game. He's older, but the eternal bachelor. I would imagine it's not easy dating a doctor of his caliber and he seems like the type that would have given up on it for the sake of his own sanity. In short, he's a pretty big geek.

"The pit that forms in my stomach the moment I let my mind wander in that direction. Sometimes the nausea isn't so bad, but it's usually enough to kill an erection."

"Have you ever tried to imagine him as a woman?"

"Uh…" I raise an eyebrow at myself in the mirror hanging on the wall across from me.

He chuckles, "Not literally, but when you look at a woman and you become attracted or aroused by her, what is it that turns you on?"

"I'm not sure I know how to answer that."

He chuckles again. "Well, next time you look at him, put him into the context of which you would apprise a woman. See if you can get or keep that erection. If you can, then it is a step in the right direction."

"Baby steps," I mutter. "I'm tired of baby steps."

"Calvin, so much of what you're feeling is truly 'mind over matter'. Yes, your repulsion is a conditioned response, but much like you did with women, you can overcome this too," he says confidently.

"I wish it were that easy."

"It wasn't easy with women, was it?"

"In a way, yes." I don't elaborate.

"How so?"

I sigh into the phone and fall back onto the bed. Eric left to run an errand, giving me the chance to call Dr. V without interruption from him.

I hate having to run away just to make these phone calls, but when you're only hearing half of it, they can sound pretty fucked up. "Because a woman is a natural partner."

"Ahh, but is a woman a natural partner to you?"

I take a deep breath and let it out slowly, "No."

"Then what's natural about it? Because society tells you that you should be with a woman?" I nod, realizing where he is going with this. "Because your father thinks that you shouldn't be with a man?" That question is followed by a pregnant pause, one filled with a promise of more to come. "Who cares?" Dr. V says softly, he knows he's breaking down that boundary, that barrier within me. "Your father certainly doesn't and society is a bitch you can't tame on your own. Society is what it is, Calvin. Just because they may not agree with it, doesn't mean it should stop you from finding happiness. It doesn't mean that you can't be with who you want to be with."

I screw my eyes closed. I can feel the wetness pooling. I don't need to cry over this, fuck, why do I have to feel this knot in my heart, this gaping hole. I rub at my chest, hoping to soothe the ache.

"I think you need to decide, for you, who it is important to. Who will care? When you've done that, once you've decided that the people who matter to you aren't going to care about who you're with, then and only then, can you start to let go. You were told that being gay is the ultimate taboo. You were shown some of the most unimaginable things in order to program your brain into liking and loving women. You were shown things that truly do not exist, not in today's society. Not in today's world." He takes a deep breath and continues, "Calvin, there will always be haters, there will always be right-wing nut jobs, religious groups, and people in society who disagree with being gay and I agree that once out, it won't be easy for you, but that is a bridge you burn when you have to. Not before you've even cleared the water from the river to start building it."

I can't respond to him, my mind is running a million miles a minute. I know deep down, in my heart of hearts, that he is right. Because I've been conditioned to believe that being gay is bad - that's putting it mildly - it's hard for me to let go of all the pressures of what I think society would tell me to do. But just because my mind agrees with the right-wing conservatives, my heart certainly does not.

After some time passes without saying anything, Dr. V breaks our silence. "You have to tell him. Telling him will put him in his place, either beside you or behind you. If he's beside you, he will help you, support you, and he will be there to stand with you. Hell, he may even stick up for you, but he needs to understand where you stand, what you feel, how you feel and where it is you want to go from there. If he doesn't know and he crosses the line, crosses into the place you cannot go, he needs to understand why."

"He has to know it isn't him," I interrupt.

"Yes, but he won't know that if you don't tell him. He's going to think it is him and that you don't want him."

I sit back up on the end of the bed. "Yeah, I know. I just...fuck, I don't know how to tell him."

"When the moment is right, you will. I can't tell you when to do it or how to do it, just that you need to do it. What about talking to someone else, someone you trust?"

"That's a mighty small list, Doc," I tell him with a humorless laugh.

"Try that first. Try it on for size, see if it fits, then decide."

"Yeah, alright. Thanks, Doc."

"Anytime. You still coming in during the break?"

"Yeah."

"Think about this, don't reject the idea so quickly, actually think about it..."

"What's that?"

"Bring him with you. Talk here, talk in front of me."

I start to object, but Doc interrupts, "Think about it. It's neutral, it's safe, and lastly, I can help you explain some things that you might not understand yourself." His voice goes distant and he tells someone something. "I have to run, my next appointment is here. Think about it."

"Yeah, alright," I tell him and we hang up. I toss my phone into the chair and put my head in my hands, allowing my vision to morph to something unreal, something dreamlike, the fantasy...the one where sex doesn't hurt so much.

chapter 4

calvin

"Why are you hiding over here?"

I turn in the direction of the voice and watch as Talon leans against the railing next to me. This probably isn't the best place to carry on a conversation. We're in a bar after all, but when Talon wants to talk, there isn't any place off limits. That's the amount of tenacity that he has. Then again, his motivation and drive have gotten us this far in our careers and that means he's someone you listen to, no matter what.

My eyes leave Talon and like a homing missile, they find *him* once again just as he throws his head back laughing at something the guy sitting next to him said. "Just people watching," I tell him.

"People or Peacock watching?"

My eyes dart to his. "Am I that obvious?" I ask, bringing the beer bottle to my lips and sucking down more than half of it. Our eyes never look away from each other.

"Yeah, maybe a little. More so to me, I think, than anyone else." Talon finally breaks our eye contact as he looks down over our group of people. The bar itself isn't packed, but it's not empty either. Just enough to mix into the crowd. "So Raine flew back to Los Angeles last night," he says out of nowhere. I want to roll my eyes because I know he won't say anything

33

more on the issue, he's waiting for me to say something, but the news surprises me.

"Well, that explains Dex's dickwad attitude."

He snorts, "She didn't even say goodbye."

"Ouch." I shudder at the thought of being abandoned.

"Pretty much. He's pissed off because he can't go running after her."

The waitress approaches us and hands me another beer. Talon orders one for himself and off she goes. "She means that much to him?" I ask skeptically.

Talon shrugs, "Yeah, I guess so. He's been in a foul mood since leaving Atlanta."

"He's dealing with a lot. I can't imagine being Raine and discovering all this bullshit about the guy you're with."

He shoulder checks me. "I'm pretty sure she knew what she was getting into but Dex doesn't see it that way. He thinks that he has to protect her from his past and that's not something he can do, no one can." He turns his back on the railing, I think he's going to leave but he leans back against it, resting his elbows and overlooking the small crowd behind us. We're elevated above the main floor and the rest of the band, but there isn't a lot going on up here, which was why I came up here in the first place.

Talon succeeds at something he's done best since we met; his quiet questions. He's waiting for me to start talking. My eyes land on Eric and the guy he's sitting with. The guy is definitely his type, well, all except for the fact that he could probably squish the wannabe with his bare hands, or step on him. My fingers flex around my beer bottle as the guy leans in and whispers something in Eric's ear and I can see the faint blush spread across his cheeks.

"If he makes you so jealous, why aren't you down there talking to him yourself?"

I grind my teeth in frustration. "If it were that easy, don't you think I would be?" I mutter then ask him, "Do you ever look at someone and all you can see when you look at them is something that can only be described as 'home'?"

"Every damn day," he grunts before turning back around. "Every time I look at either one of them, that's what I feel."

"But you're with them."

"I am, but looking back on it now, I felt it the moment I rounded that corner and she was standing there, before you, as a matter of fact," he tells me.

"But did you know immediately that's what you were feeling?"

"Aw, hell no. I just knew I saw something I wanted, but it took me a long time to realize that what I wanted wasn't something I could dispose of the next day. It was...it's hard to describe..."

"No, I get that," I cut him off. Thankfully the waitress returns with his beer and another for me. I quickly down the rest of mine and replace the fresh bottle with the old.

When the waitress leaves, Talon wastes no time in continuing the mini-inquisition he has going on. "If that's what you're seeing, why are you sitting up here watching him talk to..."

"Because it's easier this way," I say through gritted teeth.

"I highly doubt that." He turns toward me. "Listen, I can't pretend that I understand it because honestly, I don't. A part of me always thought that you were waiting for him to admit it to himself," he tells me.

I can't deny his statement. "In a way, I think I was," I say cryptically before sipping my beer.

"So he's out and I know you're not oblivious to how he feels about you." I give him a sideways glance, drinking more beer. "That's what I thought." He swallows down the last of his. "So if you know how he feels about you, I can't imagine anything in the world that would continue to keep you away from him."

"Did Addison send you up here?"

He snorts a laugh. "Nah man, it's honestly what I see when you two look at each other. There is something there, something I can't quite explain because I'm not sure I understand it myself, but you know how sometimes you just know when something is meant to be?"

I don't respond to him, I can't. I've never been able to talk about my past with him, or anyone for that matter, and I'm not about to start now. "I have my reasons for keeping my distance." Dr. V's words come creeping back into my brain about social norms and society and I start to wonder if that is really what is keeping me away from it all. Not to mention the fact that if I was to finally tell someone about my past, if it wasn't Eric, it would have to be Talon. Kyle and I are not that close, and well, Dex is a jackass and he makes no secret of that fact. While I'm confident that he could keep himself in check if it came to a heart to heart, he's far from the first person on the list that I want to spill my guts to.

Talon shrugs, sets his beer on the table next to us, turns to me and places his hand on my shoulder. "Maybe it's time to re-evaluate those reasons, brother. You should know that no one in this circle will ever judge you, or him, for your choices. Not me or Kyle - how could we? Certainly not Dex, he's not oblivious to this either. We all love you and we love Eric, there is no judgment here." He gives me a gentle squeeze before shoving off. I down the rest of my beer while I watch Eric and his new friend stand up and head toward the back of the bar.

"Damn it," I grumble to myself.

"Hey there." I turn to the voice interrupting me and find myself looking into the brown eyes of a gothic wannabe with a cute smile and hooker red lipstick.

"Hey yourself," I tell her as she steps up closer to me.

"Wanna dance?"

I smile at the escape presenting itself, the piece of attention I need to stop myself from dwelling on what Talon's just said to me. "Sure," I tell her and take her hand.

eric

I zip up my fly and leave...shit, what's his name? Fuck, it doesn't matter anyway. I leave him in the handicap stall of the men's bathroom. He had no problem kneeling before me, but anytime I tried to start anything, he shoved me off, so I gave in and let him suck.

Disgust washes through me. Why the hell do I do this shit to myself? Oh, yeah, because it's my piss poor attempt at making him jealous. Piss poor because it never fucking works.

I round the corner and freeze when my eyes lock on him from across the bar. He's sitting at the bar with some tiny trying-too-hard goth standing between his legs, kissing and licking on his neck.

What wouldn't I give to be that tongue?

Give it up...he doesn't want you.

Fuck you...

My head and my heart begin their nightly argument. The inner war is getting old. The constant tug and pull from one direction to the other is nearly too much for me to handle anymore and walking into that bathroom served three purposes. The obvious, getting off. The next obvious was to make him jealous, and then the least obvious is my pitiful attempt at forcing myself to get over him and move on. A battle that has been playing out for months, if not years.

A battle I know I am going to lose, miserably.

chapter 5

eric

I returned to the rest of our group, though the party is winding down and they're becoming more subdued. I can tell that Kyle and Talon will be taking Addison back shortly because I can see her starting to fade, that's when Kyle approaches me.

"What's goin' on, man?" he asks as he sits down next to me. I purposefully sat with my back to Mouse and his chick because I didn't want to be tempted to look.

"Nada, you?"

He shrugs. "Same as always," he says with a hint of something more simmering under the surface.

"Spit it out, man, come on."

He leans forward, closer to me. "I was just wondering if you and..."

"No, and I'm pretty sure it's never going to happen," I tell him before he can say his name.

"Why do you say that?"

I give him a very pointed look. "Can you not see what's happening behind me?"

He sighs, "I do, but um, you just crawled out of the bathroom, alone. What do you expect?" He throws the obvious back at me and I want to argue with him, but he's absolutely right.

"Yeah, well, what am I supposed to do, wait forever?"

"No," he smiles, "You fight for it. You follow your gut." I look at Kyle, unable to really say anything at the moment. Kyle's very attractive and I would have to say, I never in my wildest dreams imagined that he was bi until he met Addison and everything changed for them. Giving me hope that I didn't have before. Hope that just maybe, I might get what I think I want.

"I often wonder if it's worth it," I grumble.

"What do you mean exactly?"

"What if I'm wrong? What if I'm really chasing after something that I have no business wanting; someone that isn't at least curious," I tell him.

"Haven't you guys ever talked about…"

I can't help the sigh as my chest tightens while I remember that night… a couple years ago…

"I'm so damn drunk," Mouse laughs.

I've been fighting the urge all night, afraid that maybe, just maybe, I would be taking advantage of him, but he keeps touching me. Keeps wrapping his arms around my waist, pulling me closer. What in the hell am I supposed to do?

Finally Mouse plops down on the park bench. We've just played a show and in true 69 Bottles' fashion, we got drunk afterwards. I sit down next to him and he slides a little closer to me. He stinks of drink though I'm not sure I smell a whole lot better than he does. I think my head is a little clearer, maybe.

That's when he turns his head in my direction, looking like he wants to kiss me…

I steal the chance, placing my lips against his, firmly. There is a brief moment of warmth and electricity that passes between us and then it is suddenly wiped away when he pulls back and throws up all over the ground in front of us. Being the gentleman my mother raised me to be, I take him home. When I went to leave, he stopped me, asked me to stay, so I did.

The next morning, it was almost like nothing happened. I think my heart cracked a little that day and any time I tried to bring it up to him, ask him if it was the alcohol or if he truly felt that way about me, the subject gets changed.

"Eric."

Talon's voice brings me back to the present. "Yeah?"

"We're gonna take off," he says, looking to Kyle and Addie and then back to me.

I look at Kyle and answer his earlier question, "Not directly, no."

Kyle gives me a sad smile. "Maybe it's time you tell him."

I shrug and we all say goodnight. I decided, against my better judgment, to go and pull the chick off of Mouse, but when Talon, Kyle and Addison are gone, I turn around and so is Mouse. I look to the bathroom and standing vigil near the door is Casey. "Fuck."

I turn to Troy, "They'll be fine, right?"

"Yeah. Casey's got him."

"Good, let's go."

"You don't..."

"Nope," I snap and storm past Troy toward the door.

"But you always stay and wait." Troy tries to stop me.

"Not tonight," I tell him and I keep walking, crashing through the door and walking toward one of the two remaining vehicles.

"Yo, Peacock." I roll my eyes.

"Hey, I didn't know you were still here. Ready to go back?" I ask Dex as he runs up to me.

"Yeah," he says as he catches his breath.

"You drunk?"

He snorts. "I fucking wish."

"You holding up alright?"

"Do we really have to talk about this?" The tone of his voice tells me that if we do, it's not going to be pleasant.

"No."

"Good, so how was..."

I give him a stern look as we both reach opposite sides of the car to climb in. "How about we make a deal? You don't talk about Raine and where she is, and I won't talk about the bad blowjob I got in the bathroom stall. Deal?"

"Fine." We both open our doors. "I don't care about that. I want to talk about Calvin."

His eyes glint with a hint of mischief, something he's notorious for. "What the hell, Dex? Is this gang up on Peacock night? Because Kyle already accosted me. He's off the discussion table too." I scowl at him.

"You take away all my fun," Dex grumbles as we climb in.

"Seriously, did you guys all conspire to talk to me?"

"Yes," he says with a laugh. Though I think he intended to brush it off as a non-discussion among the four or more of them, I honestly believe this is their way of an intervention.

"Well, I'm done talking about it," I say solemnly. "What's the point in talking about it with you, Kyle, Addison or anyone else for that matter when the person I really need to talk to has been avoiding me like the plague?"

"Well, maybe it's time to trap him. Force him to talk to you. Shit, y'all are staying in the same damn hotel room and you're stuck on the same fucking bus, so maybe it's time to pull up the big girl panties and talk to him."

I scowl at him, but he drops the subject, obviously making his point in the most Dex way possible, the fewer the words the better.

We ride back to the hotel in silence, something not entirely uncommon around Dex, at least Dex pre-girlfriend. I don't know what that chick has done to him, but damn, she's sure as shit straightened his ass out.

Once in my room, I climb in the shower. I'm out and combing through my hair, realizing that I need to re-dye it before the show in Miami when there is a knock at the door. I wrap a towel around my waist and open the door.

Shit. I knew I should have looked. "Where's your key?" I ask him. Our eyes meet and grab hold of each other, refusing to let the other go. The familiar pull I feel when I look at him is there, it's always right fucking there.

"Will you let me in?"

"Do I have to? I mean, you don't even have a key."

He gives me a smirk. "Oh, I have it, just wanted to drag you out of bed." I watch as his eyes roam over my nearly naked body before finally looking away. If I didn't know better, I'd swear he was turning green.

"I…" I hesitate, "Yeah, fine, whatever." I hold the door open for him to come in, he ducks under my arm and my eyes meet Casey's in the hallway. He just gives me a smile and I close the door just as Casey's eyes dart down then back up. I look…fuck. "Give me a minute," I tell Calvin as I slip back into the bathroom, grabbing a pair of flannel pajama pants from my suitcase, not that it's going to hide the hard-on that sprouted the moment I opened the door, it's at least a little respectful and less likely to break free.

I stare at myself in the mirror, take a few deep breaths as I pull my hair back and tie it up to keep it off my face. I take one more deep breath before leaving the steamy bathroom.

When I round the corner, Mouse is sitting in the chair near the window, leaning forward, his elbows on his knees and his head in his hands. He lifts his head, his eyes are slightly red around the edges and if I didn't know better, I would think he'd been crying. "What's up?" I ask him softly.

"I need to say something that I've needed to say for a long time."

The tone in his voice is hesitant, scared even, and I take a seat on the edge of the bed, awkwardly, I might add. "So say it." Is this it?

chapter 6

calvin

"I don't want you, Eric. I'm not the type of person you think I am and I am certainly not the person you want me to be. That is impossible for me."

"Whoever said I want..." I give him a stern look. He's tried this before, or at least made an attempt at progressing our relationship in the past, opening up to me, trying to kiss me, things like that, but unfortunately, there is always copious amounts of alcohol involved and that makes it impossible to tell what's really what. Reality versus the fantasy.

"I'm not stupid, or blind, Eric. I see you watching me, waiting to see what I'm going to do or who I'm going to do it with and I can't..." The steam I thought I'd built up before coming in here tonight slowly starts to fade away. My fight draining, I close my eyes, hoping that the truth doesn't show through in my eyes.

"I'm not the only one watching, you know? I saw you tonight, standing on the balcony watching me, and after the conversations everyone keeps trying to have with me tonight, everyone already thinks there is something going on between us, they're just impatient for us to come out with it."

His eyes meet mine. "That's never going to happen, it's impossible."

"Why, Calvin? Why is it impossible? That's the part in all of this that I don't understand." He stands up and takes a step toward me.

"Remember, that night, a couple years ago, the night you kissed me?"

"The night you puked all over my shoes...yeah, I remember, Calvin, I remember it like it was fucking yesterday. The night neither one of us has ever talked about...a night I was certain you didn't remember." I watch as frustration and anger creep over Eric's features. His hands clench and unfurl, repeatedly.

"Oh, I remember, Eric. I remember it like it was fucking ten minutes ago. I can't fucking forget it, but this... between us, cannot and will never happen." I gesture between the two of us.

"Why, Calvin? Just tell me why?"

"Because I'm not..." I can't even say the word. I can't even admit it to myself, let alone him, that I'm not gay, because it's a lie, a god-awful fucking lie that I wish like hell I didn't have to use. I wish I didn't have to try and convince myself that I'm not gay, because...fuck!

"That's what I thought." Eric takes another step in my direction, followed by another, then another. I try to back away but I can't. I'm trapped against the wall of the hotel room. His approach is slow, but steady. He doesn't want to scare me, I can see that in his eyes. My body is locked down, my fists clench hard enough that I can feel my nails biting into my palms, excitement and fear play war inside me.

"Because I don't deserve you." I finally manage to speak, though barely above a whisper. "Because you deserve to be with someone who can love you back. I'm not that person, Eric. I can't love you back."

"You won't even let yourself try, so how do you know you can't love me back?"

"Because, Eric, every time I look at you I can think of nothing but you. Nothing but your lips and the way they would taste on mine, your touch against my skin and the love I know you have for me."

Eric stops in his tracks, staring me down with his eyes scared but yet that warmth, the love he has for me, shines back at me. "How?" he breathes.

"Because everything I see when I look at you, I feel it too. I know you see it in my eyes, I know it is the reason you can't let go of me. I know it's there but goddammit, Eric, it is buried so far down inside of me that I cannot unlock it. I cannot find the key. No matter how many times I try. No matter how many times I kiss you, no matter how many fucking times I tell myself it is all in my head, it's not. I can't get past it, I can't unlock it. I can't let it go."

I watch his eyes turn from warmth to confusion, my cryptic words making it hard for him to understand where it is that I am coming from. Words that I can't...

"Maybe if you explain it to him, you'll have your answers. Tell him what hides inside you and let him decide for himself."

Dr. V's words ring in my head once again. *Can I do this? Can I bring myself to explain to him exactly why I cannot love him? Why we can't be together?*

I drop my eyes from his, fighting the war inside of me isn't something I need him to see. I need to…

Suddenly, his hands are on my cheeks, his fingers in my hair, tilting my head up to look at him. "Try, Calvin," he whispers.

"I wish I could…I wish it could be different. I wish it didn't have to be like this, but it is and it has to be," I say through clenched teeth as I fight the rising bile in my stomach, fight my muscles from locking down and holding me prisoner within my own skin, but it's too late. Eric's lips land hard and fast against mine. For the briefest of moments the world washes away and I am alone. I am free, freer than anything I have ever felt before.

The feeling vanishes in the blink of an eye when my body locks down, bile rises beyond the point of managing it…beyond what I can handle. I cough and sputter while Eric pulls back, though he doesn't release me. My body shakes and convulses and he releases me in disgust. "What the fuck, Calvin?" As it should be.

I turn and dart into the bathroom to retch, instinct takes over when I see him approaching me. "Don't. Just stay there." He doesn't stop, he comes closer. "Don't fucking touch me." The urge to flee takes over. I flush the toilet and dart from the bathroom and our hotel room.

Fuck! FUCK! Fuck!
"Whoa, dude, you alright?" I look at Casey.
"No, let me into your room."
"No, not until you tell me what's wrong?"
"I'm drunk, I need to go to bed."
"Bullshit," Casey calls me out. "You've barely drank anything tonight. Try again."
"Fuck off, now move." I push on him, but he's a brick shithouse and doesn't move.

The gravity of what's happened, again, washes over me and my stomach rolls. "Seriously, I'm going to fucking hurl all over your shitkickers if you don't fucking let me in your room."
"So hurl."
"This is none of your fucking business." I punch the wall next to his door. My hand throbs briefly, but the pain is a welcome relief. It's enough

to pull the tears out of my eyes and back into my skull where they fucking belong.

"Did he hurt you?" Casey's voice turns serious and I look at him.

"Ugh! No. Why would you ask me that?"

He shrugs. "It's my job."

"Fuck off, it is not. Since when do you care about fights?"

"Because, he's your best fucking friend, Calvin, that's why I care."

Sadness washes over me. "Not anymore."

Casey and I argued for a couple more minutes before Talon came out in the hall. Casey finally let me get into his room and I slammed the door in his face, I'll apologize tomorrow.

I text Dr. V.

It happened again, only this time, I was stone cold sober...

chapter
7

calvin

Casey came in some time after I fell asleep, thank god, because I wasn't in the mood for his inquisition; which I know is coming.

I tried to sneak out before anyone else got up this morning but failed miserably. Addison, Talon, Kyle, Beck and Mills are all in the hallway when I come out of Casey's room.

"Why were you in there?" Talon asks me and all I can do is stare daggers at him, hoping like hell he won't press the subject.

"What's the plan for today?" I ask, changing the subject.

"Not much, just some shopping. We have to leave this afternoon to drive down to Miami. Did you need to go somewhere?" Mills asks.

"Anywhere but here," I say stoically.

"Mouse?" Addison says and I look at her. "Can we talk?"

I roll my eyes. "There isn't anything to talk about."

"I beg to differ. Just you and me?"

I sigh, "Fine."

She turns to the guys. "Go ahead, we'll stay here."

I watch as Talon and Kyle both nod their acceptance and kiss Addison before departing with Beck and Mills. "Come on, let's go to my room." She walks past me toward one of the doors at the far end of the hall. Once there, without a word, she slides the key into the door and opens it, gesturing me inside.

'This isn't necessary. I don't have anything that needs..."

"I'm aware. But Mouse, you've got to talk to someone."

I scrub my head with my hand and relent, stepping past her into the room. It's much bigger than ours. They usually get the bigger rooms anyway. Talon, at least, has always gotten the biggest rooms. Rooms that we used to party in, before this tour. To say that I'm a little jealous or maybe even a little hurt that things panned out the way they did is an understatement. I knew all along that eventually we'd all find our own person and the dynamic of the band would change, I just never expected it to be this soon. "How do you do it?" I say as we take a seat in the little sitting room off of the bedroom.

"Do what?" she asks innocently.

"Deal with both of them?"

She laughs, "Some days, I don't. Some days it's just easier to let them be them. Other days I feel like they can't get enough of me, no matter what I do." I watch as a warm smile spreads across her face as she talks about Talon and Kyle.

"How do they do it?"

She cocks her head at me. "You'll have to be more specific."

I let out a deep breath and start to fidget with my hands. "Is it the three of you, all the time, in bed?"

I can't look at her, my embarrassment at the question I've asked is enough for the both of us.

"No, it's not. Sometimes it's just me alone with Talon or Kyle, other times it's just the two of them though they won't admit that too much." I shiver thinking about Talon and Kyle together, my mind repels the idea.

"So," I swallow hard. "When the three of you are together, do they..." I let the question fall into silence and I see her move, getting comfortable, pulling her feet up under her as she leans into the arm of the chair she sat in.

"They do," she says so matter of fact that it causes my head to come up and look at her. My mind attempts to reject the idea, forcing my stomach to churn. She cocks her head at me. "I'm an open book, Calvin, ask me anything."

I swallow again. "I need alcohol for this conversation," I tell her as I rub my sweating palms across my thighs.

She nods with her head behind me. "Fridge is over there."

I look behind me and sure enough, there is a slightly larger than dorm sized fridge under the counter, but I don't get up. I turn back toward her, my mind going a million miles a minute with a million different questions. "That doesn't repulse you? Seeing them together like that?"

Her head cocks at me in return, questions and concern clear as day in her ice blue eyes. "No, it doesn't. In fact, it's a huge turn-on for me." Her voice is soft, nearly a whisper, almost as if she's trying to read deeper than necessary into me or my question. "Why do you think it would repulse me?"

"Because it's not natural," I grumble without a second thought.

She doesn't say anything for a few minutes and I start to grow uncomfortable and start fidgeting once again.

"Do you honestly believe that?" she finally asks and our eyes meet.

"I can't answer that question without unearthing things that I can't talk about."

She shrugs, "Okay then. I'll respond to that statement. Natural is in the eye of the beholder, Calvin. I have a hard time believing you to be the anti-gay type." My eyes leave her, a silent omission and confession that she's right, I'm not anti-gay, just anti-Calvin being gay. "I didn't think so. Talon and Kyle are not gay; at least I wouldn't consider them that by any stretch of the imagination. Neither one of them had ever considered a same-sex relationship until I came along. They both love me very much and they're both sexually attracted to me, but they're also attracted to each other. There is nothing wrong with that, at least not in my book. Whether it turned me on or not, I wouldn't have a problem with either one of them wanting to be with the other. But I refused to choose between the two of them, where they took their relationship was their choice." She starts to curl a strand of hair around her finger, the movement captures my attention and I look at her. "I never expected them to progress to having a relationship with each other. I just expected us to have wild three-way sex and," she shrugs, "I've gotten far more in the process."

I don't know how to respond to that information at first. The only thing I can think of is what if it didn't turn her on but I let that drop. This conversation has already fallen deeper into territory I would have been happy to know nothing about, I don't want to continue to press it.

"Can I ask you something?" Her voice is soft, reassuring.

I look at her, fear and concern roll around inside my mind. "Sure," I tell her after a beat.

"You said it's not natural. Why is it that you think that?"

"Because a relationship should be between a man and a woman." My voice is robotic and detached, the re-programmed version coming out.

Her eyes narrow at me. "That doesn't sound like something you believe."

I stand up in a frustrated huff. "Whether or not I believe it is irrelevant."

"I beg to differ with you." I see pity in her eyes and I want to revolt from it, but there is something there, hiding, that tells me she's the person I can trust with all my secrets, but I'm not ready to reveal them to her. "It sounds like a lie you've told yourself for years." She reads right into me and I can't stay standing anymore. My head is spinning with the idea that this woman is about to unravel everything I've ever thought I've known about myself. She's going to dig it out of me and there is nothing I can do about it.

"I haven't told myself anything," I whisper, "More like had it beaten into me. Burned into my brain."

I put my head in my hands.

"So that's why you and..."

Tears form in my eyes before I can stop them. "Have you ever wanted something so bad that you will let nothing stop you from getting it?"

"Yes," she breathes.

"Have you ever had something so close that you can taste it, only to put it in the palm of your hand and have it shatter into a million tiny pieces?" I ask.

I hear her shift, I can feel her presence drawing closer, but she doesn't touch me, she doesn't do anything for a moment, causing me to finally lift my head. She's leaning forward with her elbows on her knees, her hands clasped together. "No," she finally answers.

"Well, that is what happens every time I get close to him."

"Why?"

She asks the question I knew was coming and I scrub at my face. "I...Addison, I've never told anyone this outside of my shrink. I don't even know if I can tell you."

"So Eric doesn't know?"

"No, he's the last person on the planet I want to tell." I stand up and start to pace in front of the couch.

"Why not tell him?"

"Because...because...because I can't fucking be with him and it kills me every fucking day."

chapter 8

calvin

My conversation with Addison ended shortly after that without another word said. She didn't press the issue and I certainly couldn't explain it to her. Not explaining it to her actually made me feel guilty, which in turn makes me feel like I'm falling apart when it comes to Eric. I can't seem to bring myself to discuss it with him and if I am going to tell anyone, he deserves to be the first to know.

When I leave the room, Casey is in the hallway. "He's not here."

I nod and slide my key into the slot and step into the room I share with Eric. I can smell him, his cologne, his body wash. The room is still warm with steam from the shower and I go straight to my bag.

"Was he okay?" I ask Casey who's followed me into the room.

He shrugs, "You know how he is, sometimes you can read him and other times you can't. Today was a 'can't' kind of day. He wasn't giving anything away, but I am pretty sure you owe him an explanation."

"Jesus, if I could fucking give him one, don't you think I would have by now?"

"Hey chill, bro, I'm not trying to piss you off. But you know as well as I do that he's your best friend and I can't imagine you pissing away your years of friendship over a squabble."

"A squabble, really Casey?" I raise an eyebrow at him. "We're not six."

"You fucking know what I mean."

"He kissed me, Casey," I tell him as I toss my shave kit on the bed.

"And what, you didn't want him to?"

"No, I didn't want him to."

"Okay, seriously? Where the fuck have you been? He's hot for you, Mouse, has been since the moment I fucking met you guys in New York. You can't be oblivious to it because I see you doing the same fucking thing to him. You both pick up random people in a piss poor attempt to make the other one jealous, you fucking stare each other down like you're undressing them. If you can't fucking see that, I can see why he would be fucking pissed off at you."

Casey turns to leave. "Just because I look at him, just because I pick up random chicks doesn't mean I can fucking be with him, Casey."

"Why the fuck not?" He turns back around to face me. "Are you afraid we're going to judge you?"

"Of course not."

"Then what the fuck are you so afraid of?" he asks me, positively pissed off.

"Why the fuck do you care?"

"I don't."

"Bullshit, Casey, you wouldn't be fucking arguing with me if you didn't fucking care, why the hell does it matter to you?"

"Because you're like my two best fucking friends, you're both so goddamn miserable apart like this. It's time you fucking got out of your head and…"

"Fuck you, Casey, it's not that fucking easy." I fall into the chair I was sitting in the other night.

"I fail to see how it's not easy. You just do it." His voice is hard.

"You can't do it if you throw up in the process," I mutter.

"What the fuck does that mean?"

"Nothing, forget it."

"Fuck you, Mouse, you can't fucking say something like that and then expect me to let it go."

"I can't fucking do it because every fucking time I try, or he tries, I end up a violent, vomiting mess."

He takes a step back. "Why the hell would you do that?"

"I can't fucking help it." Rage colors my vision. He's fucking dragging this shit out of me. "I swear to fucking god, Casey, if you say anything to him I will beat the shit out of you." My hands flex repeatedly.

"What the hell am I supposed to tell him? That the idea of being with him repulses you? You can fucking tell him that shit yourself. I will not get in the middle of that. You'll fucking break his heart," He tells me as he crosses his arms across his chest.

"I've already done that. Last night. I told him to give it up, that we would never be. But he won't let it go."

"I wouldn't either. Not without an explanation first. He deserves that much."

"You know, Casey, I thought you were my friend too."

"Fuck! I am, damn it, but I won't watch you break his heart for no fucking reason or at the very least not without an explanation. If he repulses you that bad, he needs to know that. It's not fair for him to hang on to something that will never be," he tells me.

"That's what I was trying to do. I was trying to tell him it will never happen, but he's holding on to this hope that it will and I don't know what else to tell him. How the hell else do I explain it to him?"

"How about you start with the truth?" He raises an eyebrow at me. "Tell him why he repulses you."

"He doesn't repulse me, and I can't fucking tell him because I can't watch it destroy him."

"You're one seriously cryptic motherfucker, you know that?" He leans back against the wall, settling in for an explanation.

"I wish I could explain it to you, Casey, I really do, but I can't, just like I couldn't explain it to Addison. If I am going to waste the breath it is going to take to explain it to someone, it will be Peacock and no one else."

"Then explain it to him, Mouse. He needs to fucking know. If you won't be with him, he needs to know why, he needs to be able to move on if you're so hell bent on not being with him."

I stand up in frustration. "How do you let go of something you love?" I whisper.

He gives me an annoyed snort. "You don't. You set them free. He deserves to be set free."

"I don't know if he'll ever be free. I can't let him go like that. That's where this is a problem. You see, I need to set him free, he needs to love other people, he needs to find someone else, but I can't let him do that."

"Why the hell not?" He straightens.

"Because I'm in fucking love with him, I don't want him to find someone else, but I can't be with him."

"Jesus fucking Christ, Calvin, you've got to be shitting me. How in the hell can you fucking be in love with someone and not be with them?" He shakes his head at me. "This is even more fucked up than I imagined. You're so wrapped up in your head that you can't let it go."

I give him a humorless laugh. "You have no fucking idea what I've been through."

"Been through is the operative phrase in that sentence."

He pushes off the wall and takes a hardened stance, pointing at me. "You better figure your shit out, Calvin, and you better fucking tell him whatever it is that has you so screwed up in the fucking head because he deserves that much, he deserves to know why in the hell you can't be with him and he needs the fucking truth. Skirting it will not allow either one of you to move on."

With that statement he walks out the door, his piss poor attempt at slamming the door is almost comical, but I can't even begin to laugh about it.

He's fucking right. Eric deserves an explanation and I have got to find a way to tell him.

chapter 9

eric

"Seriously, you need to talk to him." Casey isn't backing down and hasn't since we came downstairs to grab a bite to eat before taking off for Miami. One more show and then a much needed, week long break.

"Don't you think I've been trying, Casey? I mean, come on, how can I not? He's been throwing me away, throwing up on me, and you think I want to sit back and do nothing about it?"

Casey's face turns somber. "No, I know you need to talk to him and I'm sure he's not making it very easy for you."

I shake my head and go back to looking at the menu, trying to decide what to eat when your appetite is slowly sliding down the drain isn't all that appealing.

"There is seriously something up with him," Casey sputters on the other side of the table.

I look over my menu at him. "Duh. Though I can't even begin to imagine what it is, other than the fact that he's repulsed by the fact that another man likes him."

Casey raises an eyebrow. "Likes? Really, Eric?"

I shrug and go back to staring blankly at my menu. Casey figured it out a long time ago that my infatuation with Calvin is deeper than liking someone. In fact, it's nearly reached my soul, but fortunately for me, there is some type of barrier there, preventing him from penetrating too deep; protecting me from pain I don't really deserve to feel. "I repulse him," I tell Casey without looking at him.

Then suddenly my menu is dipping down so that I have no choice but to look at him. "No, you don't. Whatever it is that is going on with Calvin is far deeper than superficial, and you and I both know that your feelings are not one-sided. You've seen the way he looks at you, hell, we've all seen it."

I roll my eyes. "No shit, considering that's all you guys seem to talk about with us anymore. Look, he needs his space, he needs time, he needs…"

"He needs to get over himself and tell you the truth," Casey interrupts.

That right there is the crux of this whole situation. "I can't force him to tell me anything and any more pushing might just push him away completely."

"So then what?"

"I move on."

Casey raises an eyebrow at me again, cocking his head too. "You're incapable of that and anytime you try, you feel like shit afterward. Is that really the best solution?"

I shrug. "It has to be. Until he's willing to talk to me, to tell me the truth, to explain it all to me, there is nothing I can do."

"What if the truth is something you can't live with?" Casey asks me in a tone that tells me he's channeling Calvin and not himself.

Shaking my head, I tell him the honest to god truth, "I'll never know until he tells me."

"What if he never tells you? Then what are you going to do, sit here pining over something you can never have because you weren't willing to move on when you had the chance? He told you he can't be with you, he's given you an out. If I were you, I'd take it."

"You're kidding, right? After you've sat here, telling me that he needs to tell me the truth, you turn around and tell me to take his offered out. What the fuck, Casey?"

He sighs and sets his menu down. "Look – yes, he needs to tell you the truth, but if you can't honestly tell him, to his face, that the truth doesn't matter, no matter what the situation may be, then you need to pull up your boxers and move the fuck on. Calvin will never come clean with you unless he knows that you won't run in the opposite direction. Either that or he is going to tell you the truth in an attempt to push you away. Either way, you have to be willing to stand by his side, no matter what. You're going to have to prove to him what it is that you feel for him, what it is that he means to you and that no matter what his demons are, you can overcome them together. *If* you can't commit to that, Eric, then there is no point and you should move on." He stands up and finishes, "His demons are dark, Eric. I've seen a taste of it and more importantly, I'm starting to see what it does to him when his demons hurt you. Make the choice, Eric. Decide what and who are more important. When you've done that, go to him and explain it to him."

"He won't listen to me."

He shakes his head at me. "I wouldn't dismiss that, I have a feeling that him knowing how you feel - regardless of the situation - will change his perspective on telling you, one way or another."

It's with that sentence that Casey leaves me to my table. Where he disappears to is beyond me, but I know he's watching me closely because it's his job.

He's right, of course. I can't keep pushing at Calvin without showing him some support, showing him that I am not something to be thrown away or trampled, but how? When? Where?

Not here, and not in Miami. Away from the bus, the band, the guys.

chapter 10

calvin

The moment I've been waiting for...the time I've been desperate to find has finally come.

My fingers strum along the strings, my mind clears, my body comes alive with every strum, flick, click, tap, and move of my fingers. With playing comes peace.

The silence on the bus is broken by the strings of my guitar, strumming and tuning as I play through some of my favorite songs. Songs that always seem to free my mind of everything. Songs I only wish I could play on stage. Playing always opens the world to me, like watching a movie in my head. When I'm playing, all my fucked-up-ness is gone and replaced by all the things I wish I could have. Today it's filled with Eric.

The way he looks when he has his bass in his hands, the euphoric smile on his face when he settles in to play. The smile in his eyes when he realizes I'm watching him. That is a happy place indeed.

I knew years ago, when we started this band, that playing was the same kind of therapy for Eric as it is for me.

I asked Dr. V about it once, about why playing was so freeing for me and he knew the answer immediately. I taught myself to play when I was institutionalized. Playing brought peace within me. Like reading a good book, I could escape into the music, which is how I became so good at it so fast. Playing, writing songs, discovering what I was capable of with my fingers and a guitar was more than I could have ever imagined. It would bring me hope, bring me comfort. Especially when I had bad days, at least bad days in their eyes.

When I left that place, one of the first things I did was find myself a guitar. Once I had that in my hands, street peddling became easy and profitable for me. Couple that with the fact that I could sing meant more people would watch and drop change into my case. That's how I managed to have an apartment, well, the semblance of an apartment, and how I managed to keep myself from becoming a complete street thug. It's also how I managed to get into college, which led me to the band.

The memories are flowing harder than they usually do when I play alone.

I remember meeting Talon first. We had a chemistry class together. We were two broken souls brought together as pretty close friends. After that, I met Dex, and then Eric who came with Kyle and then introduced them to Talon and everything changed. I found a home with these crazy fuckers and for the first time in my life, I felt like I belonged. For the first time ever, I felt like who I was on the inside was never a factor. In fact, the amount of women surrounding us made it that much easier to forget my past. To forget about my father and, of course, the time I spent in the institution.

But I also found alcohol and drugs. Turning to coke when I needed a pick-me-up to get through school, band practice, shows, then eventually needing it every day. It took nearly a year before anyone truly caught on to what was going on with me and ironically enough, it was Eric that figured it out. I found it easier to be myself, to live through anything, when I was high. Nothing mattered and it was through being high that I figured out how to ignore the urges I had after being with anyone. I found it easier to pass over it like it didn't matter or like it never happened.

Eric convinced me and got me off the coke. I couldn't do it by myself and Eric was always there to pick up the pieces of me when the night was over.

Unlike the rest of the guys, I never spent time in rehab. I found the strength in myself to cut back on what I was using and how often I was using it until eventually I was only using once a day. That lasted for nearly six months, before one day I got so wrapped up in school that I passed out before my nightly ritual of snorting a line. When I woke up in the morning, I felt clearer and stronger than I'd ever had before. It was literally the wake-up call that I needed in order to rid myself of the powder forever.

Oh, I remember that day like it was yesterday…

"I need you," I said into the phone.

"What did you do?"

I smile into the phone. "Nothing, that's the problem. Can you please come over?"

"I'll be there in five," Eric said before hanging up the phone. I went back to my dorm room, one that I was fortunate enough to have to myself, and I waited.

Within five minutes, Eric was there, concern etched in his features. "What's up, Mouse?" I smiled at the memory of how that nickname came to fruition.

"I need you to take this." I handed him the baggie I had in my hand. "I don't need it anymore." He cocked his head at me. "I didn't do it last night, I fell asleep before I could manage to do it. When I woke up this morning, everything made more sense. If it wasn't important enough for me to do it last night, it isn't important enough for me to do it ever again."

Peacock smiled at me, wide and gorgeous. "I knew you could do it," he said softly.

It was in that moment, though I didn't know it at the time, that I fell for Eric Richardson. His love and compassion shone through that morning brighter than anything I'd seen before. Ironically enough, I chalked it up to being free of the coke, to not being high or hungover. The clarity of it all, that's when everything changed between the two of us. Though I never had a problem avoiding the obvious, burying myself in girls without a second thought. Girls were easy. Girls I could fuck and walk away from. I never felt like I had to explain myself to them. I never felt the need to tell them why I couldn't stay, just that I wasn't going to stay. I always felt like I owed Eric an explanation for why I was the way I was.

Despite all of that, he never indicated anything about being gay until much later in the band's history. Little things started happening, like he'd find himself in the middle of a threesome with a guy and a girl, or sometimes I'd even catch him watching some guy in a way that would suggest more than just a casual glance. Then the women started to fade into the background. He'd still tag along to the bars, flirt with the girls, talk to them, whatever, but I started to notice that he'd never take anyone anywhere. He'd always be in the same spot, often times with the same girl, drinking beer and whatever. Then I started to notice the girl conversations slowing down and he'd intercede into my personal conversations and whatnot. Not that it ever bothered me, but in hindsight, I see what he was doing.

He was jealous, in his own way.

I realized he was gay right before he kissed me for the first time, right before I threw up all over the ground in front of the bench we were on.

I sigh, remembering that first kiss. I remember thinking briefly that I'd consumed enough alcohol to stop myself from falling into my body's conditioned response and that maybe all the stars finally fell into place…then it shattered into a million tiny pieces. Holding me prisoner inside my own body.

I told myself that he needed to admit to himself that he was gay, but he knew he was gay. So I rationalized it away by thinking that he needed to tell everyone. And until he came clean with Talon and the band, I couldn't act on my impulses and emotions. Then he finally fucking does it and everything I thought I knew shattered. My self-hatred has only grown.

I know that I am dragging him along, making him think that us being together is a possibility, but it is not intentional. That is why I told him that we can't be. I hoped like hell that telling him would make him see it and move on, let it go.

The disconnect between my heart and my head, between the truth and what I've been conditioned to think as truth, has only made things worse.

"You have to tell him." Addison's voice breaks me of my thoughts and I jump. I'd gotten so lost in my thoughts somewhere along the way that I stopped playing. "He deserves to know the truth. You may not want to tell me or anyone else for that matter, but you have got to tell him. Let him make that choice, Mouse. You cannot make it for him."

I give her a sad smile and nod.

She comes over to stand in front of me. She grabs my chin, raising my head up so that I can look at her. "I'm here for you, so is everyone else on this bus."

I close my eyes. "I know, but now is the wrong time."

"No time like the present."

"True, but you see," she releases my chin and I open my eyes, "He needs to be able to escape from me and right now, he can't do that. He needs to be able to walk away, to think, to process, to come to grips with what he will hear. I feel like if I tell him right now, it won't be a good thing."

"Then tell him on break."

I shake my head. "Too much, we have to be back together again too soon after."

She crosses her arms over her chest. "Is this something that's going to break up the band?" Her voice is hard, but she isn't angry, she needs answers.

I stand up and she backs away from me. "God, I hope not. I don't understand why things would be any different after I tell him. He's either going to accept it or he's not. If he accepts it, the dynamic between him and I changes. If he doesn't accept it, things go back to exactly the way they were before. We're friends and nothing more." Though I say the words, I don't feel their conviction and Addison can sense that.

"Then the sooner you tell him, the better. Let him decide for himself."

I nod and sit back down. I'd gotten up for a reason, but now it's pointless.

Addison drops the subject when Kyle comes on board, followed quickly by Talon and a very stoic looking Dex.

I quickly pack up my guitar and put it into the bench seat cubby and climb into my bunk. Dex and Raine moved back into the private room, so Mouse, Victoria and I share the three racks. I slide into the bottom one, pulling the curtain closed and putting my headphones in.

I know the moment Eric comes on board because my body comes alive. My hair stands on end, and for the first time, desire courses through my veins without revulsion to chase it away. Hope blossoms as I hash out a plan.

chapter 11

eric

Calvin hasn't said much to me since Orlando. The Miami show went great, surprising considering I felt so disconnected from Calvin while on stage.

I noticed a change in him when we got off the bus at the Miami hotel. He was different, but it wasn't something I could put my thumb on. When we got to our PR event that night, it was like nothing had transpired between us in Orlando. In fact, it was just like it had always been between us and with the band. Once I caught on to his demeanor, it made it easier for me to slip right back into my own little bubble of being the band's bassist. We were right back to the way things have always been. The next morning brings us to an appearance at a radio station before our flight home. Everything goes as expected, except for whenever I steal a glance at Calvin and he catches me. Today I get a small smile in return. That's new, and it just adds to my confusion and frustration with him. When I catch him glancing at me, I find it harder than I thought to return the sentiment.

By the time we are on board of our plane to Los Angeles, there's not a lot of conversation going on and the silence is a bit uncomfortable. Eventually, I doze off.

"We're landing." Calvin's voice wakes me. He moved to sit next to me. Odd.

"Yeah, already?" I say sleepily.

"Yup, almost home." His voice is lighter than it has been. I sit up, stretching and running a hand through my hair before fixing the ponytail.

A full five minutes passes before either one of us manages to say anything. It's him who breaks the silence. "What are you doing tonight?" he asks.

"Uh, unpacking, doing laundry, enjoying my own shower for an hour."

"So in other words, nothing?"

I roll my head in his direction. "What do you need, Mouse?"

I see him stiffen briefly. "Don't call me that."

I raise an eyebrow. "Don't like your nickname anymore?"

"Not when you say it."

"Ever?" He just shrugs and I roll my eyes. "Again with the vague explanations. You know, Mouse," I say with a sneer, "I'm getting really tired of all this beating around the bush."

"Good, be at my house at seven," he says and stands up, moving across the aisle next to Talon, Kyle and Addison, leaving no room for me and no chance for me to question him.

What the fuck? Seriously, what the fuck does he want from me? I roll my eyes and let it go as we're dropping onto the runway at the airport.

We deplane and start to load up our luggage. I finally manage to get close enough to Calvin that I grab him by the arm and push him away from the guys. "What the hell? Let me go, Eric."

"Not until you give me a goddamn explanation," I say through gritted teeth.

"I'm fucking trying, now let me go."

"What the hell does that mean?"

"It means that if you want your goddamn answers, then you'll be at my house at seven. Now, let me go." He growls the last command and I release him. I'm so stunned by the fact that he is finally going to give me the answers that I need that I just stand there as he skirts around me and goes back to helping load up the cars.

"Yo, Peacock!" Talon yells and I slowly snap out of my little moment of shock.

"What?" I shout as I turn around only to see that the ground is no longer covered with bags.

"Let's go, yo," Kyle says and we all climb into the SUV.

We spend the next thirty minutes bullshitting, laughing and enjoying the freedom of not being on tour. I'm eternally grateful that I live closest to the airport and I'm the first person to be dropped off. But I can't escape the SUV before Mouse reminds me of our seven o'clock rendezvous at his place. "Yeah, alright," I mutter as I climb out, telling the guys and Addison goodbye while Mills and Beck pull my stuff from the truck. Mouse never got out of the car.

There is nothing like coming home after having been gone for nine freaking weeks and I'm thankful for the maid service I paid for when I step inside a nice, clean, fresh smelling apartment. Aside from it being cleaned while I was away, everything is as I left it. Stepping inside, I realize just how happy I am to be home as I drop everything in the middle of the living room. My happiness about being home is thwarted when I open the fridge and realize that I need to go grocery shopping at some point. I go to the pantry, only to realize it isn't much better off, mostly box meals and macaroni and cheese. I grab a warm Mountain Dew and I roll my eyes at myself.

Fuckin' a, the least I could have done was have something decent to eat when I got home. But whatever, I look at the clock, it's three-thirty, the countdown in my head slowly starts as I drag my luggage to my room, throw my suitcases on the bed before unzipping them and tossing clothes into piles for the laundry.

As the time draws closer to six, when I need to be walking out the door to make sure I make it to Calvin's in time, I start to get a nervous excited feeling coursing through me. That feeling leads to all kinds of speculation about what he wants to talk to me about. Maybe he is finally going to tell me the truth. Tell me why he can't or doesn't want to be with me. Maybe this is what I need to hear to let him go or maybe it is what I need to pull him in closer to me. Either way, it's about time he tells me.

At six, I grab my keys and head for the door. I'm not dressed in anything fancy and my hair is pulled back, looking more like a kid's paint plate than a rainbow, but it is what it is. I've been looking forward to a solid week where I didn't have to do my hair and I have no intention of changing that now. I've got my usual black jeans on with a t-shirt. I grab my jacket off the hook and I close and lock the door. I stand there for a moment debating on whether or not I am really ready to do this. Can I really let this man go? I know I might have to. I think his heart isn't in this like mine is, so maybe it is best if we just leave things as they were before New York.

Until all this drama with him, I didn't regret coming out, but now that it is leading to this with Calvin, I kind of wish I hadn't done it. Part of me hoped that he was more confident in who he was and that he was just waiting for me to find the confidence in myself, but I see and know now that wasn't the case.

I climb into my car and drive away, headed toward Calvin's house and toward my fate with him.

Standing at his door, I can hear soft music coming from inside. He lives in an affluent apartment building near downtown Los Angeles. He's always been a big city type of person and I prefer the quiet of the 'burbs, though those don't really exist in L.A., despite their best efforts. I hesitate, second guessing myself about why I'm here. Why am I giving into him like this? Curiosity wins, and I knock.

"It's open." I hear him shout from within the apartment and I slowly turn the doorknob.

"Cal?"

"Be out in a minute, make yourself comfortable," he shouts from somewhere in the apartment. Though the building screams 'loads of money', his apartment is rather modest, with furniture that belongs in a catalog. I thought my tastes were over the top, but he's putting me to shame with his black leather sofas, larger than life flat screen hanging on the wall, below that an entertainment center that is stuffed with different gaming devices, DVD players and the like. On top of the stand are stacks of movies and games, most of which I recognize from stuff he had on the bus.

Though we never played it much, we have two different consoles on the bus, it killed time.

The living room leads into a small dining room and I'm surprised to see that the table is set with two place settings, silverware, the whole nine yards. That's when the scent of something Italian and delicious reaches me. It smells wonderful. Beyond the table is a counter that separates the dining room from the kitchen and sitting on top of that are several lowball glasses and what appear to be two or three different scotches or whiskeys. "Help yourself," Calvin says as he comes up behind me. "Trust me, you're going to want a few of those tonight."

"What you got?" I say with confusion coloring my voice.

"Scotch, whiskey, vodka?"

"Scotch. Why the dinner?"

"You haven't eaten, have you?"

I shake my head and our eyes meet. "I don't have anything in the house," I mumble.

"I figured. Come sit, it's ready," he tells me as he hands me a lowball of scotch.

I take a seat facing the kitchen as I watch him work. He pulls something from the oven and then sets it on the counter. "I didn't know you could cook."

He snorts a laugh, "I would hold judgment on that until you've tried it."

"Well, it smells delicious."

Our eyes meet and he mumbles a sheepish, "thanks." He drops his eyes from mine and finishes whatever it is that he was doing before I stole his attention. "It's just lasagna."

My stomach rumbles and I hear him laugh as he grabs a plate and brings it over, it's piled with garlic bread. "It's store bought bread, so don't get too excited." He smiles sweetly at me before returning to the kitchen to bring over the pan he's just cut up. "We haven't had a home cooked meal in weeks, I thought this would be a good ice breaker," he says solemnly as he sets the bubbling pan on the hot pads between us.

"It smells wonderful."

He smiles as he takes his seat. "You said that already. Here," he reaches his hand out, "hand me your plate."

I do and watch as he scoops a good size piece onto my plate before handing it back to me. "You really didn't have to do all this," I tell him honestly.

He looks at me while he picks up his own plate. "Yeah, I did. I owe you an explanation and it's not going to be a pretty one. I figured I'd feed you and get you drunk before I tell you everything."

"Everything," I breathe.

Our eyes meet, sincerity radiates from him in waves. "Everything," he whispers.

chapter 12

calvin

He's right, dinner was probably over the top, but I needed to find a way to put him into an agreeable mood. Alcohol is best served on a full stomach and him knowing that I cooked for him might help him see past what I'm about to tell him.

"Jesus, Cal, this is fantastic," he praises and I smile at him.

"I'm glad you like it. It's one of the only things I know how to do well."

He blushes slightly before taking another bite. Watching him eat is the kind of thing that would turn me on if that were possible. I've always found food to be arousing, but in true Calvin's dick like fashion, he sits softly inside my jeans. The disgust that makes me feel causes my whole body to lock down momentarily, but Eric is too engrossed in the food in front of him and he doesn't notice. I fight the churn of my stomach by focusing on my food.

I want him drunk, but rationally drunk. I know that sounds bad, but Eric on alcohol is a true Eric. His honesty is brutal and real and I need that tonight. I need to know what he's thinking and alcohol takes away his filter.

"You wanted to talk?" he says between bites.

"After we eat," I tell him before taking a big gulp of scotch.

"Why can't we start now?" His voice is soft and unsure. "I don't like this awkward silence between us."

I frown. "It's not intentional, I promise."

His eyes are sad when they meet mine. "I know, I guess I just wish we could go back to the way things were between us."

My heart breaks a little. "How so?" I swallow.

"Before this wedge was driven between us, before we...before you decided to tell me off in Orlando."

I set my fork down. "I told you off in Orlando because I wanted you to be free. Free of me, free of how you feel about me."

"Because you can't be with me?" he asks.

"Exactly. It's not fair for you to keep hanging on to me when there will never be an 'us'." I gesture between us.

He sets his fork down and quickly picks up his glass of scotch and downs it in a single gulp. "Is that why you brought me here tonight? To remind me that we can't be anything more than what we are?" He stands up, grabbing his glass.

"No, I brought you here tonight so that I can explain to you why we can't be together." I follow him with my eyes as he goes to the counter behind me. "Can you please finish eating? Then we will talk, Eric, I promise."

I hear his glass click with the decanter and the liquid pouring sounds a million times louder than it should be. I hear him sigh behind me and I turn. His hands are on the counter and his head is down. His pain is evident and my heart twists. I stand up and reach out for him. "Please don't," he whispers, "I don't want your comfort right now." He raises his head and our eyes meet. "I want answers. I know I'm not the only one who feels this way."

"What, about answers?"

"No, about being together."

"You're right, Eric, you're not the only one that feels this way," I tell him softly. "Please, finish eating."

"I'm full." I look at his plate, it's nearly empty, but I know he can put away way more than that. I decide not to press it.

"Help me clean up?" I ask and he nods, before taking a large pull of scotch and setting the glass down.

Moving around the kitchen, cleaning up, rinsing and loading the dishwasher starts to feel all too natural to me as we set about the task of cleaning up. Something we've certainly done before, but since New York, it takes on a whole new meaning. Since he tried to kiss me in Orlando, everything has changed between us. Now it is going to change between us forever. He will walk out of this house and sometime over the course of the next few days, he will find it in himself to get over it and we will go back to the way things were between us. Back to being Mouse and Peacock. Right? Right.

"Thanks," I tell him as I wipe down the counter one last time.

He turns around and leans against the sink. "You're welcome." He cocks his head at me, desperate to read my expression and I watch as his fingers twitch like he's aching to do something, to touch me, or something. Then he licks his lips and my mouth goes dry and my breath catches in my throat.

He takes a step toward me, then another, and I know where this is going. "Don't," I whisper.

"Why?" he counters in a voice equal parts soft and hurt.

I lean back against the counter, looking at the floor, my body tense. "Because, dinner was good, we need to talk, and I don't want to ruin it by throwing up all over everything."

He freezes. "Do I repulse you that much?" he asks, his voice laced with emotion.

"No, Eric. I want nothing more than for you to kiss me, to hold me, to show me that you love me, but you can't, I can't."

"But I can, I want to, you want me to. What's so wrong with giving into what you want?"

"Because what I want is buried deep inside my brain, hiding behind concrete walls so thick that it would take the Hulk a hundred years to even put a dent in it."

"Cal, I don't understand."

I raise my eyes to his, holding him in my gaze. "Because," a single tear escapes my eye, "Because I've been raped, beaten and tortured for being gay."

chapter
13

eric

Calvin's words knock the wind right out of me and I stumble backwards. "Because I was shown unimaginable images, forced into believing that being gay is a sin, that being gay is the highest form of blasphemy, that being gay is an abomination."

I can barely breathe, but I reach for my scotch and down the entire glass, feeling the burn slide down my throat. I look at him and there's pain in his eyes, unimaginable pain. "I was first beaten by my father, more than a few times, when he caught me with a couple guys. He'd break bones, including my cheekbone." I watch as he rubs at his left cheekbone. "When my father realized that beating me on a regular basis wasn't going to be enough to make me change who I was, he institutionalized me in a nut house. One that specialized in conditional therapy."

"I don't under..." I can't breathe enough to talk, let alone think.

Calvin sighs deeply. "You know that movie, that one where they force the rapist to watch movies of people being raped?"

"Jesus fucking Christ...that shit's real?" I finally manage.

He nods. "Well, it was fifteen years ago and where I'm from," he shrugs, "I never believed that it really worked, not until I got into the outside world and tried to have sexual thoughts about men."

"I need to sit down," I manage to say before pushing away from the counter. I go around him to the alcohol and fill my glass full of scotch before downing half of it. "Fuck me," I groan as the burn slides its way into my stomach.

"I wish I could," Calvin says and my eyes snap to him and my cock stirs involuntarily in my jeans. "I fucking love you, Eric. I've been in love with you since that morning you came to my dorm to pick up my last baggie. I fell in love with you along that entire ordeal, but I didn't realize it until I was free of the coke." He leans into the counter and I manage to fall into his chair from dinner. "I'm pretty sure I did it long before then. In fact, I like to believe that it happened the first time I saw you. But at that time I was completely and totally incapable of looking at any man long enough to feel anything for them."

"You...you love me?" My brain is hung up on what he's said to me. I'm struggling to process it all.

"I do, very much. But just because I love you, doesn't mean I can be with you," he admits with a soft smile.

"I fail to see what is standing in your way."

"Everything I've just...god, I knew I should've done this with Dr. V. Damn it." I watch as his nerves take over and he becomes frazzled. It's actually pretty cute to watch, that is until his demeanor hardens and he braces himself against the counter, staring at me with an intent expression. "Because," he swallows, "Anytime I let my mind wander into being with you, carrying on an actual relationship, having," he swallows again, "sex," the word is said through gritted teeth, "I want to vomit. My entire body physically locks down and I-," he swallows again.

I can't help but notice now the small beads of sweat forming on his forehead and his face is pale. His knuckles crack as he grips the countertop. I spring up and round the counter, not thinking, not even considering the consequences of my actions and I pin him gently against the counter, wrapping my arms around him. "Breathe, come on Cal, breathe." His entire body starts to shake and I can feel him sweating through his clothes. "Come on, Cal, please, relax. Think about something else, anything else."

"I can't," he growls.

"Yes, you can, the sunshine, oceans, cats, dogs, anything, come on, you can...."

"No, I can't."

"Why?" I breathe against his neck.

"Not until you let me go and step back. Please E, I'm begging you, let me go."

With all the strength I can muster, I release him, pulling my body off of him and I take a step back. "You make it impossible to think about anything else," he finally says in a hushed tone.

I try and find something else, something to change the subject. "You said you were raped?" Yes, that's what comes out of my mouth before my fucking filter can catch it. "Shit, don't answer that, I'm sorry."

He turns around and admonishes me, "Shh, it's alright, Eric. Yes, I was. Several times, as a matter of fact."

"How?" I ask.

He points toward the living room with his head. "Come, sit down," he tells me as he polishes off his glass and quickly pours another one. I follow his lead and take a seat on the larger of the two couches, on the far end, and he takes a seat in the chair opposite me. He leans forward with his elbows on his knees and his glass between his palms, rolling it back and forth from his wrists to the tips of his fingers.

"Can I ask something else first?" I ask.

"Go ahead," he tells me, but he doesn't look at me.

"Who's Dr. V?"

He gives me a small smile. "He's my therapist. He offered to let us talk in his office, in front of him, to let him help with this conversation, explain the things to you that I can't. I don't know much about the process of the therapy I endured, other than I was forced to watch," he shudders, "to watch some seriously nasty shit. Mostly anti-gay bigotry, religious nut jobs who talked about being gay being wrong and how being gay means you're going to hell. Those speeches were usually followed up with movies of men being raped by other men, the ugly side of society, in a nutshell." He takes a sip of his scotch before continuing, I follow suit. "Watching that kind of stuff wasn't really where the "process" came into play. If I got turned on, slightly excited emotionally, like my heartbeat or breathing changed, or god forbid I got a hard on, that would get me shocked."

I'm watching him carefully and I can see his eyes glazing over as if he is thinking back to that time.

"The shocks started off more like a tickle, then gradually progressed to voltages high enough that it would humiliate me in some fashion or another."

"How so?" I breathe out. He doesn't look at me, but I watch as he shakes off whatever it is that he was seeing and he looks at his glass.

He sighs, "I would often piss myself."

"Jesus fucking Christ, are you kidding me?" I stand up in anger. "How the fuck could anyone even consider doing-"

'Breathe Eric, please, believe me, it was all legal at the time, though it still didn't stop me from suing the shit out of them once I was able to get my head straight, but that's beside the point." He takes a huge gulp of scotch and I finish off my glass before walking to the counter. I grab the decanter and bring it back to the living room and fill up his glass. "Thanks," he whispers.

"What else?" I ask as I fill my own glass.

He frowns. "Are you sure you want to hear more of this?"

"No, but I'm still trying to understand, and I'm trying to see how this all leads back to you being raped."

"I'm getting there," he tells me before drinking down half of the scotch I just gave him. "One time I was shocked until I not only pissed myself, but I lost all control of everything." His eyes meet mine.

"Fuck, I can't even imagine what kind of force that would take."

"I thought that I was dying," he tells me. "But that was nothing compared to what happened that night and many nights after that. What happened at night were the primary grounds for my lawsuit and the criminal charges that were later brought to the person responsible. The opposite happened at night. I was forced to get hard before he would set about raping me, usually repeatedly...."

"Stop, I can't..." I stand up and start pacing, "I don't know if I can handle hearing any more about that."

I catch Calvin as he nods solemnly. "Now do you understand why no matter how much I love you, I can't be with you?"

I stop in my tracks and look at him. I don't know what to say to that. "How am I supposed to respond to that?"

"Just tell me that you agree, that you understand that you can't be with me and walk out the door. Fuck, Eric," he stands up, "You deserve someone who can love you emotionally and physically. You don't deserve my baggage and I certainly don't deserve your love when I have absolutely no way to reciprocate it."

"I don't believe that."

"Fuck Eric, damn it, you've already seen what happens, three times now. I've puked on you twice."

"That wasn't..."

"No Eric, it wasn't alcohol, either time. That is what my body does, among other things, like locking down, convulsing, puking, sweating, growing weak...those are just a few of the things that happen. The worst of it is the mental disgust I go through after the fact. It took me three years and a lot of cocaine before I could finally get an erection, get myself off, or even have sex with a woman without vomiting all over the place. Even still, to this day, being with a woman still repulses me enough that I have to fight back the bile that rises, but my body and the shame are different now. Usually, I end up feeling guilty because I've walked out, waited 'til they've fallen asleep and left or left them half-naked in a bathroom somewhere. I can't masturbate." I flinch at that idea. "If I can even manage to get hard, I usually end up in a repulsed pile of goo on my bed with a raging hard-on that I can do nothing about. Let alone even," he swallows hard, "in the kitchen when you came up behind me…"

"You freaked out," I tell him.

He nods, "Ironically, it wasn't because you touched me."

"Then what was it?"

His eyes dart to my crotch and back up. "Shit. Damn it, Cal, I…fuck."

"Stop, it's alright, Eric. You didn't know, I'd barely begun to explain anything to you, how could you have even guessed," he tells me softly before sitting back down.

"Now what?" I ask him unwillingly after a few minutes of silence.

He frowns and shakes his head. "We go back to the way we were, friends." His eyes meet mine once again and once again I am lost to them, lost in him, drawn like a moth to a flame.

I shake my head, "I can't do that."

"You don't have a choice."

"Like hell I don't, Calvin." I cock my head at him. "You told me this so that you could drive me away, so that I would find you repulsive and storm out of here, and find it within myself to get over you and we could move on?"

"Who wants to be with someone who wasn't strong enough to fend off an attacker, who wasn't man enough to…"

"Stop right fucking there, Calvin Caldwell, I will not listen to you talk like that." I round the couch to draw closer to him, moving his glass on the coffee table before sitting in front of him, my thighs on either side of his. "Look at me," I tell him.

"I can't. I think you should go."

"No, I won't. Calvin, we all have our own fucking baggage. Yes, I see what yours is and it is quite possibly the worst thing I've ever heard and three thousand times bigger than I could have ever imagined, but I'll be damned if I am going to let that stop me from trying to help you."

"You're insane. Eric, the only thing that is going to happen in all of this is that I'm going to freak the fuck out and we will never be able to be closer than we are right now. I can't have that, Eric. I can't have you being hurt every time something triggers me and I will be damned if I am going to have a sexless relationship with you."

"I want to meet Dr. V, I want the two of us to meet with him, Calvin, I want to help you get over this."

He stands up and manages to skirt past my entrapment. "I can't just get over it."

I stand up, facing him. "Bullshit, you did it with women. Why can't you do it with men? The problem with men for you, Cal, is the fact that you've had countless women to help you work through your issues, your wall that 'Hulk can't smash', but how many men have you had since the abuse?"

"None," he finally breathes.

"That's my point. You haven't had anyone to work through this with. You haven't been able to even try."

"And you think I want to do that with you? Do you honestly think that I want you to watch me puke every time you try and kiss me? Or break into the sweats when I think about you? What the fuck kind of relationship is that, Eric?" I don't answer him because I don't have an answer. "That's my point, it doesn't exist. It can't exist."

"That's where I think you're wrong and I want to prove it to you."

Our eyes meet again, this time I see some concern, fear and anxiety buried deep in his soul. "I'm not running away from this," I tell him firmly. "I haven't waited this long to just walk away. To just give up on you, on a chance for us to actually happen. Are women really what you want?" I watch as he shakes his head. "Are men?" He shakes his head again. "Then what is it, what do you want?" I ask him softly.

He looks at me, his eyes red with tears. "You," he breathes and my world stops spinning.

chapter 14

calvin

"If it's me you want, then you have got to let me help you." Eric doesn't hesitate.

"I don't know how," I tell him. "I know in my head and in my heart that you are what I want, Eric. You've been what I've wanted for a long time. I thought that if I just ignored it, just didn't do anything about it, that I could move on, that *you*," I say with emphasis, "would move on and that we would have never had to have this conversation."

"I can't help how I feel about you," he tells me in a whisper as he sits down in the chair I was just sitting in. "I've tried, trust me." His voice is soft, almost comforting in a strange way. "I've done everything I can to force myself to move on."

I cross my arms over my chest. "No, you've tried like hell to make me jealous, and let me tell you, it worked every fucking time. But fighting to make me jealous isn't getting over me, Eric, fighting to make me jealous is simply your way of forcing me. If you honestly believed that making me jealous would lead you to someone who would magically make you get over me, you didn't have much success; you still want me."

"And I'll never stop," he tells me.

"Why?"

"Because you don't give up on those you love."

"If you love someone, you set them free," I counter.

"Is that what you want me to do?" His eyes meet mine and I drop my hands in defeat.

"Sometimes yes and other times no." I raise my eyes to him. "You have to understand that this is deeper than being in my mind, Eric. This is physically something I don't know how to handle. It defines who I am. Sure, I could get into women and get over it with women, but with men, with you? I don't know if I can do that." I take a deep breath and go back to pacing. "Being with a man is exactly what I was conditioned to believe was the utmost form of blasphemy. It's everything I was conditioned to ignore, to hate." I'm practically growling by the end. "I can't just fuck it away. I can just rinse and repeat until it no longer bothers me. There is always going to be something, somewhere, in the back of my mind that tells me that what I am doing is wrong."

I watch as he leans forward with his elbows on his knees. "If it is what you want, how can it be wrong?" His question is innocent and not one that I have an answer for.

"I'm not saying that I believe it's wrong, it's what has been ingrained in me. Even after all these years, never acting on the impulses I felt about being with a man, it still makes me sick."

"Has it ever occurred to you that it's fear that is making you sick and not the desire itself?" he asks.

"I'm not sure I'm following you," I tell him because I don't know that I get where he's going with this.

"Well, think about it for a moment. You were raped, forced against your will to do unspeakable acts. Has it occurred to you that your fear is because of that? That you feel like being with a man will be like that?"

His questions make me stop pacing, and though I can't look at him, I'm hearing everything he's saying.

"Have you ever watched a gay porn? Or seen examples of real relationships?"

"Talon and Kyle."

I see him shake his head. "That's a little different. But when you see them together, how does that make you feel? Do you think that what happened to you happens with them?"

"I try not to pay much attention to them. I guess I've never really tried and I can't imagine that what happened to me is happening between the two of them."

"Okay, so what if we positively reinforce the nature of two men being together? What if we...I don't know, what if you let me show you that it's not like that, at all."

I shrug. "I've never considered that before." Which is the truth.

"You've never had anyone to help you consider that before. It's like I said, you had women to help you get over some of your fears, your issues with orgasms, things like that, but you've never had a man to help guide you, to show you what it can and really is like."

"Have you?" I counter.

"No, but I know how to treat people. I know the things that I want from a relationship and I know how I want to be treated. The foundations of relationships are all the same, Cal, whether it is with the same or opposite sex. Love is love, no matter what body parts we have."

I take a seat on the couch across from him, my desire to pace fades away as my mind wanders into the things that he's talking about. About how it shouldn't matter to me, physically or mentally, who I'm with. Then Dr. V's words about mind over matter come back into focus and how if I apply myself to this idea, I can change it, I can make it work for me. "This won't be easy, Eric."

I look at him and he gives me a reassuring smile. "I just want the chance to try, Calvin, I want the chance to help turn this around for you, to redefine you. And I honestly think that we need to start with Dr. V. We need to go to him, separately or together, or both. I know that I am nowhere near capable of handling this by myself. I need to know what I can and can't push with you, how I can push things, when to push things." He runs his hand over his hair. "My biggest fear right now is pushing you too far too fast. Like earlier, my attempt to help you turned disastrous and I need to know how to avoid that happening in the future."

"I don't know how you can help me," I whisper.

"That's why we need Dr. V. If you're truly ready and willing to commit to this, to working through this, I am here. But the bottom line in everything is that you have to be willing to do this for yourself. You have to want to make these changes. Until you know that, without a doubt, that you're committed to better yourself, we can't go further than we are right now."

"Jesus, when did you become so fucking psychological?"

He snorts a laugh, "Good question. I don't know, but I do know that I want you, I want to be with you, in every way."

"I'm not worth it," I breathe.

He smiles at me and states, "I beg to differ."

"You'll see, Eric. You'll see that I'm not worth the headache of trying to fix."

His smile grows a little bigger. "That is something I don't believe to be true."

"You'll see, I promise, you will change your mind about all this," I tell him, though the confidence in the statement is gone, thereby negating its intended reaction.

"I've had eight years to get to the point that no matter what you told me, it wouldn't change how I feel about you."

I don't say anything, what can I say to that? If the deepest, darkest part of who I am isn't enough to scare this man away from me, then I should have nothing to fear, but yet I am shaking because I'm petrified. "I'm scared," I admit so softly that I'm not sure he's heard me until he stands up and skirts the table to kneel in front of me.

He captures my eyes with his and that lost and found feeling returns with a vengeance. "I will do everything I can to protect you." His hand comes to rest on my thigh. A comforting touch that I welcome. "The hardest part of all this, right now, for me?"

"What?"

"That I desperately want to kiss you." My body tenses under his gentle touch because of the words that he's spoken. "But I know that I shouldn't."

"I can't."

"You can, and you have, but see the part where I've failed in that scenario is that I've been the one to lead that charge, not you. I think that is something you have to do for yourself."

"I don't know how."

"You do. It's no different than kissing anyone else, Calvin. Just because it's me shouldn't change your capability of doing something," he says softly.

"But it does."

He gives me a small, sad smile. "I know."

Hesitantly and with shaking fingers, I reach for his cheek, pushing a limit. Just because I have to see how it feels. See what his skin feels like under my touch. The warmth, the stubble of his beard against my palm. He doesn't move, he waits patiently until my hands finally connect. I let out a rush of breath as my fingers slide along his cheek until my palm rests under his jaw, his face in my hands. There is electricity flowing between us, a passion igniting within me that is starting to take over my body, amplified when he leans into my touch and closes his eyes.

"I've waited so long for this," he whispers as he snuggles further into my touch. His hand comes up to cover mine, holding me to him. I don't want to let him go and for the first time ever, I don't have to let him go and that idea scares me enough that I pull my hand away. "What's the matter? What's wrong?" he asks quickly, his eyes flying open to assess me.

"Nothing." I squint my eyes in thought. I can touch him. I touched him. I held him in a way that wasn't friendly, but romantic. "I...I don't know how to describe it."

"Are you in pain?" he asks somberly.

I look at him, our eyes meet, my face relaxes, my mind finds peace and quiet for the first time since I can remember and I shake my head slightly. "As a matter of fact, I...Eric, I just touched you and...and I didn't get sick, I didn't...nothing happened. I'm sorry, but I'm in shock. I've never..." I swallow hard, "I've never touched anyone like that before...I've never felt anything like that before."

"Like what?" His voice is soft but excited.

I smile. "Desire," I breathe.

His answering smile could light up a room darker than hell and for the first time in my life, I actually fight my urge to kiss him. I fight... "I have a feeling I'm going to regret this," I say hastily as I cup his face between my hands, and without thinking about it, I bring my lips to his, hard and desperate. I feel the recoil in my body, but I fight to ignore it, sliding my hands down his neck, onto his shoulders as he moves his lips against mine.

Electricity, desire, repulsion, confusion, hope...it's all there in the taste of his lips, the brush of his lips against my own.

My body starts to shake against my will and I shudder as confusion, excitement and repulsion play war inside my mind, my body. My hands tighten on his shoulders and he grunts in pain. I push him back and pull away. "Shit, shit...I'm sorry." I pull my hands from his shoulders as I take in his face, contorted in pain.

"No, no...don't be. Don't...damn it, I wish you hadn't stopped," he finally manages to say.

"I was hurting you."

He smiles. "A pain I will gladly take any day if it means I can kiss you like that again." I feel his hand gently squeeze my thigh, letting me know that he's still there, he's still with me. "I don't want to ruin this moment, but...I'm afraid to go much further. I don't want to push you beyond what you can handle, I don't want to ruin this moment between us."

He stands up and I can't help but notice the bulge in his pants and sadness washes over me as I realize my kissing him turned him on, again. And once again, I find myself soft as ever.

"What is it, Cal?" I can't meet his eyes. I can't find it in myself to look at him.

"You should probably go," I tell him.

He doesn't say anything, he doesn't have to. I can feel his frustration filling the air between us. "Not until you tell me what's wrong."

"I've told you so much tonight, Eric, I don't know if I can tell you this. Can we please just drop it?"

He sits back down on the coffee table. "No, we can't. Talk to me."

I contemplate the consequences of telling him versus not. By not telling him I'm protecting him from something that will become a very real topic of discussion. Telling him may be the straw that breaks the camel's back and my last chance to push him away completely. Despite how I feel about him, I haven't wrapped my head around the idea that he wants to help me, that regardless of what I've told him, he's still here. Jesus, he hasn't run screaming for the hills.

"Cal?" I hear him, but I can't answer him.

Fuck, he's...damn it, I can't...I want to fucking cry in frustration right now. I don't know what to do.

"Calvin."

"What?" I snap and look at him.

"Whoa, come on, you checked out on me. What's wrong?"

Because I can't say it out loud I stand up in front of him, and it's enough to draw his attention downward, then back up to my eyes. "That's what," I say before stepping away from him.

"I'm confused." he says, "Please just tell me."

"I kissed you, I fucking kissed you and for the first time in my life the desire and hope I felt outweighed the revulsion, the instinct I have to throw up all over the place and yet it still wasn't enough."

"Calvin, I'm confused."

"It wasn't enough to get me hard," I say through gritted teeth and he looks down at his own crotch and back up.

"Shit, Cal, I...fuck, I can't help it."

I grab two fists full of my hair in frustration. "Argh. I know that. I know you can't help it, I know I turn you on, I know that you want me and I...I can't even get a goddamn erection from it. I can't even...please, just go. I can't do this anymore tonight."

His face falls, defeat all over it and in his body language. "We're not done. I won't let this come between us. You didn't get hard? So what, Calvin. I was half hard when you kissed me because I was so fucking excited that you actually put your lips on me, a thousand times more excited because you didn't throw up all over me. I cannot help that I got hard when the person I've longed to kiss for years was finally kissing me. So what if you didn't get a damn hard-on, Calvin, this is not a goddamn race here. I don't fucking expect you to turn off all the shit you've been through in one night. I don't expect you to just fall to your knees and start sucking my cock and I certainly do not expect this to just magically happen between us. It doesn't work that way. But damn it, you cannot get pissed

80

off at me because I got a hard-on from kissing you. If you do that, this will never work between us."

"Please leave," I breathe.

"No." He shakes his head.

chapter 15

calvin

"I'm not leaving." His voice is unyielding.

My entire body is trembling, but I can't tell what is winning out, fear and nerves or excitement. "I'm not worth all this trouble."

I watch as his hands fist once again and he slowly rises to his feet. The phrase 'if looks could kill' comes to mind. "Do not ever say that to me again."

"Think about it, Eric. Think about it really hard because this is not going to be an easy journey. I am not just magically going to be physically okay with all this. Because believe me, Eric, I've tried. I've tried so fucking hard over the years to just wash it all away; throw everything to the wind and walk right up and wrap my arms around you." My body starts to shake harder, sweat forms on my brow and my stomach churns as I think about all the times I so desperately wanted to do those things to him. I swallow hard as he watches me closely.

"It's happening right now, isn't it?"

I wrap my arms around my stomach and cower into the wall behind me. "Yes," I breathe.

"Why? You're there and I'm here."

I just shake my head as I swallow hard. Panic overwhelms me as I worry that I'm going to make an ass out of myself by becoming sick. I just tap my head, trying to convey to him that I'm thinking about him, thinking about what I've just said to him.

"You're thinking?" I nod in answer. "About what?" I point to him. "Thinking about me makes you sick."

I let out the breath I was holding in and mutter, "Imagining." I swallow again and clear my throat, attempting to dispel the raw acid feeling. "Kissing you," I breathe.

"But you just..."

"I know, I know I just...but I..." I swallow hard once more.

"Jesus Cal, you're white as a ghost." He takes a step toward me, then another, I begin frantically shaking my head back and forth as dinner starts creeping up my throat.

"Don't, god." I cover my mouth and he freezes, backing away from me.

"I will never hurt you, Calvin." His voice is laced with anguish.

"I believe you," I tell him as the churning in my stomach settles down when he takes a seat on the couch. "You don't scare me, Eric, you've never scared me. Please," I beg him, "Please never think that you scare me, because you don't. God, this is going to sound so fucking cliché, but it's not you, it's me."

I watch as he rolls his eyes and shakes his head in my direction.

"This is what you're going to have to deal with, me - fucked up. I don't know what will trigger it, what will cause me to feel this way and I sure as shit do not want you to have to witness this. Eric, it's not fair to you."

"But it's my choice."

"No, Eric, it's not."

He stands up again and I slink back into the wall instinctively though it's the wrong response. I watch as fear and pain wash over his features as he takes in my body language. "Oh, but it is," His tone is menacing, but I feel the depth of his conviction and it slides over me like a warm breeze. "You say this isn't going to be easy, and I believe you. I'm sure there is a mountain of shit you haven't told me about what happened to you and I certainly have no fucking clue how to even start helping you work through this, but Jesus Christ, Calvin, we have too much history - too many fucking years between us. If you think I'm just going to walk away from you, run screaming in the other direction, I assure you, you have another thing coming. I have not waited this long to learn about what haunts you to just walk away from you."

"Jesus, Eric, I'm not something that you can magically put back together. It won't work like that. But this is also my choice. My choice whether or not this goes any further. It is my choice to realize and understand that every time I see fear or worry or pity in your eyes that you don't have to be here. You don't have to watch me go through this, and for what? For you? God dammit, Eric, I would walk through hell barefoot for you, but I cannot and will not put you through this. All this pain I know I am going to cause you, is it worth it?"

I watch as a smile tugs at the corner of his mouth, his hands unfurl themselves as his body relaxes. I watch as his eyes well up with unshed tears, tears of pain that I know I've caused him. My heart wrenches at knowing I'm already causing him so much pain already. Pain shoots like lightning through my body, zapping me in ways I never thought I could ever feel. I would take a dozen shattered cheekbones over witnessing this pain and my inability to comfort him crushes me. "Go home, Eric."

A single tear falls down his cheek, my hand twitches with the need to wipe it away, but I stay put. The agony of loss creeps over my entire body and I just need him to leave. Without a word, I watch as he turns toward the door. When he reaches it, he stops with his hand on the knob. I watch as he rests his head against the door. "I would walk through heaven, hell, and the Sahara without shoes, food or water for you," he says so quietly that I can barely make it out. "When you realize that I am not someone you can push away with your demons, you know where to find me."

My knees buckle and his hand turns the knob as he pulls the door open before storming out and slamming it behind him. The moment the door closes, I jump and my entire world goes blank.

Sometime around three in the morning, I wake up on the floor of my living room drenched in sweat. It takes me a few minutes to realize where I am and why I'm there. Then like a flash flood, it all comes rushing back to me.

Dinner…

Eric…

Demons…

The hurt, the pain, the desire, the love…

I let the one thing I've ever loved walk right out my door. I threw away my one chance at redemption all because I'm too goddamn stubborn to let him help me, to let him redefine me.

I punch the floor, hard. My knuckles crack on impact, but they only sting slightly as I crawl my ass down the hallway and up into my bed where for the first time since I was seven, I cry myself back to sleep.

eric

"Dude, it's three-thirty in the morning, what the hell?"
"I sneee ewe to commmme an get meee."
"Jesus Christ Eric, where are you?"
"Druunnk, in a bar,"
"Well, no shit Sherlock, where?"
"Dunno..."
"I'm tracking your phone, be there soon, don't fucking move."
I plop down on something, and wait...

chapter 16

eric

"Fuck!" I squeeze my eyes shut and throw my arm over them to block out the light pouring into my bedroom.

Jesus, I haven't been this fucking hung-over in…thinking hurts and I squeeze my eyes shut.

You're a damn idiot.

I grab a pillow and smother my face with it, growling.

I try like hell to roll over and go back to sleep, but it's pointless. The minute consciousness returns, last night comes rushing back. "Fuck," I growl as I throw my pillow across the room and open my eyes enough to see a glass of water on my table. "What the fuck?" Next to the water are a couple pills. "Who the…"

"That would be me."

"Jesus," I start and scramble, sitting up. "Fuck, what the hell are you doing here?"

"Hey fucker, you called me at three-thirty this morning."

I scowl at him. "I did?"

I watch as Casey nods behind his coffee cup.

"Goddammit, I'm sorry."

He shrugs. "You usually call before you go out."

"I really needed to be alone." I scrub at my face.

"Was it really that bad?" he asks before taking another sip from his coffee cup.

I groan, "Yes, but I'm not sure there is anything I can do about it. He said his piece then all but threw me out the door."

"Since when are you the giving up type?" Casey inquires and my heart lurches in my chest.

"I'm not," I tell him softly.

"Exactly, so what's the problem?" he urges.

"I have a headache worthy of migraine medicine and I'm hungover like a motherfucker, that's the problem." I glare at him.

He scoffs, "Pfft, whatever."

I shake my head. "Let me shower, then we can get some breakfast." He raises an eyebrow at me. "What?" I scold him.

"It's nearly two o'clock."

"Shit." I look over at the clock. "Fuuuccck!" I growl before crawling out of bed. My jeans are still on, but everything else is missing. I look over my shoulder at Casey. "Thanks."

He smirks, shrugs and walks out of my bedroom. I stumble my half drunk, fully hungover ass to the shower.

Once inside the shower, with hot water running over my head and down my back, the last pieces from Calvin's house slowly slide back into my mind. Calvin's words rattle around like a bag of popping popcorn...

"Jesus, Eric, I'm not something that you can magically put back together. It won't work like that. But this is also my choice. My choice whether or not this goes any further. It is my choice to realize and understand that every time I see fear or worry or pity in your eyes that you don't have to be here. You don't have to watch me go through this, and for what? For you? God dammit, Eric, I would walk through hell barefoot for you, but I cannot and will not put you through this. All this pain I know I am going to cause you, is it worth it?"

Even with what I said before I walked out, I knew I needed to leave. I knew that I needed to give him a chance to breathe and to take in everything. But more than anything, I needed him to be comfortable knowing that he told me his deepest secrets. I shake my head and scrub away the memory of his tortured expression when he told me to leave. A look I will not soon forget. A look of pure pain, agony and yet a detachment from the entire situation that I didn't expect. Seeing him in pain is what made me cry, knowing that he has to fight who he is every damn day breaks my heart.

"Goddammit!" I growl before punching the wall of the shower. "Fuck," I curse as I shake out my hand, dispelling the pain I've inflicted on myself. "I knew this wouldn't be easy, not with him. Nothing with Calvin is ever fucking easy but this...fuck!"

Calvin was right, is this worth it? Is it worth the pain? The heartache? The frustration I know I'm going to feel while going through this? Those are the questions I need answers to, but I can't answer those questions without first knowing more about what he's suffering from.

With newfound determination coursing through me I finish showering quickly. When I step out, I grab three ibuprofen and the Tylenol Casey left on my nightstand and I swallow the five pills before I dry off, pull my hair back and get dressed.

When I get to the living room, Casey is sitting on my cheap couch watching the flat screen, some news station is playing in the background. "World War three break out yet?" I chide.

"Nope, but Kim's ass is everywhere again." I roll my eyes.

"I need your help," I tell him as I grab my wallet and keys off of the table.

"Beck and Troy brought your car back already."

"Oh, nice. I'll text 'em later, thanks for that, but that wasn't what I was referring to."

Casey turns to look at me. "I ain't blowing you."

I roll my eyes. "Shut the hell up, I'm actually serious."

He gives me a quick half smile. "Tell me."

"I need some information."

He shrugs. "That's Mills' area, not mine. Though you might be able to get away with Beck."

"No, neither, I need it from you and you alone. You, I can trust."

"What do you need?" His casual tone makes me wonder if I could ask him to kill someone and he'd do it, but that's not what I need either.

"I need to know where Dr. V's office is."

"Who's Dr. V?" he asks and I realize that I should have asked Beck. Casey hasn't been around long enough.

"Fuck," I roll my eyes in frustration. "I probably should have asked Beck or Rusty, they've been around longer. Damn it."

"I can ask for you," he volunteers. "I might be able to get more information for you than..." His phone rings, he pulls it from his pocket and takes a look at it. "It's Calvin."

"Fuck," I growl, "Don't tell him you're here."

He gives me a sideways glance before pressing a button and bringing it to his ear. "Hey man, what's up?"

I can't hear the other side of the conversation. "Nah, I haven't talked to him." That's when Casey looks at me expectantly and I nod, telling him to stick with that lie. "I can try calling him if you want..." There's a pause, "You sure?" And another pause, "Did you need him for something?" Casey shrugs in my direction and I almost want to take the phone from his hand and talk to Mouse myself, but I fight the urge. "Alright, if I hear from him, I'll have him call you."

After that, I'm apparently dropped from the conversation and Casey sits back, chatting with him about something and I wander off into the kitchen to pour my own cup of lukewarm coffee while he finishes his call with Calvin.

"He says he's trying to call you."

"My phone isn't ringing," I tell him without even having looked at my phone.

Casey turns, grabs it off of the table and hands it to me. I set it back down on the counter without looking at the display.

"For God's sake, what the hell is wrong with you two today? When we got off that plane yesterday, you two were buddy-buddy now you're fucking cold as ice."

"None of your business, Casey, stay out of it."

"Well, for the fucking record, he's looking for you, so maybe you might want to check your fucking phone and stop being a dick. Whatever it is that happened between the two of you is hardly worth throwing away nearly a decade of friendship." He huffs and turns back into the living room, plopping back on the couch. I roll my eyes and grab my phone. I push the home button but nothing happens.

Fuck, it's dead. I try to power it on and the apple appears. Not dead. I scowl at it, I never turn off my phone. "Did you turn off my phone?" I ask Casey.

"Nah, man, I just pulled everything out of your pockets and threw it on the table."

"Okay," I say nonchalantly, not really paying much attention as I watch my phone load. Then it starts chiming with texts, voicemails and missed calls. Ironically, other than a few extra messages from Calvin, this is a normal thing for my phone, but I never turn it off, so this is odd to see it all compiled at once.

I scroll through the texts from Calvin:

Calvin to Eric: I'm sorry I threw you out. Can we talk today?
The message was sent at ten this morning.

Calvin to Eric: Hey, where are you? You're not picking up.

The message was sent around eleven thirty this morning.

Calvin to Eric: Okay, I'm really worried now, please call me. I know you're mad at me, but please, at least let me know you're okay and home safe.

The message was sent at 1:35 p.m.

Right before I woke up.

Calvin to Eric: Okay, Casey hasn't seen you either, I'm starting to freak out, I'm coming over.

The message was sent just a few minutes ago.

"You might want to take off," I tell Casey.

"Why?"

"Mouse will be here any minute. You told him you hadn't seen me."

He shrugs and stands up. "I just got here. He called me looking for you. I was worried when you didn't answer your phone so I came over."

I raise my eyebrow at him. "You mean, he didn't tell you he was coming by here?"

He snorts. "No, he didn't. But I can't say I'm surprised. But I'll take off. I'll see what I can find out about this Dr. V you asked me about."

I sigh, "Don't go overboard and please, for the love of fucking, do not let him find out I asked."

He rolls his eyes at me in exasperation. "What's the big deal?"

I lean on the counter, clasping my hands together. "Stays between us?"

"Always, man, you know that."

"Dr. V is a therapist, that's all I know." I catch Casey's movement of taking a step back. "So you weren't told he was seeing one?" I raise an eyebrow at him.

"No, I guess it wasn't pertinent information until now. Are you sure someone on the team knows about this Dr. V?"

I shake my head. "For as little as anyone seems to know about Mouse, I wouldn't be surprised if no one knows. This is why I don't want it to be a big deal, and in all honesty, just forget I asked. I will try and see if I can get the information from Mouse. I'd really rather not go behind his back because I don't need him thinking he can't trust me."

"Why do you need the information anyway?"

I pin him with a 'don't go there' look. "Now that would be telling."

"Alright, but is it something we need to know about, the team I mean?"

It's a very valid question he's asking. "If the team doesn't know by now, it's obviously not that important or at least Mouse doesn't see it that way and technically speaking, it hasn't been an issue so far, so I don't see why it would be now. It's certainly nothing new. Now scram, please."

"Yeah, yeah, I'm out. Call me if you need me and damn it, call me before you go out again so I'm not thrown off at three a.m."

"Yeah okay," I tell him half-heartedly. I'd like to tell him that it won't be that way again, but if Calvin is coming over here, I doubt that he's gonna just check on me.

"Later," Casey says as he reaches the door.

"Thanks, man, I appreciate it."

He smiles. "Anytime."

With that he leaves and I grab my phone, flipping through my messages. The only voicemails I have are from Calvin, and one from Jess. I play that one.

"Hey big guy, just wanted to check and see if you made it back to Cali okay. Haven't talked to you in a few days, give me a call when you get a chance," she sighs into the phone, "I hate to even ask, but any changes?" another pause like she's expecting me to answer, "Anyway, call me back when you get this. Later."

Instead of calling her, I text her.

Eric to Jess: home safe yesterday, long night last night, yes - everything has changed, but for the good or bad, I don't know yet. Lunch tomorrow?

She replies back quickly.

Jess to Eric: don't leave me hanging…? Glad you're home safe, I have a meeting tomorrow over lunch, dinner? Drinks? Let me know.

Eric to Jess: have to, he'll be here in a few minutes, I'll call you later and we can hash out plans. Home til Tuesday then back on the road.

Jess to Eric: just make time for me before you leave. Good luck. **hugs**

I don't reply to her. We learned early on that we both play a "who gets the last word" game and we'd end up bantering for ten messages before one of us would finally quit. I go digging for my charger and plug my phone in. No sooner does it chime with the charge tone when there is a knock on my door.

I walk over to it, realizing I'm still only in jeans, no shoes, socks or t-shirt, when I swing open the door to a very nervous, slightly strung out Calvin who is making no secret of his appraising of me.

"Thank God," he says in a rush before stepping toward me. His hands are on my face and his lips are on mine before I can even wrap my head around what's happening. Holy fuck, he's kissing me, again.

chapter 17

eric

My heart starts pounding in my chest with a little bit of excitement and fear that he will come to realize that he's kissing me and pull back. But he doesn't, no, he deepens the kiss by pulling me into him. Dumbstruck, I don't know what to do with my hands. I want to touch him, but I'm afraid of pushing him too far. He pulls back and looks at me. "Touch me," he breathes and my hands move on their own accord; with shaky fingers, I cup his cheeks in my palms.

God, he's so soft and warm. I can feel the growth of his beard beneath my fingers and every nerve in my body ignites with desire. I take a step back, pulling him with me, followed by another step and I kick the door closed. Gently I push him back against me as he tugs my bottom lip between his teeth. "Ahh." I can't control the moan, the sensation is overwhelming me. Jesus, I have got to be dreaming, this can't be fucking happening. Can it?

He breaks our kiss. "Stop," he kisses me, "Thinking."

I push my forehead against his. "I can't help it." My voice is husky, full of all the pent up lust I feel for him, even I don't recognize it. "I'm scared I'm going to overstep…"

"Shhh…" He teasingly kisses me again. "I'm alright. More relieved that you're alright than anything."

My entire body goes slack with his concern. "I...I turned my phone off last night."

"You never turn that thing off."

I snort, pulling back to look into his eyes, releasing his cheeks in favor of his biceps. "No I don't, but I was pretty drunk last night."

"That's my fault. I shouldn't have kicked you out. I saw it, in your eyes."

I cock my head at him. "Saw what, Calvin?"

"Your decision."

I shake my head. "I hadn't decided anything last night."

His eyes leave mine, looking away from me. "I saw you warring with yourself."

"Aww, Cal, I wasn't warring with myself about you, I was scared. For you. Fuck, you looked so scared last night." I push back, putting some distance between us so that I can think better. His kiss has me shaky and confused. "I cried because I didn't know how to comfort you. I, jeez Cal, I don't know how to do this and I think last night we both needed some time to breathe." I come away from the door completely, giving both of us our own air to breathe. "I thought that if I left it would give you a chance to think, to clear your head and to come to terms with the fact that you'd told me so much stuff. And I," I pause, looking at him, "I needed to try and figure out how best I can help you." I meet his eyes. "The last thing I want to do is push you beyond what you can handle."

"That's precisely why I kissed you just now."

"I don't understand."

He sighs and steps farther into my apartment. "I needed to know if you'd rejected me."

"I could never..."

He nods at me. "I know that now. But this isn't going to be easy for either one of us."

"But you kissed me and you seem to be doing okay." I give him an encouraging half smile.

He gives me a returning smile before replying, "After last night, I realized in the right frame of mind, I can do a lot of things. When I got here and you opened the door, I was so relieved to see you that I didn't know what else to do, I let instinct take over."

I smile, "Your instinct can take over anytime."

"Good."

"But I still don't know anything, Cal. I need to know more about this, more about you, more about what happens when you're triggered. I really want to talk to Dr. V."

I see sadness color his features, but he reaches into his back pocket for his wallet which he opens and he pulls out a card. He places it between his index and middle finger and extends his arm in my direction. "What's this?"

He gives me a smile, "It's Dr. V's card. You have an appointment with him tomorrow morning at ten."

"You'll be there?" I ask as I take the card from him.

He lowers his gaze and turns toward my couch. "No, tomorrow is for you."

"That's not fair, I'd feel like I was talking about you behind your back."

He turns back to me, meeting my eyes. "You're not. I made the appointment. I wanted to give you a chance to meet him by yourself, ask all the questions rattling around in your mind about me, about my situation without the burden of me being there. I thought it would make you more comfortable. I know, just like I'm sure you do, that you'd hesitate to ask something for fear of offending me and I don't want that for you. I want you to be able to ask anything of him and I have given him carte blanche to answer any and all questions you have."

"I don't know what to say."

He smiles. "Say you'll come to dinner with me tonight. Then tomorrow you can go to Dr. V's office. He's cleared his schedule for you all day tomorrow."

"I don't need all..."

"Shh, I asked him if he could, knowing the extent of the information he has, the millions of questions you have combined with the fact that we're not in town long. I thought that if you had enough time to chat with him that you could get all your answers at once."

"I'm sure I can't possibly ask him everything."

He smiles as he sits down. "No, but he's a good doctor and he's agreed to help us both. You understanding me and us." He pauses as he crosses his ankle over his knee and leans back into the couch, putting one arm on the back of it. Settling in, he continues, "I've decided that I've fought this part of me for long enough. I need to figure out how to make this work and in order for me to do this I have to have as much support on board as possible. That is, if you're willing to go through all this."

"Where did all this confidence come from?" I ask him with a playful smirk on my face.

He smiles back. "You," he states simply.

"Huh...so you mean that we could have had this conversation eight years ago?"

He laughs. "I highly doubt that. I was too caught up in 'who I was supposed to be' to see who it is that I am. But this will not be easy and a part of me already feels like giving up this battle."

"If you're not..." I interrupt and he continues anyway.

"But I know where that part comes from, that part comes from the behaviorally trained part of me. The part of my mind that doesn't want to let this go, unwillingly mind you. Eric, I want this more than anything else, which is how I know you need to start with Dr. V and we go from there."

"Alright," I agree softly.

chapter 18

calvin

"What made you change your mind?" His question is legitimate and I want to answer it, but I don't know for sure where to begin.

"A lot of things really."

He comes to sit on the couch, but on the opposite side from me and I don't like the distance between us, but I don't know if I can bring myself closer. I was honestly so overwhelmed that he was okay and with seeing him half-naked that I couldn't stop myself from kissing him when he opened the door. That was the final validation that I needed to know that I'd made the right choice.

"Can you be more specific, please?" he pleads.

"Well, Dr. V helped," I tell him.

"How so?" he asks the obvious follow-up.

I scrub at my face. "Well, I called him this morning, before I tried calling you the first time, and I told him that I needed to see him. But he didn't have a lot of free time today so we talked on the phone, which is pretty normal for him and me." I'm rambling, I know that, but I'm trying to organize all the thoughts in my head before I start spewing everything all over the place. "I told him that I told you almost everything last night. Told him that I broke it down, explaining it to you and that I'd done my best to tell you about everything." I pause, taking a deep breath. "I told him about what happened when I kissed you or what didn't happen for that matter." I watch as his nose scrunches up. "You need to understand something about Dr. V, I tell him everything. I have to. It's the only way that he's able to help me through a lot of what goes on within me when certain things happen, like kissing you, or picturing us together. Without the gory details, he can't work out ways to help me through it."

"No, I get that, and I am certainly very glad you can tell him everything, but it just feels so, I don't know, personal."

I smile at him. "It is personal. What happens to me directly affects anyone that I'm with." I stand up and start to pace again, I can't control the urge to keep moving or to keep my mind occupied on menial tasks like walking. "Being with women," I can't ignore his scoff, right as I turn back the other direction. "You need to understand that I have nothing else to compare this to," I tell him.

"What about before all this shit happened to you, you said that you were with other guys?" I turn to look at him, his face has relaxed and I'm distracted by his naked chest, the tattoos covering his chest and shoulders, down his arms, are a site to behold. A hodge-podge of life forever marking his skin but in the center of it all is his demon, with wings spread wide. My mouth waters with a desire to lick it, and him. To savor his taste…I stop the thought, knowing what will happen if I let it go any further.

I swallow and turn back around. "I was, but it's hard to compare the me then to the me now. Back then my biggest fear wasn't even about getting caught, it was more about getting hurt, emotionally. Sure, my father had caught me a few times," I subconsciously rub at my cheek, "But I tried to justify his actions, I tried to rationalize away the reason why he did the things he did."

"How so?" he asks me.

I sigh, I knew that we were going to have to talk about everything my father ever did to me, tell him the story of how my father came to be a drunk asshole, but I hadn't planned on it being today.

"Cal, if we're going to work through this, we can't keep secrets anymore."

"No, I know that. I just…" I look at him again and our eyes meet, "I hadn't planned on laying it all on the table so fast."

"How did you justify it?" he counters with a less complicated question and for that I silently thank him.

"He was a drunk. Lost in his own world. Sometimes I would think that it bothered him because he was hell bent on keeping the farm in the family. He was determined to force me into running it and somewhere in the back of his mind if I was gay, he didn't think it would be something I could do." I run a hand over my head, calming myself down about the whole mess.

"He was right, it wasn't something I wanted to do, but it wasn't because I was gay, it was because I didn't want to do it. Sure, I grew up on a farm, I knew the ins and outs of everything that happened there, had to happen and how it happened. He made sure of that. But it wasn't for me. I craved the city. I craved the big town environment. I hated the small town gossip, the small town life of church on Sunday's. Birthday parties that brought every kid in the town out, just everyone being up in your business all the time. I hated it, and as graduation drew closer, I was saving my money for college. Something else he didn't think I needed, but that was the reason I saved my money. So that I could do it without him. He knew deep down that if I ran off to college, that I would never come back."

"What about your mother?"

"She was already gone. She died when I was six."

"Fuck Cal, I didn't..."

"It's okay. Even though I was young, my mother wasn't exactly the nurturing type. She cared more about her Ladies Aide Society and the church than she did about her own family. She cared more about the image of being a farmer's wife than she did about being a mother."

"How'd she die?"

I snort. "Honesty, I'm not sure I know anymore. I was told it was a car accident throughout my childhood. But as I grew older, so did my suspicions about what really happened. I often wonder if it was my father who ran her off the road. He was a miserable son of a bitch before she was gone and her death amplified whatever demons he was hiding behind. Honestly, by the time I was old enough to question it, I was hiding behind my own problems and I gave up." I turn to him. "You know how they say hindsight is always twenty-twenty?" He nods. "Well in hindsight, when it comes to my mother, I wouldn't be surprised if she'd just run off. My father, to save face with the town, convinced the sheriff, who was his best friend, to stage an accident and he told the town she was dead." I shrug.

"That's a pretty elaborate lie to pull off."

I snort. "My father is or maybe was, a pretty powerful man in that town. He could do and say just about anything to manipulate people into believing whatever he wanted them to believe. Including me. I was too young to really know better and to be completely honest with you, I don't even remember crying afterward. That, my friend, is pretty fucked up."

"I'd say so," he agrees.

"As I got older, I started to notice certain things, boys and girls, the differences between them, and then I started to notice that boys held my attention better than any girl could. Sure, I dated a few, but I never made it past second base with most of them. You know, copping a feel and all. I never had much of a desire for them. Then finally one day, when I was fifteen, working in the field, Billy caught me staring at him and it was pretty much downhill after that. Though he was the true definition of a closet homo." I chuckle at the memories of Billy.

"Why was that?"

Our eyes meet again and I'm momentarily lost in him before I answer. "He was captain and quarterback of the football team, held that position since freshman year. Aw man, he was good looking, but he always had chicks lined up ready to drop to their knees in the middle of the hallways at school. Most of the guys in my school assumed I was gay and they made no secret of telling people that. Including Billy." I shrug, "But three times a week, after school, we'd be at my house working in the fields, side by side, eventually the looking turned to touching, then kissing and then finally blowjobs and other things. The irony about that scenario now is the fact that if he got his rocks off first, he'd be so repulsed that I usually ended up rubbing my own out while he ran screaming from the barn."

"What a dipshitidiot."

I laugh at his term. "Where the hell did you learn that phrase?"

He laughs too, "You wouldn't believe me if I told you."

I lift my chin in a challenge, "Try me."

"From Jess, though she pulled it out of a book somewhere."

I laugh, "Well, be sure to thank her for me, it suits him perfectly."

"Do you know whatever happened to him?" he asks as I come to stand in front of the patio doors, looking out across the city. Eric's apartment is high enough in the building and elevated enough by hills that Los Angeles lays out before me. Though you certainly can't see the whole city, it's still a sight to behold. I was jealous of this view when he moved in. His apartment is smaller than mine but no less luxurious.

I sigh before answering, "Nope, I don't. I don't entirely care either. Though after the second to last time my father beat me, he finally told his buddies to shut the fuck up and grow up when they'd start teasing me at school. So I guess that was his way of making amends for running like a little girl when my father caught us."

"So if you were back in school after that, what happened that got you locked up?"

I run my hand through my hair. "The same, though I'd given up on Billy after that day. I started driving to Decorah, a college town not too far from us, where I would meet guys, and you know. But one time, one of them came home with me, and I was naive enough to believe that my father would still be at the bar, but he wasn't. That time, he didn't beat me up too bad. I think he learned after the last time with Billy that I was bigger and stronger than he was and that I was going to fight back. Instead, he threw my friend out, put me in the house, locked me up in my room and he left.

If I'd had any idea of what was coming for me the next day, I would have broken out and left."

"What came?"

"Men in white coats," I say somberly. "Literally. They were men who had the same right-wing beliefs my father did that being gay was an abomination of God. That being gay was a learned trait. I think my father probably blamed himself since I never had my mother around. I grew up around him and men who worked for him, so he was pretty sure these doctors were capable of 'curing the gay' out of me."

"But it's not a choice."

I look at him and smile. "No, it's not a choice. It's what defines you, it's a part of you, whether you want it to be or not." I sigh, looking back out the window. "But my father believed it was a choice. That by sending me away to the nuthouse I could be cured of my 'gayness', and in a way, I was."

chapter 19

eric

"I don't see it that way." He looks at me, confused. "I see it as some group of crazy ass whack jobs bending you to their beliefs." I shift on the couch to look at him better and he continues, "Think about it. It's not much different than someone pushing off their religious beliefs on you to the point that you can't help but believe what they're saying is the truth. Which it might be, but some people are more susceptible to believing what they're told, versus the reality of a situation. You were manipulated to believe that being gay is a sin, that being gay is the ultimate blasphemy and nothing more."

"But it doesn't stop my physical reaction."

"No, and there is a chance that you might never be able to rid yourself of the physical reaction, but I think if you break down what exactly it is that makes you shake, what makes you sick, you might actually see that the trigger in your mind is what you were made to believe. Like that all gay men are raped or are rapists, or that all gay men are beaten or killed, which we both know is not the case. But in your mind, that's what you believe. That is ultimately what we need to reverse in your mind."

I'm confident that there is nothing I'm telling him that Dr. V hasn't already said to him, if not him then certainly someone else has. I watch him carefully, lost in thought, lost in understanding and I can see the determination on his features.

"How, though?" he finally asks.

"How, what?" I cock my head at him, vying for his attention, but he keeps staring out the window.

"How do we reverse it?"

I smile. "Time, patience, perseverance. Like anything else, Calvin, it won't be done overnight. But right now, we're taking steps in the right direction by talking about it. For me, I need to know what boundaries I can push with you. Like earlier, when you kissed me, I was afraid of touching you, afraid of triggering you and more importantly, afraid of losing the moment I was granted. I'm also afraid that if I do something, like touch you or kiss you…"

"You've touched me for years and nothing has ever happened," he interrupts.

'You're right, I have, but when I've touched you, it wasn't a lover's touch. Like touching your cheek, or hugging you - which isn't something we do often," I tell him. "I'm worried about instigating something as simple as kissing you. You've kissed me twice in less than twenty-four hours, but both of those times have been at your lead. What's going to happen if I take the lead and try and kiss you?"

I watch as he shrugs. "I honestly don't know. The two times that you did, both times I've had negative reactions."

"And they were two times where I let my hormones get the better of me and I kissed you out of nowhere with no right to do so." A lightbulb clicks in my head. "Oh my god, Cal…do you honestly believe that I would do something to you against your will?"

His eyes shoot to mine, first there is fear and concern then finally he softens and shakes his head. "No, I don't think you would."

"You're right, I wouldn't. It's not who I am and it is certainly not in my nature to do so, but if you think about it, that is your trigger."

He squints at me, trying to read me, trying to see what it is I'm trying to say.

"I went after you, both times, in unprovoked, unwarranted and certainly unwelcome circumstances," I tell him and it all starts to make sense to me, better sense than it did before.

"But none of those times did I ever feel that way."

"Consciously? No, you didn't, you wouldn't feel that way, at least not after our chats last night and now today. Don't you see, you were still fighting yourself, you still are. Fighting a battle between your mind and your heart. Ask yourself, what does my heart want? And there you will have your answer."

"I want you." His voice is soft, somber and convincing.

I smile warmly at him. "And I want you," I tell him and I stand up. "But right now, the only thing you can do is learn to trust me. Trust me wholeheartedly that I would never ever do anything to harm you. Once you've established that trust, then you will be able to see that I'm not your mind's enemy." I take a couple of steps toward him. "When you're with women, who takes the lead?"

"I do," he answers confidently.

"What happens when a woman tries to take the lead?" I take two more steps toward him.

"I get nauseous."

I take another step toward him and I watch as he stiffens. "What is happening to you right now?" I ask.

I watch as he swallows hard, so I take a step back, then another. His eyes relax and his body relaxes in response to my backing away from him. "I'm not going to take the lead here, Calvin. You are."

His eyes dart to mine, then down my body and back up again.

"We go only as far as you want this to go. Not a step further. If you want my hands on you, you put them there."

"I don't know if I'm ready for this," he breathes.

"Then don't do anything. I am not and will not force you to do anything with me that you don't want to, but think about it so far. Dinner last night. You picked it, you told me when and I was there. You kissed me first. Today, I opened the door and you all but jumped on me. I make a move toward you and…"

"I don't mean to," he practically sobs.

I freeze. "Stop, I know you don't, Calvin. Jesus, I know." My heart breaks and I don't know what to do or say and I know he sees it too.

"Please don't, don't start with the sad eyes, Eric, I can't, I can't take them. I can't…I should go."

"No," I tell him and sigh. "I am sad because I know you don't mean any of this, I know this isn't how you want this to be between us. I know you want more, you want us closer together, I know that. Unequivocally I know that and I know that you're unable to help it, you're unable to stop your body from reacting in ways that you despise. So please, my sadness is only because you're upset. Not because you can't do something." I take a deep breath. "It was the same thing last night. What you mistook for pain and pity was actually concern and confusion. Jesus Cal, I want so fucking bad to knock this out of you. To let you be the person you want to be, need to be, are destined to be and all I can do is try. All I can do is keep pressing and keep hoping that I won't turn it into something worse. Drive you away from me." Tears well in my eyes. "God forbid, push you out of my life forever."

He doesn't respond, he just keeps staring at me. "Say something." I murmur.

I watch as he shakes his head and pushes away from the window he's been leaning on. It's like watching a slow motion scene where the hottest woman you've ever seen is walking in your direction, only without the flowing hair and high-heels. He walks toward me, determination spelled out across his face. I don't know what his plans are, but I don't intend to move until I can figure it out.

He comes to stand in front of me. His eyes lock with mine. "I have complete control?" he asks.

"Yes," I breathe.

His hand grabs the back of my neck and he pulls me down, pressing his lips to mine, hot and hard. Desire, lust, need, desperation explode throughout my body. My dick hardens slightly, lengthening in my jeans. My head starts to swim as his tongue slides along the seam of my lips, coaxing me to open for him. I moan, giving him the opportunity he wants and he slides his tongue in along mine. My breathing hitches and my palms twitch with a desperate need to touch him, but I stay still.

His hand unfurls from around my neck and slides down along my shoulder, to my arm just as I feel his breathing spike. A hint of fear slides through me as I worry about him, until his other hand cups my arm. He breaks our kiss and I slowly open my eyes.

His are on fire with need. "Touch me, please, Eric?" he breathes.

"Where?"

His hands slide down my arms to my hands where he grabs my wrists and puts them on his hips. "Anywhere," he pleads.

chapter 20

calvin

I can see the concern in Eric's eyes as he rests his hands on my hips. I know I don't do a very good job of showing it, but having his hands on me feels amazing. "Kiss me," I breathe and his eyes widen momentarily so I grab him by the back of the neck again, bringing his lips to mine and he doesn't hold back. When our mouths clash together, neither one of us is breathing. I put everything I am feeling for him into my kiss, sliding my tongue past his lips and along his. I place my other hand on his shoulder and begin to slowly trace my thumb along his collarbone. He shivers and I feel his hands tighten, pulling me toward him and I slide in closer.

Then I feel his hands start to tug at my shirt, pulling it up, seeking skin contact and I don't stop him. I want to feel his hands on me, I need to feel them. He gently slides his hands up my t-shirt until he grabs hold of my sides. His fingers are rough, calloused from his bass and I shiver. His breathing hitches again and my head starts to swim and for the first time, my cock starts to harden.

Panic rises in the back of my throat, unknown emotions, and desire course hotly throughout my body. I'm losing my grip on the here and now. My hands loosen on his body and he freezes. I pull back, breathing heavy. "Shit, I'm...fuck," I growl pulling my body away from his.

I can hear him fighting to catch his own breath. "What did I do?"

I don't answer, having to honestly think through what really happened that I lost it before I can answer him. The panic in me is making it harder to breathe so I lean down, putting my hands on my knees and I can feel it. I'm still hard, maybe even harder than I was a few moments ago. Panic, pain, desire, need... Jesus, they're all coursing through me, feelings that I've never felt before and this time the panic was all on me. It wasn't anything that he's done. No, in fact, it's quite the opposite.

"Calvin, are you alright?" I'm sucking air in but finding very little relief. I can see spots behind my eyes and my legs are growing weaker the longer I let realization of what's actually happened sink in. I try desperately to think of something else, but above anything else in this situation, need and desire are overruling everything else. I feel his hand gently on my back stroking up and down. My heart rate begins to slow, though breathing is still a challenge, the longer he rubs along my back, the more relaxed I'm starting to feel.

God, he's going to think I'm a complete lunatic. I've had a damn panic attack over an erection. "This...is...so...stupid," I spit between breaths.

"I highly doubt that. Can you tell me what I did?"

I actually smile slightly through the deep breaths. "You didn't do anything, Eric. Nothing at all." Now I know I am going to have to explain myself.

"Then what happened?"

I take one big deep breath, followed by another. My equilibrium is returning to me and I almost feel comfortable enough to stand up, but then his warm hand slides along my back once again and I would much rather stay bent over like this if it means he keeps touching me. "In all the times that I've started to react, I have never been able to stomach anyone touching me. When, in fact, you touching my back has had the opposite effect. It's comforting."

"What else can I do?" he asks softly. I can't help but notice the worry in his voice.

"Don't laugh," I tell him.

"What on earth would be funny about this?"

I snort, "Just promise me you won't laugh?"

I can almost feel him rolling his eyes. "I promise."

"I got hard." I rush through the words, afraid that my admission will make me sick, but it doesn't.

"What?"

I chuckle a little and finally stand up. His hand on my back steadies me momentarily until I look him in the eyes. Then, without a second thought, I grab his free hand and place it over my crotch. "I..got...hard," I say semi-seductively as I watch his eyes widen and he takes in my erection.

He smiles and I release his hand, but he doesn't release me, instead his eyes grow soft and his hand slides along the bulge in my pants. I hiss through my teeth and claim his mouth once more. Licking his lips, begging him to open for me, his hand leaves my crotch, but I find his wrist and bring it back. "Don't stop," I tell him before I put my lips back on his. He kisses me back with abandon, his hand gently stroking along my shaft. I groan into his mouth and pull back. "I don't know how much more of this I can take," I breathe against his lips, kissing him again quickly and pulling back. At the same time, his hand comes away from my cock and it jumps. "Only for the fact that I don't know how far this will go between us right now."

"I want you so bad," he tells me and I smile.

"It scares me," I tell him honestly.

"It does me too." He rests his forehead against mine. Being close to him, like this, isn't much of a challenge and I don't know whether it is because I am letting my dick lead this ride, or if there is something unlocking itself inside me. Either way, I'm petrified that the high of Eric is going to wear off and I'm not going to be able to stop before I get to the point of full-on panic. "So why did getting hard scare you?"

I raise an eyebrow as I pull back from him. "It didn't scare me necessarily. It's just never happened before."

He gives me a questioning look. "Never?"

I shake my head. "No, never." I laugh, "Poor girls always have to suck or stroke me hard. Kissing, touching, playing with the bases have never done much for me, at least until we get to the point of naked." I laugh a little harder, "I'm pretty sure I've disappointed my fair share of women who've pulled off my pants to find a soft dick in their face." I take a step back, putting some distance between us. "You know, I'm pretty sure we don't need to talk about them."

"On the contrary, I think we do." I give him a look. "No, hear me out." I nod for him to continue. "If all you have had to experience since all of this is women, I think that things that have happened with them could be valuable to you in figuring all this out. Like maybe you couldn't get hard while making out with them because they honestly never actually turned you on. Hell, even a woman sucking on my dick gets me hard, but not so much their bodies." I watch as he shivers at more than a few memories of that.

"Have you always been gay?" I ask him, and he scoffs. "No, seriously, I'm curious. You never had a problem picking up chicks, which I guess is how I could wipe away my attraction for you. A 'you weren't into guys' kind of thing."

Eric motions for me to sit on the couch and I do. He sits down opposite me and I slide closer, our knees touching. He puts his arm along the back of the couch and I put my arm on top of his arm. Holding him. He pauses to look at our connection and then back to me and I give him a smile. I need him to know that while this is intimate between us, this doesn't bother me. It should. "I think I'm finally starting to see the friendship lines blur," I tell him.

"Explain please?"

I smile. "After you answer my question."

He gives me a playfully quizzical look, "What question?"

"Uh huh, nice try, the one about you always being gay, have you..." I swallow, anticipating the bile feeling in my throat that never comes, "Always been gay?"

"The simple answer to that question, Cal, is yes. I've known since I was about sixteen. Though girls have never disgusted me and I've even slept with more than a few, I did it because it was the social norm. Especially once I got to college and found you fuckers, and Dex, the way he's always been with his comments and shit. So I hid it. Hid who I knew I was because for me it was easier to play it straight than to play it gay."

"You certainly don't act gay," I tell him without a thought.

He doesn't take offense like I worried he would, in fact, he smiles at me. "Not all gay men are 'gay'," he says with the flick of his wrist. "Some, like me are just gay and male and not much to it. Then again, how many men do you know dye their hair?"

I can't help but snort a laugh at him. "It's not the dye, it's the fact that you take almost as long as Addison does to get ready."

"Perfection takes a while."

The tension is shattered when we both start laughing and slowly my erection subsides, bringing me back to level, slowing the driving urge I have to take this further than I know I'm ready for.

chapter 21

eric

"Put some clothes on," Calvin nods at me.

"Too distracting?" I tease him.

His answering smile is so bright and happy that my heart warms a little more. "Yes, but I can't take you out to dinner dressed like that."

I smirk. "Sure you can." He rolls his eyes. "Why go out? Why not stay here?" I say in a sultry voice full of promise.

He snorts, "Because I don't trust myself for one, and for two, you can't cook worth a fucking damn and I'm starving."

"You have a point there, but my fingers dial take-out real well." Our arms are still draped over each other's on the back of the couch and I rub my thumb along his arm.

He looks at our connection and I can see a smile playing on his lips.

"Is it getting easier?" I ask softly.

His eyes meet mine and they are soft with no trace of fear or concern. "This is, yes. I'm not sure about anything else," he says quietly.

"I'm not concerned about anything else," I tell him without hesitation. "That will come when it's time, when you're ready, when we're both ready."

That smile that was threatening his lips a moment ago spreads into a nice, soft grin. "I have to tell you that in a way, I feel ready, but..." I watch as he swallows, "There's always that other side threatening to take over."

I cup his cheek with my free hand and I notice a minuscule flinch, but the small smile on his lips never leaves as my hand touches his skin. "I'm not sure we will ever be able to rid you of that part of you, but I'm willing to try my hardest to help you."

"I know you are. I just hope it's worth it in the end."

"For who? You?" I ask.

"No, for you."

That has been his argument all along. I gently stroke my thumb along his cheek. "You're so afraid I'm going to run. Calvin, I'm not going anywhere. To be honest with you, whether we end up together for a lifetime or I help you get through this and we part ways, it will all be worth it to me. Though I hope it's not the latter of those two scenarios, I'm willing to accept the fact that I can do this, for you, as a friend. Hell, I would have started years ago if I'd known," I tell him and it's the God's honest truth.

He doesn't say anything for a few moments and I pull my hand away and watch as he shivers at the loss and my hand tingles to touch him again. "Eric," he breathes. I look at him, cocking my head and I stroke my thumb along his arm in encouragement. "I have to be honest about something."

"Anything," I tell him.

"It really wasn't until New York, when you came out to the guys and I saw their reaction, that I really let a lot of this side of me take over. I've been consumed with it since that night. Before that, I had my suspicions about you, but you'd never confirmed them. Yeah, you'd kissed me in the past, but a part of me rationalized it by thinking you were curious or bisexual. Sure, I've had feelings for you for years - thought I didn't know how to process them - but..." He pauses.

"You locked them away, unsure of what I would think?"

He gives me a sad smile. "Among other things. I worried about what the guys would say, think. In fact, I worry about it still."

I smile at him. "I wouldn't worry about them. You saw it with me, even now. Jesus, I knew that walking onto that tour bus would change so many things, but I never, in my wildest imagination, imagined that things would be happening the way they have," I tell him.

"How so?"

"Well, Talon and Kyle?" I raise an eyebrow at him and he smirks.

"No, I definitely didn't see that coming," he agrees.

"No, I didn't either, but then again, I'm not so sure those two would have ever considered being with each other if Addison hadn't come around. In fact, we have Addison to thank for a lot of shit."

He cocks his head at me, willing me to explain. Much the same way I had earlier, though in return I just give him a very pointed look. He laughs. "Yeah, I suppose. Dex and Raine - if Addison hadn't come with us, Raine would have never shown up in New York."

"Tori and Rusty."

"God, who'd have thought that those two..." he slips into his own thoughts.

"And if she hadn't encouraged me to come out..."

"We wouldn't be sitting here, like this," he finishes.

"Exactly," I agree.

We sit in silence for a few minutes before I get up. He stops me and leans in, bringing his lips to mine in a soft, 'don't go' kind of kiss. My head swims with his contact. "I'm just gonna put some clothes on." I give him a smile as I get up off of the couch and head for my bedroom. Once outside of his presence, I take a huge, comforting, cleansing breath, pulling as much air into my lungs as humanly possible.

There is a huge weight that comes with Calvin, one that I never thought to expect, but it all suddenly makes perfect sense. It makes sense why I couldn't make a move, why he never made one on his own. The fact that we both feel things for each other confirms that my own emotions weren't one sided, which fills me with relief. I knew there was no rhyme or reason for me to have feelings for someone who would never reciprocate.

Jess and I have talked about it numerous times. She'd been in situations where she'd had feelings for someone, would do almost anything for them, only to be treated like shit and only to be told years later, after the fact, that they were really in love with her but didn't know how to handle it. I'd told her that it was because they didn't have to. She willingly handed over so much of herself that the guys didn't feel the need to work for it. That was until it was gone, then all of a sudden there is so much more to it than what was on the surface.

In a way, that is how it's been with Calvin all this time. Though I was giving and willing to give him pieces of me, whether he wanted them or not, he wasn't sure how to process them, how to handle them, but all the while, he too was falling in love.

"You're not doing your hair are you?"

The sound of his voice makes me jump. "What? No, I just..."

He grins. "You okay?"

My answering smile is big and bright. "More than okay. I guess I never really gave myself time to process anything from yesterday until now. Instead I just buried it, got drunk over it and now I actually feel freer than I've felt in years and I don't know how to describe it," I tell him candidly.

Something I've always been able to do with him except when it came to my emotions. Like a shy freckle-faced teenager talking to the girl he likes for the first time.

"I understand that better than you think," he tells me as he sits on the foot of my bed.

I shiver as excitement courses through me, seeing him on my bed. I won't lie, all this talking about his past, his treatment; everything is overwhelming and scary as fuck, but seeing Calvin sitting on my bed has my cock stirring again. I swallow. "I'd imagine you do. I really hoped that you telling me would lift some of that burden from your shoulders."

He smiles as he lowers his head and clasps his hands together before his lust filled gaze meets mine. Fuck. I'm not sure, but I think he captures my reaction, the one I tried to hide, and his features shift and his demeanor changes enough to pull me back to the present and out of my fantasies. "Honestly, if I'd known that it would be like this," he gestures between the two of us, "I would've told you years ago." Then he shakes his head. "Then again, maybe not. I think that you coming out woke the beast inside me, made me take a harder, longer look at myself, who I am and who it is that I want to be."

"My coming out did all of that?" I ask, as I finally manage to straighten out my t-shirt and pull it over my head.

He sighs and my eyes meet his as I pull it down my body, that little smirk is playing at his lips again and I actually fucking blush. "That is so not fair," I mumble.

That's when he stands up and saunters toward me. Unsure of what he's going to do, I take a small step back between me and my closet door. He's still coming at me. "No, it's not," he says softly before his body is pressed against me and his lips are pressed firmly to mine.

His hands slide up my stomach, pushing my t-shirt back up. His hands are warm and rough, kneading at my flesh as he climbs higher and slides his tongue into my mouth when I gasp for breath.

Taking a cue from earlier, I put my hands on his forearms and slide them up toward his shoulders. He shudders and I'm concerned it's for the wrong reasons so I stop moving. He pulls his lips from mine and I tremble at the loss. "Don't stop," he whispers and his breath caresses along my jaw. I take his request and keep moving my hands further up his arms, going for his shoulders, then down his chest.

I feel my fingers scrape over one of his nipples and the piercing there. He shudders. I freeze, but he encourages me by bringing his hand to cup the back of my head and pulling me down to his lips. "Ahh," I moan into his mouth and pull back slightly. "You're pushing my limits of control, Calvin," I breathe.

"I know," he answers back before kissing me chastely once, twice, and a third time before releasing my head and pulling back from my body altogether.

His body locks down, and people constantly joke about turning green, but I watch Calvin, literally, turn green and pale with sweat on his forehead before he takes off into my en suite bathroom.

"Shit," I curse under my breath as I hear Calvin vomiting violently into my toilet. "Fuck! Shit! Fuck! Dammit." I stutter through every curse word I can think of under my breath as I slowly walk toward the bathroom door.

"Don't. Please," he pleads between heaves.

"Do you want me to leave?" He vehemently shakes his head.

"Just stay there." His voice is pained, softer than the last time we had an encounter like this, but I can hear it in his voice. He truly hates himself right now and that hurts me the most.

"Okay." I can't hide my own sadness and pain from my voice. I did try my hardest, but it didn't work.

Slowly his convulsions and the retching subsides, but he stays there, pulling in huge lungfuls of air and his color returns.

I'm a little anxious to know what I did to set him off, to trigger him, but it might be best to let him recover first.

chapter 22

calvin

Fuck! Fuck! Fuck!

He's going to be pissed off.

I fucking threw up, I panicked, fucking hell, I don't even know what triggered me.

Breathing becomes easier the longer I'm bent over the toilet, but I've got to get up. I either need to apologize or leave.

"If you're thinking about running out the door, you can forget it. I'm not going to let you," he tells me from his perch on the doorjamb.

How the fuck did he know I was thinking about...I look at him, his features are soft with concern, but there isn't a trace of pity in his features, not at all. In fact, it's just adoration and concern.

"I pushed you too far." His voice is soft and resentful.

I shake my head before flushing the toilet and slowly sliding onto the lid with my head down toward my knees.

"Then what happened?"

"Honestly, I'm not sure," I tell him and catch him as he pushes away from the portal and walks the few steps toward his tub where he sits down on the edge of it, facing me, but there is a lot of distance between us. I subconsciously start to fidget with my hands.

"Think about it, please. I'd really like to know what I did." There is a shy innocence in his voice and it twists my heart.

"I don't think you did anything, Eric. I was totally into it, so much so that I started to get hard..." I let the thought trail off.

"That's what happened last night though you fought it."

I shake my head. "I got hard earlier too and didn't have the same reaction. I think that when you said I was pushing the limits of your control that my mind ran wild, ran away from me, and..." I take a deep breath, "I couldn't hold it back. It swept over me so fast that..."

His face turns sad. "I'm so sorry."

"Stop, Eric, damn it, don't be like this, you can't help my imagination," I tell him in a rushed breath.

"I know, but if I hadn't said anything..."

"I'm glad you did."

He huffs. "But look at what happened, if I hadn't said anything you wouldn't have had to come in here and..."

"Okay, you need to stop right there," I tell him sternly with more force than I feel right now. In fact, I feel weaker now than I ever have before and I don't quite understand why. "I told you things like this were going to happen and I'll be damned if I want you walking on eggshells with me." I rub my sweaty palms across my thighs, attempting to dispel the sticky feeling. "I can't accurately describe the war that is raging inside of me right now, but I think I need to try." I watch as he nods. "Have you ever warred with yourself about something, like buying a new car or wanting something really bad, but you know you shouldn't or that you can't afford it?"

I watch as he processes my suggestion, no doubt thinking of a time when he'd had that thought process. "Or maybe deciding what was more important? Hmm," I say with a hum. "Or like how to spend a hundred dollars...god," I run my hand over my head, "Does this make any sense?"

"Yes, it does, and yes, I've been there before," he tells me confidently.

"Okay, so take that and amplify that by putting a time limit on something, like deciding whether to get the blue or the yellow car." He scoffs at me but smirks. "You know what I mean." He nods his understanding. "Okay, say you've got twenty seconds to decide which one and at the end of that twenty seconds, they both disappear completely?"

"Okay, I see where you're going with this. You're basically telling me that your war is between your head and your heart? Your heart wants this, between us, but your mind is refusing to let you enjoy the party."

I nod my head. "The difference is that at the end of the twenty seconds, whatever decision is before me doesn't necessarily disappear, but rather than decide, my entire body reacts, locking down, sweating, panicking in ways I'm pretty sure you've never imagined before. That is what happens when I don't make that decision. It's always been easier for me to choose the blue car, the one that is safe and effective, the route regularly traveled and to walk away. When it comes to you, the safest path isn't the one I want to take. I want to travel the road that leads to you, but I run into barriers in my head. But only in my head. When things simmer down and my heart starts to take over again, I start to freak out about upsetting you, about hurting you."

"How can I prove to you that you're not going to hurt me? That, while I can't quite comprehend your situation because I've never experienced anything like it, I can understand and do know that there is no malicious intention when it comes to me. That you sometimes just don't have a choice. How can I prove it to you?"

I can't help but smile at him. "You already are."

"Good. Now come on." He stands and holds his hand out for me to take it.

"I'm not ready to go out yet."

"Who said anything about going out? Come on," he says again and I can't help but take his hand. He steadies me as I stand up and he leads me back into his bedroom and to the side of the bed that is my favorite side. "Sit down, please," he says and I do, looking at him with confusion. "Why don't you lay down for a little bit? You still look pretty pale and frankly, after this has happened before, you've either passed out from drink or you've run out on me, so I don't honestly know what your body is doing."

I smile, "Lying down would be good." I kick off my shoes and lie down. I want so badly to ask him to join me, but I think it would be better suited for me if I just let him go for now. He pulls a blanket up from the foot of his bed and covers me up before he goes to leave. "Eric?"

He turns back to me. "Yeah?"

"Thank you."

He smiles. "You're welcome. I'll be out here if you need me."

"Thanks."

chapter 23

eric

I leave Calvin to rest in my room. He looked so beat up over what happened and ironically, I think it was the emotional side that got to him more than the physical. He seemed so torn up over the fact that he lost his hold on himself and it tore me up inside to see that.

I text Casey before he goes getting into everyone's business about Dr. V.

Eric to Casey: Disregard Dr. V - Calvin gave me the information.

I grab my bass off of the stand in the corner of my living room. Playing always gives me a sense of comfort and calm, and it gives me a chance to think. It might also be enough to block out the fact that Calvin is laying in my bed. The thought sends a shiver of excitement down my spine.

Quit thinking about it, I scold myself internally. Thinking about it is only going to make it worse.

I frown at nothing. I'm right, of course, but it's so damn hard. Yup, I totally went there. I shake my head and strum along the strings. This guitar hasn't been played since before we left for the tour and it's badly out of tune.

Just as I finish tuning her up, my phone chimes with a text.

Casey to Eric: No worries, hadn't gotten around to anything yet. Everything okay there? Are you going out tonight?

I reply to him:

Thanks, all is fine here, long story. Cal wants to go out for dinner, but not planning on drinking tonight.

Casey to Eric: Let me know where & when, I'll be there quietly.

Eric to Casey: No need. It's just him and I and dinner. I think it's best if we keep it that way. I'm hoping to convince him to stay in and eat.

Casey to Eric: I like that idea better. You know the rules.

Eric to Casey: Fuck the rules, we're not the ones you need to worry about.

Casey to Eric: who said anything about worrying?

I roll my eyes and drop it, putting my phone back on the table. I go back to checking my tune job and start to play. I'm not hooked into anything so the sound is quieter. Not exactly the soothing notes I want or need to hear, but I don't want to disturb Calvin.

I wasn't lying when I told him he was pushing the limits of my control. Fuck, he had me so riled up. Just thinking about it has my cock twitching as I play my way through some of the newer songs we've been working on.

I wonder if I let Calvin take over, just how far we would make it before reality would set in for him. I know that somewhere inside of him, his concern is more about being hurt, raped or attacked than actually being with a man, at least that's the impression I get. He has an easier time when he's in control, but if that control shifts, then so does he. I realized that when he freaked on me a little while ago. I told him something that was very obviously a trigger to him without knowing that would ignite his fears.

I vow to talk to Dr. V about that tomorrow. A conversation that I think is getting shorter and shorter the more time I spend with Cal. The more talking he and I do, the easier it seems to be for me to understand what's working in his mind. He has no doubt been shown some seriously awful things in his lifetime, maybe now it's time to show him something good, something softer, something more like reality.

I remember when I first came out to my mother. She knew all along, her mother's intuition had taken over and she knew, but her fears were logical. Growing up in Denver, there were enough openly gay areas, bars, communities, that being gay wasn't bashed as often as it was in many other places. Though hate crimes were certainly not uncommon, they were

119

localized. But it was those hate crimes that my mother feared. She worried that if I came out, like at school or other places that I would be ridiculed, beaten up, or otherwise bullied. Though I'm pretty sure being gay wasn't the reason I was bullied in high school.

I was different from the other kids, oh boy, was I different. I was tall, broad shouldered, with a linebacker's build, and until I grew into my height fully, I was fat. There's no doubt about that fact. I've always been a big guy, but as high school went on, I went to the gym, I worked out and well, things finally started to change after that. Though I never fit in anywhere, I was who I was and I accepted that.

"Why'd you stop?"

I jump at the sound of Calvin's voice behind me. "Hey," I set my bass down and turn toward him, "Feeling better?"

He gives me a smile. "I am," he says as he comes around the couch and sits next to me. "Where were you?" he asks me.

"Ah, I slipped back into the past." I scrub my face.

"Tell me?" His voice is soft, comforting in a way.

I snort, "Not much to tell really."

"I'd still like to hear it." He gives me a small smile.

"I was thinking about when I came out to my parents, about high school, things like that."

"What happened…when you told your parents?"

I turn on the couch to face him, pulling my leg up and leaning back into the corner where the arm and back meet. "My mom knew, probably long before I did. But she was scared."

"About what?" His voice is still soft, now with curiosity.

"I think I'd picked a bad time to do it. There had been several reports of hate crimes in the months leading up to my coming out. So I guess, more than anything, she was afraid for my safety," I tell him honestly.

"What about your dad?"

I chuckle. "Honestly, I don't think he heard me. He was a workaholic. Gone more than he was home, and when he was home he was usually on the phone with clients and his assistant and the office and, yeah, it was a hot mess around my house. It finally set in when I brought home my first 'boyfriend'."

"What happened then?"

"My dad just kind of laughed, shrugged it off and went on with life. It was kind of a non-discussion with him. Though he never verbally said one way or another about supporting or not supporting me, I think he just kind of rolled with it. Sometimes I wonder if maybe he thought it was a phase; that I'd grow out of it." I shrug. "If you think about it, I did - a little. But that was more for show than anything. My mom, on the other hand, she's constantly asking me about guys, who I've met, when I'm going to bring someone home, stuff like that." I take a deep breath before admitting, "She knows about you. Not the stuff I've learned about you these past few days, but - well shit, it's hard to keep that all bottled up inside." I let out a humorless laugh. "She knew something was up and I couldn't help but tell her about you."

"Does she ask about me?"

I give him a sad smile. "Not as much as she used to. I got short with her one time, shortly before New York, and I told her to drop it. I was stressed out, trying to figure out how best to tell the guys, and well, it was bad timing. I later apologized to her, but at that point, I was really starting to lose hope."

He gently places his hand on my leg as he leans back against the couch. "Well, I hope you hadn't given up completely." His voice is laced with concern.

"No, Calvin, I haven't. In fact, I'd really like to think that we're moving forward with this, with…" I hesitate, "us."

He gives me a smile. "Me too."

I play the internal debate game about telling him my revelation about what happened earlier, but I decide that maybe Dr. V is best suited for that discussion. I'd like to get his theory on it before I go bringing it up to Calvin. I have the feeling that I'm right, but I don't know if that is going to make it any easier.

"You still want to go out?" he asks, interrupting my thoughts.

"No," I shake my head, "I'd rather stay here."

He hesitates, his eyes are worried, unsure. "Then I should probably go." He moves to stand up and I grab his wrist, holding him down.

"Please stay."

He stills, looking at me. "I want to, believe me, I do, but…" he lets out a rush of air, "Sometimes when I open the shit storm, like earlier, it's really hard to close it up again. If we stay here, alone, in your apartment, I'm not sure I can keep myself in check."

"Then let's go out," I say without a second thought. "I'm not ready to let you go home just yet," I tell him, the conviction in my voice rolls over him in waves and I can see his demeanor shifting, changing and righting itself. Which was what I was hoping for. "Though I don't know that going out will…"

"I'll be better out of here."

I suddenly get the impression that he needs a public space to hide behind. Something public isn't private and in public, things are different. Even between the two of us. Looking back on it, his attitude and personality in public are that of a straight man, a man who has a mountain of secrets to hide behind. I shrug off the thoughts that start rattling around in my brain, thoughts that I don't want to venture into, not now at least. I can only imagine that his time in the institution still plays on him more in public than in private, and while I am anxious to wipe that away too, I know his public image will not be easily swayed. What happens in public, between him and I, will turn to friendship the moment we walk out those doors.

I should be scared of that, bothered by it, but I actually find it oddly comforting and I don't fully understand why that is. Maybe it's because I, myself, have only recently come out to a small handful of people and while that proved easier than I expected it to be, it's still not all of America. It's not the public side of Peacock, bassist for 69 Bottles.

chapter 24

eric

Somewhere in our conversation, we decided to take separate cars to dinner. I could see that it would make it a little easier on Calvin, though I can't say I fully understood why until the end of the night when we parted ways. He returned to his apartment and I returned to mine.

Dinner was great, just like old times. The fun and bantering back and forth took the front seat over the weight of what we'd discussed in the last twenty-four hours. Only once did the topic get brought up and it didn't come until we were saying our goodnights. He asked if I still planned to see Dr. V in the morning and I didn't hesitate to tell him yes. He seemed happy about that. I remember thinking it was odd; that he wanted me to go to the one person who likely knew him better than he knows himself, but yet I take great comfort in knowing that he trusts me enough with his secrets to go to the one man who can tell me everything.

Dr. Vincent Rocko, at least that's what the sign on the door said when I stepped into the plush waiting area. Though void of a receptionist, the sign on the door says that he is in and will be with me shortly. Okay, not me specifically, but yeah, pretty efficient if you ask me.

At ten minutes to ten, the inner office door opens and out comes a young woman with tears streaming down her face, but she thanks the doctor before quickly leaving the reception area through the door I'd come in. I did my best to avoid looking at her. I can only imagine some of the many things that happen behind that door.

"Eric?" I hear a baritone voice coming from inside the room.

"Yes, sir?" I stand and move toward the same doorway that the woman had just exited.

"Can you lock the door for me?"

"Uh, sure," I say hesitantly and turn on my heel, back toward the door I'd come in and I flip the deadbolt lock closed and return to the doorway.

"Come on in, you can close that door or leave it open. No one will be coming in here today."

I leave the door open and walk into the even plusher, oversized sitting area that is his therapy room. The room is relatively dark, considering the idea that a therapist is supposed to lift your spirits and not to bring you down. The walls are a dark gray, the furniture a mix of blacks and browns. Everything ranging from a couch, a loveseat, a couple of chairs fill the space and my eyes land on the infamous lounger you see in movies. "Oh, don't mind that thing. I never use it," Dr. V says from behind me and I turn to face him.

The man is nearly as tall as I am, skinnier, but none the less intimidating and the furthest thing I expected to see when I met him.

"I'm Dr. Vincent, or Doctor V as Calvin likes to call me. It's a pleasure to finally meet you, Eric." He extends his hand to me and I take it. His grip is firm, yet warm and comforting.

"It's nice to meet you. Though I wish I could say I knew something about you, I don't really." I'm surprisingly very nervous about this meeting.

Dr. V's warming smile is a comfort I certainly didn't expect. He gestures toward the couch. "Grab a seat and we'll get started." I nod and move to the couch, sitting in the corner, pulling my foot under my thigh and leaning into it. It's surprisingly comfortable. I watch as he finds his way back to an oversized, very comfortable looking chair and sprawled out in front of him are several manila file folders, patient folders. "If you don't mind, I'd like to talk a little bit about you before we dive into Calvin." He makes a subtle gesture over the folders laid out before him.

"Are those all his?" I swallow hard.

"They are. Not all of them are mine, however. Calvin has a long history in therapy and he and I have only been working together for a couple of years. It took me until recently to finally acquire what I believe is his entire history."

"Including the institution?" I ask.

"Yes," he nods, "including there."

I swallow, finding the strength to pull my eyes away from the stack of folders and onto Dr. V as I take a deep breath. "What would you like to know?"

He cocks his head, no doubt something all therapists love to do. "What would you like to tell me?"

I snort. "I've never done this before," I tell him and it's the truth.

"Well, why don't you start with how old you are, where you're from, about your parents, things like that."

I launch into surprising detail about being twenty-eight, from Denver and who my parents are, what they do and where they are now. All the while Dr. V listens with rapt attention and scribbles a few notes.

"Tell me, Eric, have you come out to your parents?" he finally asks the elephant question.

"I have," I tell him.

"How long ago?"

I look up like I'm thinking, counting actually. "About thirteen years ago, when I was fifteen."

"How did they take it?"

I snort. "My mom knew, probably before I did, my father never denied it or approved it. In fact, I'm pretty sure he didn't pay attention until I brought home my first guy friend."

"What happened then?"

I shake my head. "Nothing. My father was always a workaholic. Constantly on the phone, in and out of the house, things like that. My mom and I are much closer, even to this day, and my father is now retired."

"So you've had a much different experience in coming out than Calvin has. How does that make you feel?"

I roll my eyes. "It's just how it was for me, I don't know that I can honestly dwell on the differences between us when it comes to coming out, or living a more 'outed' lifestyle. Unlike Calvin, I really had nothing to fear."

He makes a few notes before he steeples his fingers under his chin. "Okay, I am sure you have a million questions about Calvin."

"My question pool has drained quite a bit over the last twenty-four hours."

He smiles in approval. "Good. But I imagine as we talk, more questions will be raised. I'd like you to start with one of your more pressing questions."

That's too easy. "How do I fix this?"

He smiles, lowers his hands and nods his head. "You can't fix it." I know my expression falls. "Only he can make that choice and all you, or even I, can do is support him in that choice."

"How do I do that exactly?" I ask. I know I can't fix him, but I want to. I want to be his salvation, but I know I'm going to have to settle for being his reason to overcome his demons.

"That, I'm pretty sure, is the reason why you're here today."

"One of them, the other is just to better understand the things that are in his head and what is going on when he panics. I've seen it three times now and the first two times I chalked it up to bad timing and too much alcohol, the other was yesterday. Though I'm pretty sure I did that."

He cocks his head questioningly. "Please explain why you say that?"

"Because I attempted to take control. He's kissed me now three times since he told me everything, each time it was at his doing. The first time was a very slow process, but he managed through it and it was…" I sigh at the memory, "amazing. The second time he took me by surprise when I opened the door to my apartment. He was so freaked out that something had happened to me, or that I'd shoved him off to the back burner, that he came to my apartment and when he saw me, he pretty much charged at me." I watch a smile spread over Dr. V's lips, it's one of genuine happiness, something I didn't expect to see with him. "The third time, he'd followed me into my bedroom so I could throw on a t-shirt and things got heated pretty quick, not to mention the fact that we were in my bedroom. I told him that he was pushing the limits of my control and that was when he locked up."

"You seem to have a theory behind why you caused that. Can you explain that to me?"

"That depends on whether or not you're going to tell me if I'm right or wrong?"

"Perhaps," he states simply.

"It's easier when he's in control. He can take the lead, control the situation, stop it from escalating too far to the point that he'll get hurt."

"You're right." He is very matter of fact with his answer. "Calvin has been raped, multiple times, more times than either one of us want to try to count or analyze, so for him, it is easier when he knows he has control of the situation. It's not dominance or posturing by any means, it is just the way he knows how to feel comfortable in the situation. It's how he is going to have to work through the numerous things that are going through his head when it comes to you, or any man for that matter." The idea of Calvin being with another man sends a shiver of disappointment through me. "He needs to be able to trust you, fully, before he will be able to turn himself over to you completely. I'm sure that if you take a look at the relationships he's had with females or his sexual exploits with them, they were easier because he could take control of the situation easier. When it comes to men, the only thing he knows anymore is what it's like to be controlled. Giving yourself over to his control is the easiest way for him to work through his side of this. Once he starts to see that what the two of you potentially have is completely different than anything he's ever known, things will start to shift inside of him. He'll start letting go of the darkness that grabs hold of him."

I ponder what Dr. V is saying, and it falls right along with my earlier theory, a theory about how he needs to feel in control in order to find his ability to trust me. "I can give that to him," I say softly, but there is a deep conviction in my words that I start to feel as soon as they're out of my mouth.

"Good."

chapter 25

calvin

"What's up, T?"

"Nada, just calling to invite you over for dinner tonight, and to see if you've talked to Eric or Dex since we got home?"

"Dinner? Tonight?"

"Yeah, Addison's cooking, wanted to see if everyone wanted to get together."

"I don't know, Talon, today's been kind of a rough day."

"How so?" he asks, and I knew he would.

"Long story. Let me get back to you on that. Eric? No, I haven't seen him today yet, but I did see him last night."

"Oh?" He does a bad job of hiding the shock from his voice. "How's that going?" he asks the obvious.

"Ahh, it's going...I think."

I'm interrupted by a knock at my door.

"You think?"

"Hey, can I call you back? Someone's here."

"No, have you heard from Dex?"

I roll my eyes as I make my way from the bedroom toward the door. "Nope, I'm pretty sure he's locked himself up with Raine by now. I don't imagine we'll see him until we board next week."

"Yeah, alright, I'll text you the address."

I open the door and standing beyond it is Eric and my heart warms when a genuine smile spreads across his face. "Actually, how about a rain check? Tomorrow night instead?" I ask.

"Yeah, alright. Whatever."

"Really? You gonna fucking whine?"

"Shut up, no, I…Addie's kind of excited to have everyone over."

I shake my head, the dude is seriously whipped. "Eric, you want to have dinner at Addison's tonight?" I ask and I hear grumbles from Talon through the phone.

"You coulda just told me he was there, fucker."

"He just got here, he was at my door."

"Oh…oh, well, fuck. Dinner's at eight, come over around seven?"

"Why so we can all sit around while Addison busts her ass?"

He snorts a laugh. "Alright, fine, seven-thirty, no later."

"Yeah, whatever," I laugh into the phone and he hangs up.

I hold the door wider for Eric to come in. "I guess we don't have a choice," I tell him and he laughs. My phone chimes with a text. It's Talon giving me Addison's address. I roll my eyes and stow my phone. The urge to kiss him is making my lips twitch. I want to so bad, but I'm not sure how to react to a; his being here and b; the fact that he's here much later than I thought he would be.

"Dinner with them sounds fun," he says and I close the door. A big fat pink fucking elephant has taken up residence in ninety percent of my apartment as we just stare at each other.

"So…" I say with deep hesitation.

"So…" he counters and I want to sock him in the shoulder, something we've always done whenever neither one of us says anything, but I resist the urge, unable to take the chance that he's on edge.

"Can I take you being here as a good sign?"

He smiles at me. "If you thought Dr. V was going to scare me away from you, you had the wrong idea. If you were hoping he would, well, I don't know what to say about that." His voice is confident at first then dips into shy uncertainty.

"I want to kiss you." The words are out before I can stop them, before I can stop myself from the admission of what I want from him.

"Nothing is stopping you, Cal."

I rush at him, throwing my arms around him and pulling his lips down to mine. He gently, slowly wraps his arms around me, holding me to him as our lips dance. I lick at his bottom lip which puckers for me and I nip it between my teeth and his breathing spikes and his arms tighten around me. I slide my tongue in along his, my head swims, lost to his warmth and the overwhelming sensation of finally having him back in my arms.

His arms loosen and his hands slide up along my back, sending a thrill through me. Sending desire through every inch of my body. I feel his cock stiffen against me and I respond the same. "Fuck," I growl before claiming his mouth with more gusto, more finesse, more desperation than I've ever felt in my entire life. Not with Billy, not with any of the other guys, and certainly not with women.

Eric's hands slide in under my t-shirt as my tongue dances with his. I run my hand into his hair and fist it. Pulling him into me tighter, hotter and harder. Letting go and losing myself in his warmth, his closeness and nothing else matters, but I start to pull back. Not for a lack of want, but for the uncertainty of what might happen if this keeps up. I know I'm not ready for that.

"Everything that happens is entirely up to you," he tells me through his heavy breathing. "I will not push you to do anything, this is your ship, you're driving it."

"What do you mean?" I ask as I pull back from him. I'm not angry, just confused.

"I think we both need to settle down a little before we can talk," he tells me as he slowly untangles his limbs from me. His hands sliding down my back cause me to shiver and that desire from a moment ago reignites.

"I'm alright. I swear," I tell him. It's true. "Each time I kiss you, I get pulled further into you, pulled further away from everything else."

"Good. That's what I hope to hear every day, but I realized something yesterday, after what happened in my bedroom."

"Oh?" I pull back from him a step. He doesn't flinch to let me go, he knows that space is good, that I need some, though I'm not angry, I'm curious.

"Well," he starts to pace away from me, "Things were good, hot and heavy, until I told you I was beyond the point of maintaining control."

"I know." I cross my arms over my chest, widening my stance, taking a defensive posture and he scowls at me.

"But what I think triggered you was that you felt like you were losing control of the situation. Somewhere in your mind, you thought that my losing control was going to be something that was going to get you hurt."

His words slide over me like black tar, killing my buzz from kissing him in an instant, the same thing that happened yesterday. The feeling is normal when I'm about to panic, when my libido is wiped clean. "I know you'd never hurt me."

He gives me a small smile from across the room. "You know that, in your heart, but what's in your mind is telling you something different, and Calvin?"

"Yeah?"

"There is no reason your mind should tell you any differently. It's how you were reprogrammed. Your mind thinks that someone else trying to take control is someone who is going to hurt you, or worse." I watch as he turns red with worry. "Fuck, I wish I could kill that son of a bitch." I watch as his hands ball into fists.

"He's already dead," I tell him. His eyes snap to mine. "No, Jesus, no, it wasn't me, but it was certainly someone else who he'd gone after. They just beat me to it," I tell him and it's the truth. I don't remember exactly how I found out about it, but I remember that I did and I remember reading the subsequent information about the trial of the man who'd killed him a couple of years after I'd walked out of that facility. I remember the sense of relief and safety that washed over me at the time.

"Dr. V and I talked about it. A lot of what needs to happen now is on you. I will do my best to stay in control of myself, to let you take over, lead the way. If you think about it, you know that I'm right, that Dr. V is right. So all of the times you've kissed me since coming clean, what's happened?"

"Nothing. I've been able to kiss you with very little repercussions."

"But what do you think would happen if I walked up to you, right now and kissed you?"

The tar is back, my body starts to shake like I'm in a freezer naked.

"Relax Calvin, I'm...look at me. I'm over here." His voice is calm, comforting and reassuring. I fight the sludge, I fight the panic and look at him, look into his eyes and slowly but surely the sweat dries up, the shivering stops and the darkness disappears. My talisman. "Better?" he asks and I nod. "Dr. V and I both agree that until you can fully, without doubt or reservation, trust me, that you have to be the one to take the lead."

"I don't know if I can do that."

He gives me a wide smile. "I believe you can. You've already proven that you can. That is where we need to start."

"I don't know how far I can take it."

"I'd chain myself to the fucking bed if that's what it would take."

I shake my head. "No, no, no because then I'd...fuck, Eric, I'd be taking advantage of you. I'd be-" I swallow instead of finishing my sentence.

"You can't take advantage of the willing, Calvin. But I know we're not at that point yet and we might not be to that point for a long time and that's okay. I'm okay with that," he tells me with so much conviction it's scary.

"But I'm not. Jesus, Eric, don't you get it?"

"Get what?"

131

"I want to be with you so fucking bad that...but...I'm afraid that if I'm not around you then you'll realize this isn't worth it..."

"Shh, stop right there. Do you honestly think that I would have gone to Dr. V if my intention was to simply fuck you and walk away? That all I want from you is sex? That all I want is for you to get over your fear of me, of men, of who you are and just let you go on your own?"

I freeze, letting his words consume me, letting his conviction wrap me in a blanket of warmth and understanding, a conviction I know I needed to hear in order to be able to do this.

"Calvin, you could go out and fuck a hundred men, right now, if it meant that when you were done, you were cured of what haunts you. If it means that when you got back here, however long it took, that I could have you so completely that I'd never have to worry about stepping too far, pushing you to the point of panic, goddammit, I would fucking let you walk out that door right now."

That statement was the driving force behind my decision to figure out a way to make this work. I knew, at that moment, that it didn't matter what I did, how I did it, or when I did it, that Eric was going to stand by my side, no matter what. I took that new knowledge and ran away with it. Letting the conviction of his words envelope me to the point of making this work, no matter what the cost.

chapter 26

calvin

"Why is this decision so hard?" I ask no one because I'm the only one here. I've been pacing my apartment for more than ninety minutes.

It's not, it shouldn't be this hard, it shouldn't. "Goddammit," I grumble.

I want to see him. I need to see him. I fucking miss him like mad. We haven't seen each other since parting ways after Addison's impromptu dinner party last week. Tomorrow we leave for Denver and the last leg of our tour.

I look at my pile of stuff, already packed and ready to go. But I don't want to stay here, not tonight. Tonight I want to spend it with Eric, but... I shudder.

I've been fighting the inner war, fighting to maintain control of myself and not let those assholes win. I've given those fucking doctors and that goddamn institution enough of myself, I'm tired of it. I'm sick of staying away from what it is that I really want, Eric.

His name in my head spurs me on. Desperate to not only see him, but to find it in myself to sleep with him, in the same bed.

After this weekend, the text messages, the bantering back and forth, the open and raw honesty between us, it seems logical, it seems like the next step. But can I do it?

I keep pacing back and forth, wearing a path in my carpet. The side of me that walks away from the door is the darkness, the idea that I'm not allowed to do this, that doing this is wrong. The side of me that walks toward the door is the side of me that needs this, wants this, craves this, no matter what the cost.

"You're only going to spend the night with him, what's the big fucking deal?"

The text messages between us play in my mind, the messages that I've read at least a thousand times…

Calvin to Eric: I want to push you up against the wall.

That message took some strength to send. Admitting to myself, without the actual ability to act on my feelings, took a lot of fight with the demons to let it out. But once it was out, I didn't feel the sludge overcome me.

Eric to Calvin: I'm ready when you are.

That was his simple response. Egging me on, reminding me that I am in charge of this bandwagon, that what happens now is solely on me. A responsibility that is starting to seem more like a burden because sometimes I just want to let it all go. Wipe out the nonsense that is in my brain, the nonsense that I know is exactly that – bullshit nonsense.

We talked about so much via text, so many different things, like what it feels like when the panic takes over. I was able to better explain it to him because I could find the right words, edit what didn't work and I think he finally understood it. I think I finally understood it better too. I think I finally realized what it is that I can do to overcome the sludge, but I haven't been able to test the theory.

Walking away from the door…damn it. Just grab your shit and fucking go. Load it up, take it with you, go to his house and…I shiver, but this time it's not in fear, but in excitement. All worry about what it is that will happen starts to slide away.

Eric to Calvin: No matter what happens, no matter how often it happens, I'm never going away.

I actually took a screenshot of that text. I had to. It was the conviction that I needed to hear or read in order to drive this ship forward. I turn, staring down at my pile. His text repeats in my head, over and over and over again.

"Is it time to put that to the test?" I ask myself.

I take the three steps toward my gear and reach for it. I freeze.

"What if he doesn't want you there?" Impossible, I try and tell myself. We've said it every day for the last five days, we miss each other, but we both stayed away. Taking care of the things we needed to manage before returning back to the bus.

Every time my phone chimed with a text, I'd get this giddy school boy grin on my face knowing that my, I swallow, boyfriend was texting me. *Is that what he is? Did we ever actually declare that?*

Instead of fear washing over me completely, I can feel the fluttering of excitement at the idea of being Eric Richardson's boyfriend.

I tremble and try again to grab my bags. Only this time to pull back wondering, *what if he's on his way over here right now, what if he's doing the same thing?* Pacing back and forth, trying to decide whether to come here or stay there...

"I can't do this...I can't do this...I can't do this..." The mantra keeps playing in my head each time I step on the gas.

"You fucking managed to pack your car, you dragged all that shit downstairs, locked up your condo, and got in your fucking car, you can do this."

Thank fuck there isn't anyone in this car. They'd think I lost my damn mind. I have lost my fucking mind, this is stupid, he's not going to want me there. Regardless of my inner musings and external beatings, I keep moving forward toward his house. I can't find the strength to turn the damn car around. I have to see him, I need to see him, maybe I can just go in, chat, talk to him, see him then go back home. Yeah, that's what I'll do. I just want to see him. Need is a better word.

With each passing mile, stoplight and stop sign, I draw closer to his place, closer to his apartment. Closer to seeing him, touching him, kissing him. I shiver. That's what I need.

By the time I'm pulling into his parking lot, the demon is winning, wanting me to turn around, telling me that I have no business being here. That I need to just go back home, but I park my car. I can see his car and that makes the demon even more excited, telling me that he doesn't want to see me or he'd be gone. But he's not, he's here.

"Just go inside, say hi, maybe you can go to dinner with him. Just spend some time just the two of you before we get back on the road with everyone." I swallow the rising bile. Fighting the inner panic threatening to overcome me and force me to drive back home.

I manage to get myself out of the car. Then I start pacing again. Jesus, you look like a fucking idiot out here. Thank god his apartment faces away from the lot.

Just grab your guitars and go upstairs.

I grab the door handle, the driver's door.

Go home.

Stay.

Go.

Stay.

Go…

eric

I meant every damn word of what I said to Calvin that afternoon. If it would abolish his demons, I would let him go. I wouldn't hesitate to do that. I made that intention as clear as I could. Then we went to dinner with Talon, Addison, Kyle, Beck, Mills, Casey, Rusty and Tori. A team that I would learn during dinner, would be ours forever. I was totally okay with that.

Calvin and I fell back into our normal routine of banter and fun. It was natural for us and though I couldn't help my sneaky glances in his direction, and I certainly couldn't ignore the electricity that hung between us, it was easier to just be us. Dex never showed up, despite messages left and whatnot. I don't know exactly where he is, but that's okay. He's Dex and he does a good job at being him, wherever he is. Addison said that she'd heard from Raine and that all was well and that she would be rejoining the tour when we take off again in a few days.

The night flowed; Dr. V and his demons were kept at bay. I can see now why no one had any clue what was lurking under Calvin's surface. He never lets on that there is anything happening inside his mind and maybe, in times like this, there isn't anything going on.

At some point during that dinner, I decided that both he and I needed some space. We both needed a chance to calm our nerves and get things done that were pressing before we take off again for Denver. Calvin agreed.

I finally got around to having dinner with Jess the night after Addison's. She was her usual cheerful, good natured self, until I broke down about Calvin. I never gave her too many details, but it was enough that she could sort of understand what was truly happening between us. She called me out on not telling her everything and while I wanted to, I couldn't violate Calvin's trust like that. I just kept it between us that whatever was building up between the two of us was going to take some serious time. Time I was more than willing to give him.

By the time Sunday rolled around, just three days before taking off again, Calvin and I were texting each other constantly. Somewhere along the way, we started this game of cat and mouse - no pun intended - about texting, talking without actually talking to each other and as each text progressed, he and I both opened up a little bit more.

By Tuesday, I couldn't take it anymore. I was missing him something awful. I needed to see him, I was desperate for it, so I decided I would surprise him. I finished packing up my shit for the road. We leave tomorrow and I want to leave from his house. I want us to go together.

I didn't let him in on my plans, which was okay, I was truly hoping to surprise him.

"Suitcases, check. Guitars, check and check, extra equipment, double check." I'm talking to myself as I go through the pile of stuff in my living room, making sure that I have all that I need. This leg of the trip is mercifully short in comparison, but I feel like I'm packing more shit than the first time around. "Ah, crap," I grumble as I start to head for my bedroom.

chapter 27

calvin

I climb out of my car after beating on the steering wheel more than a few times. Trying to convince myself to start the car and leave, fighting with myself to stay.

I'm staying, I have to. I have to see him. That drive is winning out more than anything. Just to see him, talk to him, kiss him. I sigh and my lips twitch into a smile. I can completely and wholeheartedly do this. I know I can.

I open the back door, pulling out one guitar and then the other. The rest of my stuff is in the trunk and replaceable, guitars, not so much. I sling the first one over my back and my hands are shaking as I sling the second one over. My anxiety level is rising higher with each passing second, but each minute I spend down here acting like a goddamn fool is a minute I'm wasting not with Eric. I take a deep breath, lock up my car and put my keys in my pocket.

I take another deep breath, staring into the driver's seat of my car, debating once again if this is the right choice. "Fuck it," I tell myself and I walk away from the car headed toward the entrance of his building. I have a key to his building from looking after his apartment before the tour when he went home to see his parents, and I never got around to giving it back to him. He never asked for it and I never volunteered to return it.

I reach the security door and go to unlock it. My hands are shaking like crazy and it takes me three tries to get the key into the lock. Finally free of the security door, I head to the elevator. For as posh as his apartment is, the common areas are under kempt. There are mailboxes that line the hallway to the right, before the stairs that lead to the second floor, then to the main stairwell for the rest of the building. It's eight stories tall and Eric lives on the seventh floor. I may be in shape, but taking these stairs is too much. But I debate on them anyway. Thinking that it will take longer to get to him, give me more time to work up the courage to knock on his door.

Instead I press the up arrow for the elevator and I'll be dammed, it's already here. The fates are against me this day, I muse internally as I step inside and press seven. The doors seem to take an eternity to close before the elevator begins to climb the seven floors. I watch the numbers as they climb and my panic rises with each chime of the floors until finally it beeps with its arrival on seven and the doors slide open lightning fast. "Fuck," I groan. I could just ride back down the elevator, walk back to my car, ditch the guitars in the back and drive home. I don't move. I stand there for what feels like an eternity until the doors start to close and I spring into action, stopping them, pushing them open, new determination coursing through my veins.

Necessity and desire win out over fear of what possibly lies behind the door, his door.

I reach his door, raise my hand and drop it back down. "Why the hell am I so nervous?" I whisper to myself. "It's just Eric." My heart flutters. I raise my hand again only to drop it back down. On my third attempt, I knock, but a church mouse would hardly respond to it. I take a deep breath and knock again, harder this time and I wait.

And wait...

There isn't an answer. About the time that should be acceptable to knock again, I start to freak out that he's not here. Yes, his car is here, but that doesn't mean anything. He could be out with Jess or Casey.

I can't believe I'd nearly forgotten the pallet. What I call my array of colors for my hair. I did a touch up on it earlier today so the colors are bright and ready for Denver. But I never packed it back up. It's just a long plastic tub that fits fourteen jars of Manic Panic hair dye, plus three coloring brushes and two mixing bowls. Sometimes I get creative and decide I want more vibrant colors, or I run out of something stupid like blue or purple. It also holds anything else I might need to color my hair. Yeah I know, I do my own hair, it's fucking easier than finding someone else to do it, especially considering I have to keep it up regularly, at least while we're on the road.

Before leaving the bathroom, I double check to make sure that I have everything I need. Looks okay.

When I come to back to the living room, I add the pallet to my duffle bag and there is a knock at my door. I look at my watch, it's barely three. "Who the hell?" I grumble as I turn toward the door and reach for the handle. I whip the door open and my heart explodes the moment he charges at me, two guitars strapped to his back, his arms wrapping around my neck and his lips landing awkwardly against mine, our teeth clash.

He's clumsy and desperate as he's all but climbing my body. Lust and desire ignite my veins and I cup his face in my hands, holding him to me, settling him down, calming him as I've learned I can do in some magical way. He starts to settle, his body humming with electricity, enough to ignite my apartment, his body hot with need, my own body responding, my cock stretching and hardening against my jeans. I pull back, desperate for air. "I couldn't wait 'til tomorrow," he breathes before claiming my lips once more. Desire is exploding everywhere in my body, my control slipping, my desperation to be with him outweighing rational thought. That's when things shift, his hands come off of my neck, but his lips don't stop, his teeth grab at my bottom lip, begging me to open for him and I do, letting him slide his tongue along mine.

My breathing is ragged, my head is swimming, my heart is pounding, lust and need are a river of necessity in my veins and I can't stop this, I won't stop this. Suddenly Calvin's hands are grabbing my shirt, pulling it upward toward my head, so I let go of his face and raise my hands and smile as he tries to rid me of my t-shirt. The smile breaks our kiss long enough for him to pull off my shirt and toss it aside.

He sucks in a breath as his eyes rake over my naked torso, his hands gliding gently upward, his fingers sliding along my nipples, tugging against the rings dangling from them. I moan and he presses his lips to mine once more. My head is lost in a lusty haze, fighting the urge to move this along, to make this go faster, but I manage to win that battle for control, letting

Calvin take the lead, desperate not to soil this reunion. I need it, I want it, and most importantly he wants it.

Fuck, we've teased each other so much over the last couple of days that I'm not surprised it's come to this.

His hands continue roaming all over my chest, then around and down my back as he takes control of my mouth. My cock throbs and strains against my jeans, desperate to be released. Control yourself, Eric, I scold myself. I pull back from the kiss, needing to desperately catch my breath and bring air back into my burning lungs. My lips are raw and swollen from his kisses and my eyes land on his, swollen and moist. I lick my lips, desperate to feel his on me again.

He releases me, grabbing the top strap of one guitar from his chest and pulling it over his head. He sets it down in one of my empty stands before pulling off the other one. "I want to stay the night," I hear him whisper as he sets the second guitar in another stand. Then he takes a look at my pile of stuff in the middle of the floor and his eyes meet mine.

I chuckle, "You beat me to it."

His eyes dance back and forth between me and the pile. "You were coming to my house?" His eyebrows knit together in confusion, but then he realizes that we both had the same plan.

"Ten more minutes and you might have missed me," I tell him with a smirk.

"Well then, I'm glad I'm faster." He smiles at me again before pulling his t-shirt over his head. "I cannot promise how far this will go." His tone is sad. "But I'm tired of not trying."

My eyes well with tears, though they don't spill over and I nod with enthusiasm as he claims my mouth once more.

chapter 28

calvin

Kissing Eric, that was what I needed. My mind has quieted and my desire for him is taking over. Pushing aside my demons. He is my talisman and he is the one I know that will get me through this. I pull back from our kiss and he rests his forehead against mine as we both find our center again, bringing our breathing back to normal, at least attempting to. "I missed you so much," I tell him in a hushed whisper.

"Ditto," he tells me and I smile.

I'd hesitated only briefly when he opened the door, it only took me seeing a pile that was similar to my own sitting in his living room to realize that we may both have had the same intention today. It was seeing all of that laid out that sent me slamming into him. Knowing we both wanted the same thing.

"Stay the night?" he breathes softly as both of our ragged breaths start to slow.

"Please?" I counter.

He stands up a little straighter, his hand rubbing along my arms in a comforting, spine tingling way that makes me shiver. He stops instantly and I smile. "I'm good," I tell him and his answering smile lights up the room. I grab his hand off of my shoulder, gently taking it between my fingers and backing away, bringing him with me, leading him down the hallway.

"Are you sure?" he asks me with concern in his voice.

"I told you, I don't know how far I can take this, but I am determined to try."

I push open his bedroom door and lead him inside. There is a little bit of awkwardness between us, unsure of where either one of us should go at this point and for me, the only thing I can think of is to kiss him again, so I close the door behind us and press him up against it. Releasing his hand, I trail my fingers up his arms, to his shoulders, across his collar and down his chest. He shivers and I can see the deep brown disks of his nipples pucker at my touch and his breathing turns strained with the excitement I'm eliciting in him. I tremble again, knowing that I'm doing this to him, that he's letting me have control over the situation.

I lean in and kiss the center of his chest and he moans softly. His reaction spurs me on, igniting within me a need stronger than anything I've been able to allow myself to feel before. I continue kissing him upward, toward his neck until I find that sweet spot just below his Adam's apple and he moans. His hands twitch. Deciding that he needs some encouragement, I grab his wrists and pull his hands up to my hips, hoping that's all the encouragement he needs.

He hesitates only briefly before his hands start trailing up my sides, sending goosebumps racing across my skin. I feel my nipples harden around the rings through them and that familiar ache fires up in my cock and it starts to harden. I groan as I reach up and claim his mouth with mine, not wasting a moment to slide my tongue along his, holding him to me, my hands roam over his body. His shivers of delight match mine and we're both swept away in each other.

Lust, desire, desperation overrule everything else I'm capable of feeling. A need I haven't felt in over a decade hardens my erection further, pressing and stretching against my jeans, desperate to be free. Without conscious thought, I let my hands slide south, over his stomach and down to the button of his jeans. I pull back from our kiss, through heavy eyelids I silently ask permission and he nods in understanding.

I slowly unbutton his jeans and slide the zipper down. Desperate to see the package that awaits me. I slide my hand inside, taking hold of his cock. His breathing stops and his eyes roll up as he presses his head back against the door. Opening his neck to me was what I needed and I lick, kiss and nibble along his jaw, down his neck toward his shoulder. He's shuddering and breathing heavy as I push his jeans down enough to free his cock from its confinement. When it pops free, I pull back, looking down. "Fuck me," I breathe as I take in the gorgeousness that is Eric. His cock is thick, thicker than my own, tapered to the head and I grip it in my hand. There is a momentary flash of darkness that I manage to quickly bury. Doing this, touching him, goes against everything they tried to teach me, but for the first time in my life, I decide to embrace my demon. Show him that he's no longer in charge. I stroke Eric from base to tip, until I feel the cool metal of a barbell on the underside.

My breathing hitches and my eyes meet his. There is a smug little smile playing on his lips. "Well, aren't you full of surprises?" I tease him as I rub my thumb over the frenum piercing.

"Ahh," he moans out. I know all too well what this sensation feels like, and I know all too well what makes this piecing highly erotic in so many ways.

I release his cock and bring my hand to my mouth, running a fat, wet tongue over my thumb. He watches with rapt attention before letting his eyes roll up again as I take his cock back in my hand, rubbing my thumb along the underside of his shaft. "Fuck," he cries out.

With my free hand, I pull his head back down to me, bringing his lips to mine and this time, I let him be the one to slide his tongue in, and he doesn't hesitate. I let him take the kiss from me and he devours me, his hand sliding along the back of my neck, holding me to him as my hand slides up and down his shaft.

Having his tongue in my mouth spurs me on to do what it is that I really want to do and I release his mouth and slide down onto my knees. Looking up into his eyes, I do my best to convey that this is what I want. I see he's concerned, but I see his own lust taking over. I stroke up and a bead of clear pre-cum forms on the tip. Desperate to taste him, I stick my tongue out, sliding his tip along it and he shudders, groans and throws his head back. "Jesus Cal, please?" he begs and I tense, the darkness threatens again, but I fight it, harder, with more fervor than ever as I desperately need this, want this, crave this.

Changing what defines me has always been a goal for me, but I never in my wildest dreams imagined that it would be Eric who would be that true mark of hope. I never imagined he'd be the one to change me, to help redefine me, to fight the need to prove to me that he is what I want, what I need and who I trust most.

It's that conviction that drives me to open my mouth and to wrap my lips around the head of his cock.

"Oh fuck!" he moans as I suck him slowly into my mouth, coating his cock. I flick my tongue along the underside, along his barbell, my own tongue ring clicking alongside it. I'd pierced the damn thing on a drunken whim one night and never understood the true joy it could bring me until now. It's been a part of me for so long I don't think about it, until his barbell clicks against it again. Using the hand that's wrapped around his cock to steady me, I reach for the button of my jeans, unable to hold off on at least touching myself any longer. I shift, giving myself room and pull his cock deeper into my mouth, deeper to the point of touching the back of my throat before I slowly pull back, allowing my hand to slide into the wetness left behind. Giving me a chance to hand fuck him while I divert my attention to freeing my own straining erection.

I shiver when the cool air of his room creeps into my jeans and surrounds my cock, hot with need as I manage to free it with one hand. I peek at Eric through heavy eyes as my cock slides into view. His mouth gapes, he stops breathing and I watch as he shudders and I taste another small spurt of cum in my mouth as he takes in the sight of my cock. Knowing that I've turned him on a little more, I stroke it for him and his eyes roll up as he moans out his desire.

Eric is bigger than I am in girth, maybe even in length, but we have matching piercings, so my knowing what he would like comes into focus for him.

I release his cock from my hand and mouth, stand up and back away from him. He's shocked and maybe even a little disappointed as I back into the bed, pushing my jeans down. "Stroke yourself," I tell him and he fists his cock without hesitation. I can't take my eyes off of him as his muscles flex with each stroke up and I absentmindedly start stroking my own with more vigor than I'd meant to. My toes curl in my boots and my eyes roll up. Lust and the urge to come are all I can think about, until I become conscious enough to back off.

Making myself come will bring an end to this far faster than I'm sure either one of us are ready for tonight. "Come here please?" I ask him and he steps toward me slowly, almost agonizingly slow, but he doesn't release the grip on his cock and for that I'm thankful. His arm muscles are straining with his fight to hold back. I sit up and climb off the bed. "Lay down," I whisper and he kicks off his shoes. I watch as he sheds his jeans and then his socks before climbing onto the bed, lying out on his back.

His cock stands straight out from his body and I shiver with excitement seeing him lying there for me. I walk around the bed, grabbing a pillow and bringing it toward him. He lifts his head and I slide it in under him as he settles back, his hand grabbing his cock, holding it steady.

I hesitate, unsure of what to do next. I know what I want to do, but...

Suddenly I feel his hand slide into mine, my eyes dart to his, he's concerned, that much is obvious. "We can stop." His voice is soft.

I shake my head. "I...this is going to sound so stupid..."

He smiles and shakes his head slightly. "No, it won't. Talk to me, Cal."

My eyes slide up his naked body until our eyes meet again. "I don't know what to do now," I say sheepishly.

"What do you want to do?"

"You," I breathe.

chapter 29

eric

Fuck me!

Do I just let him, can I just let him? Fuck it. I get off the bed and walk to the opposite side and my nightstand. I pull out the bottle of lube I have in there and toss it on the bed. "Are you sure?" I ask him. His eyes are staring at the bottle. I'm not really sure what's going on inside of him, he almost looks as though he's seen a ghost.

His eyes eventually land back on me. "Are *you* sure?" His voice is concerned, laced with fear.

I give him a smile. "I've never been so sure of something before in my life, Calvin." I don't need to tack on the fact that I need this as much as he does. I need to feel him wholly and completely. I need him to do the same. I know that if he can do this, if we can do this, then we just might pass the hump of what's going on inside of him.

I climb back on the bed, moving the lube closer to him, my cock still hard as steel, his hand still on his own erection. I am dying to just roll a little closer to him, take him into my mouth, taste him. I've never wanted to suck a cock more than I do right now. My little brain takes over and I roll closer to him. He doesn't flinch, he doesn't do anything but watch me closely. His eyes lock on me and I look up to him. "I want to..." I just let my eyes finish the statement as they dart to his erection, closer, more prominent up close. His barbell glistens in the light of the room.

He doesn't say anything, but I watch the haze of uncertainty fade away from his features and he steps closer to the bed. Is that an invitation? I don't know what to do, I am so scared of stepping over the line of his control, giving him a chance to let the demons I know he's fighting take over. He releases his cock and surprisingly, he reaches for mine and I slide it closer, giving him better access to it and he doesn't hesitate to take it into his hand.

With his free hand he grips the base of his cock and shakes it up and down, I look at him for confirmation and he nods. I smile and slide even closer to him. I wrap my hand around it. He's smaller than I am, but no less impressive. He shudders at my touch and he lets out a hot rush of air, desire boils hot through my veins as he strokes my cock again and again. My eyes roll up as I match his rhythm. I get the impression that if I stick with his pace, I might be able to do this without him freaking out on me.

I'm overwhelmed by how calm I am right now. But I know he needs this, I need this. I lick the tip of his cock, pulling in the bead of pre-cum sliding off. He tastes like heaven. The perfect mix of bitter and sweet. I moan, wrapping my lips around him and sucking him into my mouth. He shudders again, moaning his approval as I start to suck up and down his cock. Feeling his barbell roll across my tongue sends goosebumps everywhere and his hand continues sliding up and down my cock.

So engrossed in having him in my mouth, I'm able to tune out my own growing desire. I'm desperate to come, but equally as scared to do so, I don't want this to end. I start to pull him in and out of my mouth in perfect time with my hand. Having him inside my mouth is heaven and I'm not sure there is much more in life that would be better than this.

He is grunting and groaning above me.

With his free hand he pulls the tie from my hair, sending it falling over my face before he grips it in his hand. I moan around his cock, sending vibrations through me and onto his cock. He holds my head still long enough for me to look up and meet his hooded gaze. "Please don't make me come," he begs and I loosen my grip and he does the same to my hair so I pull my mouth off of him. "If you make me come, we're done, I can't...I've got enough control on the darkness, but I can't promise beyond an orgasm." I nod in understanding. "Roll back,' he tells me and I do. He sheds the rest of his clothes and follows me onto the bed quickly, settling between my legs and he climbs up my body, first licking and kissing my inner thighs, then along that sensitive spot in the crook where my leg meets my body, then sliding a wet, fat tongue over my cock before open mouth kissing his way up my body. He finds one of my nipples and sucks it into his mouth and my cock jumps between us as I let out a rushed breathe of desire.

I fucking love having my nipples sucked and he catches onto that quickly as he slides his way over to the other one. My cock jumps again, my desire to take it and his in my hand is growing stronger by the minute. I'm perfectly okay with not actually having sex with him, but my need to come is growing hotter by the minute. I gently glide my hands along his sides and he shivers, his breathing hitches and his movements become more urgent as he goes back to kissing along my chest toward my neck.

I move my head to the side, giving him access, letting him do to me as he wishes and he nips gently on my neck and I moan. He steals his chance, sliding his tongue in along mine, capturing my mouth, my breath and poking at my control.

I feel his hips flex. He's looking for purchase against me, looking for friction. I want to give it to him so I press down gently on his hips, urging him to grind up against me and he lowers himself. Capturing both of us between our bodies and my eyes roll up. He rears back, his breathing equally as rapid and ragged as mine.

"I have an idea," I tell him softly.

His eyes meet mine. "I'm all ears," he says and his smile is electric as he flexes his hips once again. My eyes flutter at the sensation of our two bodies rubbing together.

"Take them both, in your hand."

"Both?" His innocence throws me for a moment and I realize, for all intents and purposes, he hasn't had much experience with this.

I thrust my hips upward and watch as the lightbulb goes off in his head. He rears up, our cocks sliding closer together. "Take them into your hand, or hands." I watch as he gathers them in his hand, holding both our cocks together. I shiver. Beyond horny, beyond ready to explode. "Now do what's natural," I tell him, letting him take the control back, letting him decide. "Oh fuck," I groan as he strokes his hand up and then back down. Underside to underside, piercing to piercing.

calvin

"Ahh, fuck," I cry out and my hips start thrusting in time with my strokes and Eric follows suit. I slow my hand, holding us together as we both thrust opposite of each other, grinding our cocks against the other's.

I feel Eric's hands slide up along my thighs to my hips and I look down, watching as we're both lost in a sea of sensation. If I don't stop, I am going to come. I don't want to stop, fuck, I don't…I've reached the point where stopping is no longer an option. The overwhelming feeling of being so close to Eric is beyond anything I could have imagined, beyond any fantasy I could have managed to muster up.

His hips thrust upward as I pull back, mutually masturbating, getting each other off. "Ahh, Calvin," he cries out and I look at him. I see him straining to hold back, holding back what we both know is coming, what we both want. What I want more than anything right now.

"I'm close," I moan as he thrusts up again, rubbing himself against me, me against him. "So good," I moan, "So fucking close."

I feel his hands tighten on my thighs and I close my eyes, allowing the fantastic feeling to overcome me, consume me, devour me, "Ah! Ah!" Eric cries out, his orgasm racking his body, his cock swells against mine, pushing me over the edge and we both explode. Flying over the cliff of ecstasy. Savoring the sensation of our mutual orgasm.

Reality settles over me. We've both just come, we've shared our first orgasm together.

You have another man's jizz all over you, you dirty fucking whore.

chapter 30

eric

Calvin freezes, the air between us burns ice cold, I look at him, and he looks petrified. This is it.

"Get it off me," he growls in disgust. He pulls back off the bed, he's not looking at me, no, he's looking at the remnants of our...my blood runs cold. "Get it off me. It's so fucking dirty, so fucking wrong," he cries out, his voice is different, like a man possessed. His demons are winning.

I scramble off the bed and walk up to him, grabbing his shoulders. "Calvin?"

"It's wrong, it's fuck, get it off me, goddammit, fucking get it off of me." He pulls away from me, his eyes finally meeting mine. "Get the fuck away from me," he growls at me and I want to run from the room, but it's not him, it's not him...get away from him...shower.

I don't know how I manage to do it, but I get my feet to move, moving away from him, doing as he's asked me to. Fuck! I knew there wasn't going to be anything good to come out of this encounter, he warned me, but I'll be fucking dammed if I knew it would be something like this. I take a deep breath as I turn on the light and reach into the shower, pulling the handle. The shower immediately starts running and warming. I know this isn't him, this isn't my Calvin out there. This is the product of what he's been through, but goddammit, this fucking stings.

I fight the urge to cry, to let this envelope me too. He needs me, he needs me to be strong. I pull a pair of boxers off of the shelf in the bathroom and pull them on. He doesn't need to see me naked, not right now. I step out of the bathroom and the petrified look is still on his face but now he's pacing back and forth across my bedroom. "Calvin, come on." I wave him toward me, but he isn't hearing me.

He's mumbling something but I can't make it out. He looks down at his chest, disgust washes over his face and he tries to touch it, to brush it off, but he always stops himself. "It's not right, it's not, you don't let another man come all over you..." I'm finally able to make out his musings, but I do my best to block him out. Each time he mumbles about disgust it hurts just a little more.

"Calvin, come on, the shower's ready."

He looks at me briefly, but it's like the wheel is turning but the hamster fell off. I walk up to him, behind him as he walks away from me, and I touch his shoulder. There is something in him that shifts. I can see some of the tension leaving his body with my touch, a calming effect of sorts. "Come on Cal, the shower's ready," I whisper through heavy emotion, through the unshed tears I want to spill all over the place. I can't do it though, I have to be strong. I have to be here to pull him back.

I turn him and he follows my lead, toward the bathroom. "Come on, Cal, we'll get it off of you. We'll wash it away." I take a deep breath. The pain is almost too much to bear, but I've got to do this, I've got to show him that he's alright, that what's happened isn't disgusting but something far more amazing than that. I help him into the walk-in and he steps under the spray, putting his whole body under it.

There is a combination of things that happen. One, the proof of our orgasms slides down his body, two, he shivers, snapping out of whatever trance he was in, and three, he completely crashes. His entire body goes slack, and he starts to fall, but I'm faster. I wrap my arms tightly around him as we both slide to the floor. Full body shaking sobs rip through him as he cries out in agony. He doesn't fight me, no, he turns into me, snuggling in and burying his face in my chest.

I turn us around so that the water is sliding down my back and I could shield him from the spray. Holding him while he cries brings out every emotion I'd suppressed when this all started. Tears streak down my cheeks but they're no longer for the selfish reasons I'd had before. My heart breaks for him. Sure, seeing him throw up was one thing, but this, this is pure agony, both on his end and mine.

I gently stroke his back, running my hand through his hair and holding him close to me while he continues to work through it in his head. I don't say anything. Sometimes the best things are left unsaid and I take my own piece of selfish comfort in knowing that I'm helping calm him down. His crying is softening, he's even started to sniffle a couple of times, but then he just snuggles into me harder than before.

It isn't until the water starts to run cold and I feel him shiver against me that I finally find my voice. "Cal, we need to move or we're going to freeze to death." I try and succeed in keeping my voice light. It's light enough that he pulls back, his eyes are fire engine red with tears still sliding down his cheeks when he looks at me. "Can you stand so I can get towels?" I ask as I rub my hands up and down his biceps and he shakes his head, but he slides off of my lap and onto the colder tile. He hisses when the cold registers and I stand up, turning off the shower and stepping out, grabbing one of my big towels from the shelves and taking it back into the shower. I wrap it around him and he unfurls enough to pull it around his front and huddle into it.

"Come on, let's get you off the tile and into something warm and dry."

"My clothes are downstairs, in my car." His voice is shaky, his emotions are threatening to overcome him once again and I don't want that to happen.

"I have a pair of sweats. They're too small and I've never worn them." I feel the need to tell him that and I don't know why. Unsure of how he'd feel putting my previously worn clothes on.

"Worn or not, I'd still wear them," he tells me softly.

I give him a sad smile and grab my own towel, wrapping it around my waist and drying off the now soaked boxers I was wearing when I got into the shower and I step into the walk-in closet to grab a pair of sweatpants for me and the smaller pair for Calvin, plus one of my t-shirts for him too.

I dry myself off quickly, avoiding truly thinking about what happened not that long ago. I can't process it, let alone understand it until him and I talk about it. But that isn't going to be tonight.

Once dressed, I go back into the bathroom and set the clothes on the counter. "I'll let you do this alone…"

"No, stay, please?" His voice is barely a whisper.

"Of course." I step back into the shower with him and crouch down before him. His eyes meet mine. They are worried and lined with sadness and fear. "Are you afraid of me?" I ask him gently.

He shakes his head. "I hurt you," he mumbles.

My heart breaks again. "No, Calvin, you didn't hurt me, not at all."

He gives me quizzical look. "You're not offended by what I said?"

My mouth quirks up in half a smile, confident of his answer. "Only if you meant it."

He vehemently shakes his head. "No, I... I honestly don't know what happened, what came over me."

"I believe that. You were not yourself, you weren't the Calvin I know," I tell him with a cock of my head. "Come on, let's get you dried off." I hold out my hand and wait for him to take it. When he does I stand up, bringing him with me. I guess being taller and stronger has some advantages and he comes up willingly. I hold him steady, giving him a chance to check his balance before leading him from the shower. His entire body is shaking, though I'm not sure if it's cold or adrenaline that's crashing through him, my only goal is to get him dressed and warm.

I rub at his arms, helping him to warm up and dry off. He starts to help me enough that we can get the t-shirt on him. He's practically swimming in it, and it's kind of cute seeing him in my t-shirt. I can help but smirk. "What's so fu..nn..ny?" he says through chattering teeth.

"Not funny. I just like you in my t-shirt," I tell him and he gives me a smile before he bends down and dries off the rest of himself and pulls on the sweatpants. Once we're done, I run a brush through my hair and tie it back.

"Leave it untied," he tells me, "I like it when it's down."

Seeing my Calvin return back to me warms my heart and heals the cracks. I undo the tie and throw it back in the bowl on the counter. I turn toward him and lean against the counter. "Your wish is my command," I tease and he wraps his arms around my chest, holding onto me for dear life and I can't help but wrap my arms around him too. Nothing sexual, nothing more than him needing me to hold him and I'm okay with that.

He pulls back after a moment. "Will you lay down with me?" he asks.

I smile. "I wouldn't miss it for the world," I tell him and he leads me from the bathroom and back up onto my bed.

chapter 31

calvin

"Do you want under or on top of the covers?" Eric asks from behind me.

"On top, for now," I tell him as I climb up ahead of him and throw the pillow he was lying on back up with the rest and I lay down, kind of in the middle of the bed, but I've done that on purpose. I really need him close to me. I don't know why, and I can't explain it, but when he grabbed my shoulders in the middle of my tirade, I felt his comforting touch. I felt him pulling me back down from the ledge of panic I was riding.

It wasn't until it all washed away that I lost it and he was there to catch me. Jesus, I've never cried so hard before in my life. Eric hasn't climbed onto the bed yet and I turn toward him, reaching out for him. He looks afraid. "I need this. I need you," I whisper, conveying to him that I want this, that I won't let the darkness win again. I can't. I can't let it overcome what I feel for him and what I feel for us.

He's careful as he climbs up, his hesitation is palpable and warranted and I'm not sure how to show him that I really do need this. I roll over, facing his side of the bed. "Lay down, please Eric," I plead and he does, lying down on his back. When he's settled, I awkwardly move his arm, find a place for mine and I lay down on him, putting my head in the crook of his shoulder and wrapping my other arm around his stomach, holding him to me.

His arm wraps around me, comforting me, chasing away the darkness as his hand comes to my back, holding me to him. "I'm not ready to talk about what happened," I tell him.

"I didn't expect you to be." His hand rubs along my back, comforting me. The vibration of his voice tickles my ear as I snuggle in to him.

I never had a conscious thought about our orgasm. It was never something that I thought about. I've had cum on me before, well, my own cum, but still, there was absolutely no way to tell whose was whose, or that I actually saw any of it. The voice came from beyond, like it does often, carrying the tone of that fucked up doctor who drilled all that nonsense into my head. He prattled on and on constantly about how being gay is wrong, it goes against nature and it goes against God. The phrase he used to always refer to being with someone who was gay or had gay tendencies was to call them a whore, because only whores would willingly sleep with people of the same sex.

I can't help but wonder now how that man slept at night, or even how he sleeps today. I suppose it's easy to do if you've managed to convince yourself that what you're preaching is truth.

Though I'd won the lawsuit against him, the money was paid out to a trustee who then pays me, so whether or not the man is alive is irrelevant and after today, I hope he's dead because if he's not, there is very little in this world that would stop me from killing him.

"Can I ask you something?" Eric asks, interrupting my musings.

"Anything." I shift my head to look at him, his eyes are full of his own unshed tears and I want to wipe them away, but I stay put.

"Have you ever considered reprogramming?"

I lift my head. "Reprogramming?"

He shrugs. "I don't know what else to call what you've been through, behavior training, I don't know. I was just wondering if you'd ever considered that? Going back into intense therapy to reverse course?"

I shake my head. "One of the first doctors I'd had suggested the same thing, but unfortunately, it's not like a ninety-day rehab. It took them over two years to make me think the way that I do, it would likely take that long or longer to undo the damage that was done. Why do you ask?" By the time I ask that question, my voice is barely above a whisper and full of curiosity more than anything.

He sighs. "I just thought that it might help you more because that…" His eyes look away from me, toward the ceiling and he blinks rapidly a few times. "I won't lie, Cal, that was scary as hell."

I prop myself up on my elbow, looking at him, searching his features for any sign that this is his way of telling me good-bye, his way of telling me that he can't handle this, but I see none. I feel nothing but concern when his hand slides up and down my back again, his other hand intertwining in mine on his stomach. In a way, I can't blame him if he wants to run away from me. "It gets easier," I breathe. "Though I've never had a reaction like that before, with women, I've had the similar feelings of shame and disgust, feelings that are often washed away by a shower or two. Even still to this day, showering post-sex is a requirement. But I have never broken down like I did."

He looks at me and asks somberly, "What happened?"

I look at our joined hands, resting along his stomach. "I felt ashamed of what happened, not between us, but the way I lost it. I was scared that you were going to go running in the opposite direction from me. Then when I realized you weren't going anywhere, it all came crashing over me. All the hate, all the pain, all the unnecessary reprogramming, as you call it." I give him a small smile, letting him know that I don't disagree with his assessment of submersion therapy. "Everything that has ever been pent up inside me poured out of me in waves."

"A cathartic breakdown?" he asks.

I nod. "Though I can't say that it was completely freeing. I feel different now. I feel like I've managed to finally break one of the shackles holding me down. That I've broken down that barrier inside of me that has prevented me from doing anything remotely close to what we did today. Though there are still several walls that need breaking down, I almost feel as though the first one was obliterated." I give him a smile before I lay back down, pulling him against me, holding him there. "This, right now, like this, would in no way be possible if I hadn't lost it in there."

As the words flow from my lips, their conviction settles in my soul and in a metaphoric way, light breaks through the darkness. Beginning to split it into pieces. Pieces that need to shatter, but they are going to take some time. "I just need more time," I tell him softly.

His hand strokes along my back. "I've got nowhere else I'd rather be."

chapter 32

eric

My stomach growls and Calvin shifts for the first time in a long while. "We should get something to eat," he says as he sits up.

"I don't have anything in the house. I didn't buy much, knowing we were leaving again."

He shrugs. "So let's go out."

I frown. "Are you sure you're up for that?" I ask. He looks unsure, but nods anyway. "We could order in." I counter, "Or I can go run and get something."

He smiles then offers, "How about we both go get something and come back here to eat?"

I smile too. "I like the sound of that."

He leans down and gives me a gentle, chaste kiss and I can't help but kiss him back. We haven't talked for some time since I told him I've got nowhere better to be. He seemed to let that statement wash over him and I wonder if he spent the quiet time embracing it.

"Any ideas?" I ask him as we both climb off the bed.

"Burgers," he says so matter of fact I wonder if he'd been thinking about it all day.

I chuckle as I walk into my closet, looking for a t-shirt to throw on and a pair of jeans. I abandon that idea when I realize the only clothes I have left in here are ones I either wouldn't be caught dead in or they don't fit. Remembering that I'd packed everything but what I'd planned on wearing tomorrow. I head back into the bedroom to see Calvin, naked, bending over to put his jeans back on. My steps falter as I stare. Jesus, he's hot even from this angle. "Enjoying the view?" he teases.

"Always." I smirk as he stands up, bringing his jeans with him and covering my view. "Though the jeans covered view is just as sexy."

My seductive tone brings him up short and I watch as he shakes his head at me, but I get the impression that he's blushing, and then his shoulders start shaking in silent laughter. Deciding not to dwell on it too much and put him back in a place of panic, I find my own jeans balled up on the floor and I shake them out, tossing them on the bed and then throwing off my sweatpants before really realizing I've got a semi going. Crap. I try to get my jeans on quickly, but I catch him watching me. Something about the look in his eyes turns my semi into full-on wood. I sigh as I try to stuff him into my jeans and Calvin laughs. "You laugh, but it's all your fault," I tease him and he laughs a little harder.

"Glad to know I'm not the only one," he says through his chuckling.

I turn on him, giving him a seductive gaze. "Oh really?"

He tries to shrug it off like it's nothing, but I can see the little playful twinkle in his eye. "I like that you look at me and I like it even more that I turn you on." His face turns bright red as he blushes through our banter. I don't approach him any further. He's been through enough for one day. Though there is a sadness that creeps over me knowing that our exploits are more than likely limited to once a day. I will take what I can get. I give him a shake of my hips as I reach for my shirt. His face goes redder still and I can't help but smile.

Once my shirt is on, I look at him and demand, "Come here, you." He wraps his arms around me, squeezing me tight, and I return the gesture, holding him to me as if my life depends on it. I stroke my hand through his hair, reminding me that I need to brush mine, but not wanting to move.

"I'm so sorry," he breathes into my chest.

I grab his shoulders, pushing him back from me just enough that I can get him to look at me. "Sorry for what?" I say softly.

"What happened earlier."

I sigh. "You have nothing to be sorry for, Cal, nothing at all. It's a part of who you are and aside from wiping those thoughts from your head, I wouldn't change a single thing about what happened. I know that wasn't you. I know it wasn't who you really are. I know that it is a programmed part of you and it is one that I cannot wait to reprogram. But I will never, ever, let you feel sorry for things like that. You have nothing to be sorry for." By the time I'm done with my speech, my voice cracks with the emotion I feel looking at the fear in his eyes.

"I wish I could just turn it off, that it would just go away," he says angrily.

I smile at him and reply, "That is what you're doing now. You obviously want that part of you gone so bad it is tearing you up inside."

"I've never had a reason to want that part of me gone, not until now."

"Then let that be your motivation. Let that be the part of you that wins over your darkness. Calvin, look at what you've accomplished in a week's time. A week ago, you would never have been able to do what you did today."

"But then I spoiled it by freaking out."

"So what?" I ask, "So what if you freaked out when it was over. Calvin, do you have any idea how many times I've regretted an orgasm with someone? It's like buyer's remorse and for most men, myself included, once we orgasm, our brains start working again and the rose colored glasses come off. It happens to all of us, just in your case, you can't control how you will react when the bliss fades."

He gives me a half sob, half whine, half laugh. "But my bliss wasn't over yet."

He leans into me and I can't help but chuckle. He was so fucking cute with his statement that it warmed my heart. I can feel him laughing too. "Well, if you'd prefer, you can have the spare bedroom tonight, the door locks," I tease him and he pulls back, socking me in the shoulder.

"Fuck that, I want to sleep with you." There is a smile on his face so wide that I swear it spreads from ear to ear.

My heart swells at that idea and I smile back. "I'd like that very much."

He leans up, tilting his head back in invitation and I lean down, kissing him gently. I'm already hard, still, I don't need to go getting him all worked up again. Him, as in my dick.

When Calvin pulls back I offer, "I have an idea for dinner. If you're up to it."

He shrugs, "Fire away."

"There's a great bar and grill near the beach, on the beach actually. It's always really quiet during the week. I go there often enough that no one bothers me while I'm there. Afterward, if you're feeling up to it, we can take a walk on the beach."

He smiles. "I like that idea."

"Good, then let's go," I tell him.

We finish with our shoes and head out the door and down to our cars. "Uh, my car is full of my stuff, can we take yours?" he asks.

"Of course," I reply. I'd planned on taking mine anyway, since I know where I'm going, but we'll let that one go. I press the button and he climbs into the passenger seat before I can be gentlemanly and open the door for him. I shrug it off and climb in behind the wheel.

chapter 33

calvin

"Eric, my man, what's goin' on?" I watch as Eric and this guy shake hands, apparently Eric spends a lot of time here.

"Not much, Malcolm, how's business?"

I watch as Malcolm snorts a laugh. "Slow, it's a typical Tuesday."

"Good, that's what we were hoping for. Malcolm, this is Calvin." He introduces us.

"Mouse?" he says.

I smile and take his hand. "That's me. Nice to meet you," I tell him and he smiles back.

"Well, come on in."

It is kind of an understatement since the restaurant is wide open, though there appears to be walls that come down around the place, but for now, it's open. Good thing it's awesome weather for April in Los Angeles. Malcolm leads us to a table, toward the back and half outside. I realize quickly that if you consider the ocean side the front of the restaurant, we're in the front. "Wow, what a view," I say as Malcolm hands us menus.

"Yeah, it's pretty nice, especially on nights like this where it's calm. What can I get you two to drink?"

"I think Mouse wants to try that summer ale you have."

"Yeah?" Malcolm confirms, looking at me.

I shrug. "Sure."

"Alright, be right back." He turns on his heel and heads for the bar.

"Summer ale?" I raise an eyebrow at Eric.

"Ah man, it's home brewed and it's the best shit ever. I keep trying to convince Malcolm to bottle it and put it out there but he says it's too much work. But he puts it on tap here. It's one of the main reasons I come here," he tells me with a smirk. "That, and Malcolm's pretty fucking cool."

"How long have you been coming here?" I ask him.

"I found it by mistake actually. I'd come out here, to the beach," he nods in the direction of the waves, "and was walking along, found it. At the time it was pretty busy, but Malcolm had found me sitting at the bar, he recognized me, but never made a big fuss about it. He treated me well, served me his summer ale and the rest was history."

"A good history at that," Malcolm says as he approaches and places two big glasses on the table.

Eric gestures toward my beer. "Go for it," he encourages and I pick up the glass, unsure of what to expect, but I take a drink anyway. It's hard to describe, but it's got a hint of pineapple and a lot of apple flavor to it, very little hops.

"Damn, that's some great shit." I smile at Malcolm. "I have to agree with Eric, you need to bottle this shit like a.s.a.p."

Malcolm laughs, "Yeah, yeah, you two can pay for it."

"Fuck yeah," Eric chimes in. "I'd totally be on board with that." He laughs and takes a big drink from his own glass.

"We'll talk about it," Malcolm chides.

"Yeah yeah, you've been saying that forever and yet here we sit."

"Man, if I bottle that shit, ain't no one got a reason to come in here no more," Malcolm laughs.

"He has a point," I say to Eric.

"Fuck that, you ain't tried his burgers yet." Eric laughs.

"Alright, you two decide what you want and I'll be right back," Malcolm says before leaving us. A couple has just come in off of the beach and he's off to play host.

"Doesn't he have anyone to help him?" I ask Eric as I pick up the menu.

"Yeah, usually, but like he said, it's a slow night. I usually duck in here during the week. Come Thursday night through Sunday, this place is packed." Eric picks up his menu and continues, "I try to avoid the crowd, though Malcolm has been begging me to bring the band over here."

"We should," I tell him over my menu.

"Malcolm would flip his shit. He loves us. Though he'd never tell you that. There's a couple of our songs that make it into his weekend music rotation and sometimes he has live bands here. As much fun as it could be to play here, it would be a complete disaster. There's no real way to keep it private."

I look around and I'm inclined to agree with him. From the beach there is open access to the restaurant and the crowds we'd attract would be a mess. Though it is definitely an idea for an impromptu party. "We should talk to Talon about it. Maybe we could do a surprise show or something one night."

Eric and I continue talking about the band and getting back on the road tomorrow as we plow through our burgers. He wasn't kidding. These things are amazing and are a perfect complement to Malcolm's brew. "Thanks for bringing me here," I tell Eric as we finish eating. "I didn't realize this was what I needed until we got here."

He smiles at me, a genuine smile of appreciation and gratitude. "I'm happy you liked it." He polishes off his beer. "I like to come here on nights like this to think. To just kind of escape it all when I don't want to be pent up at home. Like I said, Malcolm is always kind and he won't hesitate to step in if people get too curious about me, or recognize me. I'm pretty sure I'm not his most famous clientele."

"Clientele or not, we have got to come back here again." My mention of 'we' isn't lost on Eric when a smile plays on his lips. "You like that idea, don't you? The idea of 'we'?" I ask softly.

The smile that was playing forms into a big wide smile accompanied by a blush in his cheeks. "Yeah Cal, I do. A lot."

"I do too," I tell him and it's the truth. Being around him, lying with him, hugging and kissing him seems easier. I don't feel the ache of nausea when I'm with him like this, intimately.

"Good." His smile gets a little wider. "Let's get out of here."

I nod and he throws a hundred on the table, without looking at the bill. "No wonder Malcolm likes you so much," I laugh and Eric joins me as he looks at the hundred on the table.

"I'm not usually so generous, but it's a slow night." He winks at me before hollering in Malcolm's direction, "See ya, man."

"Definitely, thanks guys," he hollers back and we step out onto the beach, walking toward the waves.

We walk in silence until we find the top of the dip before the surf and Eric stops, kicks off his shoes and I follow, watching him roll up his jeans and tucking his socks into his shoes as I do the same. "It's probably freezing cold, but easier to walk in the surf than on the dry," he mumbles to me, but more to himself. Seemingly nervous about something.

"What's wrong, Eric?"

I ask and he looks at me, concern on his face. "I don't know how to do this. You know, something romantic in a way, like this."

"Huh, and here I thought you knew everything," I tease him and he snorts. "Honestly, I don't know either, but..." I let my thought go unfinished, unsure of how to tell him that I'm not comfortable with the idea of holding his hand despite the fact that I really want to do just that.

"But?" he urges.

I sigh. "I'm afraid of offending you."

He snorts, "Not likely to happen. Tell me, please?" he pauses, looking away from me, "I don't know what you're thinking if you don't tell me and usually when you take on that tone of voice, it has something to do with...well, you know. So obviously whatever it is, is something I need to know."

His tone is soft, comforting, not annoyed or really concerned, it's just Eric and how I know he can be and has been when it comes to all this fucked up-ness. "I'm not sure I can handle public affection yet."

He looks at me and responds, "As in?"

"Kissing?" The word comes out more like a question than a statement.

"I'm not sure I'm ready for that either. Though I am proud of you and I would be proud to show you off as such, it's...it's different for me too and not something I've...well, I have, but in different settings, surrounded by hulking bodyguards and...but never on my own, never in a situation like this. It's fun and exciting but in the same it's scary and," he sighs heavily, "society sucks." He finally ends his little rant of word vomiting, spilling out some of his own inner concerns that outside of the bubble of our apartments, we've never considered before. He takes a deep breath before adding, "So tonight, we just walk down the beach and we talk. We enjoy each other's company, relax, whatever and well, we tackle PDA another time." He winks at me and I smile, nodding and standing up, holding my hand out to help him and he snorts.

"Yeah, yeah, shut up and get up," I tease him. The snort was because all he'll manage to do is pull my skinny ass over. He knows it and I know it, but the gesture is nice all the same.

He gets up, brushes the sand off of his ass and we start to walk along the beach.

"What do you want to talk about?" he asks me about a hundred yards into our stroll down the beach. The sound of the waves crashing against each other is soothing, almost a strange comfort, which is odd for a kid from Iowa who, until college, had never seen the ocean before.

"You're asking me?" I shoulder check him. "I don't know. Tell me more about your parents."

He shrugs. "Not much to tell really."

"What about Jess, did you tell her the other night?"

He shakes his head. "No, I just told her that the situation was deeper than I thought it would be and that we had some things to work out. I honestly didn't feel your story was mine to tell, so I skirted the issue as best I could. She knows there is more to it, but that she will either find out when the time is right, or she'll just have to accept it."

I am not really sure what to say to that, so I just whisper my thanks and he smiles. "Someday, maybe I'll be able to tell her, but I'm hoping that at some point in all of this, it will be irrelevant."

"I like the idea of that," Eric says with a playful smile.

My phone rings, I try to ignore it, it's a generic tone so it's not someone programmed into my phone.

"You going to answer that?"

I shake my head. "Nah, they can wait. Besides, it's no one I know."

"It could be important."

I shrug it off and after a few more seconds it stops shrilling from my pocket.

Another few yards and it beeps with a voicemail. "See?" I tell Eric, "They left a message." He laughs and rolls his eyes.

That's when it starts ringing again, but this time it's my ringtone of me playing guitar. Yeah, roll your eyes if you want, but I happen to like the song. "Now this should be someone I know." I smirk at Eric and pull my phone from my pocket. "It's Casey, odd." I press the green phone icon.

"Yo, what's going on?" I say into the phone while looking at Eric.

"Have you been getting weird calls?" Casey asks and I quirk an eyebrow at Eric.

"I just got one a minute ago, I didn't answer it. Didn't even look at it, why?"

Casey covers the mouth piece of the phone and talks to someone. "Who's that?" I ask.

"Rusty, listen, check your phone, the number. It caught in the tracking. Normally we wouldn't think much of it, but it called Mills too."

I pull the phone from my ear and put Casey on speaker.

"What's up?" Eric asks softly and I shrug. Unsure of what to think, I press the home button on my phone and click on the contacts button and over to missed calls.

"Oh fuck!"

"Calvin?" Casey and Eric say together, though I can barely register it. The sludge washes over me and I fall onto my ass as Eric takes my phone from my hand.

eric

"Casey, what the hell is going on?" I ask him as I look at Calvin's phone. All I see is a number, no name but below the number it says 'Iowa'.

"The number is flagged. We can't get a hold of Mills to figure out why, we just know that it called Mills' phone then turned around and called Calvin's. Do you know who it is?"

"I can't say for certain," I tell Casey. "Look we won't answer it, but I have got to attend to Mouse. Can we call you back?"

"Yeah, but we're coming to you guys. Stay where you are."

"That's not…"

Rusty hops on the line, "No argument, stay there, we'll be there in less than twenty."

"Yeah, fine, whatever." I click the red button and hang up the phone, dropping to my knees in front of Calvin.

I gently place my hands on his shoulders and he tries to shrug me off. "No, no, don't. Calvin, come on, come back to me, what the hell is going on?" I say sternly and his eyes look to mine, though they're blank, he's completely checked out. Checked out the way he was this afternoon. "Come on Cal, I'm right here. Talk to me."

"I…I can't." His eyes dart to one of my hands and then the other.

"I got you. I'm here, now I just need you to talk to me."

"My...fffaaa..."

"Your father?" Dread courses through me. Of all the times for that son of a bitch to call him, it had to be right now.

Calvin nods. His breathing starts to slow and the tension in his body starts to subside the longer I hold his shoulders. I start to rub my thumbs against his biceps, helping calm him. God, I hope I'm helping. It seems to be working the longer I work on bringing him down from his panic attack. "Breathe for me," I tell him gently and he does, taking in a huge gulp of air and releasing it slowly. "That's it, come back to me. I'm here, no one else, just me and you."

Slowly the life and light return to his eyes, and despite the darkness of the beach I can see he's coming back to me. "Hi there." I smile. "Are you back?" I ask and he nods. "Welcome back. Can you tell me what happened?"

He shakes his head and I just let it go, giving him a chance to return. "We need to go," he tells me.

I huff, "We can't. We have to wait for Rusty and Casey to get here."

"Why the fuck do we..."

I stop him with a stern 'you know the drill' look and he sags. "Please don't tell them."

"Well, they obviously know something about that phone number," I tell him as I release his shoulders.

"Please don't be mad at me."

"Calvin, I am anything but mad at you."

I sit next to him, "I gave the number to Mills, back when we hired them. The number was an emergency contact, but..." he sighs, "But I told him never to use it unless I was dead and the funeral was long over. I never told him who it was specifically that he would be calling, and well, I never thought he'd flag the fucking thing."

"Well, I would imagine he would, given the circumstances. You know Mills, ever the paranoid one." I try and laugh it off, but I seem to have lost my sense of humor somewhere tonight.

"With all the shit with Addison and then that garbage with Dex, I wouldn't be surprised. Though I'm a little irritated that they're monitoring our phones so closely."

I give him a humorless laugh, "They don't, unless it is someone that they know could potentially be a problem. Hell, I don't even know if any normal numbers pop up or if it is just certain ones."

"Hey guys," Casey says from behind us.

Calvin jumps. "Jesus, that was fast," I scold and stand up, facing Casey who has Rusty in tow. "Before we discuss anything about why you're here, tell me something. Do you two fuck-knuckles monitor all our phone calls?"

Rusty laughs. "No, dickhead, we don't. We have certain parameters set in place, like phone numbers, odd times for phone calls from specific numbers, like family." He looks at Calvin, who still hasn't stood up. "Wanted or unwanted family. Take Addison for example. If her mother is calling after the time Addison said she's usually in bed, and she doesn't answer, I'll get an alert. Then if there are multiple calls, I can make a call to Talon or Kyle to get her. Things like that."

"When did Mills flag his number?" Calvin asks, still sitting, facing away from them, toward the ocean, watching the waves.

"Uhm, shortly after we got the new tracking system. Why?"

"Did he give you a reason?" Calvin asks Rusty.

Rusty launches into a detailed explanation. "Other than the fact that there was obviously some bad blood between the person or persons on the other end of that specific number and something about emergency contact and that I wasn't allowed to call the number, regardless of the situation with you. It was fishy, but I've been around Mills long enough not to question his motives or intentions. But the only reason it set off tonight was because this number called Mills first, then you, and then called Mills again, only to hang up after a ring or two. It tripped an alert."

"Why not just block the number?" I ask Rusty.

"Because he won't block anyone from calling anyone. That's not his job. If Calvin asks for it to be blocked, we'll block it."

I hand Calvin back his phone, over his shoulder, and he takes it from me. "They left a message. Do you want to check it?" I ask him and he shakes his head, handing me back the phone.

"You do it. I can't-" I see him hesitate and swallow hard.

"I got it." I take the phone from him and click the home button, surprised to see his background image. It's a shot of me onstage playing my bass. I click over to the voicemail button and pull up the Iowa area code's message and tap it, bringing it to my ear.

"Hi Calvin," it's a female voice, "You don't know me, and I'm sorry to have to introduce myself to you like this, but...my name is Mary Beth Pickens, you might remember me from...well, I was one of the members of the church here in town. Listen, I uh, I'm calling on behalf of your father. He's not doing so well, in fact he's real sick and he's asking for you. Can you please call me back? I hate to leave all this information over this message, but...anyway I'll be here, um...I live here, so please call." The message ends and my heart sinks.

I turn to Casey and Rusty. "You guys can go, no one is out to pick a fight with Calvin."

"Can we at least escort you back to your car?"

I roll my eyes but agree, "Yeah, fine, whatever."

The two fuck-knuckles laugh and I crouch down next to Calvin. "Come on Cal, let's go home."

"What was on the message?" he asks without looking at me or moving.

"It wasn't him," I whisper into his ear.

"Then who-"

"Let's talk about it at my house. Okay?" I interrupt.

He nods, but doesn't stand up right away. I stroke his back and he flinches away from me. I let it go. Without knowing anything that the message said, he's on the defensive and I don't blame him for that. Not in the slightest. "Come on, let's go home," I tell him and he softens a little before standing up and brushing off the sand and we follow Rusty and Casey back to the restaurant and my car. We'd only made it about two hundred yards down the beach before the phone call came and I'm trying to figure out how to tell him about the voicemail. I'm completely unsure of how he will react to the news, but after his reaction to the phone number, I don't see him going home anytime soon.

chapter 35

calvin

Catatonic - that's how I feel right now. I never knew seeing that phone number would be something that would literally knock me on my ass, but fuck me, it did.

It was like everything I fought before meeting Eric, all crumpled into a fucking phone number. The sludge, the darkness, the complete and utter despair I would feel when I would even think about being with a man.

I shudder in revulsion.

"We're almost back to my place," Eric tells me, and I hear him, but I'm not sure I can process it.

"Take me to my house. I need to be alone."

"No, Calvin, that's not the way this works." His voice has an authority to it unlike anything I've ever heard from him before. "Being alone is the exact opposite of what you need right now. Besides, your car, your gear, it's all at my house."

"Why are you doing this?" My voice comes out more accusatory than I'd wanted it to.

"Doing what?"

I groan in frustration. "Making me deal with this shit."

I catch him in a silent snort. "Because dealing with it is the only way you'll be able to get past it. Dealing with it is the only way we can work this out." He looks at me, pinning me with a hard stare and adds, "Together."

"What is there to work through?"

"Why do you want to be alone?" he counters, obliterating any sense of argument I thought I might have to get him to take me home, though I could still get in my car and go home. He wouldn't leave my guitars behind. I look at him skeptically. You know what? He just might do that out of spite for me leaving him.

"I need to figure this shit out," I counter, hoping he'll see this my way and take me home, but I have a feeling it won't work.

"Figure what out? You don't even know who called you or why they called you, so what exactly is there to work out?" He sighs. "Look, if you can give me one good reason for us to not go through with our original plan, then I'm all ears, but Calvin, you're not alone, this isn't something you have to fight on your own."

"I can listen to the message," I tell him and he just shakes his head.

"If you wanted to do that, you would have done it already, your phone is right there." He nods toward my phone sitting under the radio between us. "But you haven't because you don't want to deal with it, you'd rather hide from it, so rather than secluding yourself in your house, come to my house and when you want to know what the message says, I'll tell you."

I sigh, of course he has a good fucking point. "I feel bad," I tell him honestly.

"So you'd rather run away from explaining to me why you 'feel bad'? Well, I'm pretty sure I can guess why it is that you feel bad, but the bottom line in this equation is that what happened earlier is in the past, it was a learning lesson for both of us, it was...well, it wasn't easy to deal with, but I'll be damned if I'm going to let you run away from me because you think that's what I want." He looks at me as he comes to a stop at the light, "Calvin, I didn't stay with you all afternoon and tonight because I feel sorry for you. No, I stayed with you because I wanted to be there."

"But you were so pissed," I tell him as I look away, the light changes and I nod, indicating that he should go.

"Of course I was, but I wasn't pissed at you."

"Then why?" I ask in a rushed whisper.

I watch as his knuckles tighten on the steering wheel. I've riled him back up again. This isn't going to be good.

"It's never you, Cal, never. I was pissed off because of several reasons. One, there are motherfuckers on this planet that are capable of the things they've done to you. And two, because they fucking did it to you. They fucking took you away from..."

"From you?" I breathe.

He sighs. "No, yes, maybe, I don't know, but if they hadn't done that to you, either you would have already found your happily ever after…"

"If they hadn't done that to me, Eric, I would have never learned to play guitar, I would have never gotten good enough at it to be who I am today. Without the guitar, without the delays in things like getting my GED and getting into college, I would have never met you, Talon, Dex, Kyle and we would have never formed a band, and you and I would have never met." I turn in my seat to look at him. "I never thought that I would ever think of what happened to me as a good thing, not until now. But if you think about what I've been through and how it's gotten me to this, sitting in the car with you after a wonderful date, it was meant to happen to me." I reach over and pull his hand from the steering wheel and intertwine our fingers as he looks at me briefly.

"It doesn't make what I went through any easier, it doesn't steal away the pain, the panic, the things that happened to me, but they certainly make me see that there was a higher purpose to it all," I tell him.

"Fate," he breathes.

I smile. "Exactly." I rub my thumb along his knuckles. "Until tonight, walking on the beach, doing something romantic, I never thought about things from the other side before. For the last ten years, I've let that conditioning define who I am, but now, now it's different. Everything is changing between us and…" I pause, looking down at our hands. His hands are meaty, mine are smaller, softer. The contrast is almost startling, but there is a comfort, a warmth that comes from looking at our hands. "And I don't want this to stop."

He gives me a small smile and he looks at me from the corner of his eye, thankful that he's distracted by the road.

"Tell me," My voice is hesitant.

He looks at me with alarm. "Tell you what?"

"What the message said."

He sighs. "Can't we wait until we're back at my place?"

"No, I'd like to know now. I'd like to process it before we get back to your house, talk about it in the parking lot or whatever, but I don't want it carrying over into your house."

He gives me a quizzical look. "I just mean that when we walk into your apartment, I want it to be me and you, nothing else," I tell him softly and I mean every word of it.

His hand squeezes tighter around mine. "Do you know a Mary Beth Pickens?" he asks and I'm immediately back home mentally, racking my brain through people, names, faces, places.

"I knew a Tommy Pickens. I went to school with him. He was a year younger than I was, total nerd…he didn't have a sister, I don't think…his mom maybe?"

"Does church ring a bell?"

I shudder, remembering that hell hole of a church. Okay, the church was nice, but the people in it were from another world. Hell, they all thought a lot like my father, but I seem to remember, someone around my mother's age, though I couldn't pick her out of a line up…"I don't know, maybe? I quit going to church after my mother died or ran off or-" I drop that subject, because well, it's going to dredge up too much garbage. "My father had gone for a few years afterward, then eventually he started drinking way too much and he could barely get out of bed before noon on a Sunday, but that's irrelevant. What did she want? Why was she calling from my father's house? Is that motherfucker dead?" I can't help the contempt that drips from my voice.

"Not yet." He sighs. "She lives there, at the house."

I shudder at the idea of my father with anyone long enough to move in, but Eric continues, "She says that he's sick, 'real sick'." He uses air quotes with his free hand. "She said…" he trails off, not wanting to tell me the rest.

"We're nearly to your house, Eric, spill it, please," I encourage him.

"He's really sick and…" I squeeze his hand, hoping to convey to him that I would really like him to tell me what he knows. "He's asking for you."

That bomb drops just as Eric pulls into the parking lot of his building and I drop his hand. My body begins to vibrate and I am overcome with anger, frustration, panic and an overwhelming need to snap something in half. "Stop the car." He doesn't stop. "Damn it, stop the fucking car," I growl.

"Let me park."

"No, stop the fucking car," I growl louder.

Eric screeches to a halt and I climb out of the car and growl at the top of my lungs.

chapter 36

eric

I throw the car in park and climb out, racing around the car. "Calvin, come on," I say as I round the trunk and charge toward him before he does something insanely stupid, like punch something. He goes charging in the opposite direction and I pick up my pace, running after him until I'm able to wrap my arms around his chest and hold him to me.

"Let me go, motherfucker," he growls and struggles to get free of me.

"Not until you calm down," I tell him calmly.

"Let me go," he growls again but he starts to settle a little bit.

"What are you so pissed off about?" I ask him, hoping to make him think before he keeps going half-cocked.

"Fuck off."

"Fuck you, Calvin."

"Fuck you," he grunts back as he fights me once again.

"Gladly," I murmur in his ear and he softens.

"He's dying, Eric."

"And? Why does that piss you off?"

"Because he's not dead yet." He stills in my arms completely, defeated, and he deflates.

"Is that what you want? Is that what will make you feel better?"

"Yes." His voice is harsh, but I feel his complete conviction.

"So are you pissed because she called to tell you that he's dying and not that he's dead?" I can't help my confusion of the subject, though his father is far from any person I'd want to meet face to face. I certainly can't promise not to kill him myself.

"Yes, and that he's fucking asking for me. That cocksucker sent me away to an institution when I was a teenager, then never spoke to me again. I didn't even know he knew how to reach me, and now, after all these years I get a call from his fucking bitch mistress trying to tell me that he is asking for me. Where the fuck does he get off even asking for me in the first place?"

I sigh and release him. I know he's pissed but I think he's calmed down enough to avoid doing anything stupid. "Do you think it was a ploy?" I ask in hopes of keeping him talking.

"No, I just don't see him asking for me." His voice is very matter of fact and I can't say that I blame him. "He's wanted nothing to do with me since the day my mother died. At that point I became a burden to him, hindering his drinking, at least until I was old enough to do his dirty work on the farm. Then I was okay again, but seriously, he fucking has no clue what he's put me through in my life, not just what he did to me. And he wants to fucking see me? I don't think so."

"Then your problem is solved. You don't have to see him, you don't have to talk to him, Cal, you don't have to do anything. Just let it go. Let the bastard die alone and without your sympathy." I'm not sure if that's something he can truly live with for the rest of his life, but that is his choice. I can't force him to do anything he doesn't want to do.

"I can't go to him anyway. We leave tomorrow."

"Do you want to go to him?"

He turns on me with the glare of thousand daggers. "Fuck no, I don't."

"So then what's the issue?"

He sighs, "I guess there isn't one."

I give him a small smile. "Good, now get back in the car."

"Can I walk? I need some fresh air."

I nod. "Sure. I'll meet you at my car?"

"Yeah," he says sadly and I get back in the car. I don't want to leave him alone too long but I also know that I can't force him to talk to me if he doesn't want to. I also don't want him being pissed at me or himself for the information he has and I sure as shit don't want him holding it against me someday if he doesn't go see his father before he dies.

I pull into a spot right next to his car, afraid that he planned on running toward his car and taking off. I don't want him to be alone ever, but certainly not tonight. I climb out of the car and I can see him off in the distance. We weren't all that far away, but it looks like he's really just taking his time. I rub my palms on my thighs, the urge to smoke is getting stronger than I can possibly handle. I haven't smoked regularly for a few years, but sometimes, situations are just too stressful and I need to take a moment to myself.

I crawl back into my car, hoping to find the pack I'd bought the other night on my way to Calvin's house. I thought I was going to need it and rather than smoking myself stupid, I got drunk instead. I find the pack and a lighter in the center console, and I open it, pulling out the first cigarette that I've had in a few months and lighting it before I get back out of my car.

Calvin is standing on the passenger side, closest to his car. "Can I have one?"

I raise an eyebrow at him, but decide not to argue with him and slide the pack across the roof of the car. He catches it, pulls one out, looks at it and lights it up before tossing the pack and lighter back at me. He takes a drag and looks at the cherry, not saying anything.

"You know, if you have to go, the band will understand."

"I'm not going," he says vehemently. "I have nothing to say to him and no amount of apologizing can make what he's done to me any better."

"I know but…"

"What?" he says, looking at me, and I shrug. He drops it and leans his back against my car.

Deciding there is too much distance between us, I round my car, this time the front side and slide in next to him. "I don't want you to regret it."

He sighs. "Honestly, I'd come to grips that he was dead a long time ago. Between his heavy-ass fucking drinking, his desperate need to drink and operate machinery, shit like that, the motherfucker has had a death wish ever since my mother died. I figured that if the bottle hadn't killed him, he'd killed himself or someone else." We both take drags off of our smokes. "These things suck," he chuckles.

"So are you more angry over the fact that he wants to see you or the fact that he's still alive?"

He snorts. "Pick one. I think they're both taking up the number one spot. Why is my seeing him so important to you?" The elephant I feel in my gut gets addressed.

"I guess, I'm afraid at some point you'll regret it, and that I'll be the one you blame and-"

He turns toward me, leaning his shoulder into my car. "Stop, right there. I would never blame that on you. You're not forcing me to stay here, I'm forcing myself to stay here, though force is a pretty strong word. I have nothing to say to him, there is nothing he can do, or say to me that will make up for my life being the clusterfuck that it is. I can't honestly imagine any valid reason he'd want to see me, unless he's feeling guilty, finally, and for that he needs to suffer." He takes one last drag and throws it down, stomping it out. "In fact," he says with a heavy, cleansing sigh, "That is my salvation in all of this, knowing that he felt guilty enough to ask for me and knowing that I won't be there, means that he will suffer, never getting to say goodbye before he dies."

He pushes away from my car, standing a little straighter and a little more confidently than he was when he got here. "The only thing that would make it any sweeter would be forcing him to watch me kiss you before he goes." He smirks. "That would be the ultimate 'fuck you'."

I can't help but shake my head and return his little smirk. "Well, whenever you're ready to stuff it to him, I'll be there," I tell him as I stomp out my own cigarette and he takes my hand. "Do something for me?" I ask him.

"What?"

"When the tour is over, if you haven't heard anything more from Iowa, will you consider returning?"

He drops my hand. "Why would I do that? I mean it, Eric, it means nothing to me."

"Just hear me out. One of two things can happen. One, you tell me again that you won't go, at least then you'll have had some time to process the information you have now." He goes to speak and I stop him with my finger on his lips. "Or, you will want to go back just to stuff it in his face that his treatments didn't work. Let him know that no matter what, you won, not him, not the doctors, not anyone in town. You, Calvin, you won, not him. Prove that to him."

He smiles a little at what I've said. "And what if he's gone before the tour is over?"

"Then we go back together and you can kiss me at his grave."

"You're an evil son of bitch, you know that?" he says with a laugh.

I laugh too. "I'm aware, but either way it serves a purpose."

He raises an eyebrow at me and asks, "And that is what exactly?"

I smile. "Closure. One way or another."

He nods his understanding and maybe a little bit of approval too.

"Good, now, let's go inside." I usher him toward my building and he takes the lead, but not before taking my hand back into his.

chapter 37

calvin

"What are you doing?" I ask Eric as he grabs a couple pillows off his bed.

"I thought you'd want to sleep in the guest room?" His voice is gentle and unsure.

I shake my head. "No, I'd like to sleep in here, with you."

His face lights up and he sets the pillows back on the bed. "I'd hoped that would be the case." He pauses, pretending to straighten the sheets. "After all that has happened today, I didn't want to push you."

"Well, you're not. But I do have one condition."

His eyes meet mine. "Anything?"

"With clothes, please?" He nods his approval of my request. "I just... I don't know how I would react to that, at least not while I'm asleep and I don't want a repeat performance from this afternoon either."

"I understand." He puts his arm out, an invitation. "Come here."

I smile and walk around the end of the bed and settle in against him. He slowly wraps his arms around me and I wrap my arms around him. He kisses the top of my head and the growing familiar tingle ignites within me and I want so badly to try again, but I'm scared to death of what will happen if we do. It's with that thought that I resolve myself to behave. I truly don't want to put myself back in that position twice in one day. I don't know if I can handle it. Between what happened between us earlier and that fucking phone call, I'm a fucking wreck.

"Did you bring any clothes up from your car?"

I laugh nervously. "Uhh, no. I can run down and grab some."

He kisses the top of my head again. "No need. Wear what you had on earlier."

I nod and hug him a little tighter, he does the same and I release him, grabbing the sweats off of the bed from earlier, leaving the t-shirt. I catch his playful smirk when he realizes I'm leaving it there. "I'm just gonna-" I gesture toward the bathroom door and he nods his understanding. I don't know why I feel shy about changing in front of him, maybe it's just habit, or maybe I'm worried that I'm going to start something, indirectly, that I can't finish.

Tomorrow will be a long day, flying to Denver from here isn't that big of a deal, but we have a show tomorrow night, one we added at the beginning of the tour. God, that feels like a lifetime ago. Then we're hotel bound after what will likely be a night in the bar. I shudder at the idea of being in the bar, being around the guys, and…I swallow as the burn of acid trickles up my throat. Yeah, I don't think I'm ready to tell the guys yet, let alone be next to Eric in that fashion, fuck.

How the hell am I supposed to bring that up to him? I mean, I sort of did tonight, before we went to dinner, but this is different, this is the guys.

I sigh as I pull up the sweatpants from earlier and run a hand through my hair before taking a deep breath and walking out of the bathroom.

I can't help but smile when I come out. Eric is lying on the bed, covers pulled down and he's wearing his sweatpants, sans shirt. My heart flutters at seeing him shirtless. I have to be honest and tell myself that I've always found Eric, shirtless or not, attractive, though I'd never been able to dwell on it until now. Usually it was always a fleeting thought.

I fold my arms over my chest and lean against the door jamb, watching him fiddle on his phone. I smile at some of his facial expressions. Wondering what he's looking at that would cause a scowl, then a smirk, and then finally a blush. I raise an eyebrow as something I'm unfamiliar with rolls through me while I watch him. "What you looking at?" I ask without moving. An overwhelming need to know allows the words to spill before I can stop myself.

He smiles wider and looks at me. "Our text messages."

I scowl at him. "Our texts? From when?"

His smile doesn't fade away even an ounce. "Oh, over the last week," he says in a taunting voice.

"So why the scowl before the smirk and blush?" I chide.

He laughs. "I'm not the most eloquent with words sometimes."

I roll my eyes. "Oh, on the contrary, I find your words very eloquent and very true to who you are and I like that." I push away from the door and walk around the foot of the bed.

"I guess hindsight is always twenty-twenty. I thought it sounded good in my head, but I know what I was feeling when I wrote some of these and now, reading them, they don't exactly sound, umm, good?"

"You know? I think that one thing we have going for us is that we've been around each other long enough to know what the other is trying to say or even how they're saying it. I know when I read your texts that I always felt like you were talking to me, like I could picture your face, or hear your voice. My favorite image was when the chat bubble would hang out forever, I could see you staring at your phone," I chuckle, "With your tongue pressed between your teeth, reaching for your nose."

"Oh my god," he says before he goes beet red, setting his phone down and covering his face. He is thoroughly embarrassed.

"I kind of like it when you're embarrassed," I tease him as I climb up on to the bed. I crawl over to him on my knees and sit back before pulling his arms away from his face. Okay fine, I try and pull his arms away. I start to laugh.

"I never knew you noticed that." His voice is lighthearted and muffled by his hands over his mouth.

I laugh and place a hand on his stomach. He flinches but settles quickly, my touch taking him by surprise. He can't see me, so I shouldn't expect anything else. "I always knew when you were concentrating on something, whether it was guitar or even school work back in the day. Your tongue would get mashed between your lips and," I chuckle again, "It's pretty fucking cute. You were doing it in the car tonight too."

"Gah," he groans, but he moves his hands, placing one over mine on his stomach. I intertwine our fingers but he's yet to make eye contact with me.

"I'm surprised you even know you do it. Something like that is a nervous habit most people don't know they have."

He snorts a laugh. "Oh I know, one, my mother used to always try and grab it between her fingers. Funny thing about that though, she does it too. But ultimately, I catch myself doing it and that's usually when I pull it back in my mouth."

I laugh and lay myself down next to him. He opens his arm for me to snuggle in and I do, sliding my hand across his stomach, holding him to me. He does the same with his arm, wrapping it around me. "I think it's cute," I tell him softly and he leans up, kissing the top of my head again.

"Well, then maybe I won't pull it back in anymore." His tone is light, friendly, the embarrassment seems to be gone.

"I'm sorry I embarrassed you," I tell him as I start to trace my fingers over some of his tattoos along his side, over on to his stomach. He flinches, and I watch as his stomach muscles jump and I can feel him shaking.

"Ahh, that tickles."

I smile wide and settle my hand. "Sorry."

"Don't be, for either. I guess I just didn't realize that anyone had noticed my little quirk."

"I guess it just means I've been paying attention," I tell him and it's true. "Though I couldn't dwell on it, I noticed it, a lot. Though nowhere near as much as you'd done it in college. It still comes out once in a while. Like when you put your bass down and pick up your guitar."

He laughs. "That's because I don't play it very much. I actually have to think more about what I'm doing in order to play." He laughs again. "I also do it a lot while playing video games."

"Yes, yes you do," I tease him, tickling him lightly and he squirms under me, but I stop.

Before long, we're both yawning and Eric reaches over, extinguishing the light, plunging us into darkness. I squeeze him a little harder, holding him to me before I lift up and find his lips, planting a warm, soft kiss against his lips and he returns it, equally as warm and gentle. "Good night," I tell him softly before settling back into my special place against his chest. Realizing only now just how much we mesh together like this. Molded together like we've always been meant to be.

The idea of that sends my heart racing, for the first time, in a very good way.

chapter 38

eric

"Umphh!" I start awake after something pounds on my chest.

"Get off me." There is a grunt followed by a strangled cry.

"What the fuck?" I shoot up, flipping on the light next to my bed.

"Get off of me." The voice becomes more strained, more desperate. I look over and see Cal tossing his head back and forth, his eyes are screwed shut. "No!" he cries out in his sleep.

"Shit."

I round the bed as quickly as I can, reaching his side as he continues to toss his head back and forth, he starts to thrash, his legs kicking. "Fuck. Calvin." I don't want to touch him. I don't want to freak him out. "Calvin. Come on, Calvin, you're dreaming, wake up."

God, I feel so fucking stupid, but he's obviously lost in the throes of this dream. He's moaning and if it weren't for the fact that there are no tears streaking down his face, I'd swear he was crying. "Calvin," I say again, more clipped, sharper. He jolts to a stop. "Cal, come on, wake up." He's finally still. His breathing is hard, heavy, like he's just run a marathon.

Unsure of what else to do, I reach down and tap his shoulder. He doesn't respond, no movement, no nothing. In all the time I've shared a room with him, he's never woken me up from a dream, much less a nightmare. I grab his shoulder, a little harder this time. "Calvin, come on, man, wake up," I say and his eyes open lazily.

"Hey." His voice is soft and I deflate completely, kneeling next to the bed. "What's wrong?"

Jesus, he doesn't remember. "You were having a nightmare."

"I know, but…"

"Calvin, you were thrashing all over the place, you hit me in the chest."

He scoots back away from me, fear in his eyes. "I didn't."

"You did, but I'm glad you did. It woke me up."

'Jesus Eric, I'm so sorry, I…shit, I didn't know I…I thought they were all in my head," he says as he sits up.

"There's nothing to apologize for. I'm just, I've spent so much time sharing a room with you and I've never seen or heard you like that before." I look at him, and I know the concern for him that I'm feeling is etched on my face. "What were you dreaming about?"

"They started up again after I told you." He scrubs at his face. "I've never told anyone before, and I haven't really dealt with the deep down emotions of all this shit in a really long time, couple that with the phone call, I think I'm just overwhelmed." He sighs. "I was dreaming about him, the asshole in the institution."

"Oh fuck," I breathe. Suddenly I feel very guilty because I can't help wondering if what we did earlier today played a part in pulling up that dream for him. "Cal, I'm sorry,"

His hand comes to my cheek, cupping it. "For what? You didn't do that, you didn't drudge him back up."

"No, but…what happened earlier."

"Oh, no, I don't think that had anything to do with it," he tells me.

"Are you sure?"

He nods his head. "I have regular dreams about that place. I guess I just never knew I got so violent."

"And vocal," I tell him.

He doesn't say anything, but I can see the concern and sadness in his eyes. I just give him a small smile and we sit there like that for a few more minutes.

"What time is it?" he asks and I look past him to my clock.

"Just after six."

"What time do we need to leave for the airport?" His voice is softer, calmer now.

"Around eight-thirty or so," I tell him.

"Well, I'm not going to be able to get back to sleep. Why don't we get moving and get the car packed up and grab a bite to eat on our way." His suggestion fills me with warmth and I smile widely at him. I don't want to press him any further about the dream. I know that he's told me enough about the institution and what happened to him there that I don't want him to dredge it back up.

"Sounds good to me," I tell him, thinking he's probably right and that we should just get moving.

We got moving alright. We got showered and dressed, separately, against my wishes at least. Though I never expressed those wishes to him. It just seems like every time I want to make a move, advance things between us, something stands in the way. If it wasn't his dream, it would definitely be the time issues. But we're both dressed and his car packed up with both of our stuff and we're moving by seven-thirty. Headed toward Burbank and the private plane that will take us to Denver.

Once we've sat down in a little family owned diner about ten minutes from the airport, I look at Calvin, a serious look on my face and he recoils slightly. I laugh.

"Dude, don't do that," he scolds before laughing.

"I'm sorry, though I do have a serious question to ask you."

He shrugs. "Go for it."

"Now that we're here, in one car, all of our stuff together…what exactly are we telling the guys?"

He doesn't answer. In fact, he dodges me completely and looks at the menu. What the fuck? I roll my eyes, trying not to get irritated at his complete lack of conversation on something that I need to know how he feels about. I sigh and let it go for the moment, picking up my menu, though my appetite isn't what it was when we came in.

The waitress comes, takes our drink orders and then leaves.

"Cal?"

"Yeah?" he says in a way that is almost dismissive.

"Did you hear me earlier?"

"Yeah, I heard you, I just don't know if you're going to like my answer."

I want to roll my eyes. "If you don't want to tell them about us, I'm okay with that, but you know as well as I do that they're going to figure it out eventually. They're not stupid."

He sighs like he is preparing for war, but he gets a reprieve when the waitress shows up with our drinks and takes out orders.

When she's gone I look at him, hoping he's finally going to stop dodging me. He does, briefly, while taking a sip of his coffee. "I'm not ready to tell them anything yet."

"Okay. Can you explain to me why you feel you're not?"

He picks at his placemat. He's thinking and I can tell because that's the only time he fidgets with anything, much like my tongue thing. I wait patiently for him to answer me. After a few heartbeats he finally does. "I'm not ready to explain my past to them."

I cock my head. "What does your past have to do with telling them we're together?" I ask, thoroughly confused.

"I'm not sure I can do this publicly. You saw me last night, when we went out. If we tell them that we're working on something between the two of us, but yet they don't see us together or see us acting like we're together, they are going to wonder why and in order to explain that to them, I have to explain my past and I'm not ready to do that yet." His voice is nearly a whisper before he gets to the end of his declaration.

"So we're clear, am I not allowed to…uh, are we just supposed to pretend we're friends, like we've always been?"

"If you don't mind."

Yeah, I fucking mind, but suddenly something occurs to me. "Do you want us to be together? Or are you having second thoughts?"

His eyes dart to mine, real deep down fear reflects back at me, fear of us not being together or fear that I don't want us to be together. "I want to be with you," he breathes quickly.

"Then that's all I need, Calvin," I tell him. "We don't have to tell anyone about what's between us. Yet." I tack that on because he needs to know that eventually it will come out and eventually they are going to notice, because no matter how hard either one of us tries, if this is truly what we want, then it is going to be made obvious, but I think that is what he wants, he wants it to be made obvious so that he doesn't have to actually tell anyone. "Are you afraid that if we tell them we're together that they'll hate us or judge us?"

Calvin doesn't answer that question, but he doesn't have to, it's spelled out all over his face and in the stiffness of his body when I bring it up.

"It would be awfully hypocritical of them to think that, don't you think?" I raise an eyebrow.

He just nods, but we're interrupted again by the waitress bringing us our breakfast. We drop the conversation there, for now. He seems a little upset and I don't want to make him angry, let alone put him in a foul mood when we go to get on the plane, everyone will suspect something is wrong and start poking at the bear and that won't be good for anyone.

chapter 39

calvin

Boarding the plane was interesting. We got a few weird looks from the gang when we arrived together, but no one pressed. Dex and Raine were all over each other and Addison pretty much passed out the moment the wheels left the ground. Poor girl. Talon had told me that he and Kyle wanted to leave Addison at home so she could rest, but she of course, in true Addison style, wasn't having that. When we landed in Denver, it was a flurry of activity to offload band gear and then personal gear. Casey and Troy took all of our stuff to the hotel and the rest of the gang took us to the arena. We need to run some sound checks before we can veg for a while. The bus and gear got here ahead of us on Monday, which was the plan all along. They drove up from Florida while we got to take a break.

Up on stage, I watch as Eric sets up and tunes into the amps and tests a few things. While I stand there watching I can't help but think about what I told him this morning. My delayed response had nothing to do with him, in fact, it had everything to do with what I was fighting internally. There is a huge part of me that wants to shout from the rooftops that he and I are finally together, but then there is the institutionalized side of me that can't even begin to comprehend how to do that. I fought with my internal demons before I could honestly answer him. I think I knew, somewhere in the back of my mind, that even if we choose to be quiet about what's happening between us that the intuitive people we work with regularly will figure it out.

"Enjoying the view?" I hear Addison ask me and I turn toward her.

I shrug and she smiles at me. "Maybe a little."

She smiles a little wider. "You guys showed up together this morning."

"Doesn't mean anything," I tell her in a clipped tone that comes off a little more asshole than I'd planned.

"I know that, but I remember you wanting to talk to him, then the way you guys were at my house. I was just hoping that you'd had some time to talk over the break." Her voice is soft, comforting and I am beginning to see the hold she has on Talon and Kyle.

"We talked," I whisper softly. I feel my resolve dissipating into a sea of nothing as for the first time in my life I fight the urge to explain myself. To explain everything and I don't understand why that would be.

"Good, you guys deserve a chance to work through things." She places her hand on my shoulder. There is a comfort in her touch, but it's a totally different comfort than Eric gives me.

"It's complicated."

"It doesn't have to be," she tells me while she watches the stage with me. Talon's joined Eric on stage and they're talking.

"It does have to be," I tell her cryptically.

"Regardless of your reasons, it truly doesn't have to be." I look at her, wanting to tell her that she's wrong, that it is a thousand times worse than she could possibly imagine, but I'm pretty sure it would take much more than what I'm willing to give her right now. "If he's who you want, you go for it, no matter the reasons." She presses on my shoulder, urging me to turn toward her and I do. "Life is too short for what ifs. It's way too short for never and it's never going to be long enough for you to realize you're ready. Regardless of what the past tells you, there is happiness in your future and he's right on stage." She winks at me, then leaves me standing there gaping at her.

eric

"So... did you guys get to talk?" Talon starts with me the moment he steps on stage with me.

"Yeah, we talked." And so much more, I add in my head.

"Well, then why are you two acting like you're complete strangers?"

"Drop it, Talon, it's not worth the fight you're trying to put into this."

"On the contrary, I think it is. You two are different. You seem different." He snorts. "If I didn't know better, I'd say you've put on glass shoes and you're walking on a bed of nails."

I scowl at him. "I don't know what you're talking about."

"Oh come on, Peacock, how long have I known you? I know you're hot for him. You can't tell me that one little talk has squashed all that."

It was more than a little talk and for the record, jackass, there is so much more brewing here than you can even comprehend. I don't tell him this out loud. I keep it simpler, and less dickish. "Look," I stare him down as I speak, "At the end of the day, no matter how much you press on me, it doesn't change the fact that the story behind all of this is not mine to tell. Yes, I know what I want, and no, I will not let anything stop me from getting it, but you've got to understand that it isn't as simple as wam-bam-thank-you-ma'am." I leave it there when Addison walks on stage.

I catch Calvin out of the corner of my eye and something is off. "Excuse me," I say to Talon as I walk past Addison straight to Calvin.

"What's wrong?"

"Did you tell her?"

"Oh my god, no, what makes you think that?"

"Something she said. It threw me off guard. Almost like she knows. But I know she doesn't. We have to tell them."

"Wait, what?" I don't know what caused me to say that exactly. "Come here," I tell him, ushering him toward one of the empty rooms off of the main hallway. I open the door and he steps inside ahead of me.

"I've got to tell them, I've got to explain it to them."

"Whoa, Cal, slow down. Just because you think Addison knows more than she really does isn't a reason to go getting all freaked out about it. Listen to me." I grab his shoulders, capturing his eyes with mine. "You're not ready to tell them, do not rush into this before you've had a chance to really think about this. I understand why you'd think they know more than they do, but the truth is, they don't. The bottom line in this is that you need to decide what to tell them and what to leave out. There are certain parts of your story that no one needs to know. You simply need to just let it ride its course." I take a deep breath and release his shoulders. "If we give this time, eventually you'll be more comfortable about them knowing about us, about them knowing that we're working on something. Let them learn about it then." A light bulb goes off. "Just because it was practically instant with Addison, and even with Raine, doesn't mean that it has to be that way with us. We can take our time, let them wonder, let them speculate and then, when we're both ready, we can tell them, but not a minute before. Okay?"

"You're not ready to tell them?"

Of all the things in my speech just now, he picks up on that. "I won't be ready until you are. The bottom line is I know where I stand with you. I know what it means for us to be together, I don't need the world to know. But you also need to see that your fears of rejection are unfounded when it comes to these guys. They will be on our side one thousand percent. So please, remember that."

"I know, I…alright, you're right."

I smirk. "I like the sound of that."

"Oh shut it." He teases me and can't help but laugh.

"Look, we've got a long path ahead of us. Let's not jump the gun with telling everyone. Because if we tell them now, it will raise more questions than answers. Think about it, you may feel like you're ready to tell them, but are you honestly ready to kiss me in front of them?"

I watch as a wild range of emotions crosses over his features. He swallows hard before answering, "No, I don't know that I'm ready for that."

I give him a small smile. "Then that is your answer. Better to let them speculate without confirmation. Once it's confirmed, then you need to know that they will expect certain things of us and when we don't do those things, they will be more likely to question us. I'd rather deal with speculation than anything else."

"Alright, I can live with that," He tells me before leaning up and planting a soft, chaste kiss against my lips.

I smile, fighting the urge to wrap my arms around him and turn our kiss deeper, more passionate. He shudders too, as if he's thinking the same thing as I am. "Let's get out of here before…well, come on," I say without finishing my thought. It went two directions, before it turns into something more and before they come looking for us. That is something I'm not ready to have them do, walk in on us.

chapter
40

calvin

Being back on stage has righted all the crazy turmoil inside of me these past few days. You'd think that being on stage, in front of thousands of people would make someone crazier, but for me, it's calming. It's freeing. Denver show one is in the books and we're in the bar. Who knows, maybe the bar is what I missed? Regardless, for the first time in a couple weeks, I feel grounded again. Not that everything in the last two weeks hasn't happened, because it most certainly has, but it's like it's all better again.

Toward the end of the first part of the tour, mostly in Florida, I found myself dwelling so much on what I was so certain I couldn't have that I lost touch with me.

The ship is right back where it needs to be.

The girls are flowing in and out of our little circle in the bar, though I find irony in the fact that no one is interested in any of them. Eric keeps watching me out of the corner of his eyes and each time I catch him looking at me, I nearly blush. It seems a bit uncharacteristic of me, but I think I'm really beginning to see what Eric means to me, or at the very least, what he's meant to me all along.

Dex and Raine are all over each other, no surprise there, but something has definitely shifted between the two of them. There's a distinct difference in certain things and certain ways she moves around him. It seems like I've seen it before, but I can't place it exactly. Talon, Kyle and Addison are huddled in their own little world. It's quite refreshing and maybe even a little freeing to watch Talon and Kyle being so much closer to each other than they were even two weeks ago when we left Florida, but I also notice that Addison seems a little different too. Maybe she's finally feeling better.

I am momentarily distracted when a tall, leggy blonde enters the circle. In fact, she manages to capture everyone's attention, including Eric's. But she doesn't go to Eric, or Dex, or Talon and Kyle for that matter, no, she walks right up to me. What the hell am I supposed to do now?

"You're Mouse, right?"

I manage to place a smile on my face and look up at her. "I am, and you are?"

"My name is Jenny." She smiles overly sweet in an attempt at flirting with me and I don't know what to do. For the first time in my life, I don't know how to reject a woman, and I certainly don't know how I am going to do just that with all eyes on this blonde standing before me. If I reject her, they'll know something is up.

"Nice to meet you, Jenny," I tell her and I stand up. "Can I buy you a drink?" I ask, offering her my elbow. She giggles in that way giddy school girls do and I cringe when she takes my elbow. Jesus, here I thought that being around Eric publicly would give me the creeps, but this… this is just plain wrong. Eric makes no secret that what I am doing is completely wrong by the look in his eyes, that disapproving look I've seen so many times from him. I'm just putting on a show, really, that's all… Fuck me!

eric

That bastard, dispshitidiot, motherfucker…

Rage burns through my veins like acid. Why in the fuck would he do something like that? Why…I shake my head, fine, he wants to play that way. I stand up with gusto, prepared to go track down someone, anyone I can use to make him jealous, but as soon as I do and I see our friends' eyes on me, I lose steam and head for the door. Troy is hot on my heels. "Take me back," I growl at him and he goes darting toward one of the cars we'd brought over here and he climbs in, stopping to pick me up about halfway between the door and the car. I climb in. "Step on it."

calvin

I crash through the door, just in time to see Eric climb in the car with Troy and take off. "Fuck." I turn on my heel and slam square into Dex as I get back inside. "Fucker."

"What's up, brother?"

"Nothing, forget it," I grumble and try to sidestep him but he won't let me pass. He grabs me by the shoulder and spins me around toward the door, and he pushes me through it. We're outside now.

"Forget nothing, why you so pissed off?"

"Fuck off, Dex, I need to find Casey. I need him to take me back to the hotel."

"You want to sit here and play coy, act like there ain't shit going on between you and Peacock, fine, but you're fooling no one here, Mouse. You two sit there and stare out the sides of your heads at each other, then, when some blonde floozy walks up to you, you go running off with her and Peacock takes off. Seriously? Stand here and tell me there ain't nothing happening between you and him."

"There ain't," I lie.

He snorts his disbelief at me. "What-the-fuck-ever, Mouse."

"Shut the fuck up, you have no right to stand here and tell me off like this. Fuck Dex, you hook up with Raine and now you're some fucking magical matchmaker who knows everything? Nice fucking try, you have no fucking clue."

"Oh I have a fucking clue, believe me. I've known you for how fucking long? Seriously Mouse, you can't hide this shit anymore, just fucking deal with it, get it over with. We all know and not a fucking one of us gives a shit. But what we do care about is watching someone get deliberately hurt by someone else. You all saw fit to put me in my place with Raine when I was doing the exact same shit to her that you're doing to Peacock. Don't fucking tell me you're not, because you are. Whatever has you so hung up on facing reality, get the fuck over it," he growls angrily in my face before turning on his heel and walking right back into the bar.

eric

"Can we get another room?" I ask Troy as we pull up to the hotel.

"Why?" he asks, like he has no clue why I walked out of the bar in the first place.

"I don't want to be around Mouse right now," I tell him in a huff and climb out of the car. Troy follows and tells the valet something. Casey drew the short end of the stick tonight and he has floor duty, so I know Troy will go back to the bar with the rest of the guys.

"Yeah, we'll get it taken care of."

"Who's staying with Casey?" I ask him, curious.

"I am."

"Wanna swap?"

He sighs, "Yeah, I guess. You good to get upstairs on your own?"

"Yeah, thanks Troy."

"No problem." He climbs back in the car and drives off as I clear the glass doors and walk into the lobby, straight toward the elevator that will take me up to the fifth floor and our rooms.

Once inside the elevator, I punch the wall, not hard enough to do any damage, but certainly enough to cause it to rattle as the doors close.

The ride up is mercifully short and Casey is standing by when the doors open.

"Whoa, what's wrong with you?" he asks before I even step off the elevator.

"I don't want to talk about it. Troy and I are switching places tonight. Let me grab some shit and then you can let me in your room, if you don't mind."

"Not until you give me an explanation."

I throw my head back in frustration. I want to scream. "I can't. That's half the fucking problem, I can't fucking explain it because I'll be damned if I have any fucking clue what the real problem is. Not only that, but I can't explain it to you without divulging shit I promised I wouldn't tell. So can we just fucking drop it?"

"No," his voice is a half laugh, half stern order.

I turn on him. Casey and I are about the same height, but I have some width on him. "Look, it's impossible to explain without outing someone and he's certainly not ready for that." Shit.

"Mouse?"

"Drop it Casey, please."

"No, he's on his way up. Leroy brought him back."

"Fuck, that was fast." Too fast, shit. "Stall him." I open the door to our suite and make a bad attempt at slamming the door, fucking hotel room doors. I should have just made Casey put me in his room. I can't get what I need and be back out before Cal gets up here. Fuck, he came back quick…shit, that means he knew I left. Fuck, that means… goddammit, I'm a fucking idiot.

I stop as soon as I hear the door beep, click open and then click closed again. I can barely turn around before Calvin is slamming into me, pushing me against the wall. His hand grips my neck and pulls me down, hard and fast. His lips land on mine in a harsh, yet overwhelmingly powerful kiss unlike anything I've ever felt before. He wastes no time licking along my lips, forcing me to open for him and his tongue slides in along mine. His other hand grips my belt, undoing it one-handed, stripping me of any self-control I may have had, my cock is instantly hard and throbbing.

He gets the buckle undone, then goes straight for the button and then my zipper before pulling back. "Jealousy is a shitty fucking wasted emotion," he growls before releasing my neck. Both of his hands are sliding my shirt up my stomach, my abs come into view and he licks his lips. He keeps pushing my shirt up and I raise my arms as he pulls it off of me. I try and reach for his and he steps back, subtly shaking his head at me.

"It's your fucking fault I got jealous," I bite back at him.

"No, it's yours," he says as he steps up to me. His tongue darts out across my nipple and I groan. "Did it ever occur to you that it was going to be more embarrassing to actually reject her while everyone was watching?" He licks the other nipple and the cool air of the room makes me shiver. "I simply needed her away from the group before I could send her packing with a drink in hand. Then you got all huffy and fucking puffy and out the door you went. I saw you climb into the car and take off." He licks across my peck and then he slides up higher, toward my neck before he nips at the flesh of my shoulder. "Now rather than playing things cool I had to fucking deal with Dex in my face, scolding me like an errant child and for that, I'm pissed off."

"How the fuck was I supposed to know?"

"You were supposed to trust me."

"That's kind of hard to do when it seems like one minute everything is fucking fabulous and normal and awesome and then the next thing I know, you're headed toward the bar with some blonde bimbo for a drink. Calvin, you always buy them a drink."

"I've never rejected a woman's advances either, until tonight."

With that phrase, his lips land hard and fast on mine once again, pressing me harder to the wall, most of his body aligned with mine. I can't help the thrust of my hips and the moan that escapes when his hand slides along my cock. I shiver when his hand slides past the waist band of my boxers, plunging down and taking firm grip around my rock hard cock. "Fuck," I breathe out, breaking our kiss.

chapter 41

calvin

I drop to my knees before Eric, sliding his pants down his hips, bringing his boxers with me and his cock slides free. I lick my lips. Possessed by my need to prove myself, I take his cock in my hand, firmly. I stroke upward and watch as his entire body locks down and he moans above me.

Fueled by anger and frustration over what happened tonight, I am desperate to do this, regardless of the consequences, and I don't think he's minding one bit.

I lick my tongue along the underside of his shaft and he shudders above me. Spurred by his reaction, I wrap my lips around his cock and suck him in. Flicking my tongue, coating his cock, making it easier to slide up and down. I look up at him through hooded eyelids and he's lost in the feeling of my mouth wrapped around him and it pushes me to keep going. Determined to bring him to the edge, but not over.

My mouth and hand become one along his length, sucking down while my hand slides up, slowly releasing his cock from my mouth as my hand slides down. Back and forth. Having his cock in my mouth has my blood racing, my heart pounding, desire exploding. I manage to undo the belt on my pants followed by the buttons on my fly. Freeing my cock is easier because I'm desperate for it. To touch it, to have it in my hand while I worship his cock with my hand and mouth.

"Fuck," he groans above me. I can't help the smile that forms on my lips. He's so turned on and that gives me new desire. His hand slides into my hair, though he has no intention of guiding me, his hand is gentle and it brings me back into focus on my goal. I need him, I have to show him that I want this, that I need this, and if I can't do that, we will never work.

The idea of us never working sends a wave of dread through me, this time for loss and nothing more. I release his cock from my mouth. His eyes eventually meet mine, while I stroke both his cock and mine in my hands. "I want you," I breathe.

"Take me." His voice is soft yet determined.

"No, I mean, I really want you."

Despite my hold on his cock, he slides down the wall I pinned him against so that our faces are mere inches apart from each other. "Then take me. Take what you want from me. Have it all, it's yours." His voice is filled with a conviction that drives my need for him higher than I could have thought possible.

I release my cock and grip his neck, pulling him into me for a kiss full of desperation and all the pent up frustration from all the years of denying who I am. His answering kiss is equally as determined. We're both crossing a precipice that we never could have thought we'd ever reach. A cliff that has taken us years to reach. It all unravels, and it's all laid out before us, ready for the taking. That door is wide open, he's waiting for me to step through it.

I pull back from the kiss. "Strip," I tell him and his eyes grow wide, but soft as he stands up. His cock is right back where it was moments ago and I can't resist the urge to lick it. His motions falter as he tries in vain to remove his pants.

"I can't if you don't release me." His voice is husky, full of lust. I shiver and release him while he sheds his boots and then finally his jeans and socks.

He takes his cock in his hand and I groan, watching him stroke his cock in time to my own strokes. We're both tugging and pulling, feeling the desire blossom and grow between us and I know, in this moment, nothing will stop me.

I can see worry in his eyes. He's concerned that I'm backing out of this, I'm not, but he needs to see that. He sidesteps me, going for a bag on the dresser and unzipping it. From the bag he pulls out a sleeve of condoms and a bottle. Lube, I'm guessing. The idea of seeing that on the dresser makes me think that he has wanted this all along. The idea is exciting to me in a strange way.

He says nothing, but turns and walks toward the bathroom, returning with two towels in his hands. He walks toward one of the beds, his bed.

Before climbing up, he lays out one of the towels across the bed, then he climbs up on top of it without a word. I watch him closely as he settles on his knees, giving me access to watch as he grabs hold of his cock. "Fuck." This time I'm the one groaning.

Watching him on his knees, face down, his hand stroking his cock is...wow. I'm not sure I have the right words. He's not looking at me and I'm not sure if that is in embarrassment for what he's doing or if it is to keep me focused on what he's offering. Either way, I don't care.

I get up, straightening, releasing my cock long enough to pull off my t-shirt, kick off my boots and throw my jeans down my legs, stepping out of them as I step toward the dresser. Laying out before me is a bottle of lube and five Trojan's and I rip one off the strip. Fuck, am I really going to do this? Can I do this?

Don't think about it.

Just do it.

I give myself a little pep talk before grabbing the lube and turning around.

He hasn't moved and his hand has slowed on his cock, no doubt keeping himself on the edge. I shiver as I approach him.

eric

I feel the bed dip between my legs and I shudder in anticipation. Something has fired off in him tonight and regardless of the end result, I have to give this to him. Regardless of the consequences we will face when it's over. I shiver, excitement coursing through my veins, outweighing any other emotion I could possibly imagine feeling, like fear.

I've never gone this far with a guy. It doesn't mean that I haven't done other things, like toys, fingerings, things like that, but not this. "I've never had anyone like this before," I admit, feeling the need to tell him, hoping to ease some of the nerves I feel rolling off of him.

"Never?" he breathes.

I release my cock and push myself up so that I can turn and look at him. "No one, not ever."

There is a smile playing on his lips. "Good." He leans down and kisses me. "I'm glad," he says as he backs away from me, looking down at my body. I watch as he shudders too, his nipple rings bouncing and his nipples hardening. He sets something down, the lube, against my leg and I can see him put the condom between his teeth and rip it open. Something shifts in him. I'm concerned momentarily that something is triggering him, but rather than going south, things start to go north. He's altered his expression, hardened himself. Steeling himself for what he's about to do as he pulls the condom from its wrapper.

I get the urge to roll it on him myself, but I let it slide, for now. I don't want to push him into having me do something he isn't ready for.

Then he freezes completely.

"Cal?"

He doesn't answer. He's not panicking, he's just...I don't know. "Calvin?" I ask him again and finally his eyes meet mine. There is a concerned fear in his eyes. "Talk to me?" I whisper.

"I...I don't know how to do this," he says and I smile in relief.

"Have sex?" I tease him.

He snorts. "No, I know how to do that, but...this, I've never..."

I raise an eyebrow at him. "Done anal before?"

I watch as he turns bright red before shaking his head.

"It's no different than...well you know, except, well, it's a lot tighter."

His eyes dart to mine. "How would you know?"

"Just because I've never had anyone up there doesn't mean I've never-" I stop the thought cold in its tracks, not wanting to bring up previous encounters. I turn around, facing him. "Look, if it's too much, too fast, it's alright," I tell him and reach for his hand. He flinches slightly but then comes back to me, his eyes meeting mine.

"I...I really do want to do this, Eric, I just..."

"Shhh, it's alright," I tell him as I pull the condom from his hand and reach over, throwing it on the nightstand. "Come here," I tell him and he starts to come back to me, though we're both still hard and I feel like I'm going to get blue balls. I ignore them in favor of comforting him, helping to bring him back to me. I lay down, holding out my arm, giving him a place to lie and he does.

For the first time, we're both still naked and I do everything I can to will my erection away.

I wrap my arm around his back. "Listen to me," I tell him, "We have plenty of time for this, it doesn't have to be tonight, it doesn't have to be right now."

"I know it's just-" He pauses.

"Just what?" I ask him.

"After tonight, today, all the talk about not telling anyone, Addison approaching me, then Dex, I just, I felt like I needed to prove to you that I really do want this."

I huff. "By having sex with me?" He nods. "Ah, Cal, no, no, no, not like this. You don't owe me anything, Calvin. I'm aware of what it is that you want."

"Then why did you leave?"

I sigh, "Because my gut reaction was to find some guy in the bar and make you jealous. Then I realized that while you may not have been able to help yourself with her, I could certainly help myself with some other person. Believe it or not, Cal, I understand what's going on in your head. Yes, I was jealous, but I was jealous for all the wrong reasons."

"What were those?" he asks the logical follow up.

I put my hand on top of his. "Because she had your attention."

He looks up at me and counters, "But she didn't."

I smile slightly. "I know that now, but I didn't at the time. I let my idea of how things should be between us get in the way of us being us. Being who we are."

"I think we need to tell them," he tells me with a serious look in his eyes.

"I think they already know," I retort. "But I think you're right. I think we do. I thought, this morning, that we could just fall back into a 'normal for us' routine around our friends, but it is obvious that we can't. I think we just need to let them know that we're working on it, that there may be times where things go smoothly and other times where they might not so much."

"Like in public?"

I nod. "I'm pretty sure they already have us pegged as something more than what we were before the break, but it would probably be better if we confirmed it for them. As far as everything else, well, we deal and tell them if we need to, but I don't think we will. I think any one of them would understand that while they may have had that instant connection, you and I are not so lucky."

"But we have that connection."

I smile wide at him. "Yes we do, but they don't need to know that," I tell him.

"Okay," he tells me softly before snuggling back into his special spot against me.

chapter 42

calvin

Climbing back on board the bus wasn't exactly as exciting as we'd expected it to be, at least not for me. Being back on board means going back on the road and it means that Eric and I are forced to sleep apart. Talon, Kyle and Addison all have the master bedroom at the back of the bus. The room was Talon's before, well, before this whole tour began. The other 'room' is now occupied by Dex and Raine, leaving Eric and I in our racks toward the front of the bus. Tori has moved over to the other bus with the rest of the security detail, but we still have to sleep with one on top. Leaving one rack open for the occasion where one of the bodyguards gets stuck on board. Which happens frequently.

At least now I can climb all the way up top instead of falling into my bed on the bottom. It also means that I get to sleep on top of Eric. I shake my head in silent laughter as for some reason I find that funny.

We have a show in a couple hours, but we're all working on moving back in beforehand so that we can take off after we're done in the greenroom. Somewhere along the way there was a unanimous vote of driving on to Seattle right away, giving us a couple extra days to roam around before we play our set. Then it's Portland and finally back to close out the tour in Los Angeles.

Five more shows...then what?

The idea brings me up short. Yeah, the band isn't going anywhere and we have a new album to record, but, fuck. I try and think about what I did before this tour started and well, I'm coming up empty because right now, all I can think about is Eric and where are we going to go when we're not forced back together like this.

The idea sends a bit of fear through me. What if once this is over, he's done? What if I'm just a bored infatuation? I shake my head. I'm an idiot for even thinking that.

Suddenly the hair on the back of my neck stands up and goosebumps fly over my skin and I know why almost immediately. Eric is on the bus and I smile as I throw my bag up on my bunk. "You're gonna sleep on top of me?" he whispers in my ear and I shiver as his breath flows around me.

"I've been sleeping on top of you for two nights now," I breathe back.

"True." I can feel, rather than hear his chuckle. "It's not the same though."

I sigh. "No, it most definitely is not, but it's either this or…well, nothing actually. I don't see Talon giving up his room, there are three of them after all, and Dex, yeah, you can argue with him for that one."

"We could just squeeze into one," he teases.

I snort. "Yeah, right. I may not be that big, but I am bigger than either one of those two girls and while Dex and Raine could get away with it, I highly doubt we will."

"Worth a shot," he says with a smirk.

It wasn't but a couple minutes after our exchange that Dex and Raine came on board and we shot the shit for a few minutes before Talon, Kyle and Addison came on board too. Once we were all kind of settled, Raine and Addison set about making food. Though I know Talon won't eat, it didn't stop the rest of us from diving in before our set.

When it was time to take the stage, we all proceed through our traditional kissing of Addison, though Dex now kisses Raine instead. That tradition started with our first show in San Diego and ironically enough, it started because of Dex. He was so hell bent on getting a piece of Addison that nothing was going to stand in his way. I think it helped that nothing had developed yet between Addison and the guys, because otherwise we'd have never been able to keep it up after that.

The set went amazingly well. Eric and I seemed just that much more in tune with each other and we started feeding off the energy of the other, making it one of our most animated shows so far. Maybe the break did actually help reinvigorate us. Either that or it's Eric, or the fact that our grueling tour finally has light at the end of its tunnel.

The greenroom goes about as normal, though tonight is far fuller than last night was. I think it might have to do with the other show being a late add-on. It's late when we finally climb on board the bus. Talon, Kyle and Addison disappear quickly. It's going to be a loud night by the way Talon is kissing and loving on Addison. I start to wonder if it's in the air tonight because Dex and Raine aren't much different than Talon was. I roll my eyes.

Eric is a little feisty when he climbs on board, but he knows, at least until we hear them doing their thing, that we're not entirely in the clear of being caught doing anything. He climbs into the shower, desperate to get the sweat and all that crap out of his hair before crawling into bed.

eric

The hot water slides down my body. God, that feels good. I am so sore tonight. Almost as bad as I was after Vegas when we'd just gotten this party started. I forget how intense these shows can be. Add to that the fact that I haven't had any fucking release in...I roll my eyes and sigh, too long.

That's when a noise outside the shower draws my attention and I look through water covered eyes to see Calvin standing there, naked. My breathing hitches in my throat as I wipe away the water from my eyes in order to see him better.

He steps inside the shower and presses me against the opposite wall. My breathing spikes as his hands glide all over my body, from my thighs, up my hips to my chest, along my neck and back down again. My cock grows hard, and he takes it into his hand. My eyes roll up, but I've got to stop him. He strokes up and then back down, quickly. "Cal?"

"Shhh..."

"No Cal, I have to be honest with you..."

His eyes look at me, shocked so I quickly continue, "No, no...it's, Cal, I'm getting blue balls here. I haven't...I haven't gotten off since Tuesday. If I..."

He shushes me with a finger pressed against my lips and he drops to his knees before me.

"Oh god," I groan out as he takes me into his mouth. My cock twitches and when Calvin moans around my dick, I know I've let loose some pre-cum. "Please don't stop," I beg and he starts sucking, stroking, up and down. My orgasm doesn't take long to reach the point of no return. His mouth is so fucking hot and he looks so goddamn beautiful on my cock.

Fueled by his own need, I look down to find him stroking his own cock and mine jumps again. I can't hold back much longer. "I'm so close," I breathe and he starts sucking with more gusto, more need, more everything. Fuck, he wants this, and I'll be dammed if he's not going to get it. "Don't stop," I say and he doesn't. My orgasm is riding the wave of release, my balls pull up, and everything inside me ignites. "Ahh!" I cry out as I explode down his throat.

He doesn't stop sucking, lavishing my cock as my orgasm slides down his throat and then I feel him stroking himself vigorously. His own orgasm is impending and I want to help him. I try and move and he holds me still. Flicking his tongue against my piercing, causing me to jump uncontrollably at the sensitivity. Then he groans around my cock before popping it free. He cries out as his own orgasm takes him, tipping him over the edge.

I lick my lips, wishing I could taste him, but…

It all turns and shifts in an instant. He goes stiff, cold. I grab him by the shoulders, pulling him up. "No, Calvin, no, no, no…you didn't do anything wrong." His eyes slowly slide to mine.

"I know," he breathes.

I lean back, away from him, puzzled beyond belief.

"I freaked out because I wasn't freaking out," he says with a huge smile on his face.

I smile wide. "Seriously?" I ask with immeasurable amounts of hope in my voice.

He looks at me and nods his head vigorously. "Uh huh."

I kiss him, pulling him to my lips hard and fast. He's momentarily thrown off guard but then he melts into the kiss that I'm giving him. His tongue slides in along mine and I can taste traces of myself in his mouth. I wish he was tasting the same in mine, but I'm not so sure he'd be able to handle that. It doesn't make me any less hopeful that we're finally breaking down this wall between us. His walls.

I pull back from the kiss, releasing his shoulders and I pull him into me, hugging him close. "We'd better get out of here," he says against my chest.

"Yeah, you're probably right."

Just then the bus starts to move and Calvin is pressed against me. "Time to go," he says in a rush and pulls back from me, balancing against the walls.

There is a fleeting thought that passes through my head. How did they know everyone was on board? Shit, we totally got busted. An uncontrollable laugh escapes my lips as I stand wide-legged in the shower, holding myself up.

"What's so funny?" he asks.

"I think we've been made."

His eyebrows knit together in confusion. "The headcount," is all I have to say and I watch as realization dawns on him too.

"Shit," he says, but surprises me by laughing about it rather than freaking out. "Cat's out of the bag now. I wonder who?"

I give him half a smile. "I'm going to say Dex or Raine and on a very slim chance, Kyle."

"If it was Dex, we're never going to hear the end of it," he says, but he's not upset, in fact, I think that shower was far more cathartic for him than he could have thought it would have been when he came in here. For the first time in his life, he's not repulsed by what he's done and I take great comfort in that.

chapter
43

calvin

That was intense, I won't lie. Being able to do what I just did gives me a high unlike anything I've felt in a long time, not since the days I spent with cocaine.

I climb up into my rack. I left Eric in the bathroom to finish up. There might be enough room for two in the shower, but certainly not outside of it. After straightening everything out and finding my headphones, I climb up and plug them in, but I don't put them in. I also leave my curtain open. I want to say good night to him when he comes out. Shortly after getting settled, he comes out. I give him a playful smirk.

"What are you smirking at?" he asks in a playful tone.

"You. You look sexy just after a shower," I tease him.

"I do, huh?" he says back. That little half smile he has, that I've come to enjoy, spreads over his lips.

"Yeah, you look sexy other times too, but," I give him a pointed glance, up and down, well okay, as far down as I can see from this angle. He's tall enough that he can practically see straight into my bunk and I roll toward him, putting my head in my hand to hold it up. "Right now, you look sexier."

He comes in close and whispers, "What you just did in the shower might have something to do with that."

"Yeah, you are kind of glowing."

He blushes at my compliment and it warms my heart. "This sleeping apart is gonna suck." His voice is soft, but he throws his stuff down on the bottom rack, the one no longer occupied, with a little force.

"Yeah, but it's just for tonight. We should be in Seattle tomorrow night."

"Would it be presumptuous of me to ask Mills to nab us a king?" He raises an eyebrow at me.

"Mmm, now that sounds nice." I lean closer to the edge of my bunk and look at him. "But suspicious, don't you think?"

"Hey, I thought we were gonna tell them?"

"Tell them what? I'm pretty sure they're figuring it out on their own. We've already been made by someone wise enough to know better about who was in the bathroom, so what's the-" My words are cut off when all of a sudden we hear someone, Raine or Addison, crying out. Eric and I both look at each other and burst out laughing quietly. "On that note, I think it's time for headphones."

"I think you're right," he agrees, then he grabs a hold of the side of my rack, stepping up on the ladder at our heads so that his face is close to mine. "Good night you," he whispers.

My heart starts pounding, he's so close, he smells so fucking good. I inhale his scent, letting it overwhelm my senses. "Good night," I breathe and lean in, kissing him gently on the lips. He kisses me back with some enthusiasm and I feel my cock getting hard again. "So not fair," I murmur.

"What's not?"

"That we have to sleep apart," I whisper and I can feel the warmth of a blush spreading across my cheeks.

"Just for tonight," he says as he takes my cheek in his hand and I snuggle into him. "See you in the morning," he tells me and I kiss him one more time, this time more chaste but no less desperate.

"Night."

"Night," he says before climbing down and hopping into his rack.

I still haven't put my headphones in while I listen to him get himself situated on his bunk. Then I feel him tug down on the monitor that folds up and hear him shift, settling in. That's when I see his hand come up. I smile and take his hand in mine. I lean over and kiss his knuckles and squeeze.

At some point, I fell asleep with my hand in his.

eric

"Hey man," Kyle says quietly to me as I'm standing at the stove, eggs cooking in one pan, bacon in the other and I'm waiting for the griddle to heat up for pancakes.

"Hey."

"You making enough for everyone?" he asks.

I look at him. "Yes, why wouldn't I?"

He shrugs. "Just checking. Saves me from making breakfast." He chuckles. "What can I help with?"

I nod in the direction of the pitcher of pancake batter; he gets the hint and moves around me to start pouring drops onto the griddle.

"How you been?" he asks. I'm not sure if he's probing for information or just conversation.

"Not bad, you?"

He sighs that 'I'm head over heels in love and nothing else matters' kind of sigh. "I'm great. Tired, but great."

"I didn't hear Addison this morning."

"Nah, I think she's finally moving past that phase, though she won't eat that bacon."

"Oh shit, I forgot. There's sausage in the fridge. Wanna pull some out? I'll cook it for her."

"Sure," he says as he fills the last two spots on the griddle and sets the pitcher down for the fridge.

"Can I ask you something?" I say in an uncharacteristic way for me.

"Anything," he tells me as he shuts the fridge door and hands me the package of sausage. I rip it open and throw a few links in next to the bacon.

"How'd you know, with Talon, that you wanted to…" I can't really finish my question, embarrassment floods through me, both for the question I ask and for the fact that I'm bringing it up with Kyle.

He just shrugs. "I don't know that I consciously knew anything, man, it was just something that felt right, it felt natural, like if I didn't do it, per se, I'd be missing out. It just came naturally for both of us, but I think a part of that has to do with Addison too. If she hadn't been there, encouraging us, I'm not sure we would have, well, you know." He starts fidgeting around with the pancakes, looking for something to occupy himself. "I honestly never really thought about him like that. Sure, I thought he was attractive, but…I don't know."

"Did you ever think about other guys before him?"

He blushes a little. "Yeah, I did. It wasn't a new thing for me, but it wasn't something I acted on."

"Why not?"

"I guess I just never thought about it. Girls have always been easier I guess. Not that I wouldn't have tried, with the right guy of course." He shrugs and starts to flip pancakes. "Why do you ask?"

Now it's my turn to shrug and flip around some eggs and bacon. "I guess I was just curious about how other people handled their emotions when it comes to members of the same sex. Everyone is different, so I guess I thought I would see what your thoughts were."

He leans in closer to me, lowering his voice. "Honestly, if it wasn't for the two of them, I wouldn't be with another guy. It's not something I can see myself living with for the rest of my life, but that doesn't mean I don't condone others who would. It's just not for me. I think I'm too stubborn for that." He chuckles slightly before backing away from me.

Just in time too. "Morning, boys," Raine says from behind us. Crap, how long has she been there?

"Morning, Raine," I say before grabbing a plate. "You want some of everything?" I ask her.

"What's everything?" she says as she comes to stand opposite me, looking over what's cooking. "Yeah, definitely."

I don't know where Kyle goes, but he disappears from my other side.

Raine leans in close, lowering her voice. "Your secret is safe with me," she says before snagging a hunk of egg I flipped out of the pan and tossing it in her mouth.

"How?"

"I saw him go in, someone was already in, I knew it couldn't be anyone else in the shower."

"You didn't tell him, did you?" I look at her, concerned.

She shakes her head. "No. It's between you and me. I just told the crew that we were good to go."

"Thanks," I whisper back.

Her hand rubs along my back in a comforting way. "I'm totally here, if you want to talk."

"Thanks, but I'm good."

"Since when did you become all domestic and shit?" Dex asks as he lumbers down the hall toward us.

I roll my eyes and retort, "Shut the fuck up, Dex." I hand Raine her plate and she winks at me before walking over to Dex. I watch as she leans up and kisses him on the cheek.

He tries to take her plate and she pulls it back. "Get your own." She pokes him and he growls at her. I roll my eyes and shake my head, grabbing another plate and tossing some of everything on it.

"Here," I tell Dex as I hand him a plate.

"Thank you," he says, taking it from me.

I go back to making breakfast. Tossing the griddle of pancakes onto a plate and setting it on one of the tables, Kyle comes from the back of the bus and throws on some more batter before making himself a plate, or maybe Addison? He sets it down on the table opposite Dex and Raine. I mentally shrug it off and go back to adding some more bacon and sausage to the pan and then cleaning off the eggs into a bowl and putting it on the table.

Eventually Talon and Addison emerge from the back bedroom. Addison looks like she's literally crawled out of bed and walked up here. I shake my head, but she smiles at me before sitting down and diving into breakfast. The only person missing in this equation is Cal, who obviously must still be sleeping with headphones in, but this lot should have woken him up by now.

I turn off the burners and the griddle, refilling the bowls and plates on the table before making Calvin a plate and then myself. When I'm done, I take it over to the racks and I knock on his bunk. He doesn't emerge, weird. I slide the curtain back and sure enough, he's still sound asleep. I want to kiss him awake but there is way too much of an audience so I close the curtain and put his plate in the microwave before standing against the sink eating my own.

Everyone is chatting, bantering, having a good time and I suddenly miss Calvin and wish he was awake with us right now.

"We were in Vegas."

"No shit?" Kyle says to Dex.

"Yeah, we went and saw Derek and Dacotah, remember from Cami's party?" Dex asks him.

"Oh yeah, wait, how'd you get hooked up with them?" Kyle asks.

"They came to the North Carolina show, remember?" Dex says, though there seems to be a little jab at Raine thrown in there. That was the night that jealousy got the better of her too and she'd stormed out. I look over at Calvin's rack. It seems like jealous tantrums are a requirement for this lot. I can see Raine grow a little uncomfortable about that topic of discussion.

"Oh yeah," Talon says.

"We'd swapped numbers, talked about some shit and they came over to Nashville and we went out to dinner," Dex says and Raine blushes. Uh huh, dinner, sure, I think and mentally shake my head. "Anyway, we became friends, Raine and Cotah too for that matter, and they invited us to Vegas, so we went."

"Nice," Talon and Kyle say together.

Calvin finally manages to stumble out, or fall out of his rack. "Grace," Dex chides.

"Fuck you, I'm not used to being on top." I turn beet red and turn around, hiding my redness from everyone.

"That's what he said," Dex teases him back and I roll my eyes. Fucker will never quit will he?

"Stuff it, fucker," Calvin slams back. Our eyes meet and I give him a small smile before he ducks into the bathroom.

chapter 44

calvin

Downside to being on the bus? No privacy.

After everyone finished breakfast, we all kind of hung out in the galley area talking about this, that and the other stuff. Nothing too important, but still worthy of conversation. Somewhere in Oregon, we stopped, swapped out drivers and got a chance to get out and stretch off of the bus.

Eric and I grabbed our gear and set up shop in the galley after lowering the tables. Talon joined us and we jammed for some time. Pulling up some new stuff, and then playing around with some of the old. We were all desperate to play something new but while we wanted to, Kyle couldn't get permission from the label. They're sticklers for putting something out there that they can't guarantee to make the next album and considering we've written most of it while on the road, no one besides Kyle has heard any of it.

Dex joined us for posterity purposes. The accident in New York destroyed his electric set, so him playing with us was impossible. He was supposed to replace it over the break but from the conversation I overheard earlier, they were in Vegas for the week. I didn't catch how they'd ended up there, but if I didn't know any better, I'd say that whatever happened there changed him and Raine, in a good way.

After a while, we all kind of gave up playing, all except for Eric. He was strumming away in his own little world, not playing anything we've ever played before, but it quickly caught the attention of Talon, who has an uncanny ability to hear music and match it with his own. I watch Eric play as Talon watches intently. I can see his fingers moving like he's playing his own guitar.

When Eric finishes, I'm stuck stupid and can only sit there and stare at him. "Play it again," Talon tells him.

"What?" He's looking at me, then finally pulls his eyes away from me to Talon. "Why?"

"Because I like it. Do it again."

Eric chuckles and goes back to playing. Remember this is a bass line, no drums, no guitar, no nothing and then Talon grabs his guitar and settles in, listening closely to Eric play. Talon cuts in, strumming his guitar and it's in perfect harmony to the bass. The song is bass heavy, letting the darker tone take flight over the higher wail of the guitar. Talon is playing primarily on the top strings and in the lower register. The song is heavy, but dark. It's almost as if it's telling a story.

A story that starts off sad, confused, afraid. As the song progresses, Talon quickly picks up on the lighter feel of what Eric's playing and gradually his notes get higher, more 'happy', and that's when I hear it. My eyes dart to Eric's to find he's looking at me, trying to impress upon me the meaning behind the song. The lyrics start to come to me, the story unraveling before my own eyes. It's my story.

Lost inside
Brought to the light
Engulfed in hope, I feel the life
Turning inside out, righting the wrong
Extinguishing the bad
My guiding light
My Salvation

"Fuck me," I murmur. "Do it again," I tell both of them. It's rare that I sing more than back-up for Talon, but this time I can't let it slide past.

Dex rejoins us, sticks in hand.

This is it. This is what makes 69 Bottles the unique machine that it is. Our ability to come together as a band and let it all go, to soar on the music. Music brought us together because it is something that has always brought us back to reality. It's brought us back to who we are and who we're meant to be.

Dex playing while living on the streets.

Talon seeking salvation from a mother who wanted nothing to do with him.

Me searching for something to get lost in, rather than dealing with the pain of being trapped where I was.

Eric...I cock my head at him. He probably has the most normal story of us all and yet I don't know what that story really is. Vowing to ask him about it tonight, when we're alone, I sing along with my lyrics, though making mental notes to change things on a rewrite, I get nods of approval from everyone. Thank god, Raine started writing down the lyrics.

My singing, Dex's tapping and Eric and Talon's louder playing draws the attention of Kyle and Addison from the back room. Both of which stare dumbstruck at the four of us, but more so, at me.

When we finish, Addison, Kyle and Raine all start clapping and Eric and I are lost in each other momentarily. The song is far too perfect and I give him a quick smile of appreciation.

"Oh for the love of... you two do realize that we're not completely stupid, right?" Dex says pointing between Eric and me with his sticks.

I shrug it off and raise an eyebrow at Eric with half a smirk.

"Oh come the fuck on." Dex pokes at us.

"Dex, don't," Raine interjects.

"What? They try and act all coy, and we're supposed to just ignore it?"

"Yes," Raine and Addison say in unison.

"Oh for," Dex deflates, "Fine, be that way." He stands up in an attempt at bravado. "But we're not stupid, whatever is going on between the two of you no longer stands between the two of you. For whatever reason you don't want to admit it to us, fine, be that way, but... ahh fuck it."

"Dex?" I ask.

"What?" he snaps. He's agitated and it's quite comical.

"We've got a lot of things to work out, so yes, when we're ready, we will come out."

Dex gives me his infamous, 'got you' smirk. "Yeah, alright, whatever, but I'll be dammed if I give a shit. You two are too fucking perfect for each other and damn it, you both fucking deserve to be happy." He wraps his arm around Raine and pulls her into his side; she looks up at him like he hung the moon. "God knows if I can find happiness with one woman, you two can certainly find it with each other." He kisses Raine in a way that tells me we'll all have headphones on in a matter of minutes.

"Get a room," Talon chides them and Dex laughs, breaking their kiss.

"Don't mind if I do." He scoops Raine up and carries her past Kyle and Addison into their little alcove in the back.

"Do they never stop?" Talon jokes.

I burst out laughing. "You've got less than a shoebox worth of room to talk, my friend. Who was it that started the orgasm war last night?" I rib the three of them and only Addison blushes. "Uh huh, that's what I thought."

Talon looks at me, straight faced. "So, for real?" he asks and he doesn't need to go any further. My eyes slide over to Eric who nods at me in encouragement.

I look back to Talon and respond, "For real." I smile wide.

"Fuck yeah!" he says with a huge ass smile on his face.

"But, settle down, it's complicated, alright. We have a lot of shit to work through."

"Who doesn't?" Kyle chimes in.

"It's not that simple." I sigh, fighting the urge to tell them. How do I tell them? "I wasn't raised in a family where being gay was an acceptable practice."

They all kind of perk up a little bit, which I expected.

"What Cal is trying to tell you guys is that he has a long history of abuse, among other things, for liking guys. It's not an easy thing for him to admit to, but it is something he's working on. So while we may be together, it's not as easy as it is with the three of you, or with Dex and Raine for that matter." Eric helps me explain and he does it so eloquently and without revealing too many details.

"I get that," Kyle says, sitting down between Eric and Talon. "It's probably not the same, but I understand how that could impact you and your ability to be with Eric or anyone else of the same sex. But you have to realize that if it is what you want, then you have to go for it, balls to the wall, no holds barred." Kyle smiles sweetly at me before taking Talon's hand in his. Talon looks at their connection, then at Kyle and I can truly see the love they have for each other. They both look at Addison and the same emotion is portrayed to her and from her.

"I'm doing my best. It's just a little harder and quite a bit more complicated than that. But I am working on it," I tell the three of them while looking at Eric, conveying why it is that I'm saying this. "I've found what I want and what I want is him and I don't think there is anything that will stop me from getting it."

The words spill from my mouth like something I never expected to hear. I never imagined admitting to myself, let alone anyone else, that Eric is who and what I want in life and knowing that he is what I want sends a new wave of excitement through me.

We still have a long way to go. A road that will be bumpy and full of disasters and potholes, but we will get there, one way or another.

He's claimed me.

He craves me.
He is redeeming me, taming me, and devouring me.
He's redefined me.
Now it's time to love him the way he deserves to be loved. Wholly and unconditionally.

chapter 45

eric

Something came over Calvin while we were all sitting there playing on the bus. Something that was compelling enough to bring him to the point of telling Talon, Addison and Kyle a deep part of who he is. But it wasn't just that, it was the way he looked. There was a look of resolve that came over him. He's made a decision about something, and the look he is giving me now tells me that this may be the revelation that I have been hoping he'd have.

In talking with Doctor V, I learned something about what happens when Calvin freaks out. It's a matter of his conditioning. Sometimes it is how he may feel, but other times it may actually be the darkness that overruns him and he can't control himself. Assuming it's the latter of the two, Dr. V told me that it becomes mind over matter. Calvin truly needed to decide whether or not he wanted to be with me and from there he needed to decide whether or not he was going to whole-heartedly commit to that endeavor. If he committed to being with me, that it was truly what he wanted to do, then his darkness would no longer haunt him. He would be able to overcome what he was trained to feel.

When Doctor V had told me that bit of information, I realized then that a lot of what Calvin thinks he feels is because he knows nothing else. Which is why I vowed to stick with him, vowed to keep at it, no matter what, and it was then that I realized he may have overcome this a long time ago, like he had with women, if he'd had someone around long enough, willing to work with him and not against him. Then like he'd said, he realized that I was that person and that was what was pushing him to keep going with me, to fight his inner darkness to overcome and conquer it.

The look in his eyes right now tells me that he's finally finding that resolve. Telling Talon, Kyle and Addison has put him in a different mindset.

I can completely see and understand why he would feel this is harder than it really is, he knows nothing else. What Addison told him in Denver, without knowing his past, speaks volumes about what it is he needed to hear, and in reality, the darkness he feels can be overcome that easily. When you put your mind to it, you can do anything.

I smile at him, letting him know that I am with him one hundred percent. He smiles back. The smile is bright, brilliant and every bit the confirmation that I need to know he's made his decision and for the first time, he wants to run toward it, not away from it.

Fuck, how much longer until we're in Seattle? This no privacy bullshit is for the birds.

"We're an hour out," the driver calls back to us.

"Thank god," I grumble and everyone laughs.

"Eager much?" Calvin smirks at me.

I smirk back. "Yeah, maybe a little."

On that note, Talon, Kyle and Addison head back to their room to pack up their stuff. We're hanging out in Seattle for a few days, so we're taking everything and everyone off the bus with us. I look at my watch. It's nearly seven, right on time.

There is an open invitation for everyone to go out for dinner, but if what I am hoping is about to happen happens, we won't make it. When the three of them are gone, Calvin and I are left alone, sort of. The driver is still in the same vicinity with us. Thank god for non-disclosure agreements. "Come here," I tell Calvin and he smiles, sliding along the bench seat to sit next to me.

"I really like that song."

I smile. "I'm happy you caught on so quickly. Though I didn't have lyrics for it, I knew you'd hear it." He settles in next to me and I wrap my arm around him and gently kiss the top of his head.

"Yeah, it took a couple times, but I caught it." He rests his head on my shoulder.

"So, tell me something,"

"Anything," he says back quickly.

"Did I see what I think I saw a little while ago?" I ask him and he lifts his head to look at me.

"What do you mean?"

I smile. "After you told Talon about us, more or less. Then Kyle said what he said about going after what you want. Something changed in you. I kind of like it, but I'd much rather hear it from you."

He smiles and then settles back in his spot in the crook of my arm, pressed against me. He plays with my shirt. "I'd rather show you."

I smile wider and kiss the top of his head. "So in other words, we're declining dinner?" I tease him and he laughs.

"Yeah, we are."

I squeeze him close to me. "Kiss me, please?"

I feel his cheeks harden with a smile against my chest and he lifts up. I was right, there is a wide, truly happy smile on his face before he leans in and kisses me softly on the lips. The kiss quickly turns my blood to a boil and I'm primed up pretty fast. Sensing my change in demeanor, he licks at my bottom lip and I open for him. Our tongues meet in the middle and he continues kissing me softly. Love and devotion pouring into me unlike anything I've felt from him before, telling me everything I need to know about his decision.

He pulls back, both our breathing is jagged and I can see his lips are red, swollen slightly and the sight is something to behold. I shiver with excitement.

"It was Raine, by the way."

He cocks his head at me in confusion. "For what?"

"Who knew we were in the bathroom together last night."

"How?" he breathes and I smile.

"She came around the corner, just as you went inside. She put two and two together that it was me in the shower."

"She didn't tell-" I shake my head before he can finish his question. "Thank god."

"Why does Dex knowing bother you so much?"

He shrugs. "I don't know, because he's Dex and probably the last straight one among us. His ribbing gets annoying and I'm afraid of what it will become if he knows."

"How about you flip that around and think about how it will be the longer we keep it from him? He's already figured it out."

"So let him keep guessing for a little while longer." He snorts. "In a way, it's payback."

I laugh too and concede, "Good point."

After our talk, we proceed to pack up our stuff and we pull up to the hotel about the time we finish up. Excitement and nerves run rampant through me as we draw ever closer to getting our room keys. It's like going on a first date, almost, or at least the date you just know something is going to happen for the first time. Anticipation is now killing me. "Hurry up, Mills," I grumble.

"What's the rush?" Dex says behind me with Raine in tow and bags slung over their shoulders.

"Just tired of being pent up," I say.

He shakes his head and rolls his eyes, but decides to leave it alone, wise move. Raine just smiles at me as she passes. I smile back, letting her know that all is good.

Finally Mills hits the steps, Rusty in tow. "Here you go, guys. We're up on the twelfth. We have the entire floor and it is key card access only."

"Nice," Dex says and I have to agree.

Mills hands him and Raine their keys then turns to me and hands me our keys. I am way too eager to get off of the bus and I hear Calvin laugh behind me. I don't care. I never thought I would hate being cooped up on that thing, but today, I definitely do.

Climbing off, Beck and Casey are pulling suitcases from underneath. "You guys going out later?" Casey asks just as Calvin comes off of the bus.

"I doubt it," Calvin says. "I didn't sleep well on the bus. Take a load off, Casey."

"Yeah?" There is some excitement in Casey's voice.

"Yeah, we're good."

"Sweet, thanks."

I raise an eyebrow at him. "Hot date tonight?" I ask, totally teasing and he blushes a little bit. "Whoa, Casey's got a girl in Seattle?" I ask.

He blushes, but never confirms directly, and I grab my other bass and add it to my back with the other one, then grab both my suitcases. I turn to see Calvin doing the same. Fuck me, he is so sexy like that. I shiver, excitement running wild once again as he picks up his suitcases.

Casey and Beck start bickering about something but nothing else matters, or exists, anymore. All I see is Calvin and all I want to do is get in that fucking elevator and into our room.

"Ready?" He looks up at me and suddenly I'm back to being nervous.

I nod. He takes the lead into the hotel, toward the elevators that will take us up to our room. Each step that draws me in closer to the elevator and to privacy feels like I'm walking on hotter coals, each step burning just a little more the closer I get.

Dex and Raine snag an elevator as soon as they hit the button. I notice Calvin's pace slows down ahead of me, and I wonder if it's his own nerves getting the better of him, until Dex and Raine's elevator doors close and he picks his pace back up.

Oh, I see how this is going to go. Alone in an elevator…

chapter 46

eric

Calvin hits the up button just as I enter the elevator bay. He has his keycard in hand, ready when one shows up. His eagerness seems to match mine. This is almost better than foreplay. No, this is foreplay. It's that race to be alone, no matter who gets in our way, or how many people step onto the elevator with us. I can already feel the tension and excitement mounting between us.

He gives me a sideways look, one that says I'm looking at you, but I'm trying really hard not to and I smile. He blushes.

The ping makes us jump. I turn around and see that we're the only ones here waiting and there are a couple of people that step off, talking about something as I usher Calvin in. He smirks at me and steps inside, turning to put his keycard in the slot and pressing twelve followed by 'door close'.

I'm blocking his escape, standing just inside the door as the doors draw closed. The clash and click is my key to move. I push in on Calvin and his eyes meet mine. There's no fear, no hesitation, nothing. I drop my bags in favor of his head, cradling it in my palms as if it is the most precious glass imaginable. "Kiss me, you idiot," he breathes and that's the only invitation I need and I slant my lips over his.

My heart starts to pound, sending blood rushing through my ears. I lick at his lip, this time it's my turn to coax him open and he does in a rush of

223

air as he catches his breath. I slide my tongue in along his as the elevator beeps for the fifth time, the sixth. Fuck it, I don't care. I press into him, holding him against the wall, not pressing too hard because he's strapped with gear, but enough to remind him that I'm here.

My breathing goes ragged, fighting for air, but I don't care. Beep number ten, but he's not pulling back, I do. "I've waited a long time for this," I whisper and kiss him one more time as the elevator slows. Straightening, I lean down and grab my bags. Glancing at Calvin, his lips are pink, his cheeks flush and a very satisfied smile plays on his lips in a way that makes me want to kiss him again.

The doors open and Tori is standing just outside the elevator as we step out. She smiles and I suddenly feel like the kid who's just been busted in the candy jar. I blush without preamble and quickly move toward our room. Finding it about halfway down, I set my bags down and pull the keycard from my pocket and unlock it. Everything now seems in slow motion. Everything seems like it is all about to come to a head. Everything that I have hoped for over the last decade is about to come to fruition and my hands are shaking.

It takes me three times with the keycard before I finally get it to open. I push it open and hold it for Calvin to pull his gear inside. Once he's in, I grab mine and follow him in. It's a suite. We've entered a little living area with a couch and all that good stuff. I finally catch a glimpse of Cal who is staring through a set of French doors with his jaw hanging open.

"What? What's wrong?" I move to stand next to him, looking into the bedroom. "Oh."

"You didn't-?"

"No, I didn't say anything." It's true, I didn't. I hadn't really had time. "Could Mills have mixed up the keys?"

He shakes his head. "Dex would have been in the hallway demanding our keys."

"Are you okay with this?" I ask.

He nods and I drop the bags in my hands once again, abandoning them in favor of Calvin who is still holding his. I take them from him, moving them out of my way before he turns on me, pushing me back against the door we just came in, but he stops, reaching for my top strap to remove bass one from my back. I smile, helping him with first one, then the other and I in turn do the same for him, laying them on the floor, out of the way. No time to set up stands. As soon as we're free of our hindrances, Cal pushes me against the door, pressing into me, his hands gliding up my stomach to my chest and finally latching onto my neck and pulling me down to him.

"I'm sorry it's taken so long," he breathes. "But your wait is over."

He slams his lips against mine. My head spins, my body comes alive with desire and desperate need. My hands go to his waist, pulling up his shirt, needing to see him completely and he releases my neck long enough for me to toss his shirt aside before claiming my lips once again, his tongue flicking against mine, dancing. His hands go to the hem of my shirt, lifting, pulling it over my head. In a tangle of shirt, hands and arms, we finally free it.

As soon as I'm topless, his hands glide upward along my abs, toward my pecks, flicking a nail across each nipple as he does. I moan and my body shudders under his aggressive touch. He rakes his nails down my chest and I cry out, tossing my head back against the door, my breathing coming in short gasps. My cock is as hard as titanium. Poised and ready for whatever he can throw at me.

When his hands reach my waist, he quickly undoes my belt and then the buttons on my fly, ripping them open. He wastes no time sliding his hand inside and taking hold of my cock. I moan and my eyes roll up as he strokes up and down the base of the shaft. Sending tiny waves of pleasure soaring through my body. Everything comes alive.

I slide my hands down his chest, careful to give each of his nipple rings a tug and twist. Watching his vision blur and lust overcome him in the blink of an eye is a very heady thing to experience and it spurs me to undo his pants and repay the favor of stroking and playing with his cock while he plays with mine.

However, this time, it is my turn. Before I touch his cock, I grab his shoulders, turning him, pressing him against the door and he writhes against it. His hand squeezes tighter then releases over and over again as I slide my thumbs into the band of his jeans, pushing them down. Our eyes meet and I push a little more. He nods slightly to encourage me. I pull his hand from my jeans and he pouts. I smirk and lower myself to the floor on my knees, taking his jeans with me and his cock springs free.

I lick my lips and look up to him, seeking reassurance that he's still okay and his hand slides into my hair, pulling the tie free and then he fists my hair in his hand. He uses my hair to pull me toward him and that is all the answer I need.

My tongue darts out and his cock jumps. I take it in my hand and stroke upward gently, watching his face as pleasure rolls through him, taking him to a new height. I wrap my lips around his head, flicking my tongue against his piercing before sucking him into my mouth.

"Ahh, fuck," he cries out and I watch everything I've ever hoped for fall into place.

chapter 47

calvin

Fuck, his mouth feels so amazing.

I shudder, my hand in his hair grips tighter as he continues to lick, stroke and suck his way up and down my cock. I groan and his eyes meet mine just before he flicks his tongue in a way that should be illegal and my eyes roll back into my head. I've been eager before, been so high strung that I can barely control myself, but this...this takes the fucking cake. This is years of desire, years of wanting and needing, all coming to pass as Eric lavishes my cock with his mouth. He's doing a great job of bringing me to the brink, but then backing off enough that I'm forced to settle back down.

He knows what he's doing, fuck me, he's so goddamn good at this. "Don't stop," I moan out as he squeezes a little harder before taking my balls into the palm of his other hand. "Oh god," I cry, my legs trembling, threatening to take me down.

He releases me from his mouth and his hand comes away from clutching my balls. I look at him, sad that he's stopping, when he stands up, towering over me briefly before placing his lips against mine. He still has my cock in his hands, but he just holds it, no stroking and it's almost more intimate than what he was doing moments ago. He frees me from our kiss and smiles, pressing his forehead against mine. "Let's go to bed," he breathes and I nod.

He takes a step back, pulling me gently with him, unwilling to let go of me and frankly, I don't want him to.

He leads me into the bedroom, awkwardly since my jeans are still around my calves.

Once we're there, he releases me, allowing me to kick off my shoes and take my pants all the way off. I watch as he too strips the rest of the way, his cock bobbing up and down as he moves. My mouth waters, wanting to taste him for myself, but when I make a move to get closer to him, he shakes his head. "Bed," he tells me in a way that is nearly commanding, making me shiver. Wild ideas run through my mind about what happens when Eric takes control of a situation and I climb on to the bed.

I roll on to my back as I watch him walk out of the room for one of his bags, the same bag he pulled the condom and lube from in Denver and I shiver with a slice of fear breaking through the excitement, but only for a moment, before he starts walking back toward me. I grip my cock in my hand, watching him walk toward me, naked as a jaybird. His cock bounces in all its rock hard glory. His tattoos are on full display for me to see, including those that cover his arms and a good portion of his legs. There are only two on his chest. His nightmare and his fantasy, the angel and devil, depending on how you look at them.

I can't stop stroking while I watch him wander toward me and then he climbs on to the bed, tossing a strip of condoms and a bottle of lube up near my hip and he crawls in between my legs. His hand replaces mine, stroking up and down gently and I flex. My body is able to relax now that I'm lying down and I can give over to the full sensation of his mouth wrapped around my cock as he sucks me. Warm, wet, inviting, my hips make tiny little thrusts, matching his pace, desperately trying to slide in deeper.

His eyes are on mine as I watch what he's doing. I moan.

He releases my cock from his hand, but his mouth continues sliding up and down and he breaks our eye contact as he devours me. Licking, sucking, stroking with his tongue. "Oh god," I cry out when his hands land on my thighs, sliding upward and then back toward my knees where he lifts my legs. "Oh fuck," I cry out as he drops my cock and starts licking and kissing along my thigh. I feel a drop of pre-cum land on my stomach as he makes his way back toward my cock, but rather than taking that, he goes south, licking and tickling along my sack until he finds that sweet spot just underneath. I twitch, my muscles contracting and pleasure skyrockets through every inch of my body as he dips a little further south, licking lightly around that spot.

I put my hand in his hair, desperate for purchase, and he uses his shoulders to push my hips up off of the bed. Then I feel his warm, wet tongue as it gently presses against the tight ring. I can't stop myself. My other hand, the one not in his hair, quickly fists my cock, stroking it hard and fast and he stops, his hand coming up to still mine. "Cal?"

"Hmm?" I moan back.

"You good?"

"Mhmm… please don't stop," I moan and he nods before going back to what he was doing. His tongue is like lava, hot against my entrance, but it feels so fucking good. I don't want him to stop, I need him to keep going and the need to stroke my cock grows more intense and harder to fight.

He realizes my struggle and he replaces my hand with his, gently stroking up and down my shaft. It's not as hard or fast as I want it, but I can also tell that he's trying to keep me on the edge without pushing me over.

His tongue flicks harder against the tight ring and I shudder. The pleasure sends me soaring higher. "Fuck me," I moan out. He stills and I pout.

He comes up, releasing my cock. "Are you sure?" he asks me.

"Eric, I need you. I need to feel you."

He visibly shivers and there is a worried smile that plays on his lips as he sits up, still between my legs. I push myself up and grab him by his neck and pull his lips down to mine, pulling him on top of me. Our cocks rub together and he gasps. I steal my chance, sliding my tongue against his as his hips flick against mine.

With our cocks pinned between us, we're both lost in our kiss. Flicks of hips, sliding tongues, hands sliding over bodies. Desire unlike anything I've ever felt explodes between us as I realize that I'm about to make love to Eric, my Eric.

I break our kiss, finding his eyes as I gently flick my hips. "I love you," I breathe out and Eric stills. His arms, holding his weight above me, start to shake and his lips crush hard and heavy against mine briefly before he pulls back.

"I love you." His voice is soft, nearly a whisper. There's so much love and conviction in his voice. Something I realized on that bus that I couldn't say then seemed perfect now. I kiss him again, this time softer, more passionate. I don't know how much more of this I can take.

I don't know how I manage to do it, I'm sure he helped, but we manage to roll over. Now I'm on top of him and he smiles against my lips and his hand comes up, cupping my cheek and I lean into it, savoring his warmth, needing his touch almost as much as I need him inside me. "Please Eric?" I beg him.

He cocks his head at me, unsure of what I'm begging for. "Are you sure?"

I smile and nod. "Absolutely," I breathe.

He flips us back over where he's back on top of me and I smile. "I like this rolling around game." I smirk and he laughs as he settles himself between my legs before finding the condoms.

"You should probably turn over, it will be easier," he says, his voice laced with need and concern. I nod and move my leg around him, rolling over and raising myself up onto my knees.

I feel the bed dip and flatten out as he gets up and heads into the bathroom. He comes back out with two towels. I watch as he puts one under me and I sit up on my knees and straighten it out. The other one he sets next to me before he settles back between my legs.

Though he doesn't settle in to take me, he leans in and licks me, from the underside of my sack, straight up that sensitive spot that makes me twitch with pleasure before landing square against my entrance. I cry out as the pleasure skyrockets once again and I'm lost in his mouth and the pleasure.

Nothing else matters, not my past, not the band, not the shit back home, none of it fucking matters right now. It's only me and Eric. The two of us crossing that line and I am dying for it.

chapter 48

eric

I roll the condom on, careful not to stroke myself too much; I am so primed up, it wouldn't take much and this would be over. I certainly can't stand that thought. I'm a little worried about this, I won't lie. His reaction when I was rimming him was enough to make me stop, but I realized quickly that his reaction is conditioned into him and I realized what the gravity of him wanting this means to him. But it scares the hell out of me.

Once the condom is on, I grab the lube, meeting his eyes, searching for any signs that he's backing down. God, please don't let that be the case, and it's not. There is excitement in his eyes, laced with a little concern. I give him a reassuring smile as I help lift his hips, giving me better access. Resting his butt on my thighs, I squeeze some gel onto my fingers. Warming it up before pressing it against his entrance. He flinches but settles fast. Despite my efforts, the gel was still pretty cold.

I start working my fingers along the outside and watch as his pleasure becomes more evident. I can't stop myself from pushing a finger gently inside of him. He tenses and I still, giving him a moment to adjust to the intrusion and he relaxes. Giving me more hope that this isn't going to stop. I start moving my finger in and out slowly, allowing the lube to coat both of us. I add a little more and he jumps. With a breathy laugh he says, "That's cold."

I smile. "I know, I'm sorry."

"Don't be," he says softly with a satisfied smile on his face.

Wanting him to open more for me, I slide a second finger in and his eyes roll up as I work both fingers in and out together. My cock jumps as he moans and his cock grows harder. I add a third finger. He grunts as I stretch him but it quickly turns into pleasure and I'm more satisfied with his relaxing.

I drop some more gel onto my fingers then finally over the condom before dropping the bottle on the bed and stroking my cock, adding some extra lube to the already coated condom. I really do not want to hurt him. His acceptance of this is one thing, but hurting him concerns me and may be the trigger that sets him off.

I continue working my fingers and he gently takes his cock in his hand, holding and slowly stroking it. His body shudders and I smile before gradually pulling my fingers free of him. I am eager and fighting my need to rush to be inside of him. I know that I can't do that, not today, probably not ever.

Being with Calvin, like this, naked, exposed, and vulnerable, is something to be cherished and never rushed. His hand slows as I finish pulling my fingers free and he groans at the loss when I'm completely out. I don't stay out long. I reposition, lining myself up, ready to slide inside. I rub the tip of my cock from just under his sack, down toward his tight entrance and he groans. I press the head of my cock against the tight ring of muscle and he tenses briefly but then relaxes quickly, allowing me to push in a little farther.

"Ahh!" he cries and I still, afraid I've hurt him. "Don't stop," he says.

I can't deny him anything now. I push in a little farther and a little farther, until finally the head of my cock crests that outer ring and he relaxes more, allowing me to push into him deeper.

"Ahh, fuck," I moan above him as he squeezes me and I pull back slightly before sliding in a little farther, pushing in and pulling out, allowing the uncomfortable feeling to turn to pleasure.

He moans and strokes his cock and my eyes roll up. Watching him is nearly enough to push me to the brink of orgasm and I am not ready for that, nowhere near ready for this to be over.

I grab the towel and wipe my hand off. Dropping it back to the bed, I replace his hand with mine and he shivers, his body coming alive as he melts into the mattress below me.

My thrusts are timed to my strokes and gradually my strokes become quicker and my in and out movements become longer in and farther out, bringing myself to the point of nearly coming out before sliding all the way back in. Taking him, watching him as he writhes beneath me is a miracle in itself.

I release his cock, not wanting to push him over the edge too fast and he tries to replace my hand. I grab his hand and intertwine our fingers, holding his hand. His eyes meet mine and his confession of love is written all over his face. The look in his eyes tells me everything I thought I would never get to see, let alone have, and the pleasure soars.

I take his other hand in mine, holding on to him as I continue sliding in and out. My thrusts become more urgent, more desperate with each passing heartbeat as I look into his eyes. I lean forward, releasing one hand to brace myself, not wanting to pin him down below me. He raises his head and I slant my lips over his.

Desire intensifies the moment we make contact and I can't help sliding into him a little harder, wanting to bring him to orgasm without allowing him to touch himself. I want to take that pleasure.

I slide my tongue along his and swallow his cries of pleasure and I feel him tense and relax a few times. I am so close. I want to bring him over with me so I pull back from our kiss and take his cock into my palm. "I'm so close," I breathe, "But I need you with me."

He nods and I stroke up on his cock and slide back down as I pull out, up - in, down - out. Over and over. His body starts to shake and he cries out, "Eric, damn it…fuck me." I shudder and push into him harder and faster. "Oh fuck, I'm there," he cries out and I push in, pull up and down in and out.

"Fuck, Calvin," I cry out as my orgasm takes me over the edge, pouring myself into him and his cock hardens, jerks and explodes all over him as he screams my name.

I give him a few gentle strokes as I milk out the last of my orgasm. I look at him, and his eyes are closed, satisfaction and bliss are written all over his face and I start to extract myself slowly and he grunts. A little pain, a little… I watch as he swallows hard. Not good. "Cal, talk to me."

"I…I don't know."

I wait on baited breath for the pain of that statement to hit me and it never comes. I realize that it's because at this moment, whatever is flying through his head has nothing to do with me. I watch as he flinches as the head of my now soft cock comes out and I finally release his cock as I take a deep breath.

That's when he launches off of the bed, headed straight for the bathroom and I hear the heave and my heart sinks.

chapter
49

calvin

I felt the roll as soon as my orgasm subsided. It's a roll I'm not entirely unfamiliar with, but damn it. What a fucking way to ruin pure bliss.

I heave again, but this time nothing comes up, thank god.

I sit down, making sure that I'm not going to hurl again and as my stomach settles, I remember Eric. "Eric, can you come here?" I call out and it doesn't take but a few heartbeats before he is standing next to me.

"Forgive me."

"For what?" His voice is concerned, scared even.

"For throwing up. It...that was fucking amazing, Eric." That's all I can say when I see the hurt expression on his face. "Without throwing out my past, this um, this is kind of normal for me." I look up at him. "I can usually suppress it and move past it without actually throwing up, but," I give him a smile, "But I've also never felt anything like that before. I've never been taken over the edge like that and...and I didn't get a handle on myself. I've always prepared myself, been able to fight it...but I've never been so lost in myself that I couldn't-" He leans down and silences me with a finger against my lips.

"Calvin, if I have to deal with this after having sex with you for the rest of my life, I will gladly deal with it if it means I can be with you," he tells me. His voice is sincere and the love I feel when I'm around him and that I feel for him is reflected back at me.

I give him a half smile. "I don't want to keep doing this, but…for the first time in my life, Eric, I…I feel normal, I feel happy, blissed out, at peace. I feel so much right this moment that I don't even have the words for it. That, that was pure magic," I tell him and I watch as a smile spreads across his face and his eyes light up.

"Really?" he asks and I nod. He leans in to kiss me and I turn my head. "Hey," he grumbles.

"Dude, I just threw up, you don't want to kiss me," I laugh.

He joins in and stands up. "Come on, let's get your stuff and," he wraps his arms around me, "Take a shower with me?"

I kiss his shoulder. "I'd love that," I tell him and he kisses my forehead before letting me go and leaving the bathroom.

I step into the shower, turning the knob and adjusting it as the water warms up and Eric comes back, one of my bags in his hand. The one I usually keep all my bathroom crap in and he sets it on the sink before coming over and wrapping his arms around me while I finish with the shower.

I turn in his arms and kiss along his jaw, up to his ear and down along his neck. "Brush your teeth," he growls at me and I smirk, nipping at his chin before releasing him. He lets me go so I can go to the sink.

When I start brushing my teeth, he is standing behind me, watching me. "What?" I say with toothpaste covered lips and my toothbrush still in my mouth.

He chuckles. "Nothing. Who knew something so mundane and every day could be so sexy?"

I laugh and spit toothpaste from my mouth and clean myself up before I turn around and I barely get there when his lips land on mine. I chuckle again as he kisses me hard.

I wrap my fingers in his hair and hold him to me as he continues kissing me like nothing I've ever had from him before and it steals my breath.

During our shower, Eric washed me. It was sweet and unexpected. You know, I never saw myself as the receiving type of person, but with Eric it just comes naturally to me. He's like a big-ass teddy bear who you just want to snuggle next to all night, which I get to do.

When we got out, I dressed in some sweatpants and a tank top. We both decided that we just wanted to stay in and order room service and watch some TV or whatever strikes our fancy and I'm good with that. Sure, I like to drink and go out and party and have a great time, but for the first time in my life, hanging out with him sounds like more fun.

"What do you want to eat?" Eric asks as he hands me the hotel binder.

"You," I tease him and he blushes a little.

"For dinner? Hmmm, protein? Might work." He smirks. "Pick something."

"Yes, sir," I tease him and he gives me a Cheshire grin. "Oh no, don't you dare get used to that," I tell him and he laughs.

"I won't. It's kind of weird." He gives me a scrunched up look that makes me smile. He looks so young and innocent when he does that and given what we were doing an hour ago, I know that's far from the reality.

I take a few minutes to look over the menu while Eric gets comfortable on the couch. I tell him what I want and he picks up the hotel phone and places our order while I snuggle into him on the couch. We flip through the pay-per-view movies and settle on some comedy. I didn't really pay much attention. I was too absorbed in being snuggled up to him, we could have watched Titanic for all I cared in that moment.

When our food arrived, we ate, or rather scarfed down our food. I didn't realize until the food was right in front me just how hungry I was. Staying in was an odd novelty for me because usually when we're on the road, we're always out and about, but by the looks of things, no one was heading out for the night.

I snort.

"What's so funny?"

"Have you ever thought about how much has changed since we started this tour?" I ask him, still smiling from my snort.

"No, not really, why?"

"Well, think about it. We're pent up in a hotel."

"Better than the bus," he mumbles.

"True, but we're not the only ones staying in tonight. No one seems to be going out. Dex is wrapped up in Raine, and I'm pretty sure the same goes for Talon, Kyle and Addison."

"But it's been that way since New York."

"True, but now we're included in that list. Rather than hitting some bar somewhere in a new city, we are sitting here, finishing dinner with no plans of going out," I tell him.

"Do you want to go out?" he asks, raising an eyebrow at me.

I shake my head back and forth with gusto and he laughs. "I just think it's kind of weird how much one little tour has changed all of us in ways we would have called someone crazy for before we started."

"Huh, you're absolutely right. But it's also probably a good thing. I mean, if you think about it, we've all grown up a lot on this tour."

He frowns at me. "What?" I ask.

"Well, I guess we all always knew that eventually we'd settle down with someone." I snort because I hadn't thought about it until I made the decision to get over my fears of being with Eric, to work at this. "Okay, most of us," he corrects with a snicker.

His cell phone rings then, ending our conversation and he looks at it, frowns and puts it down, "You're not gonna answer that?"

"It's Jess."

I shrug. "When was the last time you talked to her? Answer it, I don't mind."

He continues to ignore it. "Nah, come here," he says and I crawl back up on the couch and snuggle into him. He wraps his arm around me protectively before kissing my forehead. "She'll leave a voicemail if it's important," he says before turning the movie back on. I smile. Feeling warm and protected is something he has no problem doing for me. He makes me feel like I can conquer anything, regardless of what it is life has to throw at me, no matter what demons I may possess, he's going to deal with me as I am.

"I love you," I whisper and his hand comes up to my chin, lifting my head so that I can see him.

"I love you," he breathes before claiming my lips in a soft, sensual kiss that quickly turns me on, driving me toward the desire of being back in the bedroom with him. Only this time, it's my turn to claim him.

chapter 50

eric

Calvin shifts, climbing on top of me, and taking the lead. His tongue slides in wet and hungry alongside mine. My body comes alive remembering what happened only a couple of hours ago. The desperate need I felt then resurfaces now, with a vengeance, and I can barely breathe.

He presses into me, pushing my shoulders back against the couch and I moan into his mouth. His aggression is a major turn on for me. Why, I haven't a clue. His hands slide up, along my stomach, toward my chest, bringing my shirt along for the ride. Feeling it tug against my back, I lean forward, giving him the access I know he needs. He takes it. Pulling back from the kiss long enough to toss my shirt on the floor, his lips land back on mine the second we can make contact. His hands push back on my shoulders and he straddles me.

My cock is hard as a rock and I grind my hips against his and his breathing hitches as the pleasure rocks through him. My pleasure is intensified further by his kiss. He's left me at a disadvantage, holding down my shoulders, then he slides his hands along my arms until he finds my hands. He pulls back on the kiss, teasing my lips with his tongue. I groan as he takes my hands in his, pulling them up until he is pressing them against the couch. His fingers interlock with mine and I thrust my hips at him one more time.

I pull back. His eyelids are heavy with lust. His breathing is just as erratic as mine is. He presses his forehead against mine and I tease him a little with my tongue, licking at his lips and he smiles. "It's my turn," he breathes and I shudder. I know what he is referring to and I bite back the urge to tease him about it. Though he seems okay, I don't want to push the envelope and push him over the edge that I know we're balancing on.

"I'm here," I tell him, encouraging him to take the lead, take control, take what he needs or wants from me.

He pulls back, a smile still on his lips as he maneuvers off of me, standing between my legs, pulling one hand with him, encouraging me to stand up. As I do, my phone vibrates with a voicemail, but I ignore it as I follow him back into the bedroom of the suite we share.

He turns us both, putting me between him and the bed and he gently knocks me over. I pull him down with me and he slides in on top of me. He brushes the crazy hair from my face and he smiles before his lips slant over mine once more.

I can't stop my hands from roaming along his body. Feeling the contours of the muscles of his stomach. God, you'd never know it by looking at him, but all the time he spends in the gym has paid off. He's ripped, and it makes me drool to see him completely naked, which becomes a mindless goal as I pull his shirt up.

He pulls back, sitting up so that I can remove it and the pause is only that long before his lips are back on mine. Though chaste.

He starts kissing along my jaw, up toward my ear, and I turn my head, giving him access and catch a glimpse of us in the bathroom mirror. "Oh fuck," I moan as his tongue darts out, trailing along my neck, to the hollow between my shoulders. I can't take my eyes off of him in the mirror. Giving me a new angle to see him. I shiver when he slides further down my chest, toward my nipples. He nips at one then kisses and bites his way down my stomach. My cock is standing straight out, compliments of sweatpants, there's nothing to hold him down. Calvin seizes his opportunity and nips at the head of my cock through my pants and I jump and my dick pulses harder for a moment before settling back down, but not before Calvin blows a huff of hot air across it. The warmth makes me shiver at the cool air that surrounds me and his hands grip me by the waistband.

He starts to tug downward and I lift my hips, giving him easier access to shed what's in his way. Sans boxer briefs, my cock is immediately exposed and is sucked into his mouth, hard and fast. "Oh fuck!" I cry out and I slide a hand into his hair. Not meaning to guide, just simply a gesture of 'I'm with you'. I see him smile around my dick before licking at the tip, then sliding down to the base and back up.

Pleasure soars. My need for him grows hotter and more desperate with each pass up and down my erection. Then he takes me hard and deep into his mouth and I shudder, biting my tongue, holding back the impending orgasm that is likely to happen if he keeps this up. "Calvin," I practically whine and he smirks, lifting his head from my cock. "I want you to take me," I tell him and he gets a little mischievous grin on his face.

"Paybacks suck, don't they?"

I chuckle. "Yes, they do, and damn, are they amazing." I wink at him and he blushes. I adore watching him blush. I love watching him come alive under my gentle compliments. It's like a reassurance to him that yes, this is what he wants and no, nothing will stand in his way. Not his past, not his future, not even a Mack truck could stop him right now and I love that.

"Flip over." His voice is commanding. The way he gets when he's trying to maintain control of the situation so that he doesn't lose himself in the past. But there are no shadows marking his features, not tonight. He wants this as much as, if not more than, I do and I am willing to take whatever he has to throw at me. I pray that all is okay in the end.

I flip over as he's asked and he helps guide my hips up as he settles between my legs. I grab for one of the towels still on the bed and put it beneath me when he grabs the condom strip and the lube from my other side.

I don't know why I never bothered to clean it up. Maybe I was secretly hoping for this, but I certainly didn't expect it.

Following my lead from earlier, I hear him rip open the packet and I can't help the shiver of excitement that slides up my spine when I hear the cap of the gel pop open. Using what I did to him, he proves that despite the concerns he may have had at this time before, he really was paying attention. I, on the other hand, was too focused on the goal and the prize waiting for me on the other side to realize he was taking notes. That thought makes me smile.

I jump when the cold lube hits me at my entrance, but he warms it quickly by spreading it around and I bury my head in the mattress, looking for some place to channel my need to cry out. My cock jumps as he starts to push one finger inside. Though I've never actually taken a man like this before, it doesn't mean I haven't tried certain things on my own. His finger starts to slide in and out of me, the pad dragging along that glorious spot that makes my eyes roll up into my head and he doesn't stop for a few more strokes. When he does, it's only to add another finger. First the second, and then the third.

I'm so close to the point of exploding that I can't bring myself to grab hold of my cock. This has got to last and it has to last long enough for him to get off too.

"Fuck," I groan as his fingers begin working in and out of me faster and a little bit harder. My back arches up and then down as I adjust to the pain turned pleasure from his penetration.

A few more motions in and out and he stops, slowly extracting his fingers. He pops the cap on the lube once more, adding some to my entrance and the condom he's wearing.

Everything tightens and then relaxes, desperate for this to happen.

chapter 51

calvin

I line the head of my cock up with Eric's entrance, knowing now just how tight it was, I know that I need to do this slow.

I paid attention because I was determined, at some point, to return the favor.

When I push in he moans and I watch as his hands grip into the sheets on the bed. "Fuck," I murmur. He's so fucking tight, no wonder it felt so good before. I knew that if pleasure that great were possible, I owed it to him to show him the same.

I push in a little farther until I feel the head of my cock crest that tight ring and then I start making little thrusts in and out. I can see his hands gradually releasing the covers and as his back arches downward, giving me a newer, tighter angle, the pleasure starts to take over. "Oh god," he moans as I push in a little farther and a little farther with each inward thrust.

I clean off my other hand so that I can run it along his back and grab hold of his hip, just as I bottom out inside. "Fuck me," I groan as I feel him tighten down on me and release me. Jesus, that has to be the hardest, hottest thing I've ever felt in my life and I tremble behind him.

I take his hips in both hands, guiding him forward and backward along my cock, encouraging to help me go at a pace that he's comfortable with. He was so gentle with me and I know that a little too much and it could hurt like hell. He moans and increases his pace. I feel my toes curl and pleasure racks through my body and my eyes roll up. I start to match his motion, meeting his backward thrusts with my forward thrusts, finding a rhythm that works, nice and even. Not really slow, but steady.

I release his hips and slide my hands up his back and he arches into my touch. I reach into his hair, roughly grabbing hold of it and lifting his head up. He takes my guidance and adjusts himself so that I can kiss him. He's looking over his shoulder at me, but he manages to slide his tongue along mine. Sending new waves of pleasure through me and I can feel his own pleasure in his thrusting, back and forth. I stutter just a bit when the pleasure becomes too much and I pull back from the kiss.

My own pleasure skyrockets when he takes his cock in his hand. I want to do that for him. He doesn't seem to mind as the pleasure becomes so intense for him that there is a constant stream of grunts and moans rolling off his tongue.

My own pleasure sparks to a new level. Drawing me ever closer. I take his hips back into my hands and hold him steady while I push harder into him. He cries out and I repeat it again. His moaning gets a little louder and the stroking of his cock has grown feverish. "Calvin," he cries out. He's so close.

I feel my balls shrink and tighten before fireworks of pleasure ignite all over my body and I explode inside of him. The pleasure is so intense that my body is shaking uncontrollably, matched only by him as his orgasm takes him, spilling him over the edge in a strained cry of my name.

My stomach pitches and rolls.

I swallow hard, once, twice.

I can feel the cold sweat building on my forehead and I slow my pace, allowing my orgasm to try and pull me back to where I am, here with Eric. Giving him what he gave me earlier.

I swallow again and still, but only for a heartbeat before realizing I need to pull out of him, quickly but yet as painlessly as possible.

I pull back, inch by inch and he leans forward, pulling himself to the end of my cock before all that is left is the head. I extract it slowly. This is his quiet way of telling me that he knows what's about to happen.

The sweat gathering on my forehead drips down, catching him on his asscheek, and I'm free. Despite my best efforts to tame the beast inside me, I race into the bathroom.

My mind is blank, no thoughts, at least not dark thoughts, but I still cannot control the urge to vomit. Eric isn't deterred, in fact, he readies my toothbrush for me.

"Thanks," I tell him before taking it from him and putting it into my mouth with a small smile.

He smiles back. "Anytime," he says and I look into the mirror, he's watching me again and I find it rather comforting. Though this time, before I even get the toothpaste off my lips, he's kissing me, fast and furious. Though it only lasts for a moment or two, it's enough to awaken the desire in me once again.

"Let's go to bed," I whisper between kisses and he smiles at me before heading into the bedroom, leaving me bereft, hornier than I was before the second go around, and my mouth sticky with toothpaste.

My phone chiming with a text wakes me from a nightmare. I'm still snuggled up under Eric, the way we fell asleep last night, and that brings me great relief. My dream, though nowhere near as violent as the other night, still wasn't that pleasant and I'm glad to be free of it.

The text is from Talon, asking if I want to join them in going out. Shortly after I finish reading it, I hear Eric's phone go off too. I personally don't want to move. Not from this spot, except I don't have a choice.

I carefully untangle myself from Eric and climb out of bed, headed for the bathroom.

When I come out, Eric's eyes find mine in a sleepy haze. "Go back to sleep," I tell him softly as I climb back onto the bed and settle back in his open arms.

"How'd you sleep?" he asks.

"Good, still tired though." I smile as he holds me tighter against his chest. "Talon wants to know if we want to go out with them around town today."

"Grrr," he growls playfully in my ear.

"My thoughts exactly." I snuggle into him, unintentionally rubbing up against the erection I feel pressing against my back and his breathing hitches. I smile and wiggle again.

"I thought you wanted to go back to sleep?" His voice is husky, but playful.

"I do," I grind again, "later."

He puts his fingers under my chin, turning my head and he leans over me, slanting his lips against mine in a passionate kiss that is heady and makes me feel complete.

I sigh and he steals his chance, sliding his tongue in along mine and I roll toward him onto my back. He readjusts himself so that he's lying down a little more and his hand slides down along my neck, between my pecks, over my abs until he finds my dick. Still soft, but waking up. His hand cups my cock and his fingers tickle along my balls. I shiver and my dick starts to harden. He smiles, pulling back from our kiss to look me in the eyes.

I smile as he starts to gently stroke my cock as it hardens and lengthens. "The advantage of sleeping naked," he smirks before he disappears under the covers, pushing them up so that I can't see what he's about to do.

All I feel is his hot breath caressing my cock.

His tongue jets out in various spots along my pelvis. Licking, then kissing, sometimes nibbling into my flesh and I groan. Not seeing him is torture, but it's almost like closing your eyes. I have no choice but to focus on the sensations he's providing for me to feel and savor.

He pushes my leg up and out, then slides his hand up, along my thigh toward what I so desperately want him to grab on to, but he doesn't. Instead he traces his fingers around my pelvis, from one hip to the other. It almost tickles and I squirm. "Stop that," I scold him, but it only makes it worse. He rolls himself over my other leg, planting himself in the space he's made. His hands slide up my thighs, over my hips, and yet he hasn't touched me. I can see a wet spot forming on the sheet as my cock twitches with the release of pre-cum.

His hands continue to trail over my body, working their way higher, peeking out from the sheets to graze my nipples, and tug on their rings. I arch my back as pleasure overcomes every other sensation in my body the moment his tongue finally glides from base to tip of my cock. His tongue flicks against my barbell, bringing new pleasure and that small twinge of pain that comes with tugging on it. It's not really painful, it's simply a sensation that isn't soft and it never fails to bring me to new heights.

His nails glide down my chest, not scratching or painful, just sending goosebumps all over my skin. I shudder and he sucks my cock into his mouth. "Oh god," I groan as his tongue lavishes me. His mouth is hot, wet and it feels sensational along my overly sensitive erection.

His hands move further south. I feel one of his fingers tickle along that sensitive spot just under my sack and I nearly explode in his mouth.

He senses this because he slows down his ministrations, bringing me back level and out of the danger zone of coming. But he doesn't keep me there long.

When his hand returns, it is toying with the tight ring of my entrance. Only playfully, but the intention is there and I grip the sheets. "Don't stop," I say softly and he doesn't. His mouth slides up and down my cock, my hips thrust gently with him, bringing my orgasm to the surface and I put my hand on his head, stilling him. "I'm gonna come," I tell him and he settles back down, pulling his hand away from my hole and his mouth stills, wrapped around the crown of my cock and he sucks gently on it. I shudder.

"Jesus," I groan. "That...wow," I breathe out and I feel his lips stretch in a smile but he doesn't stop sucking me. His tongue dances over my piercing. I could come just from what he's doing right now.

chapter 52

calvin

After a few more sucks and licks, he slips, letting my cock fall from his mouth in an audible pop before he starts kissing his way up my abs, to my chest until he is free of the blanket. I smile when he breaks free. His hair is a wild mess of bright color against the white sheet and I reach up, smoothing it down and take his face in my hands, bringing him to my lips and I kiss him, hard.

He groans into my mouth and his hips grind against mine. Our cocks are pinned between us, the friction is enough to bring back the spark of orgasm. I pull back from kissing him to look in his eyes. They are heavy with lust, need and love. "I don't think I'll ever get tired of telling you that I love you," he whispers as he presses his forehead against mine. He grinds his hips against me, bringing back the pleasure once more. Though I wish he'd take me again, like he did yesterday, I'm sore and I think he knows that.

His hips flex and grind again and he rears up, pressing his hips against mine and I look down our bodies. Side by side. "Do that thing...like the other day," I plead.

His eyes meet mine, he's concerned, I am too a little bit, but I nod, encouraging him. "Please?" I ask softly and he leans up and settles himself on his knees, our cocks rubbing together. He gathers both of them in his meaty palm and strokes upward.

My eyes roll up, feeling the friction of our cocks rubbing together and the motion of his hand, and he continues doing just that. The pleasure I thought I was feeling earlier triples and grows hotter and more intense the longer his hand strokes our cocks together. I try my best to watch him, but the pleasure is so intense my eyes can't stay open, even in an attempt to savor the sensation.

He keeps going, my hips grinding upward and his into mine. He adds his other hand, wrapping up both of us between them as we both thrust in and out of his hand, our motions are opposite, his down to my up, and it creates more friction, our barbells clicking, the tugging and…"Ahh!" I cry out as he moans. "I'm, oh fuck." My orgasm erupts from me in a garbled mess of panting and moaning, his own orgasm matches mine and then he takes my cock into his hand, stroking out my orgasm and I can feel us both emptying, this time, all onto my stomach.

I swallow and shake my head. "No," I cry out, but his hand never leaves mine as he moves quickly, leaning down and…I open my eyes to see him, a satisfied smile on his face as his tongue strokes along my stomach, licking up our combined essence. "Oh god that…fuck me, that's hot," I breathe. The sludge disappears a little more with each lick, as each little drop disappears into his mouth.

I sigh in relief when it's been cleaned up. Eric has a smirk of satisfaction on his face. "What?" I ask him playfully.

"I didn't have a towel, so." He finds another little drop, up near my shoulder and licks it up to finish his sentence.

"Good god, how far…"

He laughs, "I think there is one on the pillow above your head, though I'm pretty sure that last one was mine."

I laugh, "Are they that distinctive?"

"Yeah, I like the taste of yours," he teases with a chuckle and I wrap my arms around his neck, pulling him down onto me and holding him close. He laughs a little harder and rolls over, pulling me with him.

I extract my arms from around his neck and I push myself up, looking at him. "I don't think I will ever get tired of hearing you tell me you love me," I whisper his words from earlier back to him and his hands stroke up along my back, comforting me.

"Good, because I love you, Calvin," he tells me in a voice dripping with love and sincerity. It sends warmth flowing in my veins and my heart rate picks up a little more.

"I love you, Eric," I breathe and he wraps his arms around me, bringing me down to kiss him, hard and heavy.

eric

We spent the rest of that day in bed. Ordering room service for breakfast, then eventually turning the TV into the bedroom and we ate junk food all damn day. That day quickly rose to the top of my 'best days ever' list. Though that list contains days that involve Calvin, literally not much more.

The next day, we went out sightseeing in Seattle. We went to the Space Needle and then down into Pike's Market where we walked around and watched the fish guys. Watching them reminded me a lot of the band and how we all function well together. Working as a team when needed, but at the end of the day, we could all go home to be ourselves.

Jessica had left me a message that I never did check. At least not until after the Seattle show where everything went to hell in a hand basket. Had I checked it, I may have been able to warn the security team, but then again, the message left a lot to be desired on the details front. Jess had called to warn me that Sam had run off somewhere and she didn't know where that somewhere was and she was concerned that it might have something to do with Dex. In the end, all any of us would have been able to do is speculate further about where Sam really went.

That didn't stop the guilt though. Raine was attacked by Sam, well more so some guy from her past, but Sam was the mastermind behind the whole scheme. Lucky for Dex's instinct and an amazing crew, we'd been able to find her.

I did eventually tell Mills about the voicemail, but he'd said that they were already on alert because of some calls that Raine had received. The message, which he listened to and promptly deleted for me, was too vague to know if she knew anything further and she'd never called again. Mills reassured me that they'd done everything they could within their protocols, but it still happened anyway. When he'd told me that, I knew he was riddled with guilt over what happened too.

With what happened, I didn't get all the gory details, it brought our family together, proving we really are more than just friends. We'd done everything we could to protect what is ours.

Dex's drums got trashed, though the chick was either extremely smart or beyond stupid. Though she'd spray painted them, she punctured the heads of some of his set which are easily replaced. He'd still have to play Portland and more than likely, Los Angeles with spray painted drums. In the end, Raine was physically okay, and though I wonder about her mentally, Dex seemed to think that with time, it would all get better.

We moved on to Portland after that and then we finally ended up home in Los Angeles - where we are now. Calvin and I have made great strides in our relationship since our time in Seattle. Though I can't say he's episode free, he's certainly getting better about it. Public displays seem to be the only thing standing between us.

We have two more shows to do and we can call this tour done, and we're all pretty fucking happy about that. In fact, we all pretty much jumped off the bus in favor of cars and homes. The shows are tomorrow and the day after, so we have a little bit of time to relax, get unpacked and whatnot.

"Where are you going?" I ask Cal, who's driving his car - we'd taken it to the airport when we left for Denver, when I realize we're not headed toward my house.

He looks over at me and smirks, "Home."

I raise an eyebrow at him and remind him, "My house is the other direction."

He laughs, "Well, I haven't been able to be with you since Seattle, so I'm taking you to the closest place I can think of, my house."

I smile wider. "Miss me that much, do you?"

He looks at me as he comes to a stop at a light, his eyes narrow, peering at me. "You have no idea."

"Well, onward, Romeo," I tease him and when the light changes, he floors it and I burst out laughing. "Easy there, cowboy, you get a speeding ticket and it's going to take us twice as long to get there."

He chuckles and settles down on the race car driving.

About fifteen minutes later, we're pulling into the underground garage of his building and parking in his stall. When we climb out, he says, "Let's just grab what we can now, we can come back down later."

I give him a mischievous smirk. "Who says I'm going to let you up later?"

He laughs and starts to pull his guitars and my two basses from the back seat. I take his guitars and gently place them over his head, giving him a chaste kiss and a taste of what's to come upstairs and he smiles. That is the first time, outside of the bus when we knew no one was around, that he's actually accepted a kiss from me. It makes me smile a little more. Progress, one step at a time.

As we finished grabbing the rest of our gear, I get to thinking about his progress and I'm nothing short of amazed at how well he's managed to put his mind in a different place, letting his heart rule him, more than the demons in his mind. But I worry that it's temporary and while I should be giving him the benefit of the doubt, I can't help it.

When Calvin snaps, it's not pretty and I'm more concerned about the emotional state he'll be in than anything if it does happen again.

As we ride up in the elevator, we're both exchanging glances, torturous ones at that, and time seems to move at a crawl and so does the elevator. My cock hardens in my jeans, desperate to be free of its confinement and into Calvin's warm, wet mouth. My jaw falls slack as the vision consumes me and I can't help the shiver that slides up my spine in excitement.

"I love it when you start thinking about me like that," he chuckles.

"Like what?" I tease back as the elevator finally chimes with his floor.

"Uh huh, keep telling yourself that you ain't thinking about me sucking your cock."

My eyes widen, how…ah forget it, I go back to thinking about his mouth wrapped around my cock as he leads me down the hallway toward his apartment door.

chapter 53

calvin

Opening the door to my apartment is proving more difficult than I'd intended it to be. Excitement is coursing through my veins knowing that I will be alone with Eric in just a few brief moments. Finally it unlocks and I kick it open.

I guess I should be happy that my brothers, Talon and Dex, were occupied with their own significant others, giving Eric and I time to talk when we'd get back on board the bus after a show, but we never really got to take it very far. Though I did sneak into the shower with him one night.

As soon as we're inside, I immediately start to pull off a guitar from my back. From the corner of my eye, I catch Eric doing the same. Watching him hustle through it puts me into motion, propping them on their stand. I grab my two spare stands, the guitars are in my spare room, and set them out for him to put his on. He does and no sooner is he free than he turns on me, pressing against me, holding me to him. His mouth comes to mine in a hot, desperate kiss and I melt into his hold.

He holds me tighter as he licks my lips, coaxing me to open for him and I smile, kissing him back and giving him the access he wants. I shiver, but something doesn't feel right, I feel...the memory of when I told him about all this slides back into my mind and I remember kissing him while we were...

I wrench myself out of his hold and swallow hard. "Oh god." My voice is strained, not understanding why I'm reacting like this, reacting this way to him all of a sudden. I swallow again as I gasp for air and clutch my knees to keep from passing out.

"What did I do?" he asks in a desperate attempt to understand.

I shake my head. "I don't, I don't know," I tell him between pants. He kneels down in front of me.

"Talk to me, Cal, tell me what's wrong."

I shake my head. "I honestly don't know. I just, I feel all discombobulated, like my body and my mind are not on the same page and I," I attempt to take a deep breath. "Just give me a minute, please?" I ask him.

He nods before standing up, putting some distance between us, and he falls out of my line of sight.

Seeing him disappear settles me, but it settles me for the wrong reasons. Disappointment runs hot and heavy through my heart and I hate it that I did this to him, tonight, after things finally seemed to be falling into place. "Eric?" I shout, calling him back to me.

"Yeah," he says from behind me.

"Come here?" I ask, taking a few deep breaths and it's helping to bring me back. I can finally stand back up. When I do, he's a couple feet away from me, giving me space, giving me a chance to right myself. "It's a memory," I tell him softly. "I didn't realize it at first, but... that night, the one where I told you?"

I watch as he works through his own memory banks and then the light bulb clicks on. "Oh, oh!" He kind of gives me that funny face.

"That night I got worked up, remember, here, in this room. I guess I never thought...I didn't know that memories like that would trigger me," I tell him, my heart breaking knowing that I'm hurting him with my issues, but in the same, he seems to understand.

What he says next solidifies it. "Your bedroom?"

I shrug. "We can try." But my hesitation is enough to anger him.

"Well, then we can very well go back to my place too," he huffs.

"Please don't be angry with me," I plead. "I didn't intend for this to happen, in fact I didn't even know it would. Eric, think about it, every place we've been has been new, has been sans memories and well, now where we've been has been good ones, but...but that doesn't mean that this won't come back from time to time. I really don't need you being cross with me for something I can't control all the time. I didn't even know I needed to control something until it was too late." I start to lose steam on my argument and Eric doesn't seem to have changed his tune very much. "Maybe this was a bad idea. I'll take you home." I stand up a little straighter, pissed off at myself for my reaction and even more pissed off at the fact that he's acting like this.

I grab my keys off of the table near the door and his hand stops me. "I'm not mad at you, Calvin, I am never mad at you. How can I be?"

His words slide over me, but I feel no relief, no resolution to how I feel about him getting pissed off. "You can be mad at *them*." The last word is dripping with disdain. "All you fucking want, Eric, but it doesn't change the fact that your being pissed at them is something I have to see."

"And what they did to you is something I have to witness and face. Do you have any idea what it's like, I mean truly like, to watch the person you love fall apart at the seams? Watching them run throwing up into the toilet after you've had sex with them? No, Calvin, you don't."

His words sting and I step back from him, taking my hand from his roughly, clutching my keys. "Get your stuff. I'm taking you home," I say sourly.

"No, I'll take a cab."

"You're being ridiculous."

He steps toward me. "No, I'm not. If you take me home, we will talk, all will be better and we will end up fucking in my stairwell because that is the only place we haven't managed to fuck everything up and that is not what I want."

"Then what the fuck do you want, Eric? Please enlighten me."

His face falls and he looks away from me. "If I have to explain it to you again, it's not worth the effort."

"You want me to be cured, you want me to magically snap my fingers and wipe away all traces of my past. You want me to be this magical perfect lover for you, Eric, and I'm not and I don't know if I ever can be." My voice grows more angry with each passing word. "You knew this, you fucking knew what I was about when you pushed for this. You said that it didn't matter, that you didn't care and that you would be here for me, to help me, to guide me. But yet every time something happens, you get all butt hurt like I stole your fucking cookie. It is not personal, Eric, none of what happens to me is. I need you, and I fucking want you and I am fighting this, fighting the man I thought I'd been conditioned to be, fighting the impulses I have to revolt from you because it's what I was trained to do. This is not easy on me and you fucking know it."

I take a deep breath and a couple of steps back, waiting for his backlash and it doesn't come, so I continue, "And no, Eric, I do not think seeing me fall to pieces is a pretty sight. In fact, it would scare the living shit out of most people, but not you, no, you turn it into some reason to be selfish, to be a baby about it. I'm sorry, Eric, but it isn't about you. It never has been and it never will be about you. If it were about you, don't you think we'd still be sucking each other off in the shower?"

"That's all we've been doing," he grumbles.

I throw my hands up in frustration. "Your dick does not rule the world, Eric Richardson," I snap, tossing my keys on the couch. "Drive yourself home," I tell him as I grab one of my suitcases and I head for my bedroom, pulling it behind me. As soon as I clear the door, I slam it hard behind me and fall against it, sliding down to my ass and banging my head against it.

"Fuck! Fuck! Fuck!" I shout with matching bangs against the door. After the fourth I stop as reality slides through me. I'll take my black sludge over this feeling any day.

chapter 54

eric

I groan in frustration as he walks away from me, slamming his bedroom door shut. I reach for my bag and decide that running away from this is the wrong reaction to have. My reaction was all wrong and while I want to walk away and let things cool down between the two of us, fear that we might never resolve this keeps me in place.

I pull the pack of smokes from my guitar case and step out onto his patio. I need to cool down before I go knocking on his door. I need to figure out how to explain to him why I said the things I did. Well, I know why. Seeing him fall apart is one of the scariest, most gut wrenching things I could ever imagine. Whether the case is mild, like just now, or severe like the first time we tried to be together, it's just all kinds of fucked up and I'm never angry at him. I'm angry at his past. Angry for all the reasons he was put into that situation, which of course brings back the memory of the phone call and that fucking voicemail. I hang my head after lighting up. The smoke fills my lungs, making them sting with their starvation for oxygen, but then I exhale.

With each exhale, I release all the tension in my body, all the hatred I have for Calvin's father and what those doctors did to him.

Fuck, he'd been doing so well and I knew, I knew the other shoe would fall eventually. I knew that eventually we would be right back here, where we are today, but I never thought I would have this type of reaction, that I would get pissed off at him, and I'm actually not. In fact, he said all the right things to make me think the opposite, to make me change my tune, but he walked away from me before I could say anything to him.

I shake my head before pulling another drag from my cigarette.

"Why are you still here?" I hear Cal behind me and I jump, turning around quickly.

"I...I'd planned on coming and talking to you, I just," I run my hand through my hair, "I needed a minute to clear my head."

"I'm not sure we have anything to talk about. You've made how you feel very clear, Eric. You say so much, say you'll be here, you'll support me, but when something happens, you...I don't know, you just make it all about you."

"I know. I, fuck Cal, I didn't mean it to come out the way that it did."

He raises an eyebrow at me. "That may be so, but it came out that way."

I pull a drag from my cigarette. "No, I was angry and frustrated because you'd lost it again. I guess some part of me had expected the shoe to finally drop but then when it did, I got so angry with everything, except you, that I just...I don't like seeing you like that. It breaks my goddamn heart and I want to take it all away from you, shoulder it for you, or at least lessen it for you."

"You can't, Eric. You know this. I don't know when something is going to trigger and god forbid it ruins your plans when it happens."

"Dammit, Calvin. That's not...that is not what any of that was about. It was my frustration spilling over about not being able to help you, not being able to fix it or take it all away. It's me being pissed off at what's been done to you, because goddamn no one deserves that history, especially not you."

"But that doesn't change the fact that it's real and it happens to me, Eric. I can't fix it. I can't make it just wash away, I can't. God knows I wish I could. I would just rip those memories from my mind if I could, but it's obvious that I can't because if I could, I would have done it by now. Whenever we are together, I fight it, and sometimes I have to fight harder than others. But today, just now, I didn't know I needed to put my blinders on, I didn't know that I needed to do everything I could to stop it from happening."

"I know and I'm sorry. I was and am being very selfish and I have no right to be that way." I snuff out my cigarette in his butt can on his balcony and step closer to him. "I'll go," I breathe. "Maybe we both just need some time to chill."

Without warning his lips are on mine, hot and hard. I pull back, shocked by his attack, though it's far from unwelcome. "Stay?" he breathes.

I give him a concerned look, the look reflects the words flowing through my mind. "When you fall apart, it scares me to death. I'm going to be selfish and tell you that I don't know if I can handle another episode today."

He cocks his head and asks me, "Why does it scare you?"

"Because I never know which you will be there, this you or dark you. Dark you isn't fun, Calvin, and that hurts me more than you throwing your keys on the couch and telling me to drive myself home. I know I'm sounding selfish again, but that side of you says some seriously hurtful stuff. And no matter how hard I try to convince myself that it isn't you, I wonder sometimes if it is."

"I cannot promise you an episode free night, unless we have a sex free night and I'm not going to lie, I do not like the idea of that one bit. I've missed you, I miss you-"

I can't stop the kiss from happening, it's like my heart took over my body and forced me to kiss him, shutting him up, and he moans, melting into my arms as I wrap my hands around him. Sliding my tongue along his sends my heart racing and blood whooshing through my ears, defining me to everything but his soft whimpers of pleasure as I kiss him harder.

After a few more strokes of his tongue, I pull back. "I'm not staying so that I can get in your pants," I tell him, feeling the need to justify why I'm kissing him. "If it happens, it happens, Calvin. I have no expectation that it will, but I'll be dammed if I don't at least hope for it. I've missed you too."

He gives me a small smile before stepping out of my embrace and grabbing my hand. "Then let's go make a new memory,'" he tells me as he leads me toward his bedroom, the one he came out of, the one he ran away to minutes ago.

"Why'd you come back out?"

He turns to look at me. "I smelled your smoke. I couldn't understand why you stayed."

I smile at him. "I stayed because leaving things unresolved isn't how this is going to work between us. We talk thought things and a lesson learned tonight is that when we're both so heated, maybe we need to separate and think before we blow up at each other for no reason."

"Or maybe we're better at this than we both think we are." Calvin smiles back at me as he ushers me into his room. Though I've crashed at his place a hundred times, I've never actually been in his room. Only caught glimpses of it through a partially opened door.

His room is decorated in browns, blacks and shades of grey; similar to the rest of his apartment. It holds a masculine touch, but yet it's something that still screams the Calvin I know and love.

He closes the door behind me and with barely a heartbeat to spare, he kisses me, pulling my lips to his as he pushes me backward toward the bed, toward what I desire most from him. I smirk. "What?" he breathes against my lips.

"Make-up sex."

"Mhmm," he murmurs before pressing his lips against mine once more.

chapter 55

calvin

Kissing Eric has made me almost frantic, eager and desperate. I've never felt the desire I'm feeling right now. I want to put our fight behind us and while sex probably isn't exactly the right way to do that, I can't stop now.

I pull his shirt over his head and I lean down, kissing along his chest, down his abs until I get to the waist of his jeans and I start to unbutton them. I want him in my mouth, need him to feel me. I don't know what has come over me, but I am more determined than ever to prove to him that I can do this, that I will do this and that we will work through all of this madness inside me.

I pull his jeans wide, pulling the button fly free quickly. "Whoa, easy champ." His hand cups my chin, lifting my face up to look at him. "Where's the fire?" he asks softly.

"I don't know, I just, I want you, Eric."

He smiles at me and releases my chin, I go back to pulling his pants down, freeing his hard-on and wasting no time I suck it into my mouth quickly. My barbell clicks against his and the sound sends shivers racing down my spine and my cock hardens in my jeans. I lower myself to my knees, stretching up, giving myself access to undo my pants.

When my cock falls free, I hear Eric hiss and I look up at him through hooded eyes, peeking through my eyelashes, and he shivers. I taste a drop of pre-cum falling from his cock and I let it slide over my tongue, coating me and coating him. He tastes sweet with only a hint of bitterness to him and it tastes like heaven, like home.

I grip my cock in my hand and start to stroke it slowly. Pleasure forces my eyes closed as I continue sliding my tongue over his cock, and bringing my other hand up to stroke him in time with my mouth.

But I don't stay there long. I let my hand slide down to his sack and I roll his orbs between my fingers. His legs are trembling with pleasure and an inability to spread his legs wider because of his jeans, but it doesn't stop me from sliding my hand along the crack of his ass and I watch his whole body as it trembles with pleasure.

A wave of my own need slithers down my spine, sending goosebumps flying over my skin.

"I have an idea," Eric says above me. His voice is full of husky lust and I'm turned on that much more. He extracts his cock from my mouth and I pout. He chuckles. "Stand up." I do and he starts to toe off his shoes. Once they're off, he goes for his socks and his pants. I am so enraptured watching him that I don't move. I catch his sly little smirk as he wiggles his ass before climbing up on the bed. He lies down on his side, then says to me, "You coming?"

I smile and very clumsily get to work on sliding my own shoes and pants off my body and I climb up on the bed. "Turn around," he says as I'm about to lay face to face with him and suddenly his idea clicks for me. I smile and turn around before laying down, my cock in his face, his cock in mine.

He wastes no time sucking me into his mouth and I'm spurred on, grabbing his cock in my hand and then placing the tip between my lips and flicking my tongue against his cock.

Fuck, it's nearly impossible to concentrate on what I'm doing with him sucking on my dick like his life depends on it. Pleasure causes me to pause more than a few times and then he lets me free of his mouth only to slide his tongue along the seam of my sack and I moan out my pleasure as he makes his way closer to my entrance. Toying with it with his tongue and then his finger. "Ah fuck," I cry out when his finger penetrates me.

That initial spark of pain fades away quickly as he continues sliding himself in and out of the tight ring. The pleasure is so intense that I forget I have his cock in my face. I suck it into my mouth a little harder than I'd intended and he grunts in shock or pain, I'm not sure which, but I back off, slowing my pace.

He continues working his finger in and out of me and the pleasure is getting to be too much that I feel my cock twitching and my orgasm is building hot and fast. I pull off his cock and cry out, "I...slow down." He slowly pulls back from me, but not before licking my cock free of the mess it's making. My whole body trembles when his tongue grazes my barbell. Unable to hold myself on my side anymore, I fall onto my back, freeing myself of his hold and he does the same thing, but not before taking my cock gently in his hand.

His intention is clear, keeping me hard, keeping me primed, and it works wonders before he lets me go and climbs off of the bed. "Where are you going?" I ask, almost a little angry.

"We need condoms and gel," he tells me with a wink as he walks out of my room, to his bag, and I shiver, grabbing hold of myself. Keeping myself primed, much like he was doing. I've noticed that the more worked up I am, the easier it is for me to stay that way. The more I give myself pleasure, or receive it, the easier it is for me to block out everything else.

Eric returns and stands at the foot of the bed, watching me stroke myself and I run my hand along my stomach, up to my chest as the pleasure of knowing he's watching me spurs me on a little more. "Fuck, that's hot," he groans as he tosses a couple condoms on the bed and the bottle of gel. He's also pulled out a towel, one of the white ones I know he carries for shows. "Can we try something?" His voice is soft, hesitant and I look up at him.

"What do you have in mind?"

"Me, taking you from behind?"

I still, trying to freeze the memories in their tracks.

"You mentioned new memories. I'd like to try and give you some new ones there too." His voice is filled with so much love and concern, but there is a hint of fear too. "I don't want to trigger you, but…but I think that if we can wipe away some of that, we can…you can move past it a little bit more."

I give him my own sad, concerned smile and I nod slightly.

"If it's too much, we will stop."

"Shh, it's alright, Eric. I'd like that very much, to have a new memory and more than anything, I want it with you." I roll over, so that I'm on my stomach, pinning my cock between me and the sheets. His cock is right in my face and I reach out with my tongue, catching the tip, and his cock jumps. I smile, pushing myself forward, pulling his cock into my mouth as far down my throat as I can manage before pulling back off of it.

"Keep that up and you'll be stroking your own cock," he teases and I smile around his erection in my mouth and let him go with an audible pop. He kneels down, capturing my mouth with his and my heart rate increases, sending desire hot and heavy through my veins as I get up on my knees, opening myself up to take him the way he wants to take me. His breath hitches when he realizes what I'm doing.

I pull back from our kiss. "Take me, Eric," I breathe and I watch as love turns to lust in his eyes and he stands up. His cock is close enough for me to grab, but I don't reach for it. Instead, I let him do what he is going to do, let him take control of the situation, if only for a few minutes.

Fear starts to replace desire in my veins and I'm scared enough that I start to tremble when Eric climbs on the bed with me.

I feel him put a towel down under me, saving the bed from getting sprayed. When he's done, I know he sees me shaking when his hand gently comes to rest on the small of my back. I jump inadvertently, but I am able to calm down quickly once his warmth registers. My heart is pounding in my chest when I hear the rip of the foil packet. I close my eyes, visualizing Eric, the first time he took me. How gentle he was, the wondrous, curious smile that spread across his lips as he pushed himself into me.

I feel both his hands glide up my back. He's attempting to relax me and it works. My back arches down and I am better able to settle into waiting for him to proceed. He keeps one hand on my back, holding me there, but also reminding me that he hasn't gone anywhere. It helps keep me here, with him, and not in my head with the sludge.

"This is gonna be cold," he warns before he drops the lube right onto my entrance. I jump again but his hand on my back moves in a soothing pattern and I feel his fingers rubbing along my entrance, working the lube on his fingers and then I feel the gentle pressure as he pushes in. His hand on my back moves once again, it's his way of helping me relax without telling me to do so.

I take a deep breath and put my head down on my forearms, holding my upper body off of the bed and I do my best to relax, to settle down, and it seems to work when he presses into me farther. The pain returns, but it doesn't last, his fingers won't let it as he strokes in and out gently, helping me to feel the pleasure coming from his actions and I can't help but feel exactly that.

I let out a rush of air from my lungs as he pushes a second finger in, joining the first, stretching me, helping me to better accommodate his girth. There is that sharp burning sensation that is cooled again when he moves his fingers in and out of me.

His hand comes off of my back and I tense up again. "Easy, Cal." His voice is soft and comforting as he adds some more lube to his hand. The cool helps settle the burn as he adds a third finger and then I hear the squirt of lube, but feel nothing more as he takes his cock in his other hand, preparing himself to take me.

When he's satisfied, he pulls his fingers out slowly before replacing them with the head of his cock, pressing against my entrance and when he pushes past that barrier, I'm immediately transported back to that hospital room, back to the room where I was... my entire world falls black.

chapter 56

eric

Blood rushes through my ears in fear and anger. "Calvin?" I shout at him from across the room.

I flipped his fucking switch, I fucking did this to him. Fuck. "Calvin?" I need to stop this, stop him, how? How do I take back control of this situation?

I couldn't pull myself out of him fast enough the moment I realized he'd completely checked out on me. His demeanor turned cold, his body tensed up in ways that should be completely unnatural for any one. What happened afterward was well, words can't even explain it. He turned possessed by something. I would have never believed a person could switch so fast before. Go from perfectly fine to manic faster than a speeding bullet.

I can't pull my eyes away, I'm frozen as I watch him writhe in pain from some unknown memory. Tears streak down his face, his body is contorted in ways that shouldn't be possible. His hand is gripping his cock so hard that I can see it turning purple. He's screaming out, begging it to stop, begging 'him' to stop.

Calvin writhes on the bed, screaming in pain, much like he was that first night, the one with the dream, but this time he has his cock in his hand. He starts stroking it like his life depends on it.

His eyes are open, wide with fear, completely glazed over as if someone has shocked him. "Calvin?" I shout again.

Realizing that my shouting at him from here is doing no good, I rip the condom off, my cock is flaccid since he checked out and freaked out. I throw the condom in the trash and go for my jeans. I can't wake him up naked. He needs to feel safe, secure.

He is grunting, crying, groaning on the bed and I want to fucking scream. I manage to pull my jeans on and then find my t-shirt. I figure the more dressed I am, the less intimidating I will be when I can finally manage to get him out of this episode.

He flips over onto his back, his hand is still stroking his cock so fucking hard that I can't...I know that can't feel good.

Finally dressed, I grab his wrist, stilling him. He switches from his hand pumping to his hips sliding up and down with his cock inside his fist. "Fuck!" I fight his strength. Fuck me, I hadn't realized he could be this strong. I struggle trying to separate his cock from his fist, pulling his arm up and away, but he is determined. The harder I pull up and the further away I get, the higher his hips get. I have got to separate him from his cock.

"I just have to come, if I come, he'll stop. It will...I just have to..." His voice is a strangled, garbled mess, I'm barely able to make it out. My heart rips in two and I'm spurred into action once again and I find the strength to finally free his cock from his grip. I watch in horror as he falls back onto the bed and the other hand finds his cock lightning fast and the process starts all over again.

"Jesus fucking Christ," I growl as I take his other hand in mine and I pull it away from his dick, adrenaline courses through my veins like fire. With nothing else to do with his hands, I manage to pin them up near his head and I lay across his stomach. I'm trying hard not to squish him, but I have to put some type of a barrier between the two of us. I have to stop him from grabbing himself. He's writhing, crying out, screaming for me to get off of him, but I know he hasn't come back to me yet.

His hips are still doing their best to thrust upward, seeking release, and I press into him a little harder.

I never, not in a million years, thought that someone could go into full nightmare mode without being asleep and this is some seriously scary shit. Finally his hips settle a little. He cries out and he shudders under me as I feel the first few drops hit my t-shirt, on my back.

"Fuck!" I growl as I realize that he's come, all over me and himself without any contact from anyone or anything, but his body instantly relaxes and his eyes close in defeat, fresh tears trickle down his temples and on to the bed.

My heart shatters into a million pieces and the adrenaline flowing through my body starts to wane a little, but I hang my head in defeat.

This is my fault. I did this to him. I set him off. He'll never forgive me for this, hell, I don't know if I can forgive me for this, not now at least.

I knew I should have let it go, after the minor episode in the living room, I knew he was primed up, I knew his darkness was lurking in the corners and I just had to ask him. I shake my head and release his arms as I feel no more fight left in him, though the tears still trickle down his temples, he still hasn't returned to me.

I don't know how to be here, to handle this, when he comes to. I haven't got a single fucking idea what frame of mind he's going to be in and all I feel like doing is falling to pieces. But I can't. Not now.

I get up off of the bed and watch him closely. He's calm, but his breathing is still pretty intense. That had to be like a workout for him. I take a deep cleansing breath and try and find my center, try to wrap my head around what's just happened.

I start to pace the room. My mind is a raceway of thoughts rolling past at two-hundred miles an hour. Stay, go, wake him, put him in the shower, clean him up, let him be, wake him…it's all a jumbled mess.

After a couple of minutes, he answers that question for me when I hear him softly snoring on the bed. Though still naked, he's managed to find some comfort somewhere and falls asleep.

Biting back my own sadness, I pull the covers from the other side of the bed, but grab the towel and gently clean him up before covering him up. He rolls over and snuggles in on himself and my heart is in my throat.

I lean down and gently kiss his forehead before walking out of the room and gently closing the door.

calvin

I vaguely remember waking up at one point during the night to throw the covers off of me because I was hot, but then I started shaking with a cold sweat. All I really remember thinking was, fuck, I hope I'm not getting sick, before rolling back over and falling back to sleep.

When I come to, I look at the clock, it's eleven-thirty. It has to be nighttime because my room is pitch black. I feel like I've slept for days and…I shake my head, dismissing a memory before I capture what it was. I get out of bed and notice that something is off. "Why I am I upside down?" I ask myself and I shrug it off, unable to fully understand how I ended up upside down on the bed. I walk around the bed, catching myself on something on the floor. I reach down and find…jeans? Why would these be on the floor? I shake that off too before I step into the bathroom, flipping on the light and I'm blinded by it. I rub my eyes to adjust to the brightness before heading toward the toilet, reaching for my boxers only to realize that I'm not wearing any. "Fuck, how drunk did I get last night?" I grumble to myself, then a massive wave of nausea overcomes me so fast I don't have time to think about it before I'm hurling into the toilet. Cold sweat breaks out over my entire body as I keep heaving into the toilet.

But I feel fine. In fact, I feel like I do when I hurl from…

It's like a sledgehammer hitting me, sending me hurling into the toilet again. The memory slides inside, flashing before me. Eric, here, kissing, fighting, arguing, talking, kissing, making up, walking into the bedroom, kissing, sucking, licking, sixty-nine, leaving, lube, condoms. I want to try something…what is it…I'd like to take you from behind.

I hurl into the toilet again as the nightmare consumes me. Sliding back into the institution and being raped, being forced to come, being…. "Oh! My! God!" I scream as I hurl into the toilet once more.

Eric…where…

Oh god…Fuck!

I manage to swallow back the nausea a little bit. My stomach is empty as hell, nothing is left to come back up anymore anyway, and I stumble into the shower. Unsure of what to do, I clean myself off, brush my teeth and get dressed as fast as I possibly can. I have to go find him, I have to… fuck, he is never going to forgive me for this. If he tucked me into bed and left me alone in the dark, then he's not here, he obviously doesn't…I hang my head, shame wracking my body to the point of throwing up again. He will never forgive me for this.

chapter 57

calvin

I race out of my room, down the hall toward the living room. "Shit." Where are my keys? The couch. I hit the light switch near the front door and turn around and scream, falling back against the door as Eric sits up stick straight on the couch.

"What the...oh shit. Cal, you all right?"

My breathing slowly settles, returning to normal. "You didn't leave," I breathe as I fall to pieces on the floor in front of my door. I slide down, putting my head in my hands as I fight to find what I need to say to him, to apologize to him, but there's nothing. He's here, he didn't leave, he didn't...sobs rack through me and the next thing I know, Eric is lifting me up off of the floor.

He carries me somewhere, the couch, and sets me back down before moving away from me. I don't blame him, I'd move away from me too. "I'd never leave you like that. I," he hesitates, "I didn't know what you were going to be like when you woke up. I figured the last place I should be was in your bed, with you."

I shake my head. "Eric, I am so fucking sorry."

He doesn't say anything.

I wipe at my eyes, trying to clear them up so that I can see and I look up, look to him, sitting on the opposite side of the couch, his hand on his forehead looking like he's been bulldozed. His expression is stoic and unreadable and I don't like that, not one single bit.

"Eric, please? I'm sorry."

"Stop, alright, just," he puts his arm down along the back of the couch, "Stop apologizing, Calvin. I don't want your apology. You're not the one who needs to apologize for any of this. I should have never even considered trying to do what I did. I knew you were already high strung because of what happened earlier, and I still pushed it. You don't need someone pushing you into something like that." He pushes himself up off of the couch and goes to stand near his stuff, which has been moved into a pile, organized and ready to go. I cock my head at him. "I'm glad you're okay," he says as he picks up his bass and throws it over his head.

I'm stunned into inaction, unsure of what I should be doing in this moment, but it is clear to me that his guilt is getting the better of him right now and I don't know what else to do besides let him walk out the door. "I don't want you to go," I breathe.

"I don't want to go either, but I, I can't look at you right now without feeling guilty."

"Feeling guilty is pointless, Eric, and you fucking know it." My voice is laced with anger and frustration. "You didn't do that to me, you didn't…it had nothing to do with you," I tell him.

"Yeah, this time it did, Cal, this time it was me. I should have known you weren't ready for that, I should have stopped or tried something else that worked better, but I didn't. I let my dick do the thinking and look where it put you. I'm surprised that you even remember any of it." His back is still turned to me, but by the time his speech is over, his voice is soft, thoughtful and laced with the pain I know he's feeling over what happened.

"I remember, though it took me more than a few minutes after waking up. But once I realized what happened, I…I was headed to your house. I only turned the light on so that I could find my keys on the couch."

He turns around to face me, pain marring his beautiful features. "I could never leave without first making sure you're okay. You are, so I'm going to go."

"But I'm not okay, Eric. I am anything but okay. I am a fucking mess. I…I'm not okay," I admit. The anger and frustration that fueled me before is subsiding. "I need you to stay."

He hangs his head before muttering, "I can't."

"Why?"

"Because every time I fucking look at you I want to cry. I want to fucking punch something or I want to get on a plane to fucking Iowa and start picking them off one by fucking one, starting with your father. You are too fucking important to me, Calvin Caldwell. Every time I watch you fall apart, every time your past takes over you, I want to kill something or someone. I want to destroy them for destroying you. It fucking kills me to watch it all come apart. To watch everything we'd built up on the road just completely unravel into a pile of garbage on the floor."

"You knew this was going to be three steps forward and ten steps back, Eric. You fucking knew that I wasn't going to be magically cured of everything and you're letting your guilt about it consume you, and drive you into doing the most ridiculous of bullshit actions. The most selfish thing you can do is walk out that door right now. Walking out that door means that you can't accept that this is a part of who I am, that this is a part of me that will likely never go away, that something some time is going to trigger me in ways even I don't know or understand. If you think what happened tonight doesn't scare the hell out of me, you're sadly mistaken." I stand up from the couch and hold my ground. "You stood here, in this very fucking room, and told me that it didn't matter, that no matter what you would be by my side, that you would help me through this, that you would be here to pick up the goddamn pieces when I fell apart and what? You want out?"

He doesn't say anything to me. He just looks away from me, his manhood and dignity fly right out the window. I stomp my way over to the front door.

"Of all the things I've known you to be, Eric Richardson, a coward was never one of them." I open the door for him. "Get out," I tell him, my voice is far stronger than I feel but it's enough to get my point across. He grabs his other bass, throws it over his back then he picks up his bags, balancing the smaller on his roller and he looks up, his eyes meeting mine. Despite the anger, the frustration, the pure hatred I have for him right now, that overwhelming connection is there between us. I know he feels it when his mouth falls slack. "Get out," I demand, unable to look at him any longer.

My fucked up night has just turned to pure utter bullshit and I want to break something.

He readjusts his bags, looking at me as he comes to stand in front of me. "I just need some time," he breathes.

"You're the one walking out the door, Eric, not me," I tell him and he nods, pulling him and his stuff past me and out the door. He turns to look back at me like he wants to say something. "Goodbye, Eric," I say and shut the door in his face.

The minute he's out of sight, I fall to pieces all over again. This time it's because I just saw my life, my future, walk right out the door.

chapter 58

eric

Standing in front of my mirror as I finish messing with my hair for the last time, I want to break down again. I want to fall to pieces, but I can't. I have a show to do, Calvin has a show to do, we all do. Two more times, then we're free. Two more times and then life can go back to normal, at least until we get into the studio again. Fortunately for me, I rarely need to be there with him. Dex and I often record together, laying the bass and drums before guitars and vocals.

I shake my head, dispelling the idea that this is going to be easy. I know it's not, but maybe it is for the best, maybe I'm not cut out to be the rock that he needs me to be for him. Maybe I'm not the right person for him in general.

"Keep telling yourself that, you idiot."

Everything on the outside screams that I'm okay, but everything on the inside is liquid disaster on so many levels.

"Pull your shit together, Peacock, you got this."

Yeah, even my own pep talk is nowhere near convincing, but it has to be. I have to be able to deal with this as a man, to deal with the fact that I'm a goddamn moron. That I walked out and away from the only person who's ever meant anything to me. The only person who's ever shown me what it means to love and be loved. My vow to love him unconditionally has faltered big time.

calvin

"I can't do this anymore. I'm done with it."

"Well, you have two choices, deny who you are or keep working at it."

"What about that place, the one you told me about?"

Doctor V raises an eyebrow at me. "You've reached that point?"

I stand up off of the couch and start pacing. "I can only imagine what Eric saw last night, but whatever it was scared him half to death. I'm tired of letting my past consume me, and overcome me at the most inconvenient times and I am so sick and tired of denying myself what it is that I want most."

"What's that?" Doctor V asks me.

"Eric," I breathe.

"What if I told you there might be another way?"

"You got acid around here to wash it out of my head?" I look at him, serious.

He snorts. "Sure, acid will cure you and kill you at the same time. But no, I'm serious, I have another idea that may be the solution you need. Though I can't promise a total cure, I think it could be something you need to consider. What I am actually thinking is similar to the other facility but the time it would take would be hours, not months or years."

"And why have you not brought this up before?" I ask him, stoic.

He sits back in his chair, setting his pen down on his tablet. "Because up until Eric came along and changed everything for you by coming out, you never acted like you are now. You've decided that in order for you to find peace and happiness, you need to get rid of this side of you because the one person you want to be with is Eric. So, if you're honest to god serious that this is the path you want to go down, then I have a suggestion."

"Hit me."

"Hypnosis."

I scowl at him. "Hypnosis? Like that shit where people make you do crazy things?"

He rolls his eyes. "That's for entertainment value, not for life value. People have been getting hypnotized for years to do things like quit smoking and drinking. It's not always a cure all, but if your mind is as pliable as it was to get you to this point, I would imagine that hypnosis will have a similar effect, allowing us to reverse course. But like any other addiction, you have a chance to relapse. There is not a one hundred percent guarantee that it will work. I also can't guarantee that it will curb the physical things, like the vomiting and things like that. But it's worth a shot."

"Let's do it," I tell him. "I will do anything to right this ship with Eric and if that is possible with hypnosis then what do I do?"

He smiles. "Good. But I can't do it."

"What do you mean you can't?"

"I could, but there is no guarantee that it will work, I'm not trained in it."

"Sooooo, who is and how do I get in touch with them?" I ask, hope and eagerness spread through me.

"I know a couple of colleagues. Let me get in touch with them. We can set up an initial meeting."

I sigh. "I'm not spilling my guts again," I tell him.

"No, you won't have to. I've gone before, with patients of mine. When it comes time for the discussion aspect, talking to you, things like that, they will usually let the one who knows the most do the talking. They just put you under. But I can't promise that one session will be enough, there is a lot inside your head that we need to unlock and re-lock back up, so to speak."

"Whatever it takes," I tell him with conviction and he smiles.

"Hey Jess." I hug her as she comes into my dressing room backstage.

"Hey you. How are you?"

I sigh. "A fucking mess."

"Oh no, what happened?" she asks as she sits down on the couch. I sit down next to her, leaning back against the back of the sofa, throwing my arm over the back.

"We don't have enough time for that," I sigh. "But let's just say that it's over."

She reaches over and smacks me. "Bullshit." She stands up and starts berating me. "You keep fucking telling yourself bullshit like that and you're the only one who believes it. Eric, what in the hell happened?"

"Jess, please, don't push it."

All of a sudden my door opens and Calvin steps inside, closing the door before turning around. "Tell her, Eric," Calvin says, his voice is laced with fear, and he looks positively strung out.

"It's not my place," I tell Calvin as concern and heartbreak tear through me from looking at him again.

"Jess, I assume?" Cal asks her and she nods, dumbstruck by Cal bursting in here. "It's nice to meet you, though I wish it was on better circumstances." He extends his hand and she takes it.

"Likewise," she says in her typical Jess fashion of quiet reservation.

"I do hope that you and I will have some more time to talk after this, but the bottom line about what happened last night has to do with some bullshit in my past. Some things that I'm not proud of and that I cannot always control. Your friend over there knew all of this before we started anything and when the shit hit the fan, he fled." Calvin gives me a very pointed look.

Jess turns around, glaring at me. "Eric Richardson, what in the fuck?" she scolds.

Calvin has a satisfied smirk on his face as he turns to leave my dressing room. "Oh no, you don't, Calvin Caldwell. You don't get to come in here and spew bullshit at my friend and turn around and walk out the door," I say after him.

"You, Eric, do not get to tell me you'll be there, be here for me, help me through everything, be there to hold my hand when shit gets real and then bolt when the proverbial shit hits the fucking fan. Face it, Eric, you got scared, you ran away from it because that was the easiest way for you to deal with it and now, rather than running away from you, I'm telling the one person on the planet I know that can get through to you that you're acting like an idiot." He grabs the knob on the door and swings it wide before stepping through the portal and slamming it shut.

Jess turns on me faster than I can even say what the fuck. "What in the fuck, Eric? I may not know the details about what his past entails, but why on God's green earth would you run away from the one thing that means anything to you?"

I fall back onto the couch and put my head in my hands. She's right, of course she's right. "I'm scared."

"So what? Isn't that what relationships are all about? Being there for each other, being there to comfort them when they need you, pick them up when they fall? God Eric, you've talked about Calvin and being in love with that man for years since the first night I met you. You get a little taste of what he has to offer and you fucking run away from it." She folds her arms over her chest. If I didn't know better I'd think she was tapping her toes on the floor like my mother does when she's pissed off. "I thought you were better than that." Her voice is soft and concerned now. Not condescending like I would expect it to be.

"I thought I was too," I breathe out.

chapter 59

eric

It's been two weeks since that first Los Angeles show, and the tour has ended. After the second show, the four of us went out, alone. Leaving the girls to fend for themselves. Raine and Addison had no problem letting the four of us loose on the town. We deserved it, after all, we'd just rounded out a twelve week monster tour that saw more changes than I could have ever imagined happening. Talon and Kyle getting together, with Addison, of course. Dex, the resident manwhore, was tamed by Raine, and I wish I could say that things between Calvin and I had mended, but they hadn't then and they still haven't now.

You would think that after two weeks, it would hurt a lot less than it does, but the truth is, it hurts even more.

Each day passes and every night when I lay down, alone, I feel like I've been shredded apart again and again. I've nearly caved so many times and I know that's what he's waiting for. I was the one that walked out. I'm the one that needs to make amends and make this right, but I'm not even sure where to start anymore.

Jessica has practically quit talking to me, except for her daily texts asking me if today is the day. Though she hasn't done that in the last two days so I'm guessing her patience with me has worn thin.

I dragged myself out of the house the other night and all I ended up doing was getting stupid drunk in some random bar and I had to take a cab home. Lucky for me, they called one of those places that drives your car home too because I would not have known where to even start looking for it.

I even tried to make it to Malcolm's but I got about a hundred yards away from it and memories of the two of us having dinner and drinks flooded me too hard, and rather than trying to walk them off on the beach, I turned around and went home.

It's pathetic, really. It is.

My phone rings, bringing me out of my stupor of 'poor-pitiful-Eric'. It's a number I don't recognize, but it is local. I raise an eyebrow before I answer it. "Yeah?" I snap into the phone.

"Eric?"

"Yeah, who's this?"

"This is Doctor V." I sit straight up.

'What can I do for you, Doc?"

"I'm wondering if you're free to meet with me at eleven this morning?" I look at the clock, it's nine-forty.

"I…uh sure." I say skeptically.

"Good, I'm going to text you an address. If you'd meet me there, that would be great."

"So not your office?" I ask.

"No, not today. I'm working out of a colleague's office. Mine is well, never mind, I'll text you the address and I'll see you there?"

I sigh. I don't want to deal with anything too emotional today, or ever again. "I'll be there."

"Good. See you then." He disconnects the call and within ten seconds, my phone chimes with an address downtown. I get out of bed and stumble numbly toward the shower.

I haven't shaved in, well, I don't remember, and I certainly haven't colored my hair since before the last show. In fact, I'm a hot fucking mess. My cheeks are little more pronounced, and my eyes darker, more hollow. I look scary almost.

I pick up the razor with the intention of shaving. "Fuck it," I grumble, putting it back down in favor of the sheers, and I trim myself up. I don't think I look half bad all grown out.

When I was done trimming, I cleaned up the edges and climbed into the shower. By the time I'm dressed, it's nearly ten-thirty and if I'm going to make it downtown in time, I need to leave now. I pull a Mountain Dew bottle from the fridge and grab my car keys and the pack of smokes I bought yesterday. Don't judge me, yes, I started smoking again. Can you blame me?

Yeah, you can, but whatever.

I leave my apartment, locking it up and heading down to my car.

With ten minutes to spare, I pull into a parking garage below the building I'm to go into. For being a weekday, it's surprisingly empty in here and I head for the elevator, hitting the "12" button and the doors close. For some reason, I am ridiculously nervous about meeting with Doctor V. Other than that one time, after Cal and I talked…I close my eyes, trying to shake the memory, but it doesn't leave me. Doctor V and I talked a lot that day about Calvin and his affliction and the issues he had, but I walked out of there feeling confident and reassured that this would be a good thing, that I would be able to handle it, but apparently I was wrong.

The elevator chimes and the doors slide open. There are a number of suites listed on the directory across from me and I find the suite and direction I want. There are a few people on the floor, going from here to there. There appears to be mostly doctors' offices on this floor, but most of them are of the mental health variety.

I get to the right door and the placard reads, "Dr. A.P. Morris - Hypnotist". I raise an eyebrow and shrug, knocking on the door. "Come in." A voice from the other side says, it sounds familiar but I can't make it out through the muffle of the door.

When I step inside and close the door behind me, I freeze.

"Jesus, you look like shit."

"Fuck you very much. You don't look much better yourself." It was a lie of course. Calvin looks fucking amazing regardless, and the time apart has only made him look that much hotter. "What am I doing here?"

"I asked you here," he tells me. "I wanted you to be here when I did this."

"Did what? What's going on, Calvin?" I can't hide the fear from my voice and Cal has no problem picking it up.

"I'm here because I need you back. I can't take this anymore, this distance, this…it's bullshit and I can't take it anymore, Eric."

My heart stops beating and my head starts to swim. "I'm supposed to be groveling, not you," I breathe.

"Well, I'm tired of waiting for you to do it. So, after some extensive conversations with Doctor V, we came up with a solution."

"Which is what exactly?"

"Well, my options were limited, give you up or go away for a while until I could right this bullshit in my head."

"Calvin, I…"

"Shh, please Eric, let me finish." I nod and he continues, "I was willing to go away, willing to check myself in, willing to do the work it took, but the thing about that part that scared me the most was not knowing what I would have with you when I came out and option one, giving you up wasn't even an option in my book." He takes a step closer to me. "You see, Eric, I fell in love with you years ago. I couldn't do a damn thing about it because I didn't think I was strong enough to face the demons inside me in order to make it right between us. When I finally confessed to you what I am and what's inside me, you promised to stand by my side no matter what." He takes another step toward me. "Then, I imagine whatever you saw that night scared you more than anything else I've done because whatever it was sent you packing. I realized after you'd left that night that I needed to find a way to make it right between us."

"No Calvin, I...I was scared, so scared. But what scared me the most was because I pushed you, I triggered your attack. Then once I managed to get over that aspect of it, I had to practically hold you down because you were..." I shudder, "Then it didn't matter, it wasn't until you exploded all over yourself and me that I realized where it was that you were and Jesus Christ, Cal, I, fuck, I didn't know what to think about it. I can't wrap my head around the things that happened to you, at least I couldn't, not until that moment and all I wanted to do was hunt those assholes down and kill them for what they did to you."

He takes another step toward me. "I didn't know that and I am truly sorry that you had to witness that, Eric. I will never be able to apologize enough for that night, but I can do everything in my power to make it right. I cannot erase your memories, or your fear that it will happen again, but I can try and take away some of that possibility. Which is why we're here." He opens his arms, gesturing around the small waiting room I'd entered when I came in. "Dr. Morris is an expert hypnotist. We've been working together for the last two weeks. It was a process to get to this point but we are finally here. This is it, this is the last day. This is the day where I am hoping to let it all go."

"What if it doesn't work?"

"Then I keep trying, keep coming back until it does. Dr. Morris is confident that we will break the barrier today, that he will be able to wipe everything that triggers me. Though I will still remember it and there is a chance that we might not be able to wipe out the physical stuff, like vomiting, but, like smoking, my body treats my conditioning as an addiction, so we hypnotize away the addiction and...well, I guess we will need to see. So far, the things he's done have worked."

"Like what?"

"Like this." He steps closer to me, we're now face to face, closer than we've been in weeks. He wraps his arms around my neck and pulls me down. "Kiss me," he breathes.

My eyes go wide for a moment but I can't resist his request and he knows that. I slant my lips over his. Tears sting the backs of my eyes. Feeling his lips against mine is like finding heaven and home all at once.

"Well done," someone says, not Doctor V, another man, and I'm the one that stiffens, but Calvin doesn't. His tongue, catching me off guard, slides in along mine and I shiver, melting back into his kiss.

Eventually Calvin pulls back, with a smile playing on his lips. "Kissing you, in front of other people, is pretty hot." He winks at me.

"Where do I sign up?" I murmur and Calvin, Doc V, and I'm assuming Morris is the third, laugh. I smile.

After introductions are done, Doctor Morris escorts us into an office. Quite different from Doc V's but still none the less impressive. There aren't several couches or chairs strewn across the room, but simply one leather lounge and a rolling stool. There are a couple more chairs that are out of place and likely added for myself and Doc V.

"Calvin, go ahead and lay down."

"Alright."

"Eric, why don't you grab one of those chairs and if Calvin is alright with it, take his hand."

I look at Calvin who nods. I grab the chair and move to the other side, sitting near him. He leans up on his elbow closest to me and his hand cups my cheek. "For the record, I like the beard." I smile at him and he smiles too before laying back down.

"Alright Doc, do your worst," he says as he lies down, getting comfortable.

My heart starts pounding, racing blood flows through my veins. Is this it, could this honestly be the moment that brings Calvin back to me, fully and completely? Is this the moment where we finally get a chance to right the wrongs that have kept us apart for far too long?

I've never been a firm believer in hypnosis, but I watch as Doctor Morris puts Calvin under, his body goes lax, but his hand in mine holds strong. He's found a grounding point, me. His talisman. Something he's often called me and I'm beyond honored that he wanted me here.

Doctor Morris and Doctor V switch places. I find it curious, but when Doc V starts to talk to him, I understand the necessity for him to be here. Doctor V knows the most about Calvin and his history. He's known Cal a long time.

"Why are you doing this?" Doctor V asks Calvin.

"For Eric and for myself." His voice is stoic, but hearing my name, even in his subconscious state of mind sends a thrill through me.

"Tell me, Calvin, what is it that you want to forget?"

"The institute, the training they put me through." Again his voice is almost mechanical, it's strange, but I know it's working. "The rapes, the fears, the worries and social stigmas of being gay."

My heart breaks listening to Calvin as he spells out the details of much of his past. But I get why he's doing it. Doctor V is trying to take those memories of Calvin away from him. He puts more emphasis on the physical and mental response that he has to things related to being gay and what they mean. Calvin's responses are sometimes revulsion until Doctor V or Morris step in and help him deal with it, pulling it from him, extracting his need to feel those things.

The longer Calvin is under, the calmer, more relaxed and complacent he becomes, the progress is staggering until I hear the words that follow. "Calvin, Doctor Morris is going to count to thirty and when you wake up, you will have no memory of the things you watched while in the institute, no memory of what happens when you think gay thoughts, no memory…" Doc V continues on for a few more minutes before switching places with Doctor Morris.

"One, two, three…"

"I think he'll be pretty good when he's done. I cannot promise to have taken it all away, but I do hope that it's enough that you two can try again." Doctor V's hand comes to my shoulder. "He really does love you." I look up to him and he smiles. "You're good for him. Despite what you might think when it comes to his triggers and his episodes, you're always what brings him out of them. Even in a subconscious state of mind. That, my friend, speaks volumes about what you mean to him."

"Twenty-six, twenty-seven," Doctor Morris continues counting.

"Thank you, Doc," I whisper.

"Bring him in, in about a week. I want to talk to him, see how he's doing. And by the way, I drove him here today. He wanted to go home with you."

I smile, "Thirty."

All of sudden Calvin's hand squeezes mine as he wakes up. I look at him to judge how he's doing. "Hi," he breathes.

I fight back the happiest tears as I smile at him. "Hi," I breathe back.

He comes up quickly, planting his lips over mine, and the kiss is desperate. I don't have a chance to figure out if it's desperation for me or something else before he pulls back with a gasp.

"What's wrong?" Doctor Morris asks quickly.

Calvin shakes his head. "Nothing." I watch as he swallows. "Nothing is wrong, nothing." His eyes dart to mine and the biggest brightest smile you can possibly imagine spreads across his lips. "Well, not nothing." He winks at me and his eyes dart quickly toward his feet and then back to looking at Doctor Morris.

My eyes trail down his body, and I snort. "Well, okay then," I murmur. He's hard and I can see the outline through his jeans. I smirk in approval.

chapter 60

eric

We stuck around the office for a little bit while the two doctors traded off asking Calvin questions, but eventually I grew impatient and so did Cal. He was eager to get out of there and I had to agree with him, I was too.

Once we are finally in the car, I am doing my best to drive, but Calvin has other ideas.

"How long until we get to your place?" he asks as soon as we get in the car.

"I don't know," I laugh. "That's going to depend on traffic."

"Well, step on it."

I look over at him and ask him, seriously, "It really worked, huh?"

"I think so, but the only way to know for sure is to get home so that I can attack you."

I laugh. "We could get a hotel room?" I tease. "There's a few places not far from here."

"Don't tempt me," he teases as I pull out of the garage.

The drive back to my place is pure torture, no thanks to Calvin. He doesn't leave me alone. Well okay, he's not torturing me on purpose, but he is definitely having a hard time keeping his hands to himself. The sexual tension between us grows hot and heavy and the closer we get to my house, the harder it falls over us and I can't wait to fucking get home.

When we finally pull into my parking lot, Cal is all but bouncing in his seat. I can't help but smile and chuckle a little bit. "You're wound up," I tell him.

He gives me a serious look as soon as I pull into a parking spot. "Make-up sex."

Those three little words have me throwing the car in park and ripping the keys from the ignition as quick as I can manage. "Well then, let's go."

I climb out of the car and he follows me as I start toward my building. "Hey," he says, stopping me in my tracks and he puts his hand in mine. "That's better." He smiles.

"I think I'm going to like this new you." I say with a grin.

"God, I hope so," he replies.

"Hey, you do understand that I was honest to god scared to death that night. I never realized the depth of the depravity that you were dealing with until that night. It was quite possibly the scariest thing I've ever seen in my entire life and I didn't know how to deal with it."

"Eric?"

"Yeah?"

"Shut up, it's in the past, I don't want to talk about it anymore. Neither one of us handled it very well and we've both suffered enough for it. So, I'd honest to god, like to move on and move forward."

I smile at him. "Alright. That I can do." I hold open the door of my building for him and he steps inside, never letting go of my hand as we walk toward the elevator and while we wait. I am desperate to kiss him, and I want to, but I'm afraid of pushing it. He took the initiative to take my hand, and until he kisses me in front of true strangers, I have no desire to test unfamiliar waters anymore. "Shit," I say as the elevator arrives.

"What's wrong?" he asks.

"I, um, I don't have any more condoms," I murmur as we step inside the elevator.

He presses me against the back wall, my cock grows hard instantly as his hand grazes over me in the lightest of touches. "I'm clean," he breathes. "I know it's not ideal but it's fine if you don't have any."

I smile. "I am too and well, it has to be, otherwise we have to go get some." He shakes his head. "Well, okay then."

He presses his lips to mine as we ride up in the elevator and I wrap my arms around him, desperately pressing him against my body. I feel like I can't get close enough to him and it takes every ounce of willpower to not strip him naked in the elevator.

Luckily, the elevator is quick and we pull back as my floor chimes, but he doesn't go far. In fact, he walks backwards and I forward, without releasing me, or me releasing him. It's awkward but it makes me smile none the less. When we reach my door, I put the key in the lock and open it.

I chuckle when he grabs me by the collar of my shirt and pulls me inside my apartment. "Come here," he says as he pulls me down for yet another kiss and I kick my apartment door closed behind us. As soon as he hears it click shut, he's practically ripping my shirt from my body and I pull back, giving him the moment he needs to toss my shirt aside.

I waste no time and pull his up and off of him as I push him backward, down the hall toward my bedroom. We're both smiling and laughing until I press him against the end of the hallway wall and drop to my knees.

"Oh god," he groans as I rip open his jeans and pull them down swiftly. His cock springs free and my hand grasps on to it. I waste no time wrapping my lips around him and sucking him down.

His hand slides into my hair, pulling off the tie so that he can fist it in his hand and I shiver. Leaning back, I release his cock from my hand and pull my own jeans open and finally free my throbbing erection and grip it in my hand.

Pleasure soars within me as I suck his cock into my mouth and stroke my own in time with my mouth.

After a few heartbeats and teasing licks of his cock, his hands come out of my hair and he takes his cock from me, fisting it in his hand as he strokes it for me, pushing out that little drop of pre-cum for me to take onto my tongue. Once it's there, he pulls back completely and leans down, kissing me, tasting himself on my tongue and he moans into my mouth. He pulls back and sidesteps me. Stepping into my bedroom, he forces me to watch his ass walk away, kicking off one shoe then the other, then finally kicking off his pants.

He climbs up on my bed, and I expect him to lie down, but he doesn't. He crawls into a facedown ass up position and a sliver of fear creeps into me. "Cal, I can't-"

"Yes, you can. This is the only way I am truly going to know if this worked."

"But what if something happens?" He climbs off of the bed and comes to kneel in front of me.

"If I trigger, walk out of the room."

"Cal, I can't do that." He brings his finger to my lips, silencing me.

"You can and you will. Nothing will hurt me in here. Let me work through it on my own. Walk out of the room, promise me?"

I reluctantly agree and he lowers his mouth down to my cock and he sucks me in, literally to the hilt before coming back up, leaving a nice coat of wetness before he stands back up and crawls back up on the bed.

Fuck it. I'll never know if I can do this either if I don't throw caution to the wind and take him the way he needs me to. At least if he triggers, I'll know what to expect and maybe I'll be able to walk away, or maybe not.

I walk up behind him, spreading his cheeks and placing my tongue right along his tight entrance. He moans for me and my cock jumps. The cool of my apartment is sending tiny waves of pleasure across my wet cock. I press my tongue inside, rimming him; he moans and writhes beneath me and I know I've found a sweet spot for him.

I pull back, replacing my tongue with a wet finger and I push inside him. He tenses briefly but then relaxes and I push in and pull back out repeatedly before licking my other finger and adding it to the first. Stretching him. I lick my palm and take my cock in my hand as I very awkwardly shed my shoes and push my jeans from my legs.

I lick my palm again, getting it wetter. I pull my hand free of him and he groans in disappointment before I climb up on the bed. His legs are spread wide for me to fit between them and I cup some saliva in my hand before rubbing it over him. It's not lube, but it will do the trick. I hesitate, remembering the last time I pressed my head inside, but he groans at the loss when I pull my hand away. Here goes.

I take a deep breath, pressing the head of my cock gently against him. He groans with pleasure and relaxes as I press into him a little farther. His body is completely relaxed. No tension, no worry. I push in a little farther until my crown breaks through that barrier and he tenses, but then quickly relaxes. "Oh god," he moans out. "Don't stop," he encourages and I breathe a sigh of relief.

chapter 61

calvin

Asking Eric to repeat what triggered me last time is a huge step for him. For some reason, I didn't feel any twinges of anything when I asked him to do it, no recollection of what happened to me. Though the memory is still there, it feels like nothing but a memory.

I feel him press farther into me. There is a slight shock of pain, but he pushes deeper, then pulls himself back and pushes in again until I feel him inside me. Taking me, consuming me.

"Ahh," I cry out when I feel his pelvis press against me. He stills, giving me a moment to adjust and it is uncomfortable but the pleasure I know he is about to bring is enough for me to grab hold of my cock. I stroke it gently as he pulls back out of me, then pushes back in. "Ahh fuck," I cry out as the pleasure rips through me in waves.

His pace is maddeningly slow and I want him to speed up, but I don't want to rush him either, so I settle into his slower pace. Pushing and pulling my hips in tune with him. The pleasure sparks white hot and I can't hold back the string of groans that rip from my throat as he finally starts to pick up the pace.

"Fuck," he grunts as he takes my hips in his hands, squeezing me tight, helping to guide me along his cock as I stroke my own. Getting an idea, I reach back for one of his hands. I take it and bring it around to take hold of my cock and while balancing myself, I reach with the other hand for his, bringing him down with me.

"Move your right leg, outside of mine."

"Huh?" His voice is heavy with the same lust I feel but he pulls his brain cells together and moves his leg.

"Now the other one," I tell him and he does, putting my legs between his. I stretch out on to the bed, bringing my hips down closer to the bed, but still leaving room for him to stroke my cock.

"Oh god," he moans and I feel him pull back and push in, harder than he was before and the pleasure that roars through me has my eyes fluttering up and my toes curling. I take his other hand and urge him to put it down on the bed and he does. Giving me something to ground myself on and I grip his wrist as I start to slide up and down his cock. His thrusting in is more urgent, more pleasurable and his pulling out is harder and faster. His hand keeps time with his strokes but I can tell his balance is off so I replace his hand and he balances out.

His thrusting increases, slamming harder into me and I moan, releasing my own cock. I steady myself, changing the angle once again and pleasure explodes.

He is literally slamming into me. His free hand digs into the flesh of my ass cheek, holding me hard and tight as he slams in and out of me. "Oh fuck," he cries out.

"Come for me, Eric, please?" I beg. I need his release. I want his release to send me over the edge.

All walls shattered, all barriers broken. No condom means he's going to pour into me and I shudder, my orgasm explodes from me and his follows. I feel his hot spurts pouring into me and his crying out of my name nearly tips the scales for me again. "I love you," I cry out as my orgasm finds the other side of the cliff.

His head rests between my shoulder blades, his breathing is shallow and rapid, matching mine. I feel him pulling himself from me. "No, stop," I tell him.

"What?"

I shake my head. "Don't pull out, please. Stay with me," I breathe and he returns to resting his head against my back. "I love you too, Calvin. I always have, I always will," he breathes and the warmth of his breath caresses me, warming not only my back, but my heart and quieting my mind.

I didn't throw up that day, and I haven't any day since then. Though there have been a few minor things that have triggered little episodes, they pass quickly and sometimes without even Eric noticing. Being with him has brought me the greatest joy, and being with him, free of my demons is better than anything I could have ever asked for.

Deciding we wanted our own place, together, after only a month, seemed heady and weird at first, but then I realized that this relationship has been ten years in the making, so why not. I'm putting my condo on the market and Eric has broken his lease. Though it was nearly up anyway. He and I were the first of the band to move to Los Angeles back in the day. It was where I wanted to go, and looking back on it now, Eric just naturally followed me out here. I bought while he leased. It's working out in our favor now.

We found a great house, along the beach, not too far up from Malcolm's. A place we frequent often. We've even brought the rest of the gang there and had a blast. I think Addison and Raine are working their magic to give Malcolm what he wants, which is a private 69 Bottles event.

Jessica has become a regular presence in our life. After the stunt I pulled in the dressing room, she surreptitiously passed me her number before the show and while I never used it, it was nice to have that connection to Eric if I needed it while we were separated.

Tonight the entire gang is coming over for a house warming party. The sun is setting low on the horizon, but our uninhibited view is enough to make anyone the happiest person in the world. Eric comes out on the patio where I am and wraps his arms around me as we watch the sunset together while we wait for our friends. "I love you," he whispers in my ear and I smile, leaning my head back against his shoulder.

"I love you too." I turn in his arms, wrapping mine around his neck and bringing him to me, slanting my lips over his in a warm, promising kiss.

My phone ringing in the house interrupts us. "Ignore it," he growls.

"It could be one of our friends." I release him and he reluctantly lets me go and I dart into the house, answering it before I even look at the number. "Yeah?" I answer. A habit I picked up from Eric.

"Calvin?" A woman's voice comes over the line, she sounds frail and upset.

"Yes," I say with hesitation before I pull the phone back from my ear to look at the number and there it is, the area code I'd hoped to never see on my phone again. "What do you want?" I snap.

"My name is Mary-Beth Pickens, I'm a friend of your father's."

"I remember your voicemail. What can I do for you, Mary-Beth?" I ask and now Eric is standing in my line of sight and he's fuming. I understand why he would be, everything between us finally balances out and now this.

"You're father passed away tonight, Calvin, I'm so sorry."

The words slide over me and I sit down in the chair behind me and Eric comes over, taking the phone from my hands. "What's going on, Mary-Beth?"

I can no longer hear the other side of the conversation. "This is Eric, have arrangements been made?" There's a pause while he listens. "Alright, we'll be in touch. Thank you," Eric says before hanging up the phone and setting it on the table a little too roughly.

chapter 62

eric

"Cal?" I ask again.

"Yeah?" he says when he finally snaps out of his daze.

"I'm going to go call everyone and tell them not to come."

"No, don't, please?" he asks. "We've been planning this for a couple weeks and I'm alright, I just need a minute."

I look at him, trying to assess him from more than just a lover perspective and it's hard. He looks all right, but I'm hesitant. "Are you sure?" I ask.

"Yes Eric, I'm alright, I promise." he stands up and kisses me softly. "I knew it was coming, I guess I just hoped that I wouldn't hear about it."

"Well, I'm not entirely convinced that this Mary-Beth knows much about your history with your father. I think she thinks she means well."

"She does, she means well. You asked her about arrangements?"

"I did, I guess I needed to know if there was a reason you had to go."

"Oh." He's still a little dazed. "I can't go, Eric. I won't."

"I think you need to reconsider that idea," I tell him.

"Eric, I love you more than life itself, but please, don't push me on this. I finally feel like everything in my life is going right, I, fuck," I watch as he runs his hand over his head, "I can't go back there and relive all that history. I don't know what it will do to me."

I smile at him. "I think it will give you the chance to have the closure you need, to finally seal off all those loose ends. Please, promise me you'll think about it?"

He sighs heavily and hangs his head. "Alright, I will think about it, but not tonight. Tonight is about us and our friends. Just give me a few minutes to compose myself and I will be better." The plea in his voice is matched by the plea in his eyes. He kisses me chastely once more before heading upstairs to our bedroom.

I can't help but watch after him and I wonder if he's just numb or if the reality hasn't set in. Either way, I will stand by my decision that he needs to go, but I also know that I need to respect his decision to stay here too. It might have been wrong of me to suggest cancelling tonight, but in doing so, I woke him up from his daze and maybe having friends here will be enough to bring him around.

I go into the kitchen, pulling the marinating steaks from the fridge and add some of the extra sauce before taking them out to the grill.

As soon as I set the plate down, the doorbell rings. I smile when I hear Calvin coming down the stairs, and when I look up, my Calvin is back, the numb daze is gone and I smile. "Good?" I ask.

He smiles wide. "Good."

We both walk to the door, opening it to find Dex and Raine on the other side.

"Hey," Raine says cheerfully, looking around as she and Dex come in.

"Hey, nice digs," he says as he hands me a bag, obviously put together by Raine. "Wow, you guys, this is really nice."

"The one next door is available, you know, if you two are in the market," Calvin teases and he gets the glare of death from Dex. "Oh come on, you're married now, you can't stay in that small as fuck studio apartment forever."

"Yeah, true, we can't, but well, I hadn't thought about it, I guess."

"Don't let him lie to you. He's been shopping houses since before we got off tour," Raine says from the dining room.

We all laugh and I close the door.

It isn't long before our doorbell is ringing again, this time with Cami, Tristan and their son Jaden, followed by Addison – who's showing off an ever expanding baby belly, Talon, Kyle, Mills, Beck, Casey, Tori and Rusty and before long the alcohol is flowing, the steaks are cooking and the food is being eaten up. Calvin really is a good cook and Talon makes no qualms about ribbing him for not cooking while on tour. Calvin is equally as playful. You'd never know that just a couple of hours ago he got a phone call telling him his father passed away.

We eat outside, on the patio, overlooking the water with tiki torches lighting up the space and surrounded by great friends, good laughs and good eats. This is truly what life is all about.

It's nice to see everyone be themselves. Tonight we're not 69 Bottles, tonight we are friends and we are family. Tonight we are everything that should be special about the bonds we've formed.

As the night winds down, Cami, Tristan and Jaden are the first to leave. It's getting late and despite our offer to let Jaden sleep in our room, they wanted to take him home. As our friends file out, I notice Calvin getting a little more distant. The facade of playing host is wearing off and reality is washing over him slowly.

Dex, Beck, Raine, Rusty, Tori, and Mills are the next to leave followed by the trio of Addison, Talon and Kyle. Leaving us with just Casey.

"I'm really happy for you guys," Casey says to me as we're standing on the patio. "It's a great place. Perfect for the two of you." He smiles wide.

Calvin joins us on the patio then, but I can tell that the numbness is winning. "You okay?" I ask him.

He shakes his head.

"What's going on?" Casey asks.

Calvin nods at me, giving me quiet permission to tell Casey what happened. "You remember that number?"

"Yeah?" Casey says curiously.

"That number was from Calvin's father's house back in Iowa. It called again tonight and Cal answered it without looking."

"Oh? And? Who was it?" Casey asks, looking between Calvin and me.

"It was a friend of Calvin's father. He passed away tonight."

Shock crosses Casey's face. "Why didn't you cancel?"

"Because, that's not how I'm wired," Calvin chimes in. "It was a great escape, but with everyone leaving, it's wearing off." Calvin's voice is sad.

"Well, I'll get out of here. You guys need to get your plans together and," he turns to me, "Take care of him."

"Casey?" Calvin asks.

"Yeah?" he turns toward him.

"Would you mind staying here, until we get back?" Calvin asks. My heart flutters. He's completely shattered but the pain he is feeling is bringing him around, forcing him to focus on what he knows he needs to do. Seeing him react like this, as twisted as it may sound, warms my heart. I was so concerned that he'd just let this roll off his back, let it go and move on, only to regret it down the road.

"Of course. When do you need me here?"

"I don't know. We haven't even started looking into tickets or anything," I tell Casey.

"Let me call Mills, see if he can help."

"No, don't. This is my business, we can handle it." Calvin doesn't hesitate.

"Why don't you just be here tomorrow around noon, unless we call you sooner?" I tell Casey.

"Absolutely." He nods. "I'm really sorry, Mouse."

"Thanks." His voice is barely audible and Casey gives me a concerned look. I nod, letting him know that I got this, we'll be good and he lets himself out.

I go over and sit next to Calvin. He's falling apart right next to me. "Come here," I tell him and he snuggles into me. I wrap my arms around him and he falls to pieces.

It takes about twenty minutes for him to settle himself back down and all I've done is hold him. I don't really know what to say to him and sometimes the quiet comfort is all one person needs. He sits up and whispers, "I'm sorry."

I brush the hair off of his forehead. "Nothing to apologize for, Cal." I kiss the forehead I just cleared. "Why don't you go upstairs, let me finish up out here and I'll get the house locked up and be up."

He nods numbly and stands up, disappearing into the house. I take a deep breath to find my center before I finish cleaning up the last of the glasses from the tables and then lock up the patio. I put everything into the sink and lock the front door, turn off lights and I head upstairs.

When I walk into our bedroom, Cal is curled up in a ball on top of the bed. He's changed into his flannel pants and my heart just breaks seeing him so shattered like this. I know, deep down, the anger will come. It's just a matter of when, but I know he needs to deal with this in his own way. Whether it's by talking or by quietly managing his emotions.

"Come on, let's climb under the covers."

"I'm not tired."

"I know, but it's warmer under there." I tell him. I try and smile, showing him that it's all okay, but he doesn't notice, he just stands up and pulls the covers back and crawls back into bed. I go into the closet and pull on my flannel pants, and turn off the lights. I crawl in bed with him, and he immediately snuggles up to me, whether out of habit or comfort, I can't be sure but we just lay there for hours in silence until eventually he falls asleep and I do too, long after the moon has started to set and I can see the slight glow of dawn in the distance.

chapter 63

eric

I didn't sleep very long. Knowing that we need to get moving on our plans to head out of town, I get out of bed, leaving Calvin to sleep. I head downstairs and make myself a pot of coffee. I don't usually drink the stuff, but I am too tired to really think about it. Calvin drinks it more than I do.

No sooner do I sit down at the table with my coffee and laptop is there a knock on the door. I raise an eyebrow and look at the clock. It's not even eight. I go to the door and look through it. "Cami?" I say as I open the door. "Everything all right?"

"Yeah, it's perfectly fine, I'm glad I caught you."

"Caught me?"

She shrugs and I open the door for her to come in. "Yeah, I, where's Mouse?"

"Still sleeping," I tell her, completely perplexed.

"Listen, I tried to pull Casey for another assignment for the next couple of weeks and he was pretty adamant about not doing it. I couldn't understand why and then he finally said that he needed to be here." She points to the floor. "Is something going on that I should know about?" She says in her authoritative tone.

"Want some coffee? It's fresh?" I ask her and she nods, reluctantly.

I usher her into the kitchen and pour her a cup, offering her some creamer and she takes it. "Let's go outside, shall we?" I ask her. "I don't want to wake him."

She nods her agreement and follows me onto the patio where we'd just hosted a fabulous party last night. "Last night was a lot of fun. Thank you again for having us."

I smile. "You're most welcome. We look forward to doing it again soon."

"Good," she smiles and takes a sip of her coffee.

"Right before you guys showed up last night, Calvin got a phone call from his father's house, though it wasn't his father but, I'm guessing it's his wife. Cal's father passed away last night."

Her hand comes to her mouth. "Oh god Eric, I am so sorry, why didn't you call us, cancel?"

"I didn't want that." I turn around to find a disheveled Calvin standing in the doorway. "Besides, you guys were practically pulling in the driveway when I got the news and I really needed the distraction."

I walk over to him. "I'm sorry, I didn't mean to wake you."

He smiles slightly. "You didn't, the coffee did." I hand him my cup and he takes it.

"We asked Casey to watch the house. I know he lives with a crappy roommate and I figured he could use the break. That's probably why he told you no."

"I'd really rather he go with you guys," Cami says, her voice firm.

"Trust me, where we're going, we don't need him. No one back home has even the slightest clue who I am or what I've been up to. My father and I have been estranged for more than ten years. I don't even want to go back, but I know if I don't, I will regret it, eventually," Calvin says with a sad smile. Good, my message was received.

"Well, where are you going?" she asks him.

"Maynard, Iowa. It's a little eye blink, podunk town northeast of Waterloo. It's a farm town where the news doesn't reach and the residents don't care when it does," Calvin says and that is the most I've ever heard him say about where he's from. It's not a happy subject to discuss for him, but I think he's made a point to focus on him and what it is that he needs to do right now.

"When are you leaving?" Cami asks.

"As soon as we figure out flights, which was what I was about to do when you came by," I tell her.

"Don't worry about that. I put my plane on standby at Burbank. They can take you."

"That's not necessary," Calvin cuts in.

"No, it's not, but I am going to do it anyway. Do you know what airport you'll want to fly into?" she asks Calvin who looks defeated and unwilling to argue with her.

"Waterloo something or other. There's a small municipal airport there."

"Great, I'll get it all arranged. When you know you want to come home," she hands me her card, "Just call. I'll make arrangements for them to come back and pick you up."

Neither one of us argue with her. We both know all too well that Cami gets what she wants and saying no is like signing your own death warrant.

"I really wish you'd consider taking someone with you, Casey or Beck, Mills even."

"No, I need to deal with this by myself. The worst thing I will have to deal with is sideways glances and exes," Calvin says with a slight chuckle, but I can tell there is very little humor in his voice.

"Alright, but keep the guys on standby, please, if you need them, or if things get out of hand. You know how word can spread fast,"

"Okay," I agree as she walks up to Calvin.

"I'm really sorry, Calvin. I've been there, so if you need anyone to talk to, I'm here."

He gives her a small smile. "Thanks, Cami, I really appreciate all that you're doing."

"Anytime guys."

With that, she secrets herself out of the house and I walk over to Cal. "How you doing?"

He takes a deep breath. "I'm better today, ready to get moving, I guess. I don't know. It's just all so surreal."

"How so?" I ask.

"Well, I guess I always thought that when I found out he was dead, I would throw a party. Though we kind of did. I guess I never thought that his death would mean anything to me and yet I feel so lost. I never wanted to step foot on the soil of that town ever again, but yet here I am, ready to pack to leave and go right back there again. And in a strange way, I find it hard to believe that I don't feel the hatred I once felt for that man."

"It's hard to hate those who are dead, regardless of the circumstances surrounding your history. Trust me, we've all tried to do it in some fashion or another. But as long as this is what you want, I will be right here with you."

"What if I asked you to stay behind?"

I cock my head at him. "Why on earth would you do that?"

He shrugs. "I think I can deal with it better, go and make arrangements, bury him and come home."

"You know it won't be that simple, right?"

He sighs. "It never is. I guess I can sit here and think that it will be just that simple all I want, but the fact of the matter is, it won't be."

"Do you honestly want me to stay here?"

"I want you to understand that if you come, you're not going to a place like Los Angeles, or Philly, or even Denver for that matter. People don't think the way that we do."

"You're worried about the perception, of you and I being together?" I ask stoically.

"Yeah, I guess I am."

"Are you worried about it for your sake or for mine?"

"Yours."

"Wrong answer," I tell him. "Calvin, you have to understand that I've already come out. I grew up knowing I was gay, knowing who I was and what I was. I also grew up in an environment that didn't always favor those that were different."

"But Eric, you grew up in a household that accepted the fact that you're gay. I grew up in a household that had no problem shipping me off to an institution to be reprogrammed to conform to their ways. I grew up in a world where being gay isn't normal, where being gay is a sin against God. Believe me, this isn't going to be easy for either one of us."

"I can deal with sideways glances and whispering behind my back. I'm not made of glass, Calvin, I will not break," I tell him and I mean every word of it. "I am not going to cause trouble for you. I am going so that you have someone to lean on when you will need them most. You've been away from that place for over a decade, no one knows you and all you're going to get are pity glances and condolences and I am pretty sure you want none of that, am I right?"

He nods his head.

"So, am I going with you?" I ask him, hope in my voice. I can't bear the thought of him going at this head on, alone and without someone to be there to pick up the pieces if things fall apart. I get his stoic, tougher than rocks exterior he is trying to portray, but I know that deep down, under the rock, there is a shit storm starting and I want to be there when it does. Show him that it doesn't matter who you love, love is love.

"Yes," he breathes. "I can't ask you to stay here. I need you by my side."

I smile. "Good, now let's get to work."

chapter 64

calvin

Mundane tasks are enough to channel my thoughts away from what I'm about to face. At least until we boarded the plane.

Casey showed up about an hour after Cami left. Cami called him to let him know she'd made arrangements for us to leave when we were ready and Eric and I decided that the sooner, the better.

Eric called Mary-Beth, or whatever her name is, to let her know that we were coming and that we would be there later this evening. Apparently she was thrilled at the idea, at the fact that the long lost son of Raymond Walter Caldwell was finally returning home. I am more convinced now that she hasn't a clue what she was asking of me when she called the first time.

As the plane takes off, my nerves take over. I haven't stepped foot on Maynard soil since they carted me away in the middle of the night and I vowed to never go back, no matter what the circumstances were. But yet, here I am, on a plane, about to land in Waterloo, Iowa.

Eric squeezes my hand as we touch down. I lean over and kiss his shoulder before resting my head on it. He returns my kiss by kissing my forehead. Reminding me that he's here and he has me.

"No matter what," I tell him. "We are not staying in that house. There's a small hotel just on the outskirts of town. Lord knows it was a dump ten years ago, I can't imagine it's gotten any better, so I'm sorry about that."

"Don't be. As long as I have you, I don't need anything else," he whispers before kissing my forehead and the wheels touch down.

I know it's hard to believe but something in me changed the moment those wheels went skidding across the runway. Everything about me shifted, and I hate to say it, but I feel cold, turned off. Determined to deal with it and get this over with.

When we land, the pilots pull our luggage from the plane. We only brought small suitcases for each of us, with no intention of staying longer than the funeral. I'm pretty sure we can make that move pretty quick and be out of here and back in California before the week is out.

"Mr. Caldwell?" I stand up from grabbing my suitcase and spin around to see a sweet, older lady standing there.

"Yes?" I answer.

And she walks over, handing me a set of keys, then points to a nice Volvo parked not too far away from us. "What's this?" I ask, confused.

"A Mrs. Michaels reserved a car for you. It's all taken care of." She turns and walks away.

Eric and I look at each other and then our phones both chime with a text. I pull mine out.

Cami to Eric, Calvin: The car is on me. You can return it to Waterloo when you fly home, or drive it to fly out commercial - I had a feeling you'd go that route. Best of luck, we're all here if you need us. Sending hugs.

Cami's text is almost my undoing. Her generosity is unmatched by anyone I've ever known.

"She's seriously something special," I hear Eric murmur.

"You can say that again," I say softly. "I'm not sure how we hooked up with her, or what magic Kyle has up his sleeve, but I cannot imagine a better person to have our backs."

We load up the car and set off on the hour or so drive to Maynard. Eric and I don't talk much. I think he's enraptured by the land around us. Literally, this is Midwestern farm country at its finest. It's late June and the fields are blossoming with their product. "It's mostly feed corn here."

"What is that?" Eric laughs.

"Cow food," I tell him with my own little smirk. "Some of it is sweet corn, human food."

"I've never even been in the country, let alone around corn and cows and…all that junk. It's weird." I watch him shudder. "I'll take my city life any day. And the smell. Ugh!"

I laugh as we pass through a rather ripe area and the answer of the source comes when we pass the fields surrounding us and there are no less than two hundred cattle grazing.

"Oh look, cows," Eric says with a laugh and I suddenly feel lighter, less confined. It just takes one little joke to bring me out of my slump and I'm happy about that. It's making what I'm about to do that much easier.

The farm is on the east side of town, but I remember the roads like it was yesterday. "You know, ten years and any other city would change its appearance dramatically. This… this is like walking back in time," I say as I come to a twenty mile an hour crawl through downtown. Thank god for tinted windows, but there is no shortage of stares glaring at us as we pass by. "This is probably the fanciest car they've ever seen," I tell Eric who's making a scrunched up face. "I'm sure the whole town knows by now that my father is dead and I am sure there are more than a few of them wondering whether or not the long lost son will return. I can only imagine the bullshit lies my father told when I didn't return to school." My voice drops a few octaves and I keep driving, finally clearing the other side of the city (I say finally, but literally that took us less than sixty seconds).

"Where we headed first?"

"The farm," I mutter. The closer we get, the more nervous I start to get. I'm not sure I'm truly ready to step foot inside that house again, but I know I have to.

Neither one of us says anything for the next ten minutes as we make our way down the gravel road that runs in front of the house and then I see it, off in the distance. "Nothing's changed," I mumble as we draw closer to the house.

Nothing has changed, not really, except for the five or so cars sitting in the driveway, including the sheriff's squad car. "What are they doing here?" Eric asks.

I shake my head. "I have no clue other than the sheriff and my father were good buddies back in the day. I'd imagine that's why he's here. Along with all these other people.

I turn into the driveway and pull off to the side, sort of on the front lawn, but out of the way for those here to leave when they want. I put the car in park and I stare blankly at the white farm house. It needs new paint and a couple of the shutters are crooked, but with my father getting up there in age I can imagine there wasn't much he could do about that kind of stuff without help.

The wraparound is the same, with the swing on the left, the wicker rockers on the right.

Eric reaches over, pulling my hand off the keys in the ignition and takes my hand in his, giving me comfort.

Seeing this house again brings back some of the strangest memories.

Playing in the yard, running around with my airplane when I was a kid, it's almost like a vision I can see in my head.

Then I remember the storming out of the house when my father was on a drinking binge, angry and frustrated that he'd continue to drink like a fish.

Smoking between the trees, around the side of the house.

The front door opens and someone in a police uniform comes out, stands on the porch with his hands on his hips. Well, one hand is on his gun.

"Told you this car stood out," I mumble.

I look at the man standing on the porch, obviously he's the sheriff, but he's not the old one I remember. What was his name?

"You ready?" Eric asks.

"No. But if we don't get out, we're gonna have more trouble than either one of us wants," I tell him.

"I'll get our stuff. Take your time."

I keep looking at the man, the one standing on the porch. There is something very familiar about him. "Oh hell to the fuck no," I growl, dislodging myself from the car.

"Calvin?" Eric asks from inside the car as I go charging up the front yard, right toward the man on the porch.

"Can I help you, son?" the man says and it all rings crystal clear. He jaunts down the steps toward me. Good, I don't have to go as far.

"Yeah, son, I'm sure you can help me just fine." Without even a second thought, I reach back and cold cock the motherfucker standing in front of me, knocking him down on the ground. "That, Billy fucking Winstrum, is for being a goddamn fucking pussy."

"Jesus, Calvin." I hear Eric as he comes skidding to a stop next to me. "What the hell was that for?"

"Eric, meet Billy."

"Billy?" He looks down at the man on the ground. "Oh…oh."

I hear a bunch of people coming out of the house and I look up. Fuck 'em. I crouch down next to Billy. "Feel better?" he grumbles.

"Yeah, maybe a little bit." I offer him my hand and he hesitates, then takes it and I help him up.

"Where the fuck have you been?" he asks once he rights himself.

"That depends, where did old Ray say I was?"

Billy snorts, "That you ran off."

I raise an eyebrow at him. "Really? That's all he could come up with?"

"Well, that was how it started, but then it turned into some bullshit about you getting locked up or something like that."

"That wasn't bullshit, though he was the reason I got locked up."

"You shittin' me?" Billy asks.

I shake my head. "Drop it, it's not worth it. Who the fuck are all these people?" I say with a gesture toward the porch and Billy turns around looking at the people watching over us.

"Uh, half the town."

I roll my eyes and look at Eric who still looks shell shocked that I cold cocked Billy. I shoulder check him. "Welcome to small town hell," I whisper and Eric just nods.

"Billy, Eric, Eric, Billy," I say introducing them. Billy holds out his hand and Eric takes it, despite the fact that I'm pretty sure he'd like to knock Billy out too. "What crazy son of a bitch gave you the sheriff's job?" I ask him.

"Uh, Amos passed away a couple years ago, I was one of his deputies and well, yeah, I guess they just passed the torch to me."

Amos, that was his name, but they called him something else.

"Well, let's get this over with," I mutter and I desperately want to take Eric's hand in mine, to have the strength and comfort, but I'd rather not start the rumors flying just yet.

chapter 65

eric

I was introduced to everyone in the house, including Billy's wife. Calvin gave me a sideways glance at that one.

We were then finally introduced to Mary-Beth Pickens, Ray's wife. They'd married about eight years ago and she'd moved in with him.

It became evident very quickly that she knew Calvin was gone, but not where or why he'd never returned home.

"We should probably head over to the funeral home," Calvin finally says. I could tell being around all these people was starting to get to him.

"Sure."

"Will you come back, when you're done?" Mary-Beth asks Calvin.

"Depends on how long it takes. We've been up since early this morning," he says.

"Oh sure, I...I'd just like a chance to talk, before things really get out of hand," she tells Calvin in a whisper.

"I, uh, sure," he says hesitantly, but I get the feeling he'll want to come back when we're done.

We say our goodbyes and then get back in the car. "Why in the hell did you punch Billy?" I ask him once we're finally alone.

"You mean to tell me you didn't want to when you found out who he was?"

I laugh. "Yeah, I did, but dang."

"I had a few years pent up in that swing. I doubt he fully understands why I knocked him out. He was never the sharpest knife in the drawer, too many hits to the head."

"I can see that. So obviously he's no longer into men." I cringe, realizing that I may have crossed a line.

"He's always been a closet case. It's no wonder he married her. She was the head cheerleader after all."

I cringe. "Why am I not surprised?"

"Small town living for you," he says. Seems to be his answer for everything. Though I can see the truth behind his words. Everyone knows everyone.

We head back out on the road.

"Your father had a directive which Mrs. Pickens sent over to us. All that really needs to be done is for the casket to be picked out and the times scheduled," the funeral director tells us after some conversation about the facility and whatnot. "We've made arrangements with St. Paul for the service. We can do visitation here Monday evening and then viewing and services at St. Paul Wednesday morning, concluding at the cemetery up in Sumner. You're father has asked to be buried next to his parents there."

I watch as Calvin nods, and I'm not sure he's really hearing everything the director is saying and that's okay. That's part of why I came along. To help ground him and remember all the things he's forgetting. "That sounds good," Calvin says.

"Your father is here, they brought him over this morning, would you like to see him before?"

"No," Calvin states matter-of-factly.

"Oh, kay," the director says pretty quickly, unsure of how to take Calvin's tone. I know that he's fighting with himself, that being here in this place is almost too much for him, but I know he's here because he has to be.

"Why don't you give us some time to look around?" I tell the director who nods.

"I'll go get all the paperwork for him to sign while you do that."

"Thanks," I tell him and he leaves me with Calvin. I turn to him. "Talk to me, Cal."

He shakes his head and stands up. "I just... I don't know, I've never done this before. I don't even know where to start or how to make decisions."

"It seems as though your father has already done all that for you."

"Then why can't Mary-Beth pick out his casket? Why do I have to handle all this? She was his wife for crying out loud. I swear to God that asshole is punishing me."

I close my eyes, take a deep breath and shake my head. "I doubt that is the case, Calvin, and you don't think that's really true. Maybe Mary-Beth wanted to give you a chance to say goodbye to your father in private. Maybe she wanted you to feel a part of this."

"And if I hadn't come?"

"Then I imagine she'd have handled it herself. But Calvin, you have to understand that her, along with the rest of this town, that town, whatever, has no idea why you left all those years ago. Billy's answers to that question make that clear enough. I am pretty sure that unless your father had a really big stroke of conscious before he died, that even Mary-Beth has no clue and maybe, maybe it's time to tell her and to tell them all."

I watch as he runs his hands over his head. Frustration, confusion and more are all being worn on his sleeve, but I really think he needs to do this. "Let's get this over with," he huffs as he puts his arms down and walks across the hall into the casket room.

After about thirty minutes, he's picked a casket and signed the paperwork to finalize everything and I think we're about to leave. "I want to see him," Calvin says to the director.

I give a sad, small smile and nod at the director. "Follow me. We've set him up for you."

Calvin doesn't say anything to me as we follow the director toward a room that is at the back of the funeral home, which is just a remodeled house.

Calvin turns to me, his eyes meet mine and he rests his hands on my chest before gripping my jacket. "I need to do this alone." He rests his head against my chest, leaning on me, pulling strength from me. It brings me great comfort to know that I'm here for him.

"Whatever you need, Cal," I whisper and he grips my jacket a little tighter before releasing me and turning around before stepping through the portal to the room where the man he's hated his entire life lays dead.

calvin

I had no idea what to expect when I walked into the room. It's lined with about ten or so silver doors with long handles on them. I shiver thinking about the bodies that could lie beyond them. But right now, the one laying out on the table in front of me is the one I'm trying to avoid.

I haven't bothered to ask how he died, because I really don't care, but the frail man lying there is nothing like the man I remember.

His cheeks are sunken in, his eyes look bruised and he's about a third of the man he was when I last saw him. Whatever it was took him hard.

A tear streaks down my cheek and I wipe them away. "I'll leave you alone for a few minutes," the director says before taking his leave.

As soon as the door clicks closed I murmur, "You son of a bitch."

I was prepared to see a burly, husky man lying on the table and instead I see a frail old one and his suffering is evident. "Good," I mumble. "You deserved to suffer, you asshole. Do you have any idea what you've put me through? No, of course you don't. You sent me packing." I lean back against the wall behind me, refusing to get any closer.

"Well, let me tell you, despite your best efforts, I'm still gay and I am with the most amazing, beautiful, sensitive, loving man a person can ask for. Despite everything you tried to do to me." I brush away the tears again. I can't quite figure out why I'm crying but I pray to God it's from anger and not sadness. "I love Eric more than life itself. Not you, not those doctors, no one, can take that away from me. I just wish you'd been smart enough to realize that a decade ago."

I push myself off of the wall. "Goodbye, old man."

I open the door to find Eric leaning against one wall and the director against the other wall. There is a small smile playing on Eric's lips that I don't quite understand and the funeral director looks positively green. "Thank you." I hand him a card with my phone number on it. "Call if you need anything else, otherwise we'll be here Monday at four."

The director clears his throat. "Uh, yes, okay, Monday at four. Thank you, Mr. Caldwell."

I shake my head like 'what the fuck' and grab Eric's arm and pull him back through the home and out the door to our car.

"What in the same hell did you say to him?" I ask as we reach the car.

He spins me around, pressing me against the car. "Amazing? Beautiful? Loving?" There is a twinkle in his eye. "Love me more than life itself?"

"You heard me?" He snorts a laugh. "Oh god, that means he heard-" I burst out laughing and Eric takes my head in his hands.

"I love you too, Calvin Caldwell, more than life itself." He slants his lips over mine, melting away the anguish, the pain, the frustration and bringing back the love, desire and lust I feel for him when his lips are on me and his body is pressed against mine. I shiver at the thought of what I plan to do to him tonight when we get to our hotel.

chapter 66

calvin

We get back in the car and head back toward the farm house, though instead of going straight there, we stop in at Sammie's, a bar and grill, I guess you could call it that, in downtown Maynard and half the town appears to be here tonight.

"Are you sure you want to do this?" Eric asks.

"I'm not sure I can stomach eating a meal in that house. This is our best option unless you want to wait until later. Fast food doesn't exist around here and most things close at like nine o'clock. So no, I don't want to do this, but I'm hungry." I smile at Eric.

"Well, okay then. Let's do it."

He opens his door and climbs out. The evening air is warmer and I watch as Eric throws his jacket in the car. His sleeves are on full display. "Besides, with you dressed like that, no one will pay any attention to me."

"Should I do my hair up real quick?" he teases.

"Oh god, talk about giving them heart attacks," I tease him back and roll up my own sleeves before walking around the car and heading into Sammie's.

"Good lord, nothing's changed in this fucking town," I mutter as I look around the bar. It's the same fucking thing it was back in high school. The same wooden stools, faux leather booths, though the pool table looks worn, it's been replaced since I was in here last and the smell of stale beers and peanuts rings heavy.

"What can I do for you fellers?"

"Sammie?" I say to the old graying man behind the bar.

"That's me, who the hell are you?" I watch as he stands up a little straighter, all eyes seem to have turned to me, and I want to roll mine.

"Calvin."

I watch as recognition hits Sammie and half the people in the bar, among other weird unnamed emotions that float through their wide eyes. "Well, holy dog shit, look what the cat dragged in," Sammie says as he walks around the bar. My father spent so much time in this bar, drunk off of his fucking ass, that I'd ride my bike up here to drive his drunken ass home. "Good lord, you've grown up," Sammie says as he takes my hand and pulls me into a hug. "Sorry about your dad," he whispers in my ear. "I'd hoped you'd come home."

"Thanks Sammie." I pull back from him and nod toward Eric. "Sam, I'd like you to meet Eric Richardson. Eric, this is Sammie, obviously. He owns this joint."

"Nice to meet you, Eric. How do you two know each other?"

"From California," Eric says.

"No shit?" Sammie can't hide his surprise. "So that's where you been hiding all these years."

"Something like that," I grumble, not wanting to go into details.

"Come on, take a seat. What can I get ya?" Sammie asks as he escorts us to an open table.

"A pitcher would be great," I tell him and Eric nods his agreement.

"You got it."

Our meal is good, just like I remember, adding to the fact that nothing changes in this town.

Eventually people get over their shock and fear and start coming over, expressing their condolences and saying hello to me like we're long lost friends. Some I've gone to high school with, others I've managed to remember, eventually, from dealings with my father.

When we're done, we head back to the farm house. I feel relief when I notice that there is only one car in the driveway, I'm assuming it's Mary-Beth's. "We won't stay long," I tell Eric when we pull up. "I'm exhausted and losing steam on my ability to smile and be cordial to people."

"We stay as long as we need to," he tells me with a smile. I lean over the console and cup his bearded cheek.

"If you ever shave this off, I might get disappointed," I tease him as I run my fingers through it and pull him toward me, kissing him, finding my center and my salvation in a single kiss.

I pull back, getting worked up before stepping back inside this house is the last thing I want to do. "Come on," he says softly. "Let's get this over with so we can be alone."

I smile. "I like the sound of that."

We both climb out of the car and walk up the porch, the door is open and the screen door is the only thing in our way. "Mary-Beth?" I call out.

"Come on in, Calvin," she says from inside the house and Eric opens the door for me.

"Where are you?" I ask.

"The kitchen," she says back and we turn left, into the dining room and then on into the kitchen.

Sitting on the kitchen table is a thick envelope of something, though I have no idea what it is. But written on the outside in my father's chicken scratch is my name. "What's this, Mary-Beth?" I ask and she sets down whatever is in her hands and comes around the counter. She's an older lady, about my father's age, and she's definitely not getting any younger.

"Your father put that together when he got his diagnosis. He wanted you to have it, though he wanted to give it to you himself."

"I'm sorry, I couldn't come." It's true, I couldn't come, not with the tour needing to be finished and then my working to get Eric back and everything else, it honestly got lost in the shuffle of my life in California.

"Oh, I know, dear, it's alright."

"Can I ask you something, Mary-Beth?" I ask her as Eric and I take a seat and she joins us.

"Sure," she says confidently.

"When you called, to tell me he was sick and ask me to come home, did you honestly know what you were asking of me?"

She puts her head down a little in shame. "He told me, what he done to you. About sending you away."

"Did he tell you why he sent me away?"

"Because he thought he was doing the right thing. Because he thought that if he sent you away that you would come home to him, the boy he wanted you to be." She looks up, bringing her hand across the table to take mine. "I was so angry with him when I found out. I made it my mission to try and figure out a way to bring the two of you back together."

"So you know that he sent Calvin away because he's gay?" Eric interjects and she squeezes my hand.

"I do," she says, honesty dripping off of her in waves. "I think it was awful what he done and I don't think he honestly knew how to handle it. He thought that if he had a gay son that he'd have no one to pass the farm down to."

I shake my head in disgust. "He was one selfish son of a bitch."

"Please don't say that," Mary-Beth interjects. "Your father knew early on that he'd messed up with you, with how he raised you and then he just threw you away like you were an empty bottle."

"You haven't a clue what he put me through sending me to that place," I tell her, pulling my hand from hers and standing up. I need to move, to pace, anything. "He never so much as visited me, called me, sent me a letter, nothing. When I walked out of that place, I left, I never came home. How could I come home to a father that was responsible for what happened to me in there?" I'm rambling and I really don't care. I need to get it off my chest. I look at Eric who is silently giving me encouragement to keep up with my tirade. "I will never forgive him," I tell Mary-Beth.

"I know you won't, and he knew it too. He knew that nothing he could do, say or try would be enough to bring you back into his life. He'd just hoped for the chance to tell you himself. When he was diagnosed, I went on a hunt to find you and it wasn't until I got to talking to Billy that he agreed to use his connections to do so."

"So that's how you found me?"

She nods. "He'd given me a number, your number, but I held on to it. Your father fought with me and with himself about calling you, but then he got to be too sick to really care so I stepped in."

"What was it that killed him?" I manage to ask.

"Small cell lung cancer. By the time he'd gotten it diagnosed, it had already spread to his liver, kidneys and was making its way to his brain."

"Did he suffer?" I ask.

"He did," she says before she starts crying. "I cannot make up for what he done to you, Calvin, but...I am sorry I wasn't around then, that I had no idea what he was planning to do. I would have stopped him."

"It wouldn't have changed anything. He tried with his own fists several times before he gave into the white coats," I mutter.

"I am so sorry," she sobs and I don't know how I'm supposed to respond.

Eventually Eric fills her in on the arrangements that were made tonight at the home and she gives me the obituary to approve.

Raymond "Ray" Walter Caldwell, of Maynard, died Friday June 26th with his wife Mary-Beth at his side.

Funeral services will be held Wednesday, 11:00am at St. Paul Lutheran Church in Maynard, with graveside at Pinhook Cemetery following.

Family and Friends may call Monday Evening from 5-7p.m., at Becker-Milnes Funeral Home in Fayette.

Ray was a hardworking man who lived his entire life outside of Maynard, tilling the land and was a continuous member of the community.

He is survived by his wife, Mary-Beth and his son Calvin (Eric) Caldwell.

He was preceded in death by his parents, his sister and his wife Anabell.

When my eyes read over Eric's name next to mine, my eyes dart to Mary-Beth. "Are you sure you want this in here?" I ask, pointing to it.

"Don't you?"

"Yes, yes I do." New tears form in my eyes as I hand it to Eric to read.

"He said that he had no idea who you were with or what you were doing, but whatever it was, he wanted it to be included. And now that you two can legally get married, I see no reason why it can't be in there."

I hear Eric's gasp as he too reaches the part I did.

"I'm pretty sure he didn't mean that specifically," I tell her.

"Well, you two are together, are you not?" Her voice is light, happy almost.

"We are," I admit to the first person, outside of our small group of friends back home, that Eric and I are together and it's freeing.

"Good. Then it stays." She takes the tablet from Eric and sets it down. "I'll drop this off tomorrow morning."

Eric and I both look at each other with a wide smile on our faces. There was once a time when that would scare the ever-loving shit out of me, and now, now I don't care. For the first time in my life, I can honestly admit that my not caring has nothing to do with being hypnotized. I take comfort in the fact that when this is all over, we can go back to our lives in California and the people of Maynard can go back to turning up their noses.

We leave the house after that. Much to Mary-Beth's chagrin, but I think she understood why I couldn't stay in that house much longer, much less overnight.

chapter 67

eric

"Well, this is quaint," I tease Calvin as we enter our little Super 8 Motel.

"This is better than the one in town, which, when we drove past it, I'm not sure is open anymore."

I set my stuff down. "It doesn't matter where." I walk up to him, wrapping my arms around him. "As long as I'm with you." I lean down and he lifts his chin and I press my lips to his and I feel the tension melt away from his body and into my hold. It doesn't take long for his breathing to become shallow and my heart to start racing. I've missed this. We've been so busy, with the move and then the party and everything, that we've both fallen into bed exhausted most nights.

I rub my hands up along his back, hoping he feels the same way I do. I really need to be with him tonight. Show him that he truly is not alone anymore. His breathing hitches a little and I know I'm not pressing too hard for something he doesn't necessarily want.

I reach for the hem of his shirt and pull it up. He breaks my hold and our kiss so that I can pull it off of him and he repeats the process with me. His hands glide over my chest and down my stomach until he reaches my waist and the buttons of my jeans. I kiss him again, this time more urgent and lust filled. His answering kiss is equally as urgent and we're both lost in arms, mouths, hands and tongues as we do everything we can to strip each other.

When we're both sort of satisfied, we part again, kicking off shoes and pants before falling onto the bed. I tower over him, pressing his back into the bed as I kiss along his jaw, toward his ear and then down his neck. He tilts his head, giving me access to the spot I love most on him. That sweet spot where the shoulder and neck come together. I kiss it, then nibble on it. He writhes beneath me.

Thrusting his hips upward, our cocks rub together and my eyes roll up. His hands glide up my back, sending goosebumps everywhere as he brings his hands around to my chest. I shiver and start kissing my way down his chest, toward his stomach. My beard tickles him and he squirms with a breathy laugh and I smile, purposefully rubbing it against him. "That is so mean." He squirms and I smile as I go back to kissing my way down his stomach, getting closer to my destination.

When I reach it, I decide to tease him a little more and I let out a warm breath, and his cock jumps up at me. "Mmm," I moan as I take him into my mouth.

He hisses above me as my tongue dances around the crown and I toy with his barbell and give him little nibbles with my teeth.

His hand slides into my hair, dislodging the tie holding it back, and he takes my head in both his hands, holding and guiding me to suck down further along his cock and I give him a small smile as I swallow him down, putting him in the back of my throat. I swallow a couple of times, and he moans above me before I pull up on his cock.

I take his sack in my hand and start to play with the happy spot just below them, working my finger down further. He lifts his hips, urging me downward. I release his cock and trade it with my finger, looking at him as he watches me suck on it, getting it wet before returning it back to his entrance and his eyes roll up.

"Please?" he begs and I can't say no to that.

I reposition his legs on my shoulders and push him up. His hips relax and he bends for me, giving me all the access I need before I slide my finger inside. "Eric," he cries out and I shiver at my name on his lips.

I rake my nails lightly down his chest before taking his cock in my other hand, and stroking him in time with my finger in and out of him. He writhes, and I feel his cock pulsing with the pleasure I'm giving him until he stills my hand. "I don't want to come like this, not tonight," he tells me softly.

"Tell me what you want," I tell him.

"I want to take you."

Pleasure radiates all over me, sending shivers through my entire body at his request. "Please?" I ask and he smiles before pulling himself off of my hand and rolling over and off of the bed. I lay down on my back, and he goes into the bag, pulling out a bottle of lube.

We ditched the condoms after his hypnosis and haven't gone back since. I think it was, in our own little way, our signifying a commitment between us.

He climbs back on the bed, tossing a towel next to my hip. I shiver and smile at him as I take my cock in my hand, stroking gently on it while he gets himself ready. I watch as he rubs himself up and down. Mutual masturbation hasn't ever been something we've done, neither one of us can seem to keep their hands off of the other long enough to make it work.

When he's ready, he cleans his hands on the towel and puts my legs up on his shoulders. "Oh god," I groan as he presses himself against me, lifting my hips up to give him better access and I go with him as he pushes into me. His cock slides all the way inside in one thrust. "Oh fuck." I stroke my cock harder, gripping it firmly and Calvin takes my hips in his hands to guide me along his shaft and I groan.

The pleasure he elicits from me as he pounds into and out of me is almost too much to maintain straight thoughts. His hand quickly replaces mine on my cock, but I fight the urge to come. "I have an idea." I smile at him.

His eyes roll around in his head momentarily before finding mine. "Oh?"

"I want you to ride me," I tell him and I can see the idea creep over him, much the way his idea did me and he pulls himself from me. I find the bottle and lube myself up while he cleans up and switches positions. Straddling me, he reaches between us, taking my cock in his hand and lining himself up to slide down my cock. Watching his cock bounce, I can't keep my hand away anymore. I take it in my hand and watch as he settles down on top of me.

The pleasure is evident, not only in the lust filled expression on his face but the drops of pre-cum falling from his cock. I rub my thumb up over his barbell as he bottoms out inside me. He settles, and I stroke his cock slowly before he starts to move up and down my shaft. "Fuck," he cries out as he pushes down and pulls up at the same time as I stroke his cock. "Jesus Eric, this is…oh my god." His eyes close and pleasure rocks through him, racing through his veins as he slides up and down on top of me.

Taken by the pleasure he's giving me, I stop moving my hand along his shaft, but he helps by putting his hand over mine. "I want your cum on me." I groan as he slams back down on me and I start to match his thrusts.

He pulls my hand off of his cock and he leans forward, pressing his hands on my chest as he brings his hips to grind against mine.

"Fuck!" I throw my head back and Calvin claims my mouth, swallowing my cries.

"I want to fuck you, come for me," he whispers in my ear as I explode inside him. He moans and shudders on top of me, swallowing me whole before stilling and then extracting me from him. "Roll over," he says and I lazily do so but I'm not a two hit wonder. He knows that, but he also knows that I can't stop until he's fully satisfied.

It only takes him a moment before he's lining up, pushing himself inside me and I can't help but take my soft cock in my hand, stroking it gently as he starts pounding into me. My cries of pleasure fill the room as Calvin isn't very gentle. My cock gets hard as steel once again and I stroke myself harder, hoping to find a second release, but it doesn't come before Calvin is crying out my name and exploding inside me.

chapter 68

calvin

We showered and snuggled into bed after that. Though he did wake me up a couple hours later, spooning me, and we both got off for a second time, we never left each other's arms that night.

We spent Sunday at the farm house with Mary-Beth and a constant flow of people, casseroles and flowers. The day was hard enough as it was without having people telling me how sorry they were. When Billy showed up, this time without his wife, he asked me to talk, outside and alone. I reluctantly agreed.

He'd brought me out there, asking me about where I'd really been, saying that when Mary-Beth asked about looking me up, I didn't have a record and it didn't make sense to him anymore that I had been locked up.

So I explained to him that my father had sent me away, to an institution that was hell bent on curing the gay from me. He caught on quickly but didn't press. He apologized profusely for what happened to me and for all the times we'd fucked around and it got me in trouble.

When I asked him about his wife, he said that she didn't know and that it really isn't a part of who is he. I wanted to think that he was lying, but there was some strange truth in his tone. He chalked it up to experimental teenage years and he moved on from it. Eric joined us after a bit, lighting up a smoke and I ended up having one too. Billy didn't say much else, other than to tell me that he was glad I'd found someone.

Who Eric and I were, celebrity wise, went unnoticed all day Sunday and then Monday too. Eric had called Addison to let her know that the regional paper would be running an obituary that would have my name, with Eric's in parenthesis next to it. She'd assured both of us not to worry. She'd put a lid on anything if it popped up Monday, which as far as I knew, it never did.

At four o'clock Monday, Eric and I walked back into the funeral home, this time with Mary-Beth. She really is a sweet lady and I made a vow to stay in touch with her.

She'd told me yesterday that some years ago, my father, unable to handle it himself, leased out the land surrounding the farmhouse but that according to my father's will, the house and land were now mine. I told her no. It was hers and I would be signing it over to her when I got the deed from the attorney's office. The same went with the money he'd left me. I don't know how much it was, but I didn't care. Mary-Beth broke down over that one pretty hard. She honestly had no idea what she was going to do now that my father was gone. I hope I brought her some peace in the chaos of the last few days.

Eric joined me casket side, and this time I was able to say good-bye to my father with a little less anger and a few more tears. After spending the time I had with Mary-Beth, I honestly believed she was trying to change the mind of my father and maybe he'd finally realized his mistakes. Though I am a very long way away from forgiving him, knowing that gave the clearance I needed in order to grieve his passing.

The true moment of collapse came a few minutes before five. Eric and I had snuck out of the room to let Mary-Beth be with her family. While we were standing in front of the funeral home smoking, something caught my attention. A lot of somethings actually. With the setting sun behind them, like a slow-motion action movie, my entire world came walking across the parking lot.

I lost it in Eric's arms as Talon, Kyle, Dex, Raine, Addison, Casey, Mills, Beck, Tori and Rusty approached us.

"We're family," Talon said as he stood next to us. "And family sticks together."

"Always," Dex agreed.

I was then swooped up in hugs, condolences and the most overwhelming love I could have ever imagined feeling.

The sound of them caused a commotion inside and Mary-Beth came out. "Calvin, who are all these people?" she asked me in a curious tone.

"Mary-Beth, I'd like you to meet my family, my friends, and my band."

"Your band?" Her tone was even more curious now.

"Yes ma'am. We're 69 Bottles."

"Oh sweetheart, if it ain't something I can square dance too, I ain't got a clue what you're talking about."

We all laughed. "Well, then let me introduce you."

I introduced Mary-Beth to everyone, explaining who they were and what they did and she accepted them all with open arms.

They all filed in and overtook the funeral home to pay their respects to my father. I noticed then that the casket spray was from Cami, Tristan and the Bold family and I nearly lost it again.

When the visitation was over, the twelve of us overtook Sammie's and he had no problem kicking out the regular crowd for us. We ate, we talked, we were the family that we've all grown to be. It was the most amazing night. I couldn't have asked for a better group of people to be surrounded by, but best of all, I had Eric by my side. He is my absolute everything. I cannot imagine my life continuing without him by my side.

The next day, while standing graveside, saying one final goodbye to my father, Addison graced the audience with a very heartfelt version of 'Amazing Grace' and it was exactly what I needed to hear.

Everyone, along with Eric, stuck around until I was ready to walk away, long after everyone else had gone on to the farm house for conversations that I didn't want to have. I was ready to leave this Podunk town once and for all.

Though I told Mary-Beth that I would be in touch and that she was more than welcome to use my phone number any time she wanted, she was satisfied with that and I told her that I would be taking off from the cemetery. I think she was a little sad to me see me go, but we said our goodbyes and off she went.

Standing in a big ol' circle, surrounded by my friends, my family and the love of my life, I realized that this all started five months ago

With a rock band.

A tour bus.

Four amazing friends who would find their soulmates along the way.

It's been one hell of a wild ride and I couldn't ask for a greater group of people to have taken that journey with.

Eric is my rock, my salvation, my hero, my talisman and the love of my life.

epilogue

6 months later...

calvin

"Are you sure you're ready to do this?" Eric asks me.

"I'm pretty sure I've put it off long enough and I know that if I don't do it now, I might never do it. Not to mention the fact that I'm tired of it haunting me," I tell him as I place the thick yellow envelope on the table. Mary-Beth had given it to me when my father passed away.

"But tonight?"

I smile at him. "Tonight."

He gives me a sad, concerned smile. Tomorrow is a big day for both of us and I can understand his concern, but right now, I need to do this.

I unclasp the metal prongs on the back of it and everything seems to slip into slow motion as I peer inside.

I can't see much, except several pages folded up, sort of sitting on top of everything else. I pull it out, then look inside. I can't quite make it out, but they look like newspaper clippings.

I open up the letter and I hand it to Eric.

He hesitantly takes it from me, and slowly flattens it out as he clears his throat.

"Dearest Calvin," Eric starts and I sit down. "I know this must come as a surprise to you, but if you're reading this, Mary-Beth has done as I asked. Not only did she type this up for you, but she made sure you received it somehow after I've passed away."

I can hear the emotion filtering into Eric's voice and my own jaw ticks with hesitation and nerves for what is going to come next.

Eric continues, "Please know that I'm including the original, handwritten letter so you know she didn't make any alterations to what I'm about to tell you. I needed you to know that what I am about to say is the truth and it is how I truly feel.

"I'm sorry," Eric breathes as he continues reading. "I am sorry for all the pain I've caused you. Sorry for the fact that I've put you through the things that I have in your life.

"I was stupid. I, at the time, couldn't wrap my head around the fact that you were gay. Gay men just didn't exist in the world that I grew up in, in the community we lived in, and I felt that I could change you into the man you were meant to be. After about a year, I finally realized that I could no longer do that. That I was never going to change you, but the doctors had told me that they were making such amazing progress. I believed them.

"I was hoodwinked into believing that when your treatment was over, you'd return home the man I thought you should have been. But you never came home. And for that, I do not blame you.

"It took me a long time to admit to myself that you being gay was not a crime, and it was more normal than I could have possibly realized and in all honesty, you can thank Mary-Beth for that. She opened my eyes to a whole new perspective on life and on love. For the same reasons I couldn't find, date and marry another woman after your mother died, those are the reasons I sent you away.

"Sending you away was the hardest thing I've ever done in my life, and I cannot ask you to forgive me, but what I can do is tell you that I never stopped loving you. That I wish like hell that we could have this conversation in person, but I understand why you won't come.

"Ultimately, my wish for you, is complete and total happiness, the greatest love you can find, and a life worth living. But your past doesn't have to rule your future.

"With all my love, your father, Ray," Eric finishes as I brush a couple of tears from my cheeks.

"P.S.," he continues, "Despite what you may believe, I really did care about you and miss you terribly. I truly do hope that maybe, one day, you can forgive me and my decisions."

I reach for the envelope and turn it upside down, spilling the contents onto our dining room table.

One article in particular catches my eye.

"69 Bottles launches their first U.S. Tour in San Diego."

My breathing stops as my eyes scan the rest of what came out of the envelope. It's article after article, some clipped, some printed, some ripped from magazines, all pertaining to 69 Bottles and me.

"Jesus," Eric and I say together.

I let out a nervous laugh and look at Eric. "Despite it all, he knew where I was, what I was doing, and how I was doing," I breathe.

A smile spreads across my lips as I realize that I can no longer hate him for his choices. Forgive him? Not yet, but maybe, someday.

eric

"Mary-Beth," I say as I approach the little, old woman that I met when Calvin's father passed away. She proved to be a very valuable ally for Calvin in the final years his father had and she's proven her friendship with Calvin time and time again. "I'm so glad you're here."

She smiles wide. "Are you kidding? I wouldn't miss this for the world."

I chuckle. "Come on, he's in here."

"Have you seen him?" she scolds me.

"Oh sweetheart, we are far from a traditional couple. I'm pretty sure that the two of us, dressed the same, takes tradition away from us."

She smacks my shoulder. "Doesn't matter," she scolds.

I laugh and admit, "No, I haven't seen him. But you can." I knock on the door.

"Who is it?"

"It's me," I say.

"Eric, get the hell away from here, we agreed."

"Well, I have a surprise for you. I'm just going to leave it here and walk away, okay?"

"Yeah okay, fine. Go away."

"Jeez, I'm just getting scolded left and right today." I get a look from Mary-Beth that tells me to back the hell away. I do and go around the corner, listening for the click of the door.

"Oh my god," Calvin squeals as he opens the door. My work here is done.

calvin

"What on earth are you doing here?" I ask Mary-Beth as she comes into my room.

"Oh, a little birdie told me you were getting married today. I wouldn't miss it for the world."

"I'd hardly call Eric a little birdie."

She laughs, "You can say that again."

I hug her again. "It's so good to see you, I'm so happy you're here."

eric

With Sam Smith's soulful voice filling Cami's backyard, my parents escort me down the aisle. I'm first, so my view is filled with my family of amazing friends and the best day of my life, the rest of my life laid out before me as I walk toward the minister who's going to marry Calvin and I.

We reach the alter and my parents take their seats just as John Legend's voice fills the air around us and Calvin walks down the aisle with Mary-Beth at his side. Tears fill my eyes as John sings about 'laying by my side'.

Today my life begins.

Today I get everything I've ever wanted in my life. The man I love, the family I adore and my best friend by my side until the end of time.

Today everything moves forward. Each day is a giant step away from Calvin's past and another step toward our future.

A year ago, Calvin and I were still best friends, then we went on tour and our lives changed forever and I truly have Addison to thank for that.

She opened up the eyes of so many of us when she fell in love with Talon and Kyle. Seeing their love for each other grow opened the manwhore to the love of his life in Raine. Dex has never been happier and I'm starting to understand why that is. Now, officially out of the closet, I get to spend the rest of my life with my soulmate.

The End

It is bittersweet… saying good-bye to a band that I have fallen head over heels in love with from the very first words typed just over a year ago.

I know many of you are anticipating what is coming next and I am eager to share it all with you.

I cannot thank you enough, from the bottom of my heart for all your love, support and more importantly, your obsessive desire for more 69 Bottles!!

If you want to be the first to know about what's coming next, please make sure you sign up for my newsletter: http://eepurl.com/TsVMr

And follow along on Facebook: https://www.facebook.com/zoey.derrick/

Sending All My Love!!

XX
Zoey